The Eleventh Plague

John S. Marr, M.D.
and John Baldwin

The Eleventh
Plague

COMPASS PRESS
AN IMPRINT OF WHEELER PUBLISHING, INC.

Published in Large Print by arrangement with HarperCollins Publishers,
Inc., in the United States and Canada

Compass Press Large Print book series;
an imprint of Wheeler Publishing Inc., USA

Set in 16 pt Plantin.

Library of Congress Cataloging-in-Publication Data

Marr, John S.
  The eleventh plague / John S. Marr and John Baldwin.
    p. (large print) cm.(Wheeler large print book series)
    ISBN 1-56895-651-7 (hardcover)
    1. Large type books. 2. Virus diseases--United States--Fiction. 3.
Epidemics--Fiction. 4. Virologists--Fiction.
I. Baldwin, John. 1944 July 22- II. Title.
[PS3563.A711E44   1998]
813'.54—dc21   98-29240
                                                              CIP

The Eleventh Plague, sui generis, is fiction. But, the men and women of the Federation of American Scientists, SatelLife and World Health Organization, who created and continue to support the concept of ProMED, are quite real. This book is dedicated to these scientists and to
                    ProMED-mail.
ProMED-mail may be our best hope should fact follow fiction.

Acknowledgments

The authors would like to acknowledge the many friends and colleagues who assisted in the development of the novel, especially Gwyneth Cravens for her meticulous refining of the document, Mark Hammer for conceptual suggestions and word-smithing, Suzanna Lesan for her editorial expertise, and Kimberly Chiarella, Curtis Malloy, and Marcy Shaffer for their critical readings and comments. We would also like to thank John Boswell, John Cathey, John Talbot, Constance Fisher, Drew Taylor, and Peter McCabe for their continuous support throughout the writing process, along with our wives, Ann and Helen, as well as Jessica Marr, who allowed us time away from family responsibilities. And particular thanks to Jack Woodall for providing inspiration. Special thanks go to Diane Reverand and Carolyn Fireside for their superior creative contributions. Also we regret the passing of four friends who were our advisors and colleagues: Kenneth Mott, M.D., E. K. Hubbard, III, David A. McCabe, and Kurt Koegler.

In addition, John Baldwin would like to offer heartfelt thanks to the following friends, family, mentors, and advisors whose belief in my writing allowed them to help me, guide me, or just tolerate me, on my way to this book: Robert, Kennon, and Alison Baldwin; Dr. Linus

Abrams; Phyllis Amicucci; Judy Asman; Doro Bachrach; Laura Benfante; Ron Bernstein; Hillel Black; Ben Blackburn; Polly and Frank Blackford; Frank and Carol Borassi; John Boswell; Stuart Bronfeld; H. Lee Browne; Patti Browne; Andy Brucker; Anthony Bueti; Ward Calhoun; Alf Callahan; Peter Cerilli; Darrell Chapnick; Dr. Debbie Choate; Dudley Cocke; Kiana Davenport; Dick Dickerson; Meaghan Dowling; Karen Eckert; Nicole Eisenman; Ken Eshelman; David Eyre; Carolyn Fireside; David Flora; Ashe Gupta; Judy Hart and Chris Lavin; Joe Heller; Craig Hurley; Whittle, Jim, Martha, and Beck Johnston; John Karoly; Sarah Kernochan and her parents John and Adelaide; Richard Kerrigan; Georgianna Koulianos; Jimmy Lathrop; David G. Lewis; Jane Lewis; Martin Mannion; Marci Mansfield; Michael Maren; John Markham and Liz Reade; Jessica Marr; Janet McCarthy-Fabis; Shaun McConnon; Gil Messenger; Mrs. Maureen Micek; Pat and Andy Micek; Andrea Molitor; Steve Morin and Claire Talbot; Michael Newbarth; Dr. Marc Newberg; Antoinette Owen and the Brooklyn Museum of Art; David Penzak; Dr. Kermit Pines; Raptor Systems Inc.; Anne Raver; Diane Reverand; Lora Richard; Matt Roshkow; David Schutts; Brian Schwartz; Milton Sherman; Arlene Shulman; Bob Solomon; Dr. John Sparks; Mark Stevenson; Dr. Richard Talbot; Ed Tedeschi; Carole Thomassy; Dr. Larry Toder; Rob Toohey; Gary Tragesser; Mikhail Tsivin; Mary Ann Tucker; Derek Uhlman; Lance Urbas; Vito Virga; Kyoko Watanabe; Ann A. White; Susanne Whittle; and Dr. Felice Zwas. It would be wrong if I failed to thank my parents, Dr. John M. Baldwin, Jr., who showed how noble a profession medicine ultimately must be, and Detty, who showed how drama can become the essence of life. I also want to thank my coauthor, Dr. John Marr, whose patience, guidance, and skill rank him with the best of all my teachers, and whose devotion to medicine and encyclopedic knowledge rank him with the finest of all physicians. I am particularly grateful to Connie Fisher, who made it all possible. I also want to thank John Talbot for teaching me so much. And, more than anyone else, I want to thank Babes, for everything.

Disclaimer

The methods and materials required for the production of the toxins used in this novel have been altered to render them harmless. However, the authors remind the reader how simple it is for almost anyone to turn these fictional threats into reality.

Huge Honey Bee Swarms Attack Downtown San Antonio, Suburbs

SPECIAL TO *THE SAN ANTONIO LIGHT*:
MONDAY, APRIL 13

Three second graders, their mother, and six other adults died yesterday evening, Easter Sunday, as swarms of aggressive honey bees engulfed sections of San Antonio's famed River Walk tourist area. Scores of others were severely hurt. Hospitals near Balcones Heights and Terrell Hills reported bee-sting emergencies. Similar swarms attacked in other suburbs, injuring fifteen members of the First Apostle Baptist Church of Alamo Heights.

During the downtown attack severe thunderstorms swept River Walk, helping fire, police, and EMS personnel as they dispersed the insects with hoses. Environmental specialists assured the public that these were not the infamous "killer bees," but common honey bees used by local growers for spring pollination. Scientists assume the swarms were blown from the fields by a funnel cloud observed in the area.

In all, five simultaneous bee swarms were reported in the city, with the attack along the crowded River Walk the most serious. Forty

1

men, women, and children were stung repeatedly. In total, fifty-seven people were hospitalized. One woman died today from an allergic reaction to bee venom.

Sunday, April 20
San Antonio

In what will always be referred to as the Easter Swarming, a beautiful spring Sunday turned into a day of wrath as tens of thousands of bees swept into the parks and businesses that line San Antonio's River Walk.

March had been uncharacteristically chilly, and this warm, inviting April day was the perfect chance for folks to show off their Easter finery; the city's charming renovated downtown River Walk became a magnet for both visitors and locals. Tour barges, their decks lined with benches, afforded a relaxing way to see the many attractions of the Alamo City.

The narrow banks of the refurbished canals were lined with trendy shops and popular restaurants, all filled by midafternoon with people browsing, reading, or simply sunning themselves. Despite the growing threat of rain, there were long lines waiting to board the gaudy tourist boats.

Restaurants along the canals serve lunch and dinner outside, and the barges are usually full of folks who want to bask on deck and wave at the diners just a few feet away, but today the clouds were clearly gathering, and the wind was rising. One tourist had already

2

picked up his laptop and asked to have his lunch served inside, behind the glass, where he could see the canal but be out of the wind and weather.

With napkins and menus were already being blown along the ground outside, only a few people even noticed the advent of the bees. At first they seemed to skim just above the water, but soon they were everywhere.

Most horrible, most indelible in the memories of those restaurant patrons was the set of adorable identical triplet girls sitting on the back of one of the barges—each carrying a white helium-filled balloon printed with a big yellow rose. The strings had been tied to each triplet's wrist, so the balloons would not be lost to the troposphere.

The triplets were six years old this very Easter day. Their mom always dressed them alike, bought them identical toys, and took them places to show them off. Her dream was for them to be child models, or at least cheerleaders. Seated near them, she encouraged the trio to wave at people on the shore. As the triplets waved, the balloons would float up and down, drawing all eyes toward the barge.

It seems possible that the first bee may actually have stung the mother; but there was general agreement that the triplets' waving their arms to ward off the bees caused the balloons to bounce and strike other bees, enraging them even more. The girls' mother swung at the bees with her purse again and again, screaming as they began to sting her through her thin spring dress.

Terror-struck, the triplets backed away in unison. When they reached out for a rail, another stream of bees seemed to skim in over the water, striking each of the six pink arms. In seconds, the insects had penetrated the girls' puff-sleeved outfits; their screams drew the attention of diners at the canalside restaurants. One woman on the barge rolled up a newspaper and, futilely trying to help the children, began to smack at the insects.

The mother grabbed one of her brood and began to look for a place to run to. The string attached to her daughter's wrist became tangled with the string tied to her sister, so as the mother ran, the second triplet, screaming even louder, was dragged down.

"Mommy... help me!" she cried. But it was her sister, back black with bees, who picked her up.

The mother was hysterical. The bees were winning, surrounding her children in a cloud of flying agony so dense it was difficult to see past it.

Just feet away on the shore, scores of people were also being stung. Even those who managed to smash a bee immediately found their hands covered with a dozen more. When they attempted to wipe the bees off by rubbing their hands against their arms and legs, those limbs were almost instantly covered.

The best refuge now seemed the water in the canal. So panicked that their common sense had left them, fully dressed people, forgetting they couldn't breathe underwater, began jumping in.

As they ran, other people yelled to the girls, "Jump... jump in the water!" but none of the triplets could hear them. By this point, they had been stung on the head so many times that their eyes were swollen shut. Two of them had dead bees jammed in their ears, forced in deep by the children's hysterical fingers trying to scrape the scourge from their faces. One of the triplets fell kicking to the deck, then another.

Suddenly one of the barge's passengers, a big Texan, came to the rescue. He waded into the cloud of bees as if they weren't there, snapped the twine on each girl's wrist, then pitched them neatly, one by one, over the railing into the canal. He hurled the mother in last, then made a shallow dive himself.

Two of the triplets had already begun to go into shock when the Texan picked them up. As their extremities began to swell, they started losing consciousness. When they hit the water, the cold revived them, but not enough to save them. They were underwater, and they had never learned to swim.

Their mother hit the canal at a steeper angle than the cowboy and stood up promptly in the chest-high water. The bees still massed in her hair, but she ignored them. Nothing mattered now that her children were drowning.

Frantic, she looked around, wading ineffectually toward one of the punctured balloons, but before she got to the spot, her face was covered with bees. Even though she submerged and tore them off with her hands, their tiny barbed stingers would remain buried in her flesh, sending dose after dose of lethal toxin into her system.

The cowboy, who called himself Cal, saw one of the girls break water and struggled toward her. Just as he reached her, she went under, but he managed to lift her to the surface. A clerk from a nearby sporting goods store, in order to help, hurled a rubber raft into the canal and tried to maneuver it toward Cal.

Just as Cal grabbed for it, the bees hit him, the girl, and the clerk, who stood up, waving his arms as the bees struck, falling backwards into the water. The raft kicked out from under the falling clerk and turned over. At last Cal had a chance. He came up underneath the raft, gasping, with the little girl in tow. Almost immediately, the clerk's head reappeared, and with trepidation, they both examined the child.

Her face looked as if it had been inflated with a basketball pump. The orange, yellow, and black bodies of hundreds of dead and dying bees clung to her hair, her ears, her nose, inserting their abdomens into her nostrils, stinging upward, relentlessly, mercilessly. The child was barely breathing; except for the furious whine of the bees, her desperate gasps were the only thing the men could hear.

As the two of them made their way under the cover of the raft down the canal and away from the swarms, Cal tried to give the girl mouth-to-mouth resuscitation, but thirty yards away, she died in his arms.

It was only later that the bodies of her two drowned sisters and fatally poisoned mother were located and removed from the canal—initially a place of refuge that had turned for them into a watery grave.

Seated safely behind the glass of the cafe, the tourist with the laptop, unlike the other patrons, barely looked up at the crisis unfolding outside. Instead, he typed almost obsessively throughout the incident, only rarely letting himself be distracted by the rampant chaos.

He didn't seem to notice when someone ran directly for the restaurant's glassed-in vestibule, cutting his head badly on the astragal as he tried to wrench the doors open. Reeling inside, with blood streaming down his face and a haze of bees blanketing his shoulders, the man shouted, "Help me!"

A waiter jerked a tablecloth from under its place setting and started to swing at the bees; then, realizing his error, he threw the cloth over the man like a net. Another tablecloth followed, and within moments, the man had calmed down. No one else tried to come in the door, and no one in the restaurant was interested in venturing out. The only people left outside were fleeing. Sirens screamed in the background, and the sky was turning iron gray.

In moments the sidewalk was as empty as it would be at dawn. Only the bees remained, their whine carrying even over the roar of the wind. Suddenly the sky grew black, and a squall of cyclonic velocity howled down the canal. Sheets of water rocked the glass windows of the cafe, and then, in what seemed to be only a few short minutes, moved on.

As the storm passed, the room quieted, and the only sound that could be heard was the angry drone of one large undamaged bee circling inside near the glass. Slowly it flew toward the bar, with people staring at it as if it was a vulture.

As a busboy swung a handful of menus at the creature, it circled back toward the man with the laptop, and landed on the elbow of his shirt.

"Hey, mister, watch it!" A waiter pointed with alarm. "There's one on your arm... "

Without apparent concern, the man looked up from his work and studied the bee, then picked up an empty water glass and in a flash scooped the bee off his sleeve and imprisoned it under the tumbler.

As people pointed at the glass, the man gathered his things.

"Kill it!" They were furious. "You saw what they did... "

The tall, thin man seemed embarrassed by the attention. Struggling into his raincoat, he picked up his belongings and backed away.

"I can't," he said in a quiet voice. "I'm allergic... I can't . . ." He turned from his table and backed off, but there was no shortage of volunteers to kill the prisoner in the glass.

Later, one of the waiters told another how calm the guy seemed, and the other nodded. "Dude was brave, man. With that thing sit-tin' on his arm. Must be some allergy he's got. I had a cousin blow up like a balloon, almost died. She won't hardly go out at all anymore. Did you see he was wearing gloves? Wonder if he has to wear them all the time 'cause he's allergic. Damn. Weird way to live!"

Wednesday, June 10
San Diego, California

Long after the tragedy, Dorothy Adams always remembered how windy it was the morning she took her first grade class to the Zoo. San Diego is often swept by late-spring rains and erratic desert breezes that shift direction as the seasons change. That Wednesday, the last weekly field trip fell on a gray, gusty day. There was an erratic undercurrent to the children's energy as they moved in a line toward the hummingbird house, stopping at the entrance, where Dorothy tried to calm them down.

A tow-headed, green-eyed imp of a six-year-old named Joey St. John was, as usual, giving his teacher a particularly trying time. He rocked on his heels, a study in agitation, as she attempted to explain how they would all have to stand still and be quiet if they wanted to see the hummingbirds. Joey had eaten a Ring-Ding, three small chocolate donuts, half a pack of Jolly Ranchers, and a peanut-butter-and-jelly sandwich—all the things his parents wouldn't let him have at home—and was in the grip of a massive sugar rush. He might have been able to stand still and be quiet in front of a living *Tyrannosaurus rex*, but mere hummingbirds were going to be quite a challenge. Dorothy Adams knew Joey well and had a fondness for the boy, who was a favorite—in several senses of the word.

Joey was the only child of one of the wealthiest and most influential men in Southern California—Joseph St. John (pronounced, as Joseph would never fail to tell you, "Sinjin"), the real estate developer who virtually ruled La Jolla—and his blonde, beautiful wife, Eleanor.

Dorothy had been surprised the St. Johns would allow their son to attend public school, but that was before she realized Joseph Senior had the school's principal as well as the entire La Jolla Board of Education in his back pocket. Joey was always treated with kid gloves, and given attention the children of normally affluent parents never got. His schoolteachers as well as his friends were carefully chosen for their families' Christian values.

Dorothy had met regularly with the St. Johns since Joey became her pupil. She had mixed feelings about them. A large, slightly overweight middle-aged man with a receding head of dusty red hair, Joseph St. John Sr. had a true believer's gaze and a brusque, dismissive manner that chilled her. His devotion to his son was genuine enough, but even that devotion was partly to the continuance of his name, his line, and his business. A fervent right-wing Christian, the world was black and white to him.

Eleanor, on the other hand, aroused more complicated feelings in the young teacher.

She was blonde, green-eyed, petite yet stat-
uesque. Though her looks suggested the
coolest of temperaments, she was all emotion
and overeagerness.

Being married to a man like Joseph could-
n't be a picnic, no matter how luxurious the
accoutrements. Her overprotectiveness toward
her son left her in a state of constant anxiety.
Dorothy thought Eleanor St. John should
relax about Joey—he was a great little kid
with just a touch of his father's toughness.
Dorothy believed Joey could take care of himself.

Having extracted yet another dazzling smile
and a promise to quiet down from Joey, who
was at the rear of the line of children, Dorothy
began leading the class through two swinging
outer doors, then through a pair of air-curtained
inner ones that sealed the gigantic aviary.
She never noticed Joey holding back. Nor
did she notice when he left the line and made
his way back to the entrance. The sense of inde-
pendence and adventure that Dorothy Adams
had so admired was compelling him away
from mere hummingbirds toward bigger,
scarier game like lions, tigers, panthers, leopards—and, although he didn't know it, toward
a far different form of man-eater, which brings
death with the same stealth, cunning, and
perfection as any of the fierce cats that Joey
was now so intent on seeing.

As the boy pushed open one of the aviary's
heavy swinging outer doors, a seedy-looking

13

old man hobbled out past him, smiling as if to thank Joey for holding the door. Joey let the door swing shut, watching to make sure the old man was out of sight, then opened the door and sprinted away. After a few yards, he left the walkway and headed down a footpath through a giant stand of eucalyptus.

"Hummingbirds... duuhh... duuhh," he muttered to himself as he ran down the dusty little path through the trees. Drunk on freedom, he didn't notice the old man watching him from a bench. The grizzled stranger arose quickly, strangely agile now, then vanished, leaving behind a small translucent yellow object on the bench.

Still running hard, Joey was nearing the lion house when he noticed the yellow object glowing in the sun. He realized to his delight that it was a plastic water pistol in the shape of a Buck Rogers ray gun, and he picked it up immediately. He saw that the fully loaded squirt gun, small enough to fit in his hand, had adhesive tape wrapped around the handle, and somebody had marked "022.9" and put some initials on the side in blue ink. Joey felt a momentary pang of conscience at making off with someone else's property—his mom would ground him for a week if she ever found out—but his instant and all-consuming desire for the gun won out. Armed with his new forbidden weapon, he scampered on, observed from behind the eucalyptus trees by the old man, now standing straight as a Marine drill sergeant—and smiling.

14

The lion house was great, just as Joey had known it would be. From there, he headed back to the aviary, waited until his class emerged, and began to stalk them as they went from building to building. Peering out of the foliage, he'd tried to get close enough to zap a couple of kids with the water gun, but failed. He'd even risked exposure by trailing them into the petting zoo, but Dorothy had led the children away, as oblivious to his reappearance as to his absence. Joey bent down to pick up a rabbit. Even though his mom never let him touch them, Joey loved animals, and this rabbit was the biggest one he'd ever seen. Without supervision, he immediately began playing with the bunny. It jumped all over him, even ripped his long, baggy shorts. He smoothed the fur on the rabbit's long white ears, looked around to see which way the class was headed, and gave the rabbit, who seemed thirsty, a few drops from the squirt gun. He was desperate to use the gun on a human being before he had to leave.

His chance came when he was right outside the monkey house. Looking down on a walkway below him, he spotted a bored-looking teenage girl with an oversized UCLA football jacket draped over her shoulders, a senior ring hanging from a chain around her neck, six little safety pins embedded in each of her ears, and what seemed to be three loops of silver wire threaded into her left nostril. Her eyelids were colored dark red, her hair a mixture of blonde, green, and magenta, and her nail polish was black. She was the perfect zap material, and Joey wasted no time.

His first shot hit her right above the chin. He was congratulating himself when she looked up, spotted him, and yelled. He responded by aiming higher and got her right in the makeup. She wiped the arm of the jacket across her eyes, smearing her mascara and making her look like a raccoon. The girl angrily gave him the finger, but Joey aimed again. This time, though, the gun hissed empty. He sucked on the barrel just to make sure it was shot, then jammed it deep into his shorts pocket and ran off to find his class.

Only as the class was about to leave did Dorothy Adams realize her most important charge had disappeared. She hadn't really looked for him in the aviary, but she could swear she'd seen him at the petting zoo. Her heart sank as she looked at each of her charges once again. No, he was definitely gone! Absolutely frantic, she was about to call the park police when she saw him walk calmly out of the hedges to the parking lot where the other children were waiting by the school bus.

"Joey, where have you been?" she practically screamed.

Once again flashing his beatific smile, Joey simply told her, "I'm sorry, Miss Adams, I had to go to the bathroom real bad."

"Joey, for heaven's sake, you know you're supposed to tell me if you have to go! You frightened me to death!"

"I'm real sorry, Miss Adams," he replied with great sincerity. "I promise I'll never do it again."

It was, sadly, a promise he would have no trouble keeping. For the man, who had seen Joey squirt the girl and suck up the few last drops of fluid himself, murmured as the school bus pulled away, "Well done... Well done," secure in the knowledge that another unimaginable horror was once again about to smite the enemy.

Wednesday, June 17
St. Roch Hospital
10:00 A.M.

Dr. "Mac" MacDonald, among America's leading authorities on pediatric thoracic surgery, and as suntanned, fit, and silver-haired as his lofty position mandated, shouldered his way through the doors of the isolation suite and reached behind his head to untie the strings of his surgical mask. There was blood on the arms of his blue gown, which he was careful to avoid as he stripped off his surgical gloves.

Preoccupied with the new symptoms his young patient had just begun manifesting, MacDonald virtually ignored the unit's other occupant, Dr. Vincent Catrini, St. Roch Hospital's Chief of Pediatrics. Catrini was certainly an excellent physician, even if he wasn't eminent, but his rumpled and slightly unshaven appearance disturbed the fastidious MacDonald. The two doctors washed and changed

17

without comment, then went together to meet with Joey St. John's parents.

Striding with Catrini through the halls, MacDonald hoped to hell Catrini would let him do the talking. After all, this was a command performance. Joey St. John was an only child, and his parents were extremely wealthy, extremely influential, and extremely worried— worried enough to send one of their private jets to fly MacDonald to La Jolla from a conference he'd been attending in Portland, Oregon. Standing silently next to Catrini on the elevator, he made sure an expression of confident determination masked his nagging uncertainty.

Vincent Catrini had taken care of Joey since he was born and for his part was relieved and impressed by the quick, effective manner in which MacDonald had performed the procedure on the boy's chest. MacDonald was tops in his field, and Catrini was thankful the St. Johns were wealthy people able to afford his services. There were, of course, good pediatric surgeons on the St. Roch staff, but the St. Johns had insisted on the top specialist in the country, and Catrini believed he had found him—even though he was admittedly less than enthusiastic about MacDonald's patronizing attitude toward the hospital staff. He checked his watch, praying as he knocked on the door of Joey's private room that the other expert who had been called in would show up soon.

Joseph and Eleanor St. John prayed, too, as

they flanked their son's bedside, deeply shaken and truly humbled. Joey's condition had reduced them to the same level of desperation any parent of a gravely and mysteriously ill child would feel. It was as if all the wealth and influence, which had for so long set the St. Johns apart, had vanished, leaving them powerless.

At the sound of the door shutting, both St. Johns went to the two physicians, terror shadowing their faces and dulling their gaze. Eleanor, a striking woman, reached out for Catrini's hand and pleaded, "Vincent, have you learned anything new? Please, please God, tell us what's wrong. Joey's never been this sick before. Nobody we've ever known has. We've been praying and praying and asking the Lord to spare Joey. Just tell us something definite. What about the exploratory surgery? What did you find?"

"Eleanor, that's Dr. MacDonald's area of expertise."

As Catrini yielded the floor to MacDonald, Eleanor walked over to the bed where the boy lay, his small, motionless left hand visible over the sheets. She touched his arm gently, careful not to disturb the intravenous line, and held it, ready to listen to what the expert had to say.

"The procedure went well, no complications." MacDonald assumed his most reassuring demeanor. "We were in and out in a few minutes, and I feel sure we'll have an answer tomorrow."

"Tomorrow?" Eleanor St. John's voice was

fierce with frustration, and her husband echoed her, "Tomorrow!"

MacDonald didn't lose a beat. He just drove straight ahead. These people might be the most important citizens in all of Southern California, private jets and all, but there was no way he was going to let them rattle him. "I'll be in touch with Dr. Catrini continually," he went on, "and when I leave here, I'll check smears from the material we took from Joey. However, there are actually no definitive conclusions we can draw until the biopsy comes back in the morning."

He judged it prudent not to mention that certain cultures could take days, even weeks to grow out. "Meanwhile," he added, "take heart from the knowledge that your son is receiving the best medical care possible."

"But we need answers, Doctor." Through his grief, Joseph St. John glared at MacDonald with a razor-sharp look that brooked no opposition. "My wife and I are terrified. He's our only child."

As if prompted by her husband's comment, Eleanor St. John reached over to stroke Joey's forehead. The boy was light-boned and green-eyed, like her. He was under seventy pounds, suntanned, and looked deathly ill. He had a nasal oxygen feed taped over his mouth and nose, and he appeared to be breathing evenly.

"I just don't know, Dr. MacDonald," she continued. "He was fine a few days ago, wasn't he, Vincent?" She turned back to Catrini, "and we brought him to you the second the fever and chills developed, didn't we? And now this. He was always so healthy, and now he's dying!" she sobbed.

"Eleanor, that is not the way we should be thinking." St. John walked over to her and put an arm around her, a gesture suggesting domination more than compassion. MacDonald was struck by the difference in their ages, a guesstimate of fifteen to twenty years—apparently in California, even devout Christians went for trophy wives.

"Let's pray for the best and look on the bright side," St. John continued. "Dr. Miller, our infectious disease specialist, is positive it's not Hodgkins' or leukemia. He told us that last night, remember? He told us he believes it'll turn out to be something treatable."

MacDonald was aware that Miller thought that Joey might have TB, or even a fungal disease called coccidiodomycosis, known as valley fever. He fervently hoped something more treatable was growing inside Joey. He cleared his throat. "I believe Dr. Miller mentioned TB or valley fever, and yes, those conditions are high on the list, but I have to be honest with you; Joey required the lymph node biopsy because his illness could still prove to be a lymphoma."

"No, not cancer!" Mrs. St. John stiffened, her right hand flying to her mouth in dread, and she rose from beside the boy.

Catrini went to her side and tried to comfort her with a hug. "Eleanor, these days lymphomas and Hodgkin's are treatable—and curable."

21

MacDonald wondered if the boy's parents realized that both he and Catrini were hedging their bets. The nodes were unquestionably the source of Joey's fever, cough, and sepsis. Whether they were cancerous, fungal, or tubercular was far from certain. If someone were holding a gun to his head, he probably would have guessed it was cocci, the symptoms of which were often confused with TB. A possibility, even a strong one, but no more than that. MacDonald, like Catrini and Miller, was mystified, but he had no intention of making it known.

"I'd like to go over a couple of questions if you're up to it, Mrs. St. John." When she tearfully nodded yes, MacDonald asked her, "Is Joey in the habit of putting things in his mouth—toys, candy, anything sharp—popsicle sticks, for instance, or toothpicks, straws, or those little wooden skewers that they use for shish kebabs? What about lollipop sticks?"

Mrs. St. John looked surprised at the question. "Why, no." She turned to Catrini. "Vince, you know we rarely allow candy, and I can assure you, Dr. MacDonald, Joey's never had lollipops at home. I'm terrified he could fall down with the stick in his mouth. We don't even keep toothpicks around the house because of that." The futility of those safety precautions in light of what they were now facing caused Eleanor to break down once more, but her husband, one tough hombre, gave the doctors a look that would melt ice and turned to Catrini. "Why is it important?"

"Because, Joseph," Catrini replied, "something is causing those lymph nodes to swell. If it's a germ, it might have gotten to them directly, and not indirectly through the lungs as pneumonia would. Germs could have been introduced directly into that space. You see, if a person accidentally swallows a toothpick and it punctures the esophagus on the way down, all sorts of germs could be introduced into the chest area that can grow there."

Refusing to be upstaged by a local, MacDonald interrupted, "What about tortilla chips, Mrs. St. John? Does Joey like them?"

"No," Mrs. St. John replied quickly, then added by way of explanation, "as a matter of fact we—he—never eats Mexican food." She paused. "Why do you ask?"

Catrini told a disbelieving Eleanor, "Chips have been known to lacerate the esophagus on the way down, as neatly as a scalpel."

MacDonald interrupted, "I've operated on three kids who wolfed chips down without softening them with saliva or soda."

Eleanor sighed, "There's really no way to be sure... just as we told Dr. Catrini when he admitted Joey."

"Has Joey traveled anyplace out of the ordinary lately, some situation that isn't habitual to him?"

Reviewing the events of her son's life before this curse was visited upon him seemed to bring Eleanor St. John to the brink of total breakdown. "The only place I can think of is the San Diego Zoo. His first grade teacher took Joey's class on a field trip there a few days ago. Wednesday, I think. Yes, Wednesday. He loved the animals, although he isn't allowed to touch them. You know, they carry disease."

"Could he have eaten something he's not used to having?"

"Oh, I don't think so," she told him. "We've taught him very strictly about the dangers of junk food, and he's a very obedient child."

Poor overprotected kid, MacDonald thought, *not much of a childhood without candy, without animals, and now this.* "Are you sure, Mrs. St. John, he didn't mention what he did at the zoo?"

"No, I've absolutely no idea what he might have eaten. Perhaps we could ask his friends and teachers... but knowing Joey, if he had a choice it would be pizza. We do allow pizza. He likes it plain, extra cheese, no mushrooms... "

It was getting harder for the woman to maintain even a modicum of composure, and her emotionalism was beginning to grate on MacDonald. Looking impatiently at the troubled couple, he announced brusquely, "Check with his teacher and friends. If you learn anything, it could be helpful. In any event, we should have the answer when the biopsy comes back. I'll be reviewing the smears and cultures for other organisms. Please be assured, whatever this thing is, it's no match for modern medical science," and with that he swept imperiously from the room, never suspecting how grievously he misspoke.

*　　*　　*

MacDonald had decided to go back to his hotel and sip a frozen margarita by the pool when Catrini beeped him. On answering the page, he was annoyed to discover that the St. Johns wanted to see him again. Hadn't he made it clear that until the tests came back, there was really nothing more he could do for Joey? Were they just pulling rank, showing that they were the Emperor and Empress of La Jolla, and he was just the hired help obliged to do their bidding, no matter how whimsical?

By the time he reached the door to Joey's room, the anger had been replaced by uneasiness. Whatever the reason for this command appearance, MacDonald's gut instinct told him he wasn't going to like it. When he entered and saw the St. Johns staring him down with ice-cold eyes, he knew his intuition had been right.

"Mr. and Mrs. St. John, Vince, what's up?" he began on an upbeat note. "Look, I understand your concern, of course, but as I told you, I believe we'll get Joey's situation under control."

"Yes, well, I'm reassured by your certainty, Doctor." Mrs. St. John looked at him with a stony composure that had been missing moments ago. "But to reassure ourselves just a bit more, we've taken the liberty of asking

25

another consultant to join us." MacDonald looked surprised.

Mr. St. John continued, "Dr. Catrini suggested there might be other bugs, maybe even a virus like that Four Corners thing a few years ago. He mentioned some diseases carried by mosquitoes, or that hantavirus, or perhaps even something Joey might have picked up at the zoo. He recommended a Dr. Jack Bryne, from New York. We just got confirmation that he will land in a few hours." Mr. St. John turned to Catrini to explain more about this new player in the game.

"He's an expert on exotic infections," Catrini told him, "particularly the newer viruses we seem to hear about every day. Dr. Miller heard him lecture in San Francisco two years ago. Brilliant. Interesting background. He's not a medical doctor. More like a scholar of unusual communicable diseases. Physicians consult him when bizarre infections have them baffled. Spent years with the World Health Organization. He tracks emerging infections as the moderator of ProMED. Perhaps you've heard of it."

Mac hadn't a clue, and it must have shown on his face because Catrini continued, "As I explained to Mr. and Mrs. St. John, ProMED was set up in '93 by the Federation of American Scientists to maintain global surveillance of these new pathogens. Scientists from one hundred and forty-six countries now belong—largely because Jack Bryne is head man. My CDC friends admit it's far superior to their own e-mail system, WONDER. Bryne's responsible for screening incoming messages for urgency. ProMED could very well provide us with the key to Joey's illness, and Bryne *is* ProMED."

MacDonald, outflanked, nodded. "I've got considerable faith in Dr. Catrini's judgment. I'm sure he's recommended the top people." MacDonald spun Catrini's recommendation around into a bit of flattery for himself. "This Bryne sounds outstanding."

"Well, then, we are relieved, Dr. MacDonald," said Eleanor. "We'll be hearing from you soon?" She cocked her head and smiled icily. MacDonald nodded.

Mr. St. John went on, "Thanks again, Dr. MacDonald. When Dr. Catrini mentioned the possibility of hantavirus last night, you know, when Joey was first having trouble breathing, we wanted the best."

"Fine, then," he said diplomatically. "This Bryne, where's he from?"

"Albany," Catrini answered. "I thought that seemed a bit strange, his not being from New York City, but that's where ProMED's based. I was assured he was the man to call. And he has two Ph.D.s, if that means anything."

"Well, these days, with the world becoming such a small place, an expert on these new emerging viruses might be a good choice."

"I want us all to meet this evening. Early, if you would," said Mrs. St. John. "I want to know what is happening here, and I want you to call me the moment you get any results. I'm

27

sure Dr. Catrini will let you know when Dr. Bryne arrives," and she turned from Mac-Donald with a look of sheer disdain that told him he was now utterly irrelevant.

Mac MacDonald strode away from Joey's room pissed as hell at how badly things were going. Now some computer specialist who wasn't even a physician was stealing his thunder just because he was a so-called expert on weird infectious diseases! After all, hanta was only one explanation for the St. John boy's condition—and Joey's symptoms didn't even fit with it, no hemoconcentration, no whiteout on the X-ray of his lungs, meaning the boy's illness was not caused by fluids filling his lungs. The problem was outside the lungs, in the space behind the breast bone. Other organisms could do that, many other organisms, but none of them were viruses.

It still could be TB, MacDonald pondered as he stepped into the elevator and pressed the button for the lobby. Yes, TB wasn't a bad guess, or maybe an atypical mycobacterium, legionnaires', cocci, or some filthy anaerobe that could have come from the boy's teeth and somehow entered the mediastinum through a perforation. Anaerobes—bugs that grew without the presence of oxygen—were almost impossible to treat even with intravenous antibiotics if they got into the mediastinum.

As the elevator stopped at every floor and more and more people piled in, MacDonald mused that cocci was not unlikely. He recalled

28

reading a few years back about a rash of cocci cases tied directly to the North Ridge earthquake. The quake had stirred up surface dust for hundreds of miles, and that dust was laden with the fungal spores. The fungus, *Coccidioides immitis*, was endemic to the entire Sonora plateau, a dry highland extending from Arizona into California's San Joaquin Valley. Winds had kicked up the spores from their nests and blown them for weeks back over the Valley. The term "valley fever" had been coined by early settlers of the region to describe the strange, flulike illness which, in rare instances, could kill. With valley fever came desert bumps—a manifestation of the disease that caused painful, hot red lumps on the shins.

As the elevator at last made it to the lobby and the passengers shuffled out, MacDonald realized that he'd forgotten to ask Catrini if he'd checked the boy's legs. Well, tomorrow would tell. If the kid survived that long.

Walking to the parking lot to pick up his rental car, MacDonald felt his anger dissipate and a steely indifference set in. Hell, the case wasn't his problem anymore. It was Bryne's. The St. Johns had treated him like he was history, and history was just what he was going to be.

Then and there, MacDonald decided to sign off before they fired him. Later that day, he'd turn the case over to Catrini and the new expert, then summarize his findings for the high and mighty St. Johns at the evening meeting. He'd be out of there and back to Santa Barbara like a shot. Until then, he wanted nothing more from this case but that frozen margarita and a long swim in the chlorinated pool. As he exhaled with sheer relief, it struck MacDonald that whether this Bryne was the world's greatest virus hunter or a total fraud, he surely didn't envy him.

2

Wednesday, June 17
San Diego, California

Vince Catrini had been waiting for Dr. John Bryne in the lobby of the luxurious Hotel Del Coronado—the crown jewel in Joseph St. John's real estate empire—for what seemed like hours, but was more likely fifteen minutes. As his eyes continually scanned the long covered awning over the entrance to the hotel, Catrini could not help wondering why Joseph St. John had chosen this particular location for their meeting. For one thing, it was inconveniently and unnecessarily far from the hospital. For another, its very lavishness mocked the severity of the meeting's occasion. After all, this was not a physicians' junket. It was a race against time with a child's life at stake.

Bryne and that ass MacDonald had been assigned suites on the top floor overlooking the ocean—a view Catrini felt sure they wouldn't be admiring much. He had been in charge of assembling the chart and lab reports, reproducing the CT and MRI scans, and delivering copies of them to the makeshift conference room that had been set up with a slide projector, a fax, and the dedicated line Bryne had requested in advance for his laptop.

The meeting was to have commenced at 8:00 P.M., but it seemed the St. John's Gulfstream bearing Bryne had been delayed almost an hour, stacked up over Lindbergh Field in a holding pattern. Still, that didn't mean the fireworks would not go off on time—thanks to MacDonald. He'd delivered in spades on what Catrini had been sure would be his next move. Precisely at eight, MacDonald strode into the conference room, announcing he had some hopeful news. "Joey's had a much easier afternoon than yesterday," he pontificated. "Your boy's a tough little soldier, and I'm optimistic the antibiotics will hold him."

MacDonald added that he was sure they weren't dealing with a malignancy and that Joey was under the best of care. Then came the clincher. "I'll oversee the case from Santa Barbara. Now I want to say a few words to you which have helped so many distressed parents... "

Mrs. St. John grimaced. Not only was the jerk walking away, he was following it up with his patented "Parental Stress Reduction Talk."

"That'll be quite enough," Eleanor had snapped at him, making it clear she wanted nothing more to do with the man they had counted on to save their son. A man who was now running away from a sick little boy.

31

One and a half hours later, with final confirmation that the jet had landed, Catrini had been dispatched to greet Dr. John Bryne. While waiting, he reviewed the extensive dossier on John Drake Bryne, Ph.D., he'd gotten from his colleagues at the Centers for Disease Control.

Dr. John Bryne had been born to an English Anglican minister and his American wife as they traveled to China in 1937 to be missionaries. An orphan of war, Bryne had been repatriated by the American Army and hadn't seen England until many years later. It was known around the virus-hunting world that his wartime experience had been extremely traumatic, but, by virtue of that fact, was never discussed by him or his colleagues. Whatever the horror, its trauma had not turned John Bryne into a monster, but instead into a thoroughly good man who lived to help the sick. He had risked his own life over and over to do so.

Catrini was aware that everybody who knew Jack Bryne liked and respected him; that he was one of the preeminent virologists in the world; that his ProMED system offered a lone hope—and only a distant one—of riding herd over global disease; that he could speak nine languages; and that he was his own man, with a deep ambivalence for authority. Catrini knew all too well how that could be a problem with the St. Johns. He'd just have to wait and see.

The other fascinating item of Bryne's dossier was his wife, top New York City public health official Mia Hart, a strikingly beautiful woman with a steel-trap mind. Vince had seen her at a conference once, and never forgotten her. This was the first time since he'd seen Mia that Vince wasn't jealous of Bryne—who sure had his work cut out for him.

Checking his watch, Catrini shook his head. Only seven minutes had passed since last he'd looked. When he'd talked to Bryne on the phone, Jack had described himself in an unmistakable English accent as "Six-four, middle-aged, thin, tie." Yet, since he'd been waiting at their agreed-upon rendezvous point, the central lobby, no one even remotely fitting that description had passed by.

And suddenly, there he was. A tall, distinguished, middle-aged man emerging from the antique elevator, pausing to straighten his tie. As Vince hurried over to meet him, the man headed toward the desk clerk.

"Doctor." Catrini held up his hand. "Oh, Doctor."

"Yes?" When the man turned and his eyes met Catrini's, there was not a hint of welcome; instead, a strange deadness sent a shiver through Catrini and slowed him down.

"Dr. Bryne? Dr. Jack Bryne?" Vince thought he saw a sudden glint in the stranger's eyes at the mention of Bryne's name, and extended his hand. The man simply looked down at it.

"I'm sorry, sir," the desk clerk broke in, "this is our guest, Dr. Thomas Kay."

"Oh, sorry," Catrini apologized to the man. "I'm looking for somebody else." The man turned and immediately disappeared into the crowded lobby. Catrini rolled his eyes, and the desk clerk nodded and smiled. "That guy's a real character. Hardly ever leaves his room. Maybe a couple hours a day tops. Orders room service. And did you notice those... gloves. He never takes them off. Some people. Go figure..."

Amused, Catrini returned to his station, unaware that Dr. Kay was watching him from across the room.

It was the tie, Vince surmised, that had made him stop the stranger, since neckwear was rare at the "Del." When the next person entering the lobby was also wearing a tie, Catrini was sure he had his man—although he couldn't have been more off in his fantasy of the new arrival's appearance. After all, he'd expected Bryne to look almost as run-of-the-mill as that queer duck for whom he'd mistaken him.

If the man walking in was indeed Bryne, he looked right in place in Southern California: long silver-streaked hair pulled back in a ponytail and tied with a red ribbon, jeans, denim shirt with tie, tweed jacket, loafers, confident step, athletic bearing, craggy features. He had brilliant blue eyes, a deep tan, and a sort of Clint Eastwood awareness of who he was and what was going on around him—a troubleshooter for sure. Vince was glad to see him.

Catrini waved and stepped over toward the man he hoped was Bryne, noticing as he did that his tie was ornamented with clawlike crimson symbols—the biohazard icon used everywhere in hospitals, from the sharps receptacles for used needles to the door leading to the pathology lab. That proved it. It had to be Bryne.

"Breen?" he asked, looking up into a pair of alert eyes, clouded a bit by jet lag, and extended his hand.

"That's close enough. Call me Jack. 'Brin,' actually, although it's spelled like 'Breen,' it's pronounced 'Brin' as in 'gin.'" He smiled and offered his hand in introduction. "Dr. Catrini, I presume?"

Jack Bryne was the taller of the two men by a head, but he sensed there was a physical—or energetic—equality between them. He didn't need to bend down to greet the Chief of Pediatrics' grip. It came right up to Bryne and held in a gentle, comforting manner that soon strengthened to exude a joyous vivacity. Bryne could feel the power in Catrini's hands and noticed the thick muscles of his neck. This guy, like himself, was a fighter born and bred—but one who radiated kindness and compassion. Jack liked him immediately.

"I must apologize for not being suitably dressed," Bryne grinned. "I had no idea we'd be so late landing. I was planning to change in my room."

"Don't give it a thought," Catrini told him. "It's California. I'm just so glad you could make it, Bryne.... Come on, we'll go upstairs." As Catrini began to steer him across the lobby, he attempted to fill Bryne in about Joey's case, speaking with his hands, gesturing to make every point. It was obvious that Catrini was terribly concerned about the boy. What was less obvious was another, unvoiced concern that was clearly adding to his anxiety.

By the time they'd entered the ornate old elevator and after Catrini had asked the requisite questions about Bryne's flight—"Posh" was the virologist's only comment—the pediatrician came clean about the matter that had been plaguing him. "Ummm," Catrini murmured, "this is going to be tough news to break. The Intensive Care nurse called me half an hour ago to say that the boy's condition has been downgraded."

Bryne nodded sympathetically, appreciating Catrini's problem. "The St. Johns don't know?"

"Not yet." Vince shook his head mournfully. "He's developed pneumonia with bilateral effusions. You guessed it. The hard part is going to be telling the parents without crying myself."

In only a few seconds, Bryne had seen the immense amount of love and dedication Catrini had devoted to his small patient. "I'll do all I can to help, Vince," he assured him as they got off the elevator and made their way to the conference room.

The room itself was early-California ornate: gilded pilasters, hand-carved moldings with floral motifs circling the ceiling, every detail

36

proclaiming that only the most important events took place in this space.

As the two men entered, Mac MacDonald rushed over to Catrini shouting, "I paged you all afternoon!"

"You paged *me*..." Catrini was incredulous. The jerk hadn't answered his beeper at all, much less used it!

"Gentlemen, please." Bryne deftly separated them before things got physical, the last thing needed in an already turbulent situation. As he did so, he caught the gaze of Mrs. St. John. He could read the terror in her eyes, along with the desperate hope that he, Jack Bryne, was the miracle who could save her son. She almost relaxed.

He had a rare talent for calming distressed women. It had something to do with his rugged handsomeness, with the comforting informality of the ponytail, the intense blue eyes, his easy grin. As his feelings of concern flowed out to Mrs. St. John, he could detect a momentary lightening in her eyes.

"I'm afraid it's my fault we're starting so late," Bryne addressed the room, with his gaze still directed at Mrs. St. John. "It was kind of Dr. Catrini to wait for me so long in the lobby." He turned to MacDonald. "Vince has been telling me what a fine job you did on Joey."

Catrini walked over to talk to the St. Johns.

"Joseph, Eleanor," Catrini said softly, "I just got off the phone with the hospital. They've moved Joey back to ICU. It seems he's developed a secondary lung infection, pneumonia, and has fluid in his lungs—a bilateral effusion. We've changed antibiotics and—"

"Stop it!" Suddenly Eleanor shot up from her chair and held out her hand in a gesture meant to silence him. "Stop it," she screamed. "Please, please, stop using those meaningless medical terms. If I hear one more buzzword, I'll... I'll... Can't one of you simply tell us what's making Joey sick?" She turned to her husband. "Joe, why is this happening to us?"

Putting his arm around her, St. John told her, "We both know we're being tested by the Lord, Eleanor. And we must be strong before Him."

"Oh, yes, yes," Eleanor replied more calmly. "Of course, the Lord is testing us. You're right, Joseph, we must be strong before Him."

Hearing this, Jack Bryne almost wished he had that kind of faith, then remembered the powerful amount of bigotry that sometimes accompanied it. The St. Johns had that same infallibly certain lock on truth, that same fundamentalist vision that could so easily become catastrophic. He'd seen deeply held beliefs destroy people, villages, tribes, cities, even nations. Approaching Mrs. St. John gently, not coming threateningly close, Jack urged her to sit. When she did, he took the chair Catrini had recently vacated.

"Mrs. St. John," he began, leaning toward her, "if I may say . . ." Already he could see her relax slightly, probably out of gratitude that there was a new presence in attendance, someone who might have an answer. "May I say that

38

I spent virtually my entire flight studying Joey's medical history, which Dr. Catrini overnighted.

"So what can I tell you that you don't already know? That Joey has an infection which has proved very difficult to diagnose? You know that. That Joey's condition is serious? You know that all too well. But, listen to me, don't overreact. There are a few bacterial and some unusual viral illnesses that often present with these symptoms. The good news is that even after a tough few days, most of them can be treated."

"Such as? Such as?" Joseph St. John broke in. "Do you have any idea?"

"No, I haven't any at this point." Bryne continued speaking principally to Eleanor, maybe because she seemed more receptive than her overbearing husband, maybe because she was the mother of a very sick little boy. "No definite ideas." he went on. "You've probably heard of tularemia—rabbit fever—and that can reverse course dramatically after the first thirty-six hours with the right antibiotics. Joey's illness could easily be something simple like that, or some infection carried by animals or picked up outside, even in the back yard. Does Joey have any pets?"

"No, no, no, no!" Overwrought, Eleanor St. John banged her first on the arms of the chair. "We've been over this again and again with the other doctors!"

"Hon," Joseph St. John's stentorian voice boomed. "Hon, the man has to ask... How

39

about I get Reverend Ford to join us and help us pray?"

"Listen to me, all of you." Eleanor spoke as if demon-possessed—cold, determined, running the show. "My boy, my only child, is dying." She stood up to continue. "The best medical minds in the country have been flown in here and all they do is cut into Joey and ask me a lot of stupid questions about his nonexistent pets or eating razor-sharp corn chips or swallowing pointed sticks!" Quiet for a moment, she looked around the room, then sat again, her head bowed mournfully.

"I'm sorry, I'm sorry," she said to no one in particular. "It's just that my Joey is dying and nobody's doing *anything*...!" Now she sank limply back in the chair, her head in her hands.

The silence that followed Eleanor St. John's outburst seemed to Bryne to be more articulate than any words could have been. It spoke of powerlessness and hopelessness and profound human suffering and grief. How pompous any of them would be if they thought differently.

"*Reep-reep-reep!*" From out of nowhere, the silence was broken by the annoying and insistent beeper on Bryne's belt. "*Reep-reep-reep... reep-reep-reep!*" His hand flew to his waist, quashing the intrusive sound, and he examined the pager's message. It was from Drew Lawrence, his best friend, closest compatriot, and invaluable lab assistant at ProMED, who in an urgent, ten-word message told him to call him, and to turn on his laptop and check the ProMED bulletins—NOW!

When Bryne glanced up, he saw Eleanor St. John staring at him with fear and despair, afraid that Joey wasn't his top priority any more than he had been MacDonald's.

"I'm terribly sorry, Mrs. St. John," he explained. "I had no idea the beeper was switched on. I've just gotten an urgent message from my assistant at the lab in Albany. It could very well have to do with Joey's case. I must take it, but I assure you, I'll be right back. And also please remember," he smiled, "Joey's recovery is my first and primary concern."

Bryne went into an adjoining room, sat at a desk, and speed-dialed Drew Lawrence's number on his cell phone. It was well past the time he'd normally be closing up, yet the phone rang only once before a weary but cheerful voice announced, "Drew Lawrence, Arbovirus Lab, how may I help?"

"Drew, it's me. Just got your pager message. I'm in a very emotional meeting with the parents of the sick kid, so we've got to make it brief. What's up?"

"Jack, you know I wouldn't bother you without cause, but it's after eleven here, and I haven't seen you log on for hours. I got a *SatelLife* report from Colombia and one from Kentucky. And yes, they're important." Bryne could picture Drew sitting in front of his Hewlett-Packard workstation, calling up the entire ProMED database with a few keystrokes.

"Oh," he added, "and you've been getting all

41

sorts of urgent phone calls. Let me just get my notebook out of my pocket.... Yes... Your wife called, Dr. Lown called, said you're supposed to have some budget projection for him for next quarter and said it is urgent. We had a new member log onto ProMED today—our ten-thousandth subscriber—a high school kid from Brooklyn named Berger. He sent us a news clip on what looks like a killer bee incident in Texas back in April. Wait till you see it. I think it should go on ProMED."

"Come on, Drew, we've posted killer bees before."

"Yeah, but this one is stranger."

"Okay—sorry to be so short—I have to get back to the parents."

"You really should glance at the Kentucky report; it's a horse die-off, cause unknown. A Dr. Enoch Tucker has been calling, thinks it might be some kind of rabies, and wants to talk to you. Know him?"

"Tucker's one of the most experienced old-line vets in America, Drew. He was Assistant Surgeon General in the seventies and wrote the definitive text on zoonotic diseases."

"Was?"

"Exactly," Bryne answered ruefully. "He disappeared into the private sector when Reagan came in, like many of the CDC's best people. If Tucker's calling us, it has to be unusual."

Bryne's deference to the veterinarian was justified. He was the authority on bizarre disease spinoffs from animals, the diseases and parasites that occasionally infected humans, the so-called zoonoses.

42

"Dr. Tucker also FedExed us an envelope here marked 'PERSONAL' with a return address in Louisville."

"You got the package right there? Well, open it, let's see what he sent."

Bryne heard the sound of paper tearing, and in a second Lawrence came back on the line. "It's reprints, four old journal articles on horses. There's a note on Tucker's memo paper, and all it says is 'FYI Call if possible.' He initialed it. And he had also sent an e-mail marked 'URGENT' for ProMED."

"What's the scoop? I haven't been able to get to my laptop for hours."

"Seems there have been seventeen dead racehorses in six stables during the past three weeks. Tucker's asking for advice. He's now lost six horses in two days. It's a lethal disease with no diagnosis and no reliable treatment. He said that locals were calling it an epidemic."

"Sounds serious," Bryne told him.

"Oh, and just by the way," Drew continued "you and ProMED were recommended to him by your old buddy, that hotshot TV reporter Victoria Wade. She's been calling you, too." The disapproval in Drew's voice was obvious. "A lot."

"Vicky Wade." Bryne tried to sound as unaffected as possible by the mention of her name. "What's she doing there?"

"She thinks it's another insurance fraud, like the Connecticut horse assassinations a few years ago. *Hot Line* apparently sent her to research the story. It seems the horses can't eat... "

Bryne tried to focus on what Drew was telling him, but the image of Vicky Wade's lovely face suffused his concentration with affectionate memories. It had been years since they had seen each other, but he could visualize her smile, her lips, her radiance, as if it had been only days. He would always remember how close they had been, how close to happiness, and he would always think of their parting with regret. His love for Vicky had been so different from his love for his wife, Mia Hart, and the difference still struck him, even now that he was with Mia. But, Vicky. Wouldn't you know she'd wind up back in his life?

"Any clues?" he asked Drew, forcing his focus back to the subject at hand. "What's Tucker come up with?"

"Not much. Of the three horses autopsied, one had a benign growth at the bottom of the esophagus, another gastric erosions, the third an infection of myiasis—a maggot infestation of botfly larvae in the folds of its stomach. Nothing to explain the deaths."

"What about path reports?" He could hear Drew sifting through the paperwork.

"Brain sections are still being processed, results are pending. Breeder's horses are also dying in other parts of the Midwest. The cause is also unknown, the disease almost always fatal. And Jack, there's a rumor that some sheep may be dying."

"Drew," Bryne said with some urgency,

"add a summary of the details and put it up on ProMED. Here's your headline: *CRITICAL: ProMED request: What is the differential diagnosis of a horse die-off, location: Kentucky.*"

Before he left the lab for the night, Lawrence would include a complete list of symptoms and laboratory results and add it to the ProMED report. Every ProMED subscriber would see the posting. Often, even with puzzles about human patients, veterinarians were better than physicians. Both Bryne and Lawrence wished that more like Tucker would join.

These zoonoses frightened Lawrence: infections of animals that jumped species and infected humans. A species jump from monkey to man, like HIV, was one of the most unpredictable, the most inevitable, the most lethal ways for these pathogens—the bulk of the so-called "new" diseases—to emerge. And he worked with so many samples every day. No one knew what damage they could create, what human weaknesses they would exploit. Hosts with neither inherited nor acquired defenses could be invaded by sophisticated pieces of nucleic acid capable of operating with no game plan. What a single animal virus might do, evolving for millions of years in an isolated monkey population in central Africa, could be catastrophic if introduced into the population of Manhattan.

"It'll be a new one, Drew. Whatever Tucker finds. He knows it all, and if this one has stumped him, then I hope we get a little help from our friends."

So few experts had the opportunity to collaborate. ProMED provided the first forum for an exchange of information among specialists, vets, Ph.D.s, M.D.s, entomologists, and cadres of infectious disease researchers. The forum was an equal opportunity employer of other scientists' expertise.

Bryne wondered how long it would take for the first response, how long before the horses stopped dying. Other "ProMEDers" on line would soon be sending him suggestions, one of which might be the key.

"You hope, Jack," Drew said wryly. "I believe I'll pray."

"Okay, Drew, I might too. But listen, I've really got to go." Bryne tried to sign off. "Thanks for using the beeper. So long. Sorry I kept you so late."

"No Jack, wait. Not yet. I'm afraid I saved the worst for last. Just open ProMED. I've already posted this one. You better look."

"I'll log on to ProMED right now."

"Fine."

"Night, Drew." He closed the cell phone and reached for his laptop.

The conversation with Bryne left Drew Lawrence more than uneasy. Jack's impatience and distraction had been obvious, and he really hadn't discussed the St. John boy's case at all, which was not a good sign. Drew knew Jack about as well as he knew himself, and he could always tell when something wasn't right. After working together for years, they were practically married.

46

A powerfully built African-American with a congenitally arthritic left hip, Lawrence, a devout Baptist, had always seen his affliction as a divine challenge, and vowed at fourteen never to let the chronic pain and limited mobility get the better of him. Then and there he had decided to be successful. Sports, of course, were out automatically, and he had chosen science, where he excelled.

A longtime Harlem resident, Drew had been ambivalent about moving his family to Albany when the State Health Department's Wadsworth Laboratory made him an offer he couldn't refuse. Life in Albany had been good to all the Lawrences. His wife, Elise, stayed at home, although she was active in black professional social circles and in restoring the beautiful old Baptist church two blocks from the capitol building. His son, Ali, had gone to SUNY and then on to NYU Law School. Despite the chronic pain and the limp, Drew Lawrence considered himself a very lucky man.

That's what he was thinking when sometime later he switched off his computer, took off his lab coat, and turned to his notebook. He penciled a tiny checkmark next to Victoria Wade's messages. Drew wasn't a man to meddle in other people's business, but he knew enough about Victoria Wade's history with Jack Bryne, as well as the strained state of Jack's marriage, to feel anything but disturbed that Wade seemed to be back in the picture.

"Damn!" was the strongest expletive in

Lawrence's vocabulary, and when uttered by this gentle man, it had enormous force. "Damn!" Next he turned the notebook's page, made a notation about the bees, and underlined it to remind himself. He had very badly wanted to tell Bryne about this kid Berger's message. He would be intrigued.

The last thing Bryne wanted to do was keep the St. Johns waiting, but after talking to Drew, it was imperative he log onto ProMED and read the two new messages Drew had mentioned.

The first was an urgent entry from an old friend, Carlos Garcia, who was with WHO in Geneva. As Bryne scrolled down the lines of Garcia's message, his eyes widened. He could have kicked himself. He'd spent most of the flight studying Joey St. John's medical records. He'd missed more than the horse situation. What was happening in Colombia was worse. What Garcia was reporting was an epidemic. Colombian doctors were treating thousands of stricken villagers. Bryne scanned the information rapidly.

```
Jack, please post this on ProMED:
La Guajira, Colombia:
250,000 people exposed to growing
epidemic of dengue fever, complicated
now by dengue hemorrhagic fever and
shock syndrome. Epidemic out of con-
trol… hospitals overwhelmed… mortali-
ty estimates minimum 13,000 locals
```

previous week... Undetermined but close
to catastrophic deaths in indigenous
people, especially children... Mosquito
breeding sites still unidentified...
Concerns will spread to Caribbean...
Help desperately needed and welcomed...
Carlos G.

Oh no, thought Bryne, *it can't have gotten into that many humans.* Why hadn't they believed him? God help those poor people.... He shook his head. Drew was right to beep him.

It was with sorrow that Jack realized he had predicted this turn of events when he consulted down there years ago. Back then, he had been naive about American business's utterly uncaring attitude toward the Third World. He had actually thought the mining company might listen when he urged them not to build the road with "borrow pits" running alongside, but they had anyway, hundreds of miles of them, creating the perfect mosquito breeding grounds. And now mosquito-borne viral diseases were causing this epidemic: hemorrhagic dengue so far, very possibly to be followed by yellow fever. How terrible to be right at such a cost.

The second message read:

Jack Bryne:
Request your presence, Louisville
area, to assist in investigation of
recent equine deaths reported on
ProMED. Will coordinate all trans-

portation. Appreciate your help. Victoria Wade sends warm regards. Enoch Tucker, D.V.M.

"Vicky, Vicky," Bryne found himself chuckling aloud, "always around a story!"

"Just what is it you're doing, Dr. Bryne? My husband and I didn't fly you out here so you could play computer games!" Jack almost jumped when he heard Eleanor St. John's voice behind him, then turned around to face her embarrassment.

Already the anger in her face was dissipating, turning rapidly to misery. "I'm sorry, Dr. Bryne," she told him. "My remark was uncalled-for... "

"No, no, Mrs. St. John." Bryne stood and waved off her apology. "I realize I haven't helped much—yet, but if you'll sit down, I'd like to show you what I'm doing. I've got a good feeling it can be used to help Joey."

"Dr. Catrini said we could count on you. We heard that you were the best."

"No, no, I'm no better than any other good researcher. I get the credit because I have so many dedicated people behind me. I'm only as good as the men and women who contribute to ProMED."

He pulled out a chair for her, then explained that through ProMED, he could access thousands of doctors from all over the world in minutes. "With complete privacy," he continued, "I can tell them all about Joey's case. We can have hundreds of experts giving us help, new ideas, even a diagnosis, Mrs. St. John."

"Call me Eleanor. Formality seems so out of place in the middle of a crisis."

"Well, only if you call me Jack," he smiled.

"It's a deal." She almost smiled herself. "So, Jack, how can you do all that from that little machine?" Eleanor St. John still was not convinced.

"First of all, Eleanor," Bryne began, "as I've already told you, I spent the entire flight examining Joey's medical records, which Dr. Catrini sent to me in New York. Now I've transferred all those records into a single file. I've scanned every record, lab report, X-ray, and CT and MRI. Last thing tonight and early tomorrow morning I'll add the most recent reports from St. Roch's lab. See."

As she watched, he scrolled through files outlining everything about Joey's case history.

"So with your permission, I'm prepared to put Joey's case on ProMED, requesting any help we could possibly get."

Her face brightened at the prospect of more aid, much, much more. "Of course. Just hurry!"

After tagging the request with an URGENT icon, Bryne pointed at the screen. "Within a matter of minutes now we'll have experts from more than a hundred and forty different countries taking a look at Joey's case. Other virologists like myself, some of the best epidemiologists, infectious disease specialists, microbiologists, entomologists, vets... "

51

He tapped in the final short command codes that unleashed the entire flood of data before noticing that Eleanor was frozen in fear, oblivious to what he was doing.

"Eleanor! Eleanor, what is it?" he pleaded with her.

"Vets." She answered in a monotone. "You mean veterinarians?" And when he nodded, she began literally to tremble. "Vets. Oh, God. That zoo. What if it was that zoo?"

While Bryne worked his laptop and Eleanor watched, Catrini brought them all ice water. Eleanor thanked him, and drank deeply. Seeing Bryne sending Joey's records out on his computer calmed her considerably, and the tension began to go out of the room. MacDonald had been busily reassuring Joseph St. John, who soon came over and put his hand on his wife's shoulder. "Anything I can do?" he asked Bryne.

"No, that's it for now, folks." When he rose, St. John shook his hand.

Bryne and Catrini had been aware of the St. Johns' resolve. Once the couple understood what Joey's doctors had done, and were doing, for their child, that resolve had finally turned to trust.

"If you feel comfortable letting me leave," Bryne spoke up, "I want to go to the hospital immediately so I can see Joey for myself."

"Of course, Dr. Bryne, whenever you're ready." Mrs. St. John reached for the telephone.

"I would be most grateful for a ride," admitted Bryne. "I'm no match for freeways."

"Certainly," Catrini offered, reaching for his briefcase and keys. "I'll take him myself."

"Then I'm sending the limo to bring you back for the night, Dr. Bryne," Eleanor St. John insisted. "Your bags are in your suite already. Please, if you're ready to leave." Seeing her hands start to clench again, Bryne knew it was pointless to protest.

Before leaving, Catrini urged the couple to go back up to La Jolla and get some rest, promising to call them as soon as anything came in. When they tried to object, he insisted.

Grateful to be underway, the two men buckled themselves into Catrini's vintage Jaguar and left the garage well ahead of the Town Car. Catrini drove with both hands on the wheel, taking the convoluted road back like a Formula 1 driver, the gas floored at ninety. As they hit the crest of the Coronado Bridge, Bryne felt close to weightless.

"Vince. Slow down. C'mon. You'll kill us all."

"Welcome to California, Jack. Everybody drives like this. I fit right in. Plus most of the San Diego police know my car. Not to worry. Now, what was Eleanor talking about when she got so upset?"

"It was the animals," Bryne answered, "a near-phobia about small animals. No pets, no access to neighbors' pets. When it sank in that we're contacting vets, the phobia really hit home. She started talking about his field trip to the lion house. I took it all down. Of course, she needs to see every animal at the zoo as a potential time bomb."

"Well, Jack, who can blame her? I feel like a first-year med student around this one. What about some zoonosis that might fit the profile?"

"Animal diseases?" Bryne thought out loud. "Nothing much comes to mind. The boy apparently broke away from his teacher at the zoo, but no, I don't think it's a zoonosis. What I do think is that we've got a parent on the edge here. If you know her personal physician, you probably ought to give him a call."

Catrini nodded in agreement, then returned to the subject of Joey. "What about some kind of poison? A pesticide, maybe?"

"Doubt it, it sounds like an infection, Vince," Bryne replied as Catrini slid into his parking slot and turned off the car.

"C'mon, let's get upstairs." Catrini leapt from the Jag, then pointed to the road. "See, here's your limo now. I told you. Everybody drives like me." Bryne smiled as he unwound his long body from the tiny car and followed Catrini from the parking garage and into the staff entrance. Catrini waved to the guard and escorted Bryne to the ICU.

Joey St. John was sleeping when Catrini opened his chart and systematically thumbed through the thick collection of papers and reports. Two nurses stood behind the two doctors.

"Damn, the blood cultures are still pending and the biopsy won't be back until tomorrow." Bryne felt the pediatrician's urgency as he flipped to the end of the chart and checked the nurses' notes.

"He looks dehydrated. Has he taken any fluids by mouth?" Bryne asked.

"I.V. only since yesterday, I. and O. are okay, vital signs stable." Then Catrini whistled in amazement. "The white count's up to twenty-seven thousand despite the change in antibiotics."

"Look at that dressing, Vince. I think it should be changed." Bryne pointed to the four-by-four bandage over the boy's collarbone.

One of the nurses handed Catrini a box of disposable latex gloves. He slipped them on and gently removed the dressing. The other nurse held out a small towel and took the soiled bandage.

"According to the chart, this was changed only an hour ago, but look, Jack."

The small incision MacDonald had made to introduce his instrument had been closed by three black silk sutures, which were all bulging outward as if confining some inner pressure. A thick green pus oozed out around each stitch.

"Come on now, Stacey," Catrini ordered, "change this thing, stat." One of the nurses ran off to get a fresh dressing as he confessed to Bryne, "Jack, we're in trouble. Nothing's holding the kid, thank God he's holding his own." He gave the chart to the other nurse. "Call me if there's anything new. I'm ordering a portable chest X-ray, stat. He's too critical to send him for another CT." He turned to Bryne, clearly exhausted. "Jack, we both better get some rest; do you want to spend the night at our house? It's a few blocks away."

Bryne thanked Catrini for the invitation, but knew he would be more comfortable on his own. He shook hands, grateful for Catrini's support. After promising to join him at six the next morning, Bryne took the elevator down to the garage, where he tumbled with relief into the back seat of the St. Johns' limo, and stretched out his legs at last.

Wednesday, June 17
San Diego
11:00 P.M.

As the limo sped him back to the luxury of the Del, Jack contrasted the rich, elegant interior of the vehicle with his spare, cluttered office in New York. He was, to tell the truth, a little ashamed of the mess he'd left behind when he so abruptly answered the governor's personal request to help the St. John boy. Oh, that desk: textbooks, journals, printouts, handwritten reports, faxes, downloaded e-mail, and mountains of memos slurried off his desk onto the floor. Thank God for Drew Lawrence, who was capably running the show in his absence. Thank God, in fact, for a lot of unexpected things that had come to him.

Gazing at the splashes of silver moonlight glistening on the ebony ocean, Bryne mused about the strange turns his life had insisted on taking since the waking nightmare of his childhood. After earning his Ph.D.s, one at Cambridge and one at the University of Virginia, he'd joined the World Health Organization in Geneva, a stint he'd never regretted. He had visited many of the most fascinating places in the world—from the most godforsaken to the divinely lush. He had lectured frequently at the Swiss Academy of Sciences, and advised physicians who attended to heads of state, many of whom desperately turned to WHO for advice.

Bryne had flown in private planes long before the St. Johns' summons, had slept in presidential palaces as well as pitiful village clinics. He had helped train physicians all over the globe, only to see them and their dreams destroyed by senseless genocidal wars. Back then, his life had been one devoted entirely to service, and family had never mattered much to him.

Abruptly, in his late twenties, he had fallen in love and married—Lisle Barclay, his delicate blond lab assistant. They worked extremely well together, and that helped convince him they could just as amiably be private partners, and so they wed. Their supposition had turned out to be accurate. The radiant first days of their marriage were rich with work and pleasure. They were even considering starting a family when Lisle was struck fatally by a car in a crosswalk accident that should never have happened. But it had, and the days of sunlight seemed to have ended forever. At first Bryne had chosen solitude to hide his grief, turning back full-time to his research.

Then, after a long and bitter season in purgatory, came four blessings. The first, which got him out of Europe and off to America, a place with no bad memories, was an offer from the New York State Health Commissioner to serve as chief virologist at the prestigious New York State Zoonosis Laboratory. His office and research facility, ten miles west of Albany, was a complex of modular one-story buildings connected to an old farmhouse by covered walkways. From the driveway, the pre-war, four-room country house seemed bucolic. It had a stout stone chimney overgrown with honeysuckle vines and a beautiful view west toward the Adirondacks.

Inside, the lab was anything but peaceful. It contained the emergency isolation facilities used by the New York State Department of Health for the containment and diagnosis of various "hot" infectious agents: rabies, hantavirus, and other lethal insect-borne viruses.

The second gift was Drew Lawrence. Lawrence, in his younger days, had been a tech in a lab at New York Medical College, under Eileen P. Halsey, Ph.D., widely regarded as "The Queen of Stool," and also the best parasitologist that the medical school, any medical school, would ever know. Halsey had been Drew Lawrence's mentor for years. When she died, Lawrence decided to opt for other labs, other agencies, other cities. He had carefully chosen the job with New York State's prominent research facility several years before Bryne arrived.

The two men had worked beside each other as equals, sharing their knowledge. Lawrence was now as skilled in epidemiology and virology as he had been in parasitology after Halsey had trained him.

The third astonishing opportunity to come looking for Jack Bryne was ProMED. As ProMED's monitor, he was the one who screened each of the incoming calls for urgency, appropriateness, and legitimacy. He admired the system not simply because it allowed for an almost instantaneous exchange of information on emerging disease activities, but because he saw it as a system free from meddlesome government controls. It was Bryne who had coined the word "bureaupathic" to describe the illnesses caused more by government meddling than by microbes alone. Good intentions truly pave the road to hell, he thought ruefully. Plagues, starvation, civil wars, and beyond—he saw it all each day.

Of all the doctors and scientists linked into the system across the globe, Bryne was the one who read what he called the "Holy Shit List" first. He edited it, frequently late at night from his home computer. As a result, Bryne was often the one to sound the alarm when there was a crisis. Even Mia, the woman who would become his wife, a doctor and an understanding human being, grew irritated at the ceaseless diseases and had once called him Jeremiah, a prophet of gloom.

And she had been the fourth miraculous event. It occurred in the late eighties, when Jack had given up on ever finding love again. It happened at a WHO conference in Paris, where he happened to hear a speaker named Mia Hart, M.D., M.P.H., who had impressed her audience, most especially Jack, with her recognition and documentation of yet another fatal infection of the immunocompromised, an obscure parasite called cryptosporidium that had been killing people in New York City.

From the first moment he saw this poised, resourceful, intelligent, and beautiful brunette behind the podium, Jack was smitten, even cowed. He had approached her shyly, almost haltingly, to compliment her after the day's session had ended. She'd smiled, taken his hand in a warm, firm grip, and allowed her eyes to meet his.

Those eyes. It was those pure sky-blue eyes that had captivated him forever. As Mia noticed Jack's intensity and inherent tenderness, he watched a blush rise from her neck and spread evenly across her cheeks until her face glowed against the frame of her lustrous raven hair.

She shifted her stance. He lowered his eyes. Bryne noted how lithe she was, how gracefully she manipulated every one of her sixty-six inches, and just how her torso moved within her blue tailored business suit, which seemed like skin about to be shed. Was she a dancer, a skier?

"WHO." She glanced at the card he had given her. "From Geneva. I've never been there. Is it beautiful?" The dusky, rich tone of her voice mesmerized with every word. "I've heard about the fountains..."

Without a second thought, Bryne took her cue and offered Mia Hart a tour of Geneva when the conference ended. On pure instinct, she accepted. Yet almost four years would pass before they married. On some of those nights so far from New York, Bryne lay with other women, one in particular. But he and Mia shared a bond of reliability and trust and were never out of touch for long: the airfares, not to mention the phone bills, were astronomical. Finally, they made it official by flying to the Alps to be married. It had been five years now.

There were times—and Jack was well aware of them—when Mia felt that being married to him was as much a challenge as a reward. It wasn't the difference in their ages, a fact that didn't concern either one of them. She had always been mature for her age, and he maintained the trim physique, boundless stamina, and free spirit of a twenty-five-year-old. She knew he loved her, knew it with absolute conviction, knew he would always be there for her, knew he shared her life with medicine. Dr. Mia Hart also knew that their respective professions were going to take up an extraordinary amount of both their lives—time she wasn't sure either of them would willingly surrender.

Being a "babe" in medical school had, if anything, made Mia's education rougher, not easier. Defensively, she'd created a steely professional persona which, if not 100 percent real, was convincing enough to have stuck with her to this day. Funny, he was the only one who'd seen through the armor—and the first time he'd met her, at that.

A dedicated physician, Mia completed a

three-year infectious diseases fellowship at New York Medical College, a Master's in Public Health from Harvard, and then took a position as Principal Epidemiologist for the New York City Health Department. After only two years, finding that beauty was not the liability it had been in med school, she'd been promoted to First Deputy Commissioner, second in command only to the Commissioner of Health. Many of her friends and colleagues were stunned by how rapidly she had scaled the bureaucratic ladder, but a series of urgent medical crises had come at the moment when she had already mastered the ability to charm the press and deal with New York City officialdom. When plague broke out in India in 1993, some people wanted JFK closed. Hart had averted a New York City crisis by simply suggesting to the mayor that passengers on all flights from India should be screened. She had dealt with a legionnaires' outbreak in a West Side hospital and a cyclospora outbreak traced to imported raspberries, and pinpointed pigeon droppings as a source of a water-borne *E. coli* outbreak in Greenwich Village.

Demanding veto power over the recommissioning of a historic East River fountain, Hart determined that aerosolized river waters could be far too dangerous to spray into the air and— after organizing a media brouhaha that culminated in a *Village Voice* headline, "AIRBORNE TYPHOID?"—finally approved the plan only with the addition of a chlorination system. After years of neglect, the fountain was now being restored and was scheduled to be dedicated at an A-list gala in the fall.

Jack Bryne was married to one very powerful woman, Mia Hart to one very important man. They still loved and desired each other with the incandescence of first passion, but both their careers had burgeoned before they met, and work put a terrible strain on intimacy. They needed each other constantly, but had to make do with a long-distance marriage. Along with commuting to work from separate weekday residences, weekend travel also became a routine part of their lives. Both had learned to read and study on the run, knowing that they worked to save untold human lives not for greed, fame, or glamour.

How many millions of lives were at risk Bryne couldn't even calculate, but he'd seen the handwriting on the wall, as Mia had also. It would be viruses that provided the new challenges: Marburg, Sabiá, HTLV-I and II, mad cow disease, and Bornavirus. He had met them on their own turf: led field investigations to Bolivia in the sixties, later the Sudan, Thailand, Cambodia, China, and Lake Baykal in eastern Russia in 1992.

Since then, it had been Geneva, London, New York. Over the years, as he tracked exotic forms of life—and death, he'd rubbed elbows on the crusade with some of the greatest virus cowboys—Johnson, Frazer, Woodall, and McCormick. Some had retired, like his old friend Carl Rader, while others still had jobs at WHO—Jan de Reuters in Amsterdam, Matt Liang in Shanghai. After the Reagan Administration's purge of the Centers for Disease Control, some very bright guys had found themselves out in the cold and had sort of fallen through the cracks and vanished, like Frank Bishop and Ted Kameron. And others, many others, had died—grotesquely—having contracted the diseases they were studying.

All these brilliant minds had been devoted to a single task—collecting viruses, the weird ones, the lethal ones, and especially the new ones. Now, with many soldiers having departed the fray, Bryne found himself virtually alone on the quest of quests: locating the "Big One"—the virus that would eclipse HIV and Ebola. While he fervently searched for it, Bryne hoped to God he'd never find it. He hoped he hadn't stumbled on it in La Jolla.

Seeing his plush suite for the first time, Jack felt a pang that he'd agreed to give up his regular obligations, pack it all in, and, on the spur of the moment, jet out to California at the behest of rich and powerful people with a sick kid. One sick kid—when there were billions all over the globe whose parents couldn't even afford a doctor, much less a consultant. But Joey St. John's case was very strange and frighteningly unique, which was why he'd immediately put it on ProMED.

Too wired to sleep, he poured himself a hefty dose of twenty-year-old Scotch from the wet bar. Then he sat down by the phone to leave a warmer message than his previous note on

Mia's machine so something affectionate would be waiting for her at their country house when she arrived from the city in the morning.

The phone rang the required five times, but, instead of his own voice on the tape, he heard a very sleepy Mia say, "Dr. Hart."

For a moment Bryne considered hanging up rather than disturbing her rest, but he wanted—no, needed—her now.

"Mia, it's me. I'm so sorry. I assumed you'd still be in the city and wanted to make sure you got my message when you arrived in the morning."

"Jack," she paused, clearly searching for the bedside clock. "It's the middle of the night. Where are you?" She was slowly waking up. "Is everything all right?"

Taking a deep drink of the Scotch, he told her, "No, it's not, but I'm fine, not to worry. I'm in San Diego. Got called in to consult about a kid with a very baffling, very terrifying illness."

"What do you think it is?" Though Mia might be sleepy, she always was a public health professional.

"Not now, darling, it's late," he said. "I haven't—nobody has—the foggiest! We should know more in the morning. I'm just praying the boy makes it till then."

"And how long do you think you'll be needed?" He detected a slight edge in her voice.

"No idea, none. Darling, I'm really sorry I had to take off so suddenly."

"Oh, Jack, it's fine." Now he was picking up the tone of resignation he dreaded. "It's okay..."

"Thanks for understanding," Bryne said, knowing she didn't entirely and really couldn't. "Big kiss, sweetheart, and I'm sorry I woke you up. I'll call tomorrow when I have a better sense of what's going down."

"Jack, wait! Don't hang up yet. Your old flame Vicky Wade is simply dying to talk to you."

"For Christ's sake, that's ancient history, Mia!"

"Whatever. When I got up here last night, there were at least six messages from her on the machine. She sounded practically hysterical. The seventh time she called, I told her she could reach you through ProMED. I hope that was okay."

"Sure, thanks."

"Does that mean you're going to be on *Hot Line*?" Vicky Wade, after all, was a senior correspondent on the network newsmagazine that was giving *60 Minutes* a run for its money. "'Cause if she's doing the story, you know I'm going to be jealous..."

"I doubt it. Drew says she called about some new bug she's researching. Who knows? But Jesus, Mia, you have absolutely no reason to be jealous!"

"Just because she's super-famous, super-gorgeous, super-connected, and has lusted after you for years? You're right," she laughed, "I must be getting paranoid."

"Enough," Bryne chuckled. "You know how much I love you."

"I do, I do. It's just that I'm beginning to forget what you look like."

"Darling, I don't think I'll be out here long, and then we'll be able to spend some time together, fix dinner, sip champagne, make love in front of the fire for days and days..."

"From your mouth to God's ears."

"Exactly. Now go back to sleep and remember, darling, you are my one and greatest love."

"Well, since you put it that way, I'll start gathering wood for that fire as soon as we hang up."

"Wait till it's light out. I love you, Mia," he said softly.

To which she replied, "Good night, Jack," and hung up.

Quelling a new rush of guilt with another Scotch, Bryne sat staring into space, wondering if saving mankind was worth wrecking a marriage. Then he turned his attention back to the critical state of Joey St. John—and the guilt gave way to fear.

3

Thursday, June 18
San Diego
5:50 A.M.

Jack Bryne walked through the lobby of St. Roch's Hospital, found the stairwell, took the steps two at a time to the second floor, and headed down the hall toward the pathology lab.

He hoped that Joey had lived through the night, but Bryne had a nagging sense of dread about what the biopsy would reveal.

"Hey, Jack!" Catrini strode toward him, smiling.

"Vince!" Bryne grinned back, aware that a smile was Catrini's only defense against the menacing darkness of Joey's condition. Nodding toward the doors of the path lab, he told the pediatrician, "Let's hope that with the St. Johns' connections to the almighty, we can call on a little divine help for Joey."

Catrini shook his head mournfully. "You saw last night's records?"

"Sure did. He never had an indication of ARDS, so it's probably not hanta. But something very weird is happening. The nodes are getting bigger." As they walked down the hall, Jack asked, "You saw the new CT? Things are bursting out all over. Say, Vince, he is negative for cocci, isn't he?"

"San Joaquin fever?" Catrini seemed shocked. "Sure, Joey's serology and smears were negative, he wasn't in the desert, and he didn't have the bumps. He definitely does not have San Joaquin valley fever."

"And that's some relief."

"Yeah," Catrini replied. "Any relief, small as it is, will do…. Hey, speaking as an Italian and a Roman Catholic, I bet you a buck you can't even tell me who St. Roch was."

Bryne grinned. "Vince, you're definitely a dollar richer! Never heard the name."

"Well, most folks don't know either, you see

68

St. Roch is the patron saint of plague, bubonic plague. He replaced St. Sebastian, who hadn't been able to help much." Catrini paused before asking slowly, "Did you consider plague, Jack?"

"Why no, no I didn't..." Bryne admitted.

"Not to worry." Catrini slapped him on the back in a gesture of companionship. "So far those tests are also negative. St. Roch will not need to visit St. Roch's today!"

As they pushed through the door of the pathology lab, a technician almost shouted, "Hey, Vinnie, Dr. Hubert has something for you. He's over there, under the hood."

Catrini walked Bryne over to a robust personage who appeared to be Santa Claus in a white lab coat. Hunched over a photomicroscope, the pathologist was staring down with total focus.

Catrini touched Hubert's shoulder lightly but urgently, attempting to get his attention. The pathologist jerked up from his stool, startled even by a gentle nudge, surprised at the company.

"Dr. Hubert," Catrini began, "this is Dr. Jack Bryne, he's the virologist from New York that the St. Johns asked in to consult. Jack, this is Henry Hubert, our pathologist." The two men shook hands.

"I'm glad you're both here." Hubert frowned. "Take a peek at what we got from the boy's chest."

"What is it?" Catrini asked. "Can you pin it down?"

"No, Vince, I'm still not prepared to hazard a guess," Hubert replied, "but this one is bad. I'm worried. It looks like we may have a really lethal bug underneath there this time. It can't know that it's eating into another living being in order to grow, but it is."

He gazed down upon the slide; thousands of tiny *Good & Plenties* appeared to be frozen in a bluish goo—but they only seemed like candy to a layman. To a professional, they were Gram-positives—tiny, dreadful, spherical killers, some elongated, others shaped like cannonballs.

It struck Catrini that in all the years they'd worked together, he'd never before seen horror in the old pathologist's eyes, and it only intensified as he went on.

"If I'm right, no one, no one in the United States anyway, has seen this for years, many decades... See, the frozen section on the St. John kid didn't show any initial blasts or malignant cells, so I thought I'd take a look for bacteria first..."

"Okay." Vince waited to hear the rest as Hubert passed him another slide.

"All the fungal stains are still drying, but it's clear to me we're not looking at cocci. It's not Hodgkins', a lymphoma, or a leukemia."

"Isn't that good news?" Catrini asked.

"In a way," the pathologist said somberly. "But I decided to do a quick check for bacteria with a Gram stain. And wow! Whatever it is, it's Gram-positive *and* it's producing spores."

"*Bacillus subtilis*?" Catrini ventured, "or a *Clostridium?*"

"Nah."

"Well, for God's sake, Henry, if not those, then what? The kid was healthy until about two days ago, and he doesn't have HIV, so it's unlikely to be *subtilis*. What about *Actino*?"

Hubert peered into a second microscope. "No, I don't think so. Take a look. No sulfur granules. I've got to tell you, I'm stymied. We're only a BL–2 facility here." He shook his head. "This safety hood is good for most things, but to be on the safe side, I'm going to put this slide in the hood and work on it myself. I'll call in the San Diego Health Department. They might want to call Sacramento on this one—and maybe the cowboys at CDC."

"Please, Lord, no!" Catrini exploded. "Not the feds!" Catrini could see a mountain of paperwork start to rise before his eyes and stretch off forever into the future, scutwork that would keep him from his patients. "Why do we have to call the Feds? The State Health people are pretty damned savvy. Most came out of the CDC."

Hubert didn't answer, just proceeded to lift the slide from its seat on the microscope, place it in a small glass dish, and walk over to a large canopy that looked like the vent for a commercial stove. The fan's forced air created a negative pressure inside the machine, wafting any airborne germs upward through a large HEPA filter in the ceiling—and from there out through a maze of ductwork to an exhaust vent on the exterior of the hospital, out into the clear, warm San Diego air, ensuring that the filter trapped any dangerous bacterial lab contaminants.

The Occupational Safety and Health Administration—OSHA—had required that hospital intake vents never be closer than one hundred feet to those exhausts in order to prevent nosocomial outbreaks—infectious outbreaks of diseases occurring within hospitals. OSHA had discovered that the clean air intakes could actually suck germs back into the hospital from an institution's own microbiology laboratory, and then spray them directly into the fresh air system. Before this revelation, dozens of doctors, nurses, staffers, even patients had gotten sick over the years.

Hubert was clearly thinking worst-case scenario, and that could include them all. Having upped the danger from a Biological Lab Two to a BL–3 threat suggested they were dealing with an organism equal to the plague. Each increasing level of BL implied a more serious threat.

"You'll have to bear with me for a while," Hubert told them, looking at the sample. "I'll let you know as soon as I can pin this down. We might try some *Bac-tec* on the culture to speed it up. But I'd prefer the Sacramento guys do that. It's too risky." He turned to Catrini. "What've you got the kid on?"

"Floxacillin."

"Good. That should cover about everything," the pathologist replied, and as Bryne nodded his agreement, he noticed that the older man was bathed in sweat.

At that moment a young nurse came through

the door, carrying a microscope slide as if it were a precious jewel. Cowed to be in such eminent company, she stammered a bit before interrupting the pathologist, "Dr. Hubert, Dr. Alvarez wanted you to look at this right away. It's from the Emergency Department. The nurse is sending more smears and a culture, but Dr. Alvarez wanted a stat report on this one. A girl up there is in a real bad way..."

Bryne and Catrini stood aside as Hubert took the slide between his thumb and forefinger.

"Where's it from?" he asked, walking to a series of metal trays next to a binocular microscope. "Is this above or below the belt? What's the history?"

Reddening with embarrassment, the nurse confessed, "I don't know. My supervisor saw me walking by, then Dr. Alvarez started yelling. He wanted this brought to you stat. So she gave it to me."

Hubert was clearly exasperated. "Just tell me, did you see the patient or see where Alvarez took the smear?"

"I certainly did," the nurse said, gaining courage. "It was horrible. There was something wrong with her eyes—Dr. Alvarez says he might do an enucleation. She's only a teenager, too. Nose rings, earrings, all sorts of rings, and black nail polish and red and green hair. She's real sick. I saw Dr. Alvarez take some black pus from her left eye. And she had these black spots on her neck—like moles or ticks, but they weren't," she wound down. "That's all I know."

The pathologist shook his head as he slipped the slide into a low beaker of clear fluid for a few seconds and let it rest. Next he slipped the slide into another beaker, then into a third beaker for the final strain.

Bryne nodded. He understood that what Hubert had done was a quick and easy method of staining for bacteria and knew that only two possibilities existed—Gram-negative or Gram-positive. A Gram-negative strain was not negative in the usual sense. Gram-negative meant the bacteria had been stained a reddish color.

Everybody in medicine knew that most truly serious bacterial infections were Gram-negatives: bacteria that came from the gut. Like the *Salmonellas,* most Gram-negatives were enteric organisms living in the bowel. The more toxic ones, if they could make it into the bloodstream, caused sepsis and death. Other, less serious strains lived on the skin, especially below the beltline, and usually did not cause problems.

Since this new smear was from a facial lesion, an eye, Bryne knew it was probably going to be Gram-positive. As Hubert dried the slide by waving it back and forth through the air, Bryne guessed strep, but maybe one of the recently emerged antibiotic-resistant strains of staph. This deadly new staph was making young physicians again respectful of their ancient foe—the cause of boils, furuncles, carbuncles, and, in the proper milieu, toxic shock syndrome. Strep caused sore throats and the fast-spread skin infections known as cellulitis. Deeper-spreading strep caused "flesh-eating" infections and the pneumonia that killed Muppets creator Jim Henson.

"Let's have a look now." Hubert carefully placed the dry slide on the stage of a third microscope and adjusted the fine focus. "You did say Alvarez is standing by for an answer?"

"Yes, Doctor," the nurse replied, "he was in the ER when I left."

Hubert readjusted the microscope, added a drop of oil to the sample, and refocused once more. Delicately twisting two small knobs and watching intently, he moved the slide around the stage. "*Verrrry interesting, jah?*" the pathologist asked in broad stage German. He stood up, moved over to the other B–3 microscope, the one with Joey's slide, and peered down at it, saying nothing; then he reexamined the second slide under the oil-immersion technique, adjusting the focus carefully.

"Very interesting." This time he repeated the phrase without a comic touch, and Bryne picked up a new intonation—no longer professional curiosity, now real fear.

"They look the same." Hubert finally spoke, twirled around on his stool and told them, "I'd swear we have the same bug from the St. John case, and I do not like this at all." Spinning around once more, he checked the samples again. "Both of these show occasional and distinct bamboo-shaped configurations. It's clear... Look, there's another clump."

"But," Bryne interrupted, "you can't deduce that by examining only an oil immersion." He knew all too well that most bacteria look the same, either red or blue, *cocci* or rods. "What makes you think that the boy's case is in any way caused by the same bug?"

"Years of experience learning to hate the little guys," Hubert answered. "And while *Bergey's Manual* may define only one or two, or actually three, shapes and two colors, I can definitely detect morphological subtleties that the Bible of Bacteriology doesn't even list."

To prove his point, he motioned toward the microscope. "This one and the one from the girl have big, robust bodies. And... this one also. It's unmistakable. Both of them have spores mixed in with the rods. Big fat spores looking exactly like time bombs, which is exactly what they are. Take a look." He invited Bryne over to the microscope.

Bryne bent over, resting his elbows on the counter and peering at the array of dark blue spots below him. It seemed as if a swarm of tiny, elongated eggplants, curved slightly at one end, were floating in the field. He squinted and adjusted the focus. Mixed in with the rods were occasional globose forms, slightly larger than the bamboo-shaped rods, but with a much smoother surface.

The fear Bryne had been feeling turned abruptly to anger, then to overwhelming rage: he was only inches from the enemy and its incalculable potency. These tiny germs were immortal. They could easily win in the end.

Bryne remembered with blinding clarity the words from an address Joshua Lederberg had given a few years ago at the Academy of

Medicine: "They have the genes, we have the brains, but I do not know who will end up victorious." Personally, Bryne knew it was already too late; he was already exposed.

"Vince," Bryne called over the pediatrician, "these bigger ones, the one with that smooth outline are the spores.... It's just like Dr. Hubert said."

"And those particular spores," Hubert added, "are smooth because they have an extra coat of protective polysaccharides. That makes them resistant to freezing, boiling, and of course to antibiotics. Until they choose to break out of the spores, you have a chance. But the big question is when they might choose to do so. It could be years..." His voice trailed off, then picked up after a moment of meditation. "But I still can't tell you what this thing is. I'm sorry, I just plain don't know..."

"But," Catrini insisted, "you can't keep a person on antibiotics for years!"

Rather than answer him, Hubert turned to the nurse. "I'm calling Alvarez in Emergency immediately. Extension 2224, right?" The nurse nodded, and Hubert dialed.

While he held the phone to his ear, the pathologist gestured at the slides. "I'll FedEx these new ones from the girl up to Sacramento. They're already working on the St. John boy's culture. They'll have them in the morning. Meanwhile, I'll keep working here... Oh." He listened as the phone was answered on the other end, then cursed. "The girl's had a seizure. Alvarez's taken her to ICU."

A neurologist and neurosurgeon were being paged stat over the hospital's intercom as Bryne turned away from the microscope—disturbed as much by what he'd heard as by what he'd seen. Now he addressed Catrini urgently. "Vince, it's critical that we know what this new kid and the St. John boy have in common. We need to find that out right now. How are we going to be able to do that? Where are her parents? Can either of those kids even talk to us?"

Catrini immediately headed for the door, not holding back for Bryne. "Let's find Alvarez. I want to see this girl. We can check on Joey at the same time. I'll make some calls. Come on, Jack, you're right, let's see if she can tell us something."

As the door of the pathology lab closed behind them, Bryne looked Catrini directly in the eye and told him, "Hubert's good, Vinnie. If he's right, and these two kids have the same bug, somebody better call the other hospitals. There may be more cases."

When Jody Davis was first admitted to St. Roch's, she had been running a high fever—105 degrees rectal. She had gotten wildly delirious in the emergency room, screaming, punching, violent. By the time Bryne and Catrini reached pediatric ICU, she had been considerably quieted. Since Alvarez had given her a shot of intravenous Valium for her seizure, her breathing seemed almost regular.

Jody's long hair, a matted mixture of green

and red, was splayed grotesquely over the pillow. Her eyes were the horrifying part. The ICU nurses had never seen anything like those eyes.

They had swollen and festered, turned the size and color of rotting plums. The thick, greenish lids were pushed by the swelling until they had been forced fully open so that both pupils stared ahead, sightless, the irises a deep purplish brown, the corneas bloody and torn. Out of the corners of her lids and from each of her tear ducts oozed a brown necrotic fluid, and her wrists were restrained to keep her from running her arms across her face. She was thrashing in slow motion, her sores clearly agonizing, and over and over she kept repeating she'd been shot—shot in the eyes.

Catrini's attention was caught by the floor nurse motioning through the glass window with a phone in her hand. Catrini and Bryne left the room together. The call was from Hubert, and they went on speaker so they could both hear the pathologist's announcement of doom: "Vincent," he barked, "get those patients into isolation right away. Her white count shot up to fifty-five thousand, toxic granulations, an extreme shift to the left, a few blasts. She's got a leukemoid reaction, and I can actually see rods—bacteria—in the peripheral smear. Bamboo!"

Catrini hung up and ran back inside. He saw the girl start struggling and the gown fell back from her neck. There were half a dozen black sores oozing a foul greenish pus on her upper chest. Abrasions, puncture wounds? He looked again. No, they were... *boils*—large, festering boils erupting on her chest, in her armpits.

"Masks on! Masks on! That patient may have plague!" Catrini yelled as he started toward the isolation cubicle where Joey lay.

As he ran, Bryne put out a hand to stop him. "Vince, no!" He made him listen. "It's not plague in there. I saw more plague in Cambodia than I want to remember... And they never look like that. Think. Plague doesn't form those spores. This is something different, something worse. We need those lab reports immediately."

Before Catrini could answer, a candy-striper came running breathlessly down the hall. "Oh, Dr. Catrini, I'm so glad you're here. It's Dr. Hubert again. He told me to find you right away. They called him from Sacramento."

"Go ahead, what's the message?"

Looking puzzled, the young woman delivered her message: "He said to tell you 'ant tracks.' But, Dr. Catrini, what are 'ant tracks?'"

"Anthrax!" Bryne hissed. "God almighty, she means anthrax!" Abruptly he turned away and looked back through the glass toward the girl, and Catrini joined him as they watched the doors of hell swing open.

Two nurses, neither with isolation masks nor standard surgical masks, had been trying to hold the girl down, but now they backed away as if she were going to burst into flame.

Abruptly Jody Davis began screaming insanely, threw back her head, and arched her back. Her one single wail grew louder and louder, and a thin, bloody fluid began to stream out of her eyes, ears, and nose. Now the screaming was replaced by her gasping for air—gasping repeatedly in agony and panic until her heart began to give out. As the ICU staff struggled into their gowns and masks, Jody trembled and died.

It was her last and most pitiful scream that awakened Joey St. John from twelve hours of semiconsciousness. His bed was directly across the intensive care unit from hers, and he had been sleeping fitfully since early that morning. Then the wailing had begun.

Suddenly Joey sat straight up, a terrified look in his eyes, and began clawing at the bandage over his shoulder. The tape started to give way, and he tore at it, gasping in agony, struggling for breath, clawing at the wound above his collarbone. Suddenly he began to cough, a hard and racking spasm, then reached out and grabbed both sides of the bed. Looking straight up in the air, he managed to inhale heavingly and gagged.

Bryne and Catrini, paralyzed by their own powerlessness, watched Joey's eyes roll slowly back in his head and his small right hand claw one last time at MacDonald's incision. The stitches hooked in the boy's fingernails and ripped loose from the soft skin of his neck.

As Joey tried to scream, the dank and septic fluid that had built up in his chest with enough force to suffocate him began to spray from the freshly opened neck wound.

Outward and upward shot an obscene coffee-colored liquid, emerging with such force that it actually hit the ceiling tiles seven feet straight above the boy's head. The stream continued to jet out of his neck, even as Joey fell backwards. The vile fluid shot forth until it hosed completely across the ceiling to the wall, and down the wall to the floor and under the boy's bed. And there it stopped. Along with Joey St. John's heart.

The two of them stood at the foot of the bed, Catrini crossing himself and Bryne murmuring, "Those poor innocent children, God bless them." Neither spoke further, and both knew that the very worst—informing the St. Johns—was still to come.

As they backed out of ICU, a nurse built like a linebacker burst through the door at the end of the hall, her voice the very symbol of authority as she ordered them, "Hey, you two, do not leave the area!" She pushed past nurses, orderlies, a volunteer manning a cart of comic books and magazines, a few weary parents with children in ICU, and two terrified medical students.

"Everybody listen up!" she barked.

Striding up to Bryne and Catrini, she paused before them, erect in true military fashion, and announced, "For those of you who don't know, I am Deborah Gaynor, the infection control nurse. All of you," her sweeping hand movement indicated everyone in the area, "I said *all of you* stay put!" Fishing into a container of HEPA masks, she bellowed, "All right, now… put these on—everyone!"

"Agent Gaynor on another mission," Catrini muttered under his breath. "Deborah Gaynor, nurse from hell—she might as well have come from *The X-Files*!"

Bryne wasn't the least surprised by Gaynor's behavior. Whatever the venue, the ICN, or infection control nurse, always seemed to be a martinet with dictatorial powers over the entire hospital staff. It was far from amusing to see Gaynor behave according to type, stamping down the corridor and shouting orders: "Now, everyone from ICU and in this corridor, stop everything! Get those three other kids into isolation. Negative-pressure rooms. Now move!"

When Gaynor caught Bryne and Catrini hesitating, she barked, "You two get in here and get those clothes off!" They didn't argue.

Bryne stood in the shower and lathered himself with soap. As ordered, he'd left his clothes in a red bio-bag to be burned. He had soaked his watch in a vile solution of Clorox and hydrogen peroxide. He could keep some of the bleachable contents of his wallet—like credit cards, driver's license, and ID card. He had been told to get his hair cut short as soon as possible, since anthrax has an affinity for hair.

There must be Samson genes in every man,

Jack thought, mourning the loss of his shoulder-length ponytail. "Vince, please help me with this." He fingered the ponytail one last time. "I'll have to grow it back." Without a word, the pediatrician snipped it off with a pair of surgical scissors and disposed of it and the red ribbon in a nearby bin.

Bryne could hear the isolation personnel still running through the halls outside the showers where he had been shoehorned into the tiny stall. *Auschwitz,* he thought. Then other images, deeply buried, images and words he fought recalling, the trauma he had repressed for an entire lifetime but could not root out. *Get hold of yourself, Bryne, get hold of yourself. There's no time for this now,* he thought as he tried to get a grip. He realized what lay ahead.

After he'd showered and regained what passed for composure, Bryne took the surgical scissors from Catrini and clipped off the rest of his hair, cutting forward to the crown. He looked in the mirror to even off the front above his widow's peak. When the process ended, Bryne had a serviceable self-administered field cut that wouldn't cause undue attention. Nobody was being summoned here for his fashion sense.

The emergency meeting Bryne knew was soon to commence would bring a top-level cadre of epidemiologists, plague fighters, and the people from the CDC, seasoned professionals, many of whose lives had been lived in that infinitesimal space between civilization and catastrophe.

The ones who plied their strange trade in the Third World always took everything about the business with dead seriousness. These were the field physicians. These were the men and women who had found the blackened bodies stacked up like construction debris; seen the insects so thick on piles of human remains that a blanket of swollen flies and their maggots, often inches thick, rippled and writhed as if blown by the most ill of winds, while beneath them a parasitic hierarchy scavenged.

Stepping back under the shower spray, Bryne let the chlorinated water run directly back into his nose, burning as it descended to the top of his throat, at which point he gargled and spit it out. He made a cup of his hands, gathered more water, drew it to his face and sucked it into his nose, splashed it in his eyes, worked it into his ears, and drank it. He wanted to kill the damned anthrax, wanted to make sure any airborne spores weren't inside him. He blew his nose with his fingers and made sure the mucus went down the drain without hitting him. He cleaned under his fingernails with an orange stick, and scoured his fingers with a brush.

Was Catrini being as thorough as he was? Somehow Bryne doubted it, but hoped to heaven he overestimated the pediatrician's naïveté. At least they would both be taking antibiotics and plenty of them as soon as they toweled off. When he stepped out of the shower, Jack found Catrini, naked, drying himself and using the phone at the same time.

Bryne reached for scrub suits for both of them and motioned to Vince that he needed a word with him.

Catrini covered the phone and told Jack, "It's the St. Johns. I'm calling Eleanor now. Phone's ringing... no answer yet," and Bryne saw the sadness in his eyes. Then he held up his hand and turned as someone picked up on the other end.

Catrini, wrapping one towel around his midriff, another over his shoulders, now concentrated on the phone he had commandeered. Lights were flashing on every line.

Jack realized he could hear not only sirens screaming outside the hospital, but also a chopper's staccato wing beat as it landed on the roof. Byrne shook his head. This was going to be one hell of a day.

A frantic nurse was trying and failing to get Catrini's attention. He put down the phone, unaware.

"Was that Eleanor, Vincent?" Bryne asked with concern.

"No, and thank God for small favors. It was her maid, told me that Joseph and Eleanor were in the pool. I dreaded telling them over the phone. I'm going to drive over and tell them in person, Jack. Just as soon as we clear infection control."

"Would you let me ride over with you?" Bryne asked, and he could see the relief on Catrini's face as he nodded immediately.

The nurse finally got Catrini's attention, motioned to the phone in his hand, and Catrini turned to the phone again. This time he hung up smiling a bit and joined Bryne as they dried themselves.

"My wife Kathy's got a six-foot brother-in-law. She's bringing you some clothes. Like sharkskin?"

"Sure, and Vinnie, something special for you too, I take it?"

"Naturally, I thought perhaps the tux..." Catrini flinched as he saw Bryne toweling off his shoulders. "Good Lord, Jack, where did you get that thing?" He was looking at the scar sluicing down from Bryne's left shoulder to the interior of his elbow, the soft crease where blood samples are drawn.

On either side of the thin red line was a gauntlet of a dozen pairs of blanched stitch scars, a line of old punctures paralleling the main incision. "You needed a better surgeon, Jack," Catrini commented wryly. "How'd you get that thing in the first place?"

The question had been asked innumerable times. For Bryne, telling the truth was completely out of the question. The true story always dragged up those hideous images he'd had to push back down inside himself in the shower; the true story took too much from him, was too threatening to the man he had become. When he was young, he had occasionally come out with the truth. But he had stopped that completely years ago.

"Hang-gliding, Vince, hang-gliding in Switzerland. Got caught in a tree." Somehow the idea of a crazy scientist gliding over the

87

Alps and into a pine tree seemed to satisfy people; in any case, it satisfied Catrini.

"A lousy job, Jack," Vinnie finally concluded.

"No, Vincent," Bryne said, touching the old wound, "a beautiful one."

Through a window, Jack could see the morning sun making the Pacific shimmer in the distance and used it to change the subject. "Such horror in here. Such beauty out there. Hey, when are they springing us?"

"Soon... we'll be getting enough antibiotics to induce *C. difficile* diarrhea in three days." Bryne understood Catrini was referring to bacterial intoxication, a strange side effect of taking too many antibiotics, like Ceclor, which they were about to start taking in big blue-and-white 250-milligram capsules. Lots of them. It was their best defense against exposure to the anthrax bacilli aerosolized during the final moments of Joey and the girl.

Together, they donned the scrub suits and went out to the nurses' station, where Vinnie filled out a brief questionnaire for them both. Gaynor, the nurse from hell, dispensed their medications, giving Catrini enough pills for five people. He slipped a handful in the pocket of the scrub suit and, with Jack in tow, headed off to his office, where his wife would have their clothes.

When Catrini offered dinner and lodging for the night, Bryne accepted gratefully. He was relieved to be leaving the Del and found that spending time with Vinnie was strangely comforting, since both had shared the horror. Anthrax. The fact was that both men were facing a horrible death, perhaps within days. The battle was under way within them, the winner undecided.

Bryne envisioned organisms afloat inside him because they were almost inhaled, certainly inside him, despite everything. The imminence of his mortality chilled him. He wondered how Catrini, the good Catholic, would feel.

Jack would have been pleased to know that Vinnie also was comforted by his presence. It helped to keep the fear at bay. Anyway, he felt that he and Jack had founded a genuine intimacy, one built on mutual respect. The media would be swarming soon, and he was sure the virologist could use some down time, along with privacy and home cooking. Maybe a nice rack of New Zealand lamb and a really good bottle of wine. Maybe even that '78 Romanée-Conti he'd been saving for so many years. He'd ask Bryne for dinner this evening. Yeah, they'd better drink it tonight—in case the years ran out tomorrow!

Thursday, June 18
La Jolla
10:00 A.M.

The drive to the St. Johns' seemed to go by much too quickly, with neither man having much to say. "You know, Jack," Catrini said at last, "Joey was really overprotected; he was sort of a poor little rich kid. No pets, no games or toys that struck his very conservative mom as 'violent.' No *Star Trek* laser guns, no G.I. Joes, no Space Invaders. He had everything except a normal boyhood."

"Absolutely, Vince," Bryne agreed as they turned into the St. Johns' estate. "Until we pin this down, we have to assume the parents are at some small risk. Don't you agree?"

"Well," Catrini told him, "I've brought a pocketful of antibiotics, and I'll want them both down for a screening, X-rays, blood test, the works."

"God, as if the death of their son isn't enough of a curse!"

"Remember, Jack," Catrini thought aloud, "Eleanor wanted to stay last night, and I was the one who pressured her to go home." He shook his head. "I could have bent the rules. Now I almost wish I'd let her stay. At least she would have been there at the end."

"Would you really have wanted that, my friend?" Bryne asked gently. Without waiting for an answer, he reached out and gave Catrini's shoulder an affectionate shake. "We both know you did the right thing." Still, Catrini sighed as he parked the car.

"Is Mrs...." Catrini started to ask when a uniformed maid answered their ring, but she immediately beckoned them inside with a sweep of her hand.

Before them was a brilliant white marble room with a great alabaster staircase sweeping up to a landing with a curved glass window over twenty feet across affording a dazzling ocean view.

Silhouetted against the window with the Pacific at their backs stood the St. Johns. Eleanor reached out for her husband's hand, and together they walked down the stairs to the door.

As she neared the bottom of the stairs and saw the expression on Catrini's face, Eleanor shuddered. She dropped her husband's hand and ran toward the two men. Seeing the tears in Catrini's eyes, she screamed, "NO! NO!" and almost collapsed, but Bryne reached out to keep her from falling.

"Oh, Vince, no. Please say he's okay, please!" Eleanor began to sob, then abruptly stopped herself, blotting her eyes. With extraordinary self-control, this sensitive, damaged woman pulled herself together, rising in stature before Bryne's eyes. He watched her reach out and touch Catrini's cheek, where the tears were.

"It's all right," she told him firmly, "I know you did all you could. Vincent, you mustn't blame yourself. Joseph and I understand." Her husband nodded, slipping his arms around Eleanor's shoulders.

"We could lose our tempers," he told them. "I'm sure people have threatened to sue, and you must know how profound this loss is for us." St. John seemed to tower over all of them, his rage and grief almost palpable. The veins in his neck were distended and his eyes filled with tears. Still, there seemed to come from him an air of stoic resignation, of acceptance rather than torment. Once again, Bryne envied these people their religious faith.

"Thank you, Joseph, Eleanor," Catrini spoke at last. "I know how impossibly difficult this is, but I'd like to have a few words with Eleanor, if that's all right."

"Of course," she agreed graciously. "Come upstairs with me, Vincent. There's a sunny place where we can sit. And I'd like to show you something."

After Catrini and Eleanor had disappeared up the staircase, Bryne turned to Joseph St. John. "I'm so deeply sorry for your loss. No one expected this. The hospital did everything— but no one, no one, suspected anthrax." Bryne went on to explain about the infection.

St. John sat down in an armchair and looked up at Bryne. "Anthrax. That's something from the Middle Ages, isn't it? How could he have gotten it? Where? This is simply not real!" He was staring straight ahead when suddenly fear swept over his face. "We're not going to get it, are we? Shouldn't Eleanor and I be checked?"

Bryne pulled up a chair and sat facing St. John, choosing his words carefully. "I don't believe you have to worry, although I'm sure Dr. Catrini will give you both antibiotics, just to be on the safe side. Although it's lethal, the strange thing about anthrax is that it's not normally spread by close contact through the air."

Bryne knew that when a human contracts anthrax, the organisms multiply in the chest's lymph nodes. In Joey's case, there was almost certainly no danger of transmission until the final hours, when the bug broke into his lungs. Even though anthrax caused fulminant infections, as did legionnaires' disease, it normally didn't spread to others.

Picturing Joey's agonized scream and the explosive wound dehiscence, Bryne also knew full well that anthrax, at that stage, particularly since it was airborne, could be very dangerous. That was why it was a favorite biological warfare tool: spores could be sent miles in artillery shells to infect enemy troops.

"I know that all of us are puzzled about how Joey contracted this," Bryne continued. "It hasn't been a problem in this country for half a century."

He went on to explain that hunters used to get it when they dressed down deer, usually on their fingers, causing a black ulcer that spreads—occasionally to an eye. Thinking of the girl, Bryne decided not to pursue the subject of the eyes further.

"I'd say that of the less than ten cases we've had in the U.S. in the last fifty years, all came from imported sources—foreign animal products like goatskins and Afghan yarns. Back in the twenties, a man who carved ivory billiard balls for a living got it from African elephant tusks." He looked around the room. "Mr. St. John, did anyone in the family receive a gift recently, something from a friend?"

"What do you mean?"

"For example, an ivory figurine, woven wall hangings, exotic gifts from overseas?

You see, the anthrax organism can live for years on hair, or in small cracks in tusks or natural ivory. It normally lives in dirt, and animals pick it up from the grass. Humans can get anthrax from soil, but it's still mostly from animal contact."

"No, no gifts." St. John paused, then said, "Elephants. You said elephants. Could Joey have gotten it from the elephants at the zoo?"

"I simply don't know, sir," Bryne confessed. "There's to be a major meeting at noon. State and federal health people are flying in. We should know more after that."

"Eleanor and I should be present at the meeting."

Bryne frowned. "I don't think that would be a good idea. I know your feelings, but stay here with your wife. She needs you just now. If anything of note transpires, believe me, sir, you and Mrs. St. John will be the first to know."

But he knew they wouldn't be. Not if this thing was really big. Not if Joey was only the first victim...

As Catrini drove them back, he said to Jack, "You know what Eleanor wanted to show me?" He fished around in the pocket of his rumpled linen suit. "This!" He held out an object sealed in a Ziploc bag, which glinted as Bryne reached for it, peered at it, and simply said, "Goddamn!"

Catrini was allowed to drive back onto the grounds of the hospital, but they knew what would lie ahead: reporters and probably camera crews.

"There they are." Catrini gestured toward the satellite monitors on the broadcast trucks. "Looks like CNN has already heard. You go on up to the meeting, Jack. I want to stop by my office for a second and check something. I'll meet you up on twelve, the big conference room for the Board of Directors. Seats almost thirty, and I bet you it'll be filled to the rafters.

"And," Catrini added, patting the pocket where he'd replaced the object Eleanor St. John had given him, "I bet you they'll all pee in their pants when I come up with our shiny little bombshell!"

4

Thursday, June 18
St. Roch Hospital Board Room
Noon

Getting through the media barricade outside the hospital had been like breaking through a goal line defense, but somehow Bryne and Catrini had managed it without sustaining a scratch or uttering a word that could be quoted. Now they were facing dozens of grim people standing in a cluster around a conference table in the hospital board room.

As a low-flying helicopter turned toward the zoo, someone looked through the window and commented, "I hope to hell those CNN bastards don't take those choppers over to the zoo. Some of the animals are going to panic. And when they do, who knows what will be picked up and blown over Southern California by the blades!"

Another voice joined the irritated chorus: "Shit! If it's in the soil, we're going to have an epidemic on our hands! Those frigging idiots. Can't somebody get the governor to order the choppers to stay clear of the zoo?"

"That has already been done, my friend," a calm voice assured the others. "No more overflights. That's the last of them leaving." The speaker was a slim man dressed in a summer suit. Most of the other local attendees were more casually dressed, in part due to the haste with which they had been summoned by the mayor.

The man in the suit, Catrini whispered to Bryne, was Don Lesan, Director of the California State Health Department. Since he was leading the meeting, Lesan walked to the far end of the large conference table and banged on it with a coffee mug for quiet.

"Okay, okay, people!" he had to shout over the background noise, "let's get started. Everyone... Please!" Most of the crowd slipped into the empty chairs remaining around the large rectangular table. Catrini took a seat next to Lesan, but Bryne, sipping coffee from a styrofoam cup, chose to stand against a wall well away from the action.

"Thanks so much for coming on such short notice," Lesan began when silence had at last been achieved. "We're all busy, some of us were even on well-deserved vacations, so I'll try to be brief, as I hope all of us will. Okay, here goes. For those of you who don't know me, I'm Donald Lesan, State Health, Sacramento, and I've been asked by the governor and the mayor to chair this meeting. Now, a few ground rules."

He directed the crowd's attention to a trim, athletic woman who was sitting off to one side. "This is Ms. Fisher, who will be the only—and I mean the only—person talking to reporters. None of you, none of us, will give interviews. Understood?"

There were a few moans, but only a few, since most of the people in the room had been through media blackouts before and knew they were standard operating procedure for this sort of emergency.

"Secondly," Lesan continued, "the mayor regrets the sparse accommodations for you out-of-towners. We wanted a block of rooms together so you could compare notes at the end of the day—"

"But *Motel Six*!" a young woman shouted. "Was the city jail booked?"

Lesan chuckled along with the rest of the attendees, but not for long. "Seriously, we saw the motel as a plus because they always leave the lights on. Make no mistake, this is going to be a day-and-night operation until we get a handle on the situation. We're dealing with anthrax, my friends, not a day at the beach... Now, let's go around the table, and each person will give name, rank, and serial number, as it were. Ms. Fisher will also pass around a legal pad on which each of you are to write your name, agency, business telephone, fax and beeper numbers, and in the case of out-of-towners, your room number. Okay, let's start."

As Fisher rose and placed a yellow legal pad on the table, indicating it should be filled in and then passed clockwise, Lesan nodded to the man on his left, who looked around the table and cleared his throat.

"Gordon Lubold," the man announced, "Epidemic Intelligence Service, CDC, Atlanta," then nodded to the person on his left. "Jack Haser, Research Director, Special Pathogens Division, Centers for Disease Control, Atlanta through Fort Collins." After Haser came "Donnie Huber, Plant and Animal Service, United States Department of Agriculture, Rockville, Maryland," and "Leo English, chief vet, San Diego Zoo."

"Scott Hubbard, Washington, D.C." The next person, rising from his chair, spoke in a soft, even Southern drawl, which contrasted with a powerful air of authority that drew all eyes to him even before he identified himself: "Special Agent, FBI."

Hubbard was a lean, sharp-featured man of about forty whose clear green eyes sought out every other person at the table and seemed to take note when someone's gaze dropped under the pressure of his. He glanced at his watch before continuing to speak, indicating he was in a hurry but willing to wait until the room had calmed.

"Look, everybody," Hubbard told them,

98

"I basically want to reinforce that we would like to keep all specifics away from the media, but I'm sure you understand the necessity for the blackout.... Now, I have an additional request for anyone who had direct contact with the two patients and/or their physicians."

Hearing those words, Catrini, brows arched in surprise and uncertainty, swiveled his chair just enough to make eye contact with Bryne, who, in response, shrugged slightly to indicate that he had no idea what was coming next. Neither had long to wait for an answer, as Hubbard immediately said, "If those of you who have had any contact with the victims could give the Bureau a few minutes of your valuable time after the meeting, we'd be deeply grateful. The Bureau is according this incident top priority, and we expect you to adjust your schedules to cooperate."

Amidst a chorus of barely disguised grumbles, Hubbard sat down and passed a hand slowly over his closely cropped dirty-blond hair, again defying the crowd to meet his stare, but finding no takers. They had all expected the unexpected, but the FBI? Why? What could it mean?

Hubbard nodded impatiently to the man on his left, who was so flustered, he almost stumbled over his own name: "Jerry Borden, San Diego County Health Department." They continued around the table with "Maryann Connelly, mayor's Public Relations Office rep," "Mike Schultz, USDA, L.A. Animal Quarantine Station," "Jimmy Edwards, Epi Division, California State Health, Sacramento," and a very young man who presented himself as "Charles Smithers, summer intern, second-year medical student on elective, Stanford Medical School, assigned to work with the California State Health Department... Ummm... I'm not sure I should be here. They said I should come down, so I—"

"Okay, Smithers," Lesan interrupted him, "you can stay."

In this room of seasoned professionals, the young medical student was obviously unnerved. Several nodded and winked at him as if to tell him, "Welcome to the funhouse!"

Next came a suave, handsome man who looked as if Ferragamo designed for him. "Armand de'Isle, pro tem president of the San Diego Zoo," modestly announced the internationally noted billionaire philanthropist, despite the fact that practically everybody present knew who he was.

And then it was Vince Catrini's turn. Everyone had been watching him discreetly, but closely. He let them all take a good look at him before stating, "Dr. Vincent Catrini. I was the boy's pediatrician." He immediately sat back down while the people on the periphery gave their names and associations. Bryne managed to make his credentials all but inaudible.

"Okay," Lesan addressed the room, "we all know who we are. Now, to save time, let me tell you what we've learned so far. New info from any of you will, of course, be deeply appreciated."

He looked down at a note-filled pad and commenced his remarks. "Dr. Catrini's case, the St. John boy, died at six-eleven this morning here at St. Roch, the same time as the girl. Early today, our labs confirmed that both cases were anthrax. We believe the two deceased are linked only by having been at the San Diego Zoo on the same day. Ergo, the common denominator must be the zoo, and the most likely source an animal kept there."

Armand de'Isle raised a hand to be called on. "Don, we've checked our animals, our new inventory, recent animal deaths, employee sickness reports. The only piece of data that might be worthwhile, and I will defer to Dr. English on this, is the death of one specific animal. Dr. English will also comment on the imported animals we've recently acquired."

The zoo's chief veterinarian rose on cue and began to speak. "As you probably know, anthrax is not found in the U.S., so we've been checking quarantine records for every animal in the zoo. All San Diego animals coming by air from outside the United States must pass through either JFK, LAX, or San Francisco. The big ones and all the African animals have to go through Kennedy. Ruminants and equids are quarantined in Newburgh, New York—ruminants for thirty days, equids for sixty because of African horse sickness—after which they're trans-shipped here. All elephants are deticked at Kennedy, then sent on."

"What about Asia?" someone asked.

"Seattle or Los Angeles," English continued. "Not much of a problem except for the

Ebola thing at Reston a few years ago. Those monkeys came from the Philippines."

"Did you find any anthrax-positive animals at your zoo?" asked Haser from CDC.

"Yes," the vet answered, to a chorus of gasps. "Yes, we did. We have a positive in one recent death."

"A vulture?" The question was asked by a biologist, who knew that although birds could not get anthrax, their droppings could spread it if they had eaten contaminated carrion.

"Not a vulture, but I wish it had been. This is much worse—a rabbit from the petting zoo. Born and raised here. Not in contact with other animals except her pal, another female, which we have identified, and which appears healthy. However, we're isolating her and giving her antibiotics."

English went on to explain that while a vulture would have been a "normal" explanation for the catastrophe, wild rabbits are never natural reservoirs for anthrax. "Rabbits, ladies and gentlemen, can get anthrax only in a lab, and somebody has to give it to them. I've seen it happen—during my investigation of the Sverdlovsk blow-up in 1979. Hundreds of animals and people died of anthrax after an explosion in a BW research facility. It ended up killing forty-two people, all of whom inhaled the germs."

"So what are you suggesting?" Lesan demanded. "Bio-warfare?"

"Don't know," English continued. "That rabbit was born in the zoo and had never been sick.

But an anthrax outbreak doesn't necessarily imply a terrorist action. Nearly forty-five hundred pigs died of anthrax and were incinerated in Wales in 1989. The farms, buildings, and roadways had to be hosed down with formalin. We are not looking forward to doing that at Balboa Park, but we may have to."

"But what about the risk to humans?" someone asked.

"If you want human data," English responded, "look at Zimbabwe in the eighties. Nearly ten thousand people, many of them children, died from anthrax. In the U.S. it's rare—no cases in the last ten years—but it's out there in developing countries."

There were those in the room who knew he was slightly overstating his case. Anthrax had killed a weaver in California as recently as 1974 through spores imbedded in the Pakistani yarn he was working with. Spores had also been found in hides from the Middle East and goatskin drums from Haiti. Statistically, English was nearly right, but numbers meant little now.

"Gentlemen, people, please." Catrini had virtually jumped out of his chair. "This is not about something from Africa. This is about two California kids, and it's about everyone in this room!"

He looked toward Bryne for a nod of encouragement and went on, "As you know, the two children died in tandem. Both in ICU, both within minutes of each other.... I was attending on the first case. The boy got the best of care. No one, I mean no one, thought of anthrax. We had three consultants, one our ID consultant, two from outside, all the best. No one came up with anthrax. And why should we? No one dies of it in the United States." He almost sneered with irony.

"At first," the pediatrician went on, "we figured both children contracted the anthrax from a zoo animal. But we were wrong."

"And just what, Dr. Catrini," Lesan barked, "makes you so sure?"

"This," Catrini announced, pulling from his jacket the plastic Ziploc he'd shown Jack in the car. "This little yellow plastic water pistol. This is what killed them!"

Near pandemonium broke out in the room at Catrini's revelation. He managed to quiet the group enough to go on. "Dr. Alvarez admitted the girl, Jody Davis, and was able to talk to her and her parents before she died. The patient thought she'd gotten her eyes infected with mascara. Later, when she was almost delirious, she remembered she'd been squirted in the eyes by a kid at the Zoo with a water pistol... I'm sure now it must have been Joey."

"Why?" Lesan demanded.

"Because," Catrini explained, "when we went to tell the St. Johns the sad news, Eleanor said there was something she wanted to show me, something unusual. Their housekeeper found this under the boy's mattress this morning when she was changing his sheets— I guess they were hoping that he'd be home soon.

104

You see, the thing is—strict rule—Joey was never allowed to have toy guns."

"Hey, wait a minute—" Lesan could see things spinning out of control, attempted to wrest the meeting back, but Catrini wouldn't be stopped. He held the Baggie out for everyone to see.

"Take a look at the handle here." He pointed to the pistol inside the Baggie, then directed his next remark to Special Agent Hubbard. "There's a piece of surgical tape wrapped around the handle with some numbers and the letters 'LMPG.' I haven't got a clue what the letters mean, but the numbers are a different matter."

Catrini indicated the taped handle to the crowd, then continued, "We all have codes, abbreviations, and the like. I have to code all my goddamned diagnoses and procedures in order to get reimbursed by the HMOs. The coding sequence looked familiar to me... Zero-two-two point nine. Does anyone use the International Classification of Diseases code?"

The experts seemed bemused. Of course they used the code occasionally, but not nearly as often as tens of thousands of physicians who were forced to by the bottom-liners constantly depersonalizing patients. Having brought the meeting to a standstill, the pediatrician repeated the numbers. "Zero-two-two point nine. Still stumped? I'm not, not anymore. And now I'm damned glad the FBI is here... because these numbers are from the code. I looked it up, and zero-two-two point nine is... the code for anthrax!"

Catrini paused for a moment, then slid the Baggie across the conference table to Agent Hubbard, saying, "Don't worry about touching it. Dr. Bryne over there assures me that the anthrax is only *inside* the gun and it's probably dried up by now. The only possible health risk would be if someone decided to break the gun apart."

"So what exactly are you trying to tell us, Dr. Catrini?" Hubbard asked sternly.

"What I'm trying to tell you, Agent Hubbard," Catrini announced, "is that it wasn't accidental anthrax that killed Joey and Jody. It was intentional. Someone, some twisted human being, put anthrax in this squirt gun with an express intent to kill and from the coding on the handle, wanted the whole wide world to know about it!"

Thursday, June 18
Hotel Del Coronado
San Diego, California

The man whom Vinnie Catrini had mistaken for Jack Bryne and then promptly forgotten sat on a king-size bed, chain-smoking and eagerly awaiting room service. Fulfilling a mission always left him ravenous, sometimes for days, and he'd ordered a veritable feast for himself. He scratched his palms, then forced himself to read, to test his patience, then gave up and opened his laptop and, with a few clicks, accessed the Centers for Disease Control's WONDER log-in screen. He chose from his impressive collection a five-digit user ID, not his own, and the matching password.

It was amazing to him that more people didn't realize that computer passwords were as easy to come by as keys under mats: names of wives and children, initials, birthdays, ZIP codes. He had, in fact, ordered the Centers' complete Epidemic Intelligence Service Directory; as far as the Centers' computers were concerned, if a password matched, he was in. From the main CDC menu he downloaded the waiting e-mail files and announcements, then hit the search command on five key words—*ciguatera, hylae, ergot, Apis,* and anthrax. Nothing. Annoyed and frustrated, he logged off WONDER and onto another medical database, MEDNET, and ran the same search, then logged onto ProMED and read the latest updates. Eureka!

He realized that brief incident in the lobby with the little man mistaking him for Jack Bryne had been an omen, a superb one. For here on ProMED he now read postings for the first time on his bees—Apis—on his creations. Here, for all the world to see, were the swarm, and the horses, and the children at the zoo! God indeed was good—even it if took Job's patience to see it. God delivered on His promises. Here, in California, He had even granted him his fondest wish—to be on-site when all his intricate planning bore its gruesome fruit.

Sooner or later, some smartass like his old Haitian drinking buddy, Jack Bryne, would put two and two together, and immediately there would be an entire posse after him, probably headed by some bureaucrat from the FBI.

The FBI did things by the book, and he wasn't worried about them. It was the people whom the FBI turned to, the smart independent scientists like Bryne, not the CDC or the Feds, who would be worrisome. That good old Boy Scout Jack was already on the scene. Well, he'd just have to outwit Bryne—and make his life a good deal more difficult.

He doubted anyone would ever figure out the Grand Design.

He wondered if putting the code on the squirt gun was too obvious. After all, he had already given them many clues. Maybe this time, between the "LMPG" code and the new data on ProMED, there would be someone to run from. He had to stay alert and think like a hunter. He began to make a list.

For the last months, as he pursued his lethal mission, he'd pretended to be abroad on sabbatical in Scotland. Now, he decided, was the time to reappear to the world of science, to renew himself, to hide in plain sight, not as God's avenger, but as the groundbreaking toxicologist who had been terribly, terribly wronged. Who had been denied a chance not only to change forever the face of science but to be recognized as the most gifted toxicologist in the world, Dr. Theodore Graham Kameron.

When room service arrived, Kameron tipped the waiter lavishly—as befit the lavishness of the meal: champagne, Krug—only the best—oysters, caviar, Caesar salad with raw egg and anchovies, T-bone steak practically raw, a cheese tray, and hot fudge sundae. Ah, the thrill of the kill—and the thrill of the chase!

5

Thursday, June 18
San Diego, California

Bryne had been able to extricate himself from most of the St. Roch meetings after assuring a nurse-epidemiologist that he was taking antibiotics. The card the nurse handed him instructed him to call if he developed any symptoms such as fevers, chills, or headaches, and went on to add, "A case worker will call once a week. This is a routine precaution used when there has been intimate exposure to airborne pathogens such as TB, measles, plague..." Bryne noticed anthrax wasn't even on the list.

In any case, he had little to add to what was already known. He had taken all the leave time the St. John case could justify, and it had done little, if any, good. He'd given the St. Johns his deepest sympathies, but there was nothing more he could do to help.

While he waited for the long-delayed meeting with the FBI, Bryne ran his phone card through the slot and punched in Tucker's private number. The vet answered on the first ring.

"Dr. Tucker, Jack Bryne here. I've been delayed. The best I can do is a late flight into Indianapolis tonight. I could rent a—"

"No, no. I'm just glad you can get out here, Jack. Someone will pick you up and drive you to Churchill Downs in the morning. I'll arrange for a room at the Suisse Chalet Motel. At our expense, of course. It's not the spiffiest place in the town, but it's close to the airport."

"I'm most grateful, Dr. Tucker. I'll be ready early."

"No, Dr. Bryne, it's we who are grateful. The driver will pick you up at seven." Jack hung up, then guiltily called Mia's machine, and left a message telling her he had to make a detour to Indianapolis and where he'd be staying. Checking his watch, he shook his head impatiently, hoping the FBI guys would get their act together soon. But they didn't.

When it finally happened, Agent Hubbard's methodical interview, almost an interrogation, went on so long that Bryne missed his flight and had, once more, to reschedule with Tucker. Hubbard and the four additional feds he'd called in to interview everyone connected with the incident had pressed Jack particularly hard on the extent of his world travel.

"You don't seem to understand, Agent Hubbard," Jack, deeply frustrated, had found himself trying to persuade the man. "I'm a troubleshooter. It's my job to go where I'm needed. England, for mad cow disease. Japan, if there's word of bioterrorism. Or San Diego, when I'm called. Even Churchill Downs, where I'm headed next—at the request of one of the world's foremost veterinarians."

"Nevertheless, Dr. Bryne," the agent had retorted, "wherever you are, there *is* trouble."

"I don't know how else to explain the obvious to you, Mr. Hubbard." Jack had felt he was one moment away from decking the guy. "Let me repeat, I don't just up and go places at whim. I'm called in to consult."

"Now we'd like to know in slightly more detail exactly what your involvement in germ warfare was at the World Health Organization."

"But we've been through all—"

"Only a few more questions, Dr. Bryne." Hubbard had smiled a mirthless smile. "Then you'll be a free man!"

"Free? It sounds as if you're accusing me of something. Are you serious, Agent Hubbard? Do I need a lawyer?"

"Of course not, nothing of the sort. This is merely another routine interview."

But the "routine" interview lasted for another hour before the FBI men seemed to realize there was little more Bryne could tell them. So Bryne went gratefully with Catrini for a welcome, if unscheduled, overnight.

When they arrived home from the FBI interviews, they found that the entire Catrini clan had gone to sleep. The pediatrician, anticipating that Jack wasn't getting out of California that fast, shared an excellent bottle of port accompanied by a wedge of the creamiest Gorgonzola, Bath Oliver biscuits, a bowl of fruit, and a couple of Cuban cigars.

Catrini, exhausted, soon went to bed.

Jack took the tray to the garden, sat alone by the pool, and enjoyed the perfumy aroma of the California night. The luxuries Vinnie had bestowed on him delighted his palate, but did nothing to calm his hideous speculations.

What kind of mind would you have to have to do something as dreadful as what had been done to those children? How sick would you have to be? Perhaps more to the point, if you were that sick, how would you actually procure anthrax in the first place?

Virtually no anthrax existed in the New World, which meant the primary source must have been Africa or, even more likely, endemic areas in the Middle East. Still, you could look for a long time without any assurance that you were going to find a case of human anthrax. You'd be more likely to discover it in sick livestock, but at the very least you would have to leave the country.

When the World Health Organization had asked him to review the background reports on the Japanese sarin terrorists, Jack had discovered Interpol files on their "Sacred Expedition" in 1992, when six of the cultists traveled to Zaire looking for the Ebola virus. They had combed five hospitals in and around Kikwit. Finding no active human cases, they went home empty-handed. The cult's leader had been secretly taped telling a meeting of his followers his plans to drop the virus over ten U.S. cities—just to see what would happen. Recreational Ebola. Bryne shook his head.

God, now they were dealing with recreational

anthrax—not from some crazed cultists who didn't know what they were doing, but from someone who *did* know, someone who knew far too well.

The disparity between his ghastly thoughts and the idyllic setting in which he found himself was almost amusing. Bryne sipped his port and savored the cigar—and that was when it hit him. Cuba—the Caribbean! Of course! He had been wrong about the source of the anthrax. It was not the Old World. It was just twenty minutes away from Miami, right here in the Western hemisphere, an elaborate repository of infectious diseases that rightfully belong in the Middle Ages. Anthrax exists in the New World all right, in Haiti. And Bryne realized almost immediately that it would actually be easy to get the culture and transport, grow, and deliver it—if you were twisted enough to want to do it.

Bryne leaned back in the lawn chair, stretched out his long legs, remembering those months when he'd worked at the Albert Schweitzer Hospital in the sixties. Haiti back then, as today, was desperately impoverished: marasmus, kwashiorkor, malnutrition, dehydration, diarrhea, dementia, death.

The Albert Schweitzer Hospital survived for a few years, even after its founder, Dr. Mellon, died. His wife had remained in the tiny oasis of healing surrounded by thousands of people dying of tuberculosis, typhoid fever, malaria, leprosy, and the new scourge that would come to be known as AIDS. The hospital had shown Bryne human afflictions so macabre he hoped never to see them again.

Yes, it had to be Haiti. Bryne realized how straightforward it would be to obtain a culture of anthrax. The goats. He remembered that when they died, they would lie by the side of the road until something—dogs, rats, or vultures—consumed them. Goats died from anthrax. You could see the open black sores, fluid draining. You could hear the swarms of flies that carried the disease to other animals. All you needed to produce anthrax bacilli was a small specimen: find a sick goat, swab the sore, get the bacteria, put it into a test tube.

Bryne knew exactly how it would be done from there. He had first read the formula in a pamphlet called *Uncle Fester's Cookbook*, a terrorist primer. Simple, but effective. A recipe from *The Anarchist's Cookbook* had gone even further. It recommended inoculating anthrax on the eye of a sheep, pointing out that sheep eyes were easily obtained in any Greek market. He'd read both books while in Geneva at a bioterrorism conference and had been chilled.

The formulas were child's play, they would work, and they could be obtained in magazines sold on most newsstands; certain recipes had appeared on the World Wide Web for some time now. He'd warned his WHO colleagues that the recipes would work and told them he was frightened by their widespread availability.

One anthrax concoction called for Jell-O (any flavor), a few tablespoons of sugar, and two cups of water. Three blood sausages and two whole eggs were mixed in, then set aside. Next the preparer was to sprinkle bone meal on top of the broth and gently heat it, using a coffee warmer set on low. When it was warmed, a test tube of pus containing anthrax was added.

After two hours, the mixture was poured into a petri dish, an Erlenmeyer flask, Tupperware, even a plastic garbage container—anything would work.

Close the lid tight, wait, and open it when you're ready to use it. Easy. But why? Why?

Suddenly, overcome with fatigue, Bryne put out the cigar, finished his wine, then took the tray back inside, opting for a few hours of sleep if he could snatch them. The instant he lay down, his mind began racing again. Why? Who? There was nothing to do but think and wait for dawn.

Friday, June 19
San Diego

Morning came at last, and Jack prepared to go on to his next crisis. He and Catrini parted, bound by the knowledge that they were possibly facing the same horrible death they had witnessed the day before. Weeks would pass before they could stop taking the antibiotics, but years might pass before the spores began to multiply deep in the sequestered alveoli of their lungs or in a hilar lymph node.

They exchanged telephone numbers and e-mail addresses, and intended to use them. Catrini, eager enough to get out of St. Roch's, insisted on driving Bryne to the airport.

On the way, neither of the two men used the word "anthrax," and neither noticed Scott Hubbard in the car behind them.

Hubbard had a lot on his mind, not the least of which was the man in the car ahead of him. When he'd walked out of their first San Diego meeting, the FBI man had immediately arranged for the yellow water pistol to be taken by courier to the J. Edgar Hoover FBI Building in Washington. He next faxed the list of the interviewees to the Bureau for routine security checks. Hubbard would coordinate the research, cross-referencing individual backgrounds and security histories to see if anything popped up from similar lists being generated by the Bureau offices in other major cities. Work had already begun on the zoo personnel by local field staff. Hubbard himself interviewed the boy's physician and the outside consultants, Bryne and MacDonald.

Once in D.C., the water pistol underwent a microscopic inspection. The adhesive tape on the plastic handle had been carefully removed under a shielded stereomicroscope and examined fiber by fiber. The ink would be analyzed, its manufacturer identified. Each component would be subjected to exhaustive analysis. The letters "LMPG" had been forwarded to cryptographers at the National Security Agency.

The Chinese manufacturer of the squirt gun as well as its Korean distributors and U.S. retailers were identified within hours. Endless leads would be generated. Endless dead ends. The pistol had been sold as part of a bulk lot Wal-Mart had trucked around from store to store. The inventory had been pawed over by the time it got to the cash register, and there would never be a way to trace the gun to a particular point of sale.

All the distributors could say was that more than 26,000 squirt guns exactly like Joey's had been sold in the Wal-Mart system since 1991. They had no idea how many were yellow.

Hubbard was convinced they had come to a dead end—until the names and backgrounds of all attendees at the San Diego meeting were cross-indexed by computer. Three people had files, two of which were routine. Then, bingo! The third file was thick, full of shocking background material, and it belonged to John (Jack) Drake Bryne. The file was copied in its entirety, then attached to a preliminary report on the zoo incident. Offices in all major cities would receive it.

The FBI team had grilled Bryne intensely for hours, but he'd revealed nothing. Hubbard prided himself on being a good agent with excellent instincts, and something about this Bryne character hadn't rung true. Maybe it was his extremely obvious and deep-seated resentment of authority—a streak of the obsessive hatred of government those militia guys out west all had. Or maybe it was the fervor of his dedication, almost too convincing to be real. Those reasons could be part of why Scott Hubbard had his eye on Bryne, but not the main one. It was sheer instinct, but the FBI man was convinced that Bryne had a secret, something he wasn't about to divulge.

Then Bryne's file came up, and Hubbard knew not only that he'd been right but that after what he'd read, he would follow his prime suspect not just to the airport, but anywhere in the world.

Friday, June 19
Indianapolis, Indiana

As the airport shuttle bus bore him from the terminal to the motel, Bryne managed to fall asleep, but as soon as he did, a nightmare began: horses, dozens of beautiful horses, dying in a field, falling into a pit, dying horribly. Choking, gasping, trying to run, falling. He jerked awake with a start, drenched in sweat. Embarrassed, unable to shake the images, he was glad the bus was empty.

Even after checking into the Suisse Chalet Motel, Jack found that the dream—the horrible reality that awaited—still haunted him. All those poor sick horses. Tucker's epidemic would have to be Eastern equine encephalitis, of course. He hoped he was wrong, hoped it was one of the many other things it could be, even some kind of food poisoning: plants like catclaw, bahia, florestina, queen's delight, vetch. They all contained cyanide. If the horses were free-ranging, they could have

118

gotten into these wildflowers and plants. He knew that even apple seeds contained cyanide. A single cup could kill a man. One cup of apricot pits could kill an elephant. Ricin, the by-product of castor beans—the same one used to make castor oil—was deadly. Back in December, Bryne recalled, a man had been found in Arkansas with enough ricin to kill one thousand people, or hundreds of horses.

My God, Jack thought, could this horse sickness be a second "recreational" nightmare, created by yet another madman? Or was it some sort of financial scam? Were the horses insured? After all, Grand Prix jumpers had been electrocuted in Connecticut a few years before for more money than the owners would have gotten from a lifetime of prizes. But the few electrocuted horses had all been Grand Prix jumpers—not stables full of racehorses.

Truly exhausted, Bryne decided to lie down for a few minutes, but he slept deeply for what turned out to be almost an hour—until the phone began to ring. The shrieking machine at first failed to awaken him, but it kept on howling until Bryne wrenched the handset off its cradle and held it to his ear.

"Hello, hello," he mumbled.

"Jack, it's your wife, you know, Mia Hart," she said archly. "Why did you tell me you would be at this number last night? I kept trying you, but they said you hadn't checked in."

"Oh, no!" He struck his forehead with his fist when he realized he'd forgotten to call her back after he'd changed flights. "Mia, I'm

119

so sorry... I meant to phone you. Shit! You see, the feds insisted on questioning anyone involved in the St. John case, but they didn't get around to me until it was too late to make the plane. I've been in five airports since lunch. I just got here."

"The FBI, what on earth! Did they give you a hard time?"

"Well, they didn't use the rack or thumbscrews, but it wasn't my idea of fun. I understand what they are up against, but couldn't really tell them anything anyway. Made for one long night, though. The head fed's a real bastard."

"Oh, Jack, I'm sorry I woke you. We always seem to be doing that to each other."

Picturing her loveliness and knowing how hard his frequent absences were for her, Bryne said in his most romantic voice, "Hon, don't apologize. There's nothing more luxurious than being awakened by a beautiful woman with a sexy voice."

"You are so full of it, Dr. Bryne." She tried to be stern, but he could sense the pleasure behind her words. Then she was serious. "Jack, after what I've been reading and seeing on the tube, I'm glad you're out of San Diego; this business really sounds hairy!"

"That, my dear, is an understatement. There's more going on than CNN can possibly tell you." He shook his head, still groggy, the fatigue of the last few days catching up with him.

"Listen, Jack, you really sound exhausted. Get some sleep, do whatever you have to do at Churchill Downs, and get back here. I want you in my arms immediately, if not sooner."

Momentarily Bryne chose to ignore the reality that awaited him at the stables and told his wife sincerely, "I'll be in your arms tomorrow night. And believe me, darling, I'm looking forward to every moment. If I can make the last train to Albany, I'll be in before midnight."

"Couldn't we go ahead and stay in the city tomorrow night?"

Bryne felt the old pull, and with it, the old tension penetrated his voice. "If I'm lucky, I'll make the late train, it's the best I can—"

"I know, love, but..." he felt her enthusiasm waning.

"Mia, I haven't been in the lab for days!"

"But do you have to spend the entire day in Kentucky?"

"I have to allow for it. It's a bad outbreak, but I can't see it taking overnight, and if I can get an early flight, you can bet I will."

"Yeah," she soured, "I hope someone else is paying."

Bryne could feel his patience beginning to wear thin. "We'll ask Churchill Downs to pick up the tab. It's damned critical, Mia. Some of the exposed horses have already been sent out to stables all over the country, two to Saratoga. Mia, I'll be back when I can. I've seen these things happen before, and I *need* to help."

Jack could feel the chilly silence growing

121

between them even as she spoke. "Jack, for God's sake, what's driving you? What do you mean, 'I've seen this before'?"

Her words were causing him to raise his guard. He knew she knew it, but he couldn't stop himself. "Mia, please, I didn't mean anything by it. Just being theatrical, making a bad joke... But darling, I can't do any more scheduling right now. Let me call you from Churchill Downs when I have a better idea of what's going on. Okay?"

"Jack, don't hang up. I wasn't trying to start a fight, but sometimes you get these 'projects' in your head, and the next thing I know I haven't seen you in weeks. You literally get carried away from me." He could tell she was halfway between anger and tears. "You've got more frequent flier miles than a politician, and right now we need to see each other more, not less. Yes, you do get carried away... Is it me?"

"Oh, Mia, no, no, no. It's not you, sweetie. I've never been able to slow down. I guess I've never really wanted to. And now I do. I want to be able to please you. I feel rotten when we're apart, and I feel neurotic when I realize how much I annoy you. I don't mean to."

"I'm not annoyed," she said strongly. "I'm in love with all of you, Jack. With your flakiness, your dedication, with all the things that make you what you are. But Jack, I must tell you, I know there is something eating away at you, and if you ever decide to let me see that hidden part of you, please understand I'm not here to judge, but to comfort you."

"I love you, Mia. Thanks."

"I love you too, Jack. And don't forget to give my best to Victoria Wade."

He groaned a mock groan, again told her he loved her, hung up, and began to think once more of the horses.

Saturday, June 20
Indianapolis

Bryne stood in front of the motel, waiting in the bright morning sunlight for Tucker's driver, when he looked up from the paper he was reading and saw a silver Lexus pull in from the highway. Whoever the driver was, he was really pushing it, careening toward him at top speed. When the car was close enough for Jack to spot the driver, his heart skipped a beat: it was Vicky. Even with her hair tied in a bandanna and wearing dark driving glasses, Victoria Wade was unmistakable. The shock of recognition was enough to bring all their shared history back to Bryne, and with it came a rush of feelings as intense as if they had parted only the night before.

Some things don't change: He was never in one place for more than a few moments; Vicky Wade was never late. Promptness was a matter of honor for her, a reason—if not an excuse—for her driving as recklessly as she did. Her inside tires chirped as she turned into the motel drop zone, where she braked abruptly and came to a stop.

Jack pulled open the passenger door and was greeted by that same beautiful smile he

123

remembered. And that same extraordinary voice asked, "Jack, it's really you?"

"Victoria Wade, what are you doing here? I expected you to be at Churchill Downs."

"What am I doing here?" repeated one of television journalism's most well-known and respected women. "Running after you, Jack Bryne. Same as always. Seriously, Tucker sent me. Jump in. Jack, Tucker needs your help. He's depressed; his staff told me that he's not the same."

"That's not good," Bryne said, concerned immediately. "But Tucker sounded fine when I talked to him."

"It comes and goes, but he's been fine while I've been here. And by the way, it's good to see you looking so hot," she purred provocatively.

"This is such a surprise." Bryne suddenly felt reduced to the conversational level of a twelve-year-old. "When Dr. Tucker mentioned a driver, I had no idea he... ummm... meant... you."

"Well, the network lets me moonlight as a cabbie, and you looked like a big tipper."

He grinned.

"Hop in. We've got a bit of a trip." She gestured with her chin. He tossed his luggage in the back seat. "I'll explain while we drive."

Bryne nodded, lowered himself in, and turned to face her.

"Vicky, it's great to see you. You look wonderful, not a day older. I can't believe it's been fifteen years."

"Yikes, you're right. I'd only been with the network for a couple of years." Beneath the bandanna, he could see her hair was the same rich, thick, flaxen gold; even seated behind the wheel, her body still radiated grace. And the voice familiar to millions seemed to grow even more mellifluous as she recalled, "Fifteen years. South America. Colombia. I was on that Exxon coal mining story."

"Yes, Vicky, and my prediction about the borrow pits recently came true."

"I saw the story, Jack. Let's change the subject."

"Sure, remember our dinner in Barranquilla after it was all over? The aguardiente?"

"Yes, Jack, we played that board game, *Careers*."

"Right, and the winner had to buy a round of aguardiente. As I recall, you beat all of us, Victoria."

In fact, Bryne remembered every drop of the potent sugar-cane liquor, every moment of the game, which seemed to prefigure both their lives. To play *Careers*, each player secretly selects game points from three categories, Love, Fame, and Money. Wade, the winner, had placed all her points on Fame. Dividing his goal among the three objectives, Jack lost, but that loss hadn't prevented them from attempting to adjust their own life strategies during the following weekend in Cartagena. At the end of the weekend, neither player had won: *Fame* flew back to the States to cover a story; *Love-Fame-Money* returned alone to Geneva, having lost another gamble.

Vicky was looking him over. "You look as trim as you did in Cartagena," she told him.

"Sweet of you, my dear, but the truth of it is, I've put on a few pounds and gotten some gray hair. But you, you really do still look like a young woman up close."

She smiled wryly. "Well, if a personal trainer and all the jogging I do can't keep me in shape, we're all doomed. I'm running fourteen miles a week when I can."

"Impressive as always."

"It really has been a long time, Jack." He heard the tenderness in her voice, as comforting now as years before.

Strangely, that comfort left him tongue-tied again, and he had to fight for something to say. "I see you on television."

"Don't lie to me, Jack Bryne. I bet you don't watch any more TV now than you ever did!"

"Unfair! I always check the listings and never miss *Hot Line* when you're doing a piece."

"That's sweet of you, Jack." When she looked at him, he was aware they still felt the same affection they'd felt years ago. "Are you blushing, Jack? Now I'm going to be forced to believe you really do look for my shows. And I'm flattered. I know how busy you must be. No, not flattered, touched."

And with that, she loosened her seat belt and kissed him full on the mouth before turning her eyes back to the road.

"Just another technique I've added to my driving skills," she laughed.

"God, I didn't think it could be done without causing a twelve-car pileup, at least."

"Ah, Jack, you've only scratched the surface of my hidden talents."

"That's a frightening thought."

Changing the subject, she told him, "Jack, you seem very happy."

"I've remarried, you know. I have a wonderful wife." He was shocked by his hope that she might be a little jealous; if she was, she clearly wasn't about to let it show.

"Happiness suits you. I'm glad you found someone," she announced, heartily adding, "I was sorry to hear about Lisle. It must have been horrible. I didn't even know she'd passed away until a few years ago. And when I heard, I felt badly for you. I almost called so many times, but I didn't know if you'd want to hear from me—after I used your off-the-record remarks about Ebola on the air."

"That's, as they say, 'old news.'" Jack dismissed her concern. "I wish you had called..."

In response, she leaned over and kissed him again, this time more innocently on the cheek. "I'm glad you're okay. You know, I've never stopped missing you."

Deciding to change the topic, Jack smiled. "And I still can't believe I'm sitting next to *the* Vicky Wade."

"Want an autograph to prove you really know me?" she joked. "No, seriously, Jack, don't give me any of that nonsense. You knew me way back—"

"Long before you had to teach me that 'The Story Is Always King...'"

"Hey, kiddo," she said, this time keeping her eyes straight ahead, "I never tried to fool you. Speak to me, you speak to the world. Which reminds me, my producers tell me there's a huge breaking story in San Diego, and I know you were there. If there's anything you'd like to add to my meager knowledge—I'm speaking as a representative of ATV now—I'd be eager to listen. If you know what I mean, Dr. Bryne."

Bryne responded, "You mean, Ms. Wade, that anything I tell you about San Diego will be all over the evening news."

"For instance, if you'd like to tell me why they decided to close the zoo?"

"Well, actually, it's a bit complicated... I'd rather not say..."

She held up her hand. "I hear you. Case closed. Now let's get down to business closer to home. Let me tell you why ATV has me down here working with Dr. Tucker. I backstop all the medical stories for *Hot Line* because of my Peace Corps training. And this one is very strange. It makes me wish I'd gone into medicine instead of media. Anyway, Tucker and the breeders all wanted to go to the press, and they decided to go with *Hot Line*... More than half of our stories start out as tips, many of them from ProMED. Keep that in mind."

"Tucker hasn't given me or ProMED much in the way of details," Jack said. "Will he be meeting us at the track?"

"I'm sure he'll still be there. He needs you to take a look at the brains of those dead horses. The Churchill Downs veterinary pathologists didn't find rabies or prions or anything, because most of the brains were liquefied. Frankly, and you didn't hear this from me, Tucker said they don't have anything near your experience with rabies. I got the impression he thinks a raccoon strain may have mutated, if that's possible. It was something to do with *Negri* bodies. Am I saying that right?"

"Exactly," Bryne said.

"He stayed up all last night. It's bad. They've lost horses at half a dozen farms south of here down toward the Ohio Basin. It was a terrible summer for mosquitoes, and a lot of the farms had standing water problems. The sentinel birds showed no evidence of viral infection. Tucker's people sampled scores of wild birds, free-range chickens, nothing. The entomologists dipped for mosquito larvae at each of the farms and found no real evidence of a problem. They did find some Culex mosquitoes capable of spreading viral diseases like equine encephalitis."

"Any linkages between the horses other than location? Like common owners, owners in trouble, busted syndicates?" he asked, impressed again by her personal research.

"You're suggesting someone deliberately murdered all these animals, killed them for money. Actually, that's what brought us down here in the first place. But it doesn't seem likely, as far as I can tell."

"It does happen."

"It happens all the time, no doubt," she conceded. "But when somebody kills a horse, it's because it won't run. Not a horse that's able to produce twenty-five-thousand-dollar vials of semen anytime the owner wants. And killing a single horse for the insurance makes sense, but unless somebody is trying to bankrupt these stable owners, I can't see a motive for this—much less a way to do it. These days, if you're going to kill an also-ran for the policy money, you use a cattle prod set for two hundred and twenty volts. Stops their hearts, looks like a coronary. Most carriers pay right away. But that's not the point here. Tucker knows all the local breeders, and he feels sure they're legit. Frankly, he's baffled."

"Tucker, baffled?" Bryne arched an eyebrow.

"Yes, baffled," she continued. "Like every other vet I talk to. There were a couple of similar cases in Illinois a few months ago. Early symptoms in each case were a rapid onset of trembling, then the animals stopped eating, and subsequently you saw serious hind leg weakness. Then they collapsed and died..." She shook her head sadly as Bryne looked at her. Maybe he shouldn't have been so unreceptive to her kiss. She was beautiful, but... back to business.

"Twenty-seven horses from five different stables are dead as of yesterday," he mused. "And they still don't know what's causing it."

"And I still don't know what you intend to do to stop it," she challenged him.

To which his only reply was, "You will, Ms. Wade, you will."

130

6

Saturday, June 20
Churchill Downs, Kentucky

The lawns of Churchill Downs were manicured, the setting serene. It was a relief for Bryne and Wade to turn into the grounds of the racetrack after battling Louisville's morning traffic. Wade slowed the Lexus to a crawl at the gate as Jack looked up at the immense building beside them—perhaps the premier architectural landmark in American horse racing. The pines. The flowering gardens. The calm.

With its dark-roofed turrets, huge glazed windows, and enameled layer of colonial white seven generations thick, the Clubhouse at Churchill Downs always seems grander from without than within. As they passed, Bryne was surprised to see that age had taken its toll and afforded a certain seediness to the place.

"It's the horses that matter here," Wade said as she observed him eyeing the place.

"Maybe to the owners, but it's what's killing the horses that matters to me."

Wade smiled wryly. "I can assure you that the horses running at Churchill Downs get better medical care than most of the human beings on the planet. From feed to vets, bedding hay to vitamins, some sort of expert consultant has a say. These animals are multimillion-dollar financial syndicates. They have staffs of dozens of people."

"Who oversees the various feed supplies?"

"This is really something," she told him. "The horses' diets are supervised by teams of equine nutritionists. Special blends of oats before workouts, special blends of wheat, barley, and alfalfa before races. Each mix is based on a trainer's personal evaluation. I bet you thought only megacelebrities had their own chefs and trainers."

"What about security around the horses during the race?"

"Security, as a matter of fact, is the crown jewel of this track's reputation," Wade announced. "The reasons the owners want ATV here at all is to confirm—when and if *Hot Line* runs the story—that the track is safe. Dr. Tucker understands that people aren't much interested in a tragedy like this unless somebody tries to cover it up."

Jack followed Wade to the director's suite, where six obviously concerned men, all in suits and ties, awaited them. The round mahogany table held only a large, well-worn Bible. When Vicky and Jack appeared, all six men rose, their relief apparent.

Enoch Tucker, a small, intense man whose thin white hair framed a bald pate, greeted the two of them and then introduced them to the board in a direct, professional manner. He cited Jack's work on Eastern equine encephalitis, then made it clear that there was no time to waste with pleasantries. The five owners of Churchill

Downs had been terrified by the epidemic from the beginning, and Tucker, having treated more of the stricken animals than any other vet, now shared that terror. He had known these men for years, and they trusted him, paying him handsomely for his reliability, honesty, and discretion. He was frustrated that he personally could do nothing to make the crisis end and prayed that Jack Bryne could. His remarks were as terse as possible.

The one commonality among the owners was that thus far every stricken horse had either been entered as a three-year-old in the Kentucky Derby in May or had a stall adjoining one. Almost all the dead horses had bedded at Churchill Downs before the race. To date, the deaths were similar but the cause unknown, yet everything pointed to something they had been exposed to while they were at the track—perhaps even on race day.

Tucker then went on to update the group on the number of deaths, reviewed the list of sick animals, and outlined the ways in which the horses had been linked, one way or another, to the Derby. He also described his ProMED questionnaire asking if there had been more cases elsewhere. It seemed clear that if someone wanted to infect horses at stables besides Churchill Downs, he could.

Tucker was suggesting the possibility of sabotage. The bombshell dropped in the laps of the owners caused a heavy silence to fall over the room.

"However," Tucker continued, "I'm convinced

that if we handle this correctly, we can protect the reputation of Churchill Downs, save the season, and keep the track open next spring."

Could Tucker actually mean that the track might somehow close? Bryne wondered. Why would he even consider closing the track?

"There are so many factors that could cause this sort of epidemic," Tucker explained, "that it would be virtually impossible to involve the track directly. In fact, the more we know, the more agents, or potential agents, we can identify, the more inconclusive the situation becomes. Naturally, the more inconclusive the situation becomes, the harder it is to affix any sort of liability. Therefore, the more research we do, the more difficult blaming the track becomes. With that in mind, I want you to listen to Dr. Bryne."

Jack stood up and began to speak. "I in no way want to suggest that your excellent staff hasn't done all it could to give you a diagnosis. But there are new bugs out there, ones that have yet to get into the literature and may not have been considered, or tested for."

"For example?" one of the owners demanded.

"For example, a new morbilliform virus, a variant on the distemper virus. Now, distemper usually infects carnivores—dogs, captive lions, tigers, leopards."

"But not horses, for God's sake," one of the older owners, Leigh S. Connors, broke in. He was an intelligent, aristocratic man whose family had entered horses in the Derby for more than a hundred years.

"Leigh, let him finish!" Tucker insisted.

"Thanks," Bryne nodded to the vet. "It might surprise you to know that distemper's related to measles, which affects humans, and to rinderpest, which infects cattle. Another morbilliform is *peste de petit ruminants*, which targets sheep and goats. The same for phocid distemper in seals."

"In seals?" asked a younger man seated at the far end of the table.

"That's right. In the early nineties, thousands of seals began to die in Russia, around Lake Baykal. After numerous discussions and international exchanges on an early ProMED system, the cause has now been shown to be an entirely new morbilliform virus, closely akin to distemper. The seals ate infected dog carcasses, and the virus jumped species."

Bryne then told them he mentioned such diseases because a few years ago a new morbilliform virus had broken out in Australian horses. But this virus had then spread to humans, killing them as well. "All morbilliform viruses are airborne," he added, "and highly infectious."

"Do you think our horses got that virus?" the younger man asked. "Some of them were in Australia. Are people going to start getting this disease?"

"It's not impossible. But you've also hosted horses from England, Spain, Saudi Arabia. Look, the virus could have been imported, or, indeed, be a completely new morbilliform."

"But didn't you say viruses attack specific hosts?" asked Leigh Connors.

Bryne shrugged his shoulders, telling him, "That's the orthodoxy today. But keep in mind the best new thinking suggests that Ebola, for instance, could even be a plant virus. That's not merely a *species* jump; it's a jump from one kingdom, Plantae, to another, Animalia. Which only goes to show how little we know. For example, the closest virus to the rabies virus infects cabbage. We will have a lot of tests to run, gentlemen. Thank you."

Bryne sat down as Tucker stood up to announce, "So it's set. I'll give Dr. Bryne all the material he needs from here, and he'll pick up the other specimens when Ms. Wade drives him back to Indianapolis. The research botanists at the Lilly research facility will also have their initial results on plant intoxicants." He turned to Bryne. "How long do you think it will take for an answer?"

Although he actually had no idea, Jack heard himself volunteer, "Something definitive might take a matter of weeks. But the New York lab is as fast as any—"

"No!" shouted Leigh Connors, rising from his chair. "There's not gonna be any more damned *'specialists'* in on this thing. The Lord looks after us here." He started for the door, then stopped and turned to Enoch Tucker. "People hear we're calling in fancy experts from New York City and now these TV people. Rumors will spread. Well, damn it, I just won't have it!"

Two of the board members seemed visibly relieved when Connors stormed out, slamming the heavy door behind him. The younger man who had questioned Jack seemed to be speaking for all the remaining owners when he apologized. "All Leigh wants," the man explained, "is to reassure the breeders and the public that the track is safe. Then the whole incident could disappear. We would be most grateful for your help."

"Good." Tucker stood again. "Now, Dr. Bryne has been kind enough to interrupt a cross-country trip to come to Kentucky, and he did so at my request. It was a costly disruption for Dr. Bryne, and I intend to include his expenses and fees in my next invoice." He grinned. "We don't want Leigh to see checks made out to 'some fancy expert from New York City,' now, do we?"

With Wade driving, Tucker took them to three of the nearby stables. At each farm Bryne was able to take a few smears. For the next few hours, Jack reexperienced a vision of hell: once-sleek stallions trying to remain on all fours, ears back, breathing labored, gagging; others prostrate, kicking in their stalls. It was awful, and the worst part was that nothing could be done to stop the dying. At least, not yet.

By midafternoon, Jack and Wade had dropped Tucker off and were heading back to the famous Eli Lilly Botanical Gardens in Indianapolis. As he tried to clear his mind of the gruesome images of the sick horses, Wade mentioned that she'd gotten a fax from the two veterinarians at Indiana University suggesting that the horses might be chewing yellow star thistle and saying that trembling was often caused by white snakeroot. Cyanide poisoning from naturally occurring sources had already been ruled out. They suggested Wade talk with the experts in poisonous plants at the Botanical Gardens, and that was where she was headed now.

Wade exited the highway and headed directly for the Gardens. While she drove, she joked with Bryne about the way Tucker had persuaded the board to fund Jack's lab work and research.

"Can't keep the money even if I get it," Jack explained. "I'll have to turn it over to New York State."

"Damn it, Bryne, keep it!" she said intently. "You saw those poor horses! Connors needs the information whether he pays for it or not. More important, so does Dr. Tucker."

When Bryne asked, "And so does ATV?" she looked away.

By the time she'd thought up an answer, Bryne had tipped back his seat and fallen asleep, to awake to the sounds of a fountain. He peered out of the car and saw a huge, circular pool with sculptural cubes of concrete around the rim, and cool, inviting lawns. He felt Vicky's hand on his sleeve.

"Wake up, Jack, we're here. I'm going inside. Your beeper kept going off, but I overpowered it." She unfastened her seat belt. "C'mon."

"And good morning to you, Ms. Wade," he joked. "Now where in heaven *is* my beeper?"

Opening the glove compartment, she grabbed his pager and handed it to him.

Jack checked the message. Lawrence again. He reached back to get his laptop from the back seat. "I'll meet you back here. I like the outdoors if you don't mind," he called as she stepped out of the car.

In a few moments, he had scrolled past ProMED's highlights and was reading the message. Lawrence had finished the draft of the funding proposal and the budget projections that he'd mentioned—when? How many days ago had he arrived in California? It must have been the jet lag. Bryne felt he was losing track of time. Lawrence wanted to know if he'd be staying in Indianapolis and if he needed the entire proposal e-mailed to him. Why would Lawrence hit the beeper over something this routine?

Bryne tapped in a short reply message asking Lawrence to hold onto the file, since he was on his way back. Next he scrolled up and read the ProMED highlights.

An update on therapeutic uses for certain hymenoptera toxins looked interesting; several incidents of type A flu seemed urgent; and a severe Listeria outbreak in France. Nothing on Tucker's horses.

Then he saw *it*. A polite, discreet note from a Pakistani physician commenting on the unusual case of the sick boy in San Diego. Bryne had sent out a summary of Joey's lab tests and clinical picture before the anthrax diagnosis, which the Pakistani ProMEDer had picked up:

For ProMed:
As strange as it may seem in your won-
derful country, I suggest you consider
anthrax. Respectfully, Sirhan Khan,
M.D., Aga Khan Hospital, Karachi,
Pakistan

Bryne first shook his head, checked the posting time, then swore—the message had been only a few hours too late! Others would get it right and send messages similar to this one, but they would all be too late. If Jack had gotten on ProMED faster, and if Joey and the young girl had been given massive doses of the correct antibiotics, they might still be alive.

He turned off the laptop, tucked it under his arm, and headed off toward the sunlit fields beyond the fountain, beyond the colonnades of the building. It felt good to be outdoors. The temperature was warmer than in New York, the air fresh and inviting. Jack realized how much he could use some sunlight and how much he needed to rest.

Looking up toward the museum's main building, he noticed a clear blue banner with subtle slits that allowed the wind to waft through. It was hung to announce a major new exhibition: THE ANCIENT ARTS OF EGYPT. The banner undulated in the breeze, beckoning him toward the garden, but he decided to be dutiful, turned away from the sunlight, and entered the cool darkness of the museum's galleries.

Suddenly, from out of nowhere, an

140

overwhelming dizziness struck Bryne. The room seemed to shift around the margins. He desperately needed to sit down. He felt a twinge in his chest. If this was not simply *déjà vu*, it was not a faint, inexplicable sensation; it was tremendously potent and actually frightening. What could it be? Too much coffee, too little sleep? So many possibilities. Anthrax? No, he told himself, no.

Sugar shock, he decided. Must be. He hadn't eaten in seven hours, because Wade never bothered to stop to eat. He shook his head to clear it. Better. Relieved, he headed off toward the restaurant. He would catch up with Wade later.

Making his way through the corridors, Bryne found himself standing before a profoundly disturbing vision, Turner's massive painting of Yahweh's revenge, *The Fifth Plague*. The huge canvas depicted Jehovah's punishment visited on Pharaoh and his Egyptian subjects for keeping the Chosen People in bondage. Horrible death to the overlords and to their beasts. Ominous black clouds raced past, tempests rimmed the horizon. Cattle and horses lay dead in the foreground. A pyramid glowed in the background.

The images pulsed with screaming, suffering, flight, and death. Bryne was frozen—immobile. He had to tell himself it was only oil on canvas and only a coincidence. Still, there they were, all those dying horses.

Eventually Wade found him standing before the painting, shivering. "Hey, are you okay?

C'mon, Jack," she urged, tugging his arm. "Let's get out of here. I've got some food." She looked up at the painting. "What a horribly depressing painting. What is it?"

"It's the wrath of God, Vicky."

She slipped her hand in his and led him away, and he was relieved.

Over sandwiches eaten on the road, Wade gave Jack a copy of the reports from the plant specialists.

"Jack, these names are all Greek—or Latin—to me. Can you take a look?" she asked him. "The botanists agree with Dr. Tucker. The horses appear to be dying from a pharmacological cause, not an infectious agent. Whatever it is, it damages a specific portion of their brains—either slowly or quickly, depending on the assumed dose and duration of exposure."

Bryne shrugged. "The main question is still what is the toxic agent. Corollary questions are: When exactly did the affliction begin? How widespread is this epizootic? And which horses were preferentially affected?"

Vicky nodded. "One of the veterinarians did not agree with you. He suggested that a slow virus—a prion variant—could have been introduced into the equine population. 'Mad horse disease,' he called it. Is that possible?" she asked, sensing a story.

"Prions are quite real. England's experience with mad cow disease is only the beginning."

As Wade was adjusting the mirror, Bryne

noticed that a fast-moving blue van was approaching them from behind as if preparing to pass them. Instead it slowed, keeping a uniform distance right behind their car. Looking back, Bryne at first thought they were being followed, but he then decided his fatigue was just making him paranoid.

"The Lilly folks," Vicky went on, "speculated that the source could also be adulterated feed. If cows can get prions from infected feed, maybe horses can as well."

"It's a real possibility," Bryne agreed. "Keep in mind, the Brits are still hurting and will be for a long time because the bovine incubation period for mad cow is about ten years. It may be less in humans. And if these horses have something new…"

"It could spread to humans?"

"Right. With mad cow we're looking at a potential pandemic. And the public doesn't know that prions can be in organs other than the brain, such as the spinal column or nervous tissue in regular meat. You know, that's how the cows got it, by eating offal, including sheep remains in fortified feed. It all started with Gajdusek's work with kuru, and nearly fifty years later Prusiner wins a Nobel Prize for the idea."

Bryne didn't want to ask, but wondered if Wade gardened, since prions are found in bone meal. It was thought that even the tiniest particle making its way into an eye might be enough to infect. He also knew that cow brains are used as an additive for women's skin creams, moisturizers, and body lotions, because sphingomyelin gives the creams a smooth texture and the fluid in the eyeballs is used to thicken milk shakes. Instead he said, "And by the way, if you want a real story, wait and see what's going to happen in Japan. It was the one market the Brits had for cow spinal columns. The Japanese eat it raw, thinly sliced like sashimi. They swear it's safe. It's considered a delicacy." Wade looked at him in disbelief.

Bryne continued, "Believe it. Denial is not just a river in Egypt." She smiled, and he went on, "The Japanese even denied they had an AIDS problem until those businessmen's weekend tours to the Bangkok brothels finally caught up with them. The same may be true with bovine spongiform encephalopathy. Remember, it takes a decade to incubate. Japan is one huge test tube."

Glancing behind him, Bryne noticed that the blue van was still following them. "Or it could be rabies without Negri bodies. Although Negri bodies are generally the hallmark of rabies, you don't find them in the brains of rabid bats. It could be that kind of mutation. In fact, the Churchill Downs pathologists may have missed it if they were looking for Negri bodies. Our lab can do the fluorescent antibody tests for bat, fox, skunk, and so on. But Vicky, if we do have some sort of mutated rabies strain or a new prion disease here, Tucker's going to need expert assistance."

Bryne nodded his head toward a package on

the seat. "Tucker's given me slides with corneal impressions, follicular samples from neck areas, and some biopsies near the hooves. His staff must have been taking these samples for weeks. It's a lot of work, means dozens of tests to run. Really, Vicky, why me? My budget's a mess. I'm already behind with the routine work."

"To be frank," she grinned sheepishly, "Enoch asked you down to Louisville before he had any way to pay you. But don't worry, the network is going to be funding whatever we need to do, just so you'd be clear on the budget for this research..." She stopped in mid-sentence, smiled, and turned to him. "Now who is holding up whom?"

"Well," he shook his head, "I'm learning from a master. But I'd do it for nothing if Enoch asked. Of course, I'll need more brain sections from the others, too."

"Tucker saved what he could, but I told you some were virtually dissolved, turned to liquid. It's as if battery acid ate its way into their skulls and destroyed most of the structure."

"That's not typical for either rabies or mad cow," Bryne muttered.

"Well, what kind of things *do* that?"

"Christ, Vicky, I don't know. I'm good, but what makes you think I'm *that* good?

"Because, my darling, you are."

They got to the airport early enough to talk over a drink at one of the terminal bars.

Jack took a swig of his Watney's and told her,

"I couldn't be happier to see you, but I have to ask what you're really doing here."

Vicky smiled. "I'm the reporter. I'm the one who's supposed to ask the questions."

"I didn't know this was an interview."

"It isn't." She sipped her white wine. "It's two old... ummm... *friends*... having a drink at an airport."

"So you're not going to tell me why you're here."

"Sure, I thought I had. It's not a secret. It's just what it seems. Look, I'm a damned good journalist, and I can smell a breaking story from a mile away. This horse thing, I'm not sure why, but I *know* it'll turn out to be major. I don't really know if I mean it's some kind of scam, blackmail, rabies, or even a new virus. There's enough of them emerging every day, and *Hot Line* prides itself on staying on top of all the new pathogens. You know, we did the first mad cow story."

"I do indeed. I saw it."

"And my curiosity about the horses is further whetted by the fact that Enoch Tucker's completely in the dark. That's rare for him."

"So your intuition is telling you it's bioterrorism, using a new virus we can't yet test for?"

"Well, sort of. Maybe. Frankly, that's why I had Tucker call you."

"God, I hope I can help."

"Me, too. I may seem like a stonehearted journalist, but it breaks my heart to see those beautiful animals suffer."

"Yes, me, too. And the thought that it

could spread to humans is horrific." Jack happened to focus on the clock above the bar. "My God, I've got to catch another plane." He quickly picked up the bill, which she snatched from him. After she paid, they walked together to the gate. He slid his overnight bag, now housing all the material Wade had given him, through the metal detector, then turned to say good-bye.

"Jack," she began, "if you even try to thank me for buying you a beer, I swear I'll kiss you again."

"I'm sorry, Vicky, it's just..." He felt flustered, lost, as she reached up with both her arms and offered her lips. Bryne kissed her cheek. As he turned away to walk through the gate, she smiled sadly and blew him a kiss in return.

"Jack," he heard her call him, and looked back. "Jack, I want you to call me when you get to New York. I really mean it, Mister. We have to find out what's doing this."

Or *who's* doing this, Bryne thought, giving her a mock salute before boarding the 737 that would take him back to Mia.

"Ms. Wade? Vicky Wade?" She had taken only a few steps away from the gate when Vicky heard her name called. She turned and saw a man in a gray suit approaching her carrying a folded newspaper. As he fell into step beside her, he smiled, but there was an edge to the warmth. She nodded, eyeing him nervously.

As if sensing her edginess, the man, who had

a Southern drawl, introduced himself as "Scott Hubbard, FBI," and discreetly showed her his identification as they walked. "Ms. Wade, I wonder if we might chat for a few minutes."

Vicky didn't know what this was about, but she didn't like it. "I'm as busy as I've ever been, Mr. Hubbard," she told him tersely, hoping to blow him off.

He continued to smile, saying, "I promise you, ma'am, this won't take but a few minutes."

Vicky, who never panicked, was suddenly on the verge of terrifying uncertainty. She thought about ditching him by walking calmly into the ladies room, then calling New York on her cell phone and discussing her next move. Then she changed her mind.

An ATV reporter and the FBI have a little informal chat in the Indianapolis airport. Why? She was getting the first whiff of what might turn out to be another big story. "Okay, over here." She pointed to a row of chairs in an empty boarding area.

"They've got an interview room we can use—"

"Here's the deal," she broke in. "I'm sure you know I'm with ATV. If I miss my flight, I'm in trouble. But if I talk to you without informing the legal department, I'll certainly be fired. Now if you're willing to talk to me informally, here's what we'll do. We sit where I indicated for ten minutes max. I tape the entire conversation. I make my plane, keep my job, and we get on with our lives."

"Sure, Ms. Wade," Hubbard nodded, "let's both record it. And I'll be happy to keep our conversation brief."

They walked over to the chairs, took seats, dug out their respective tape recorders, and announced date, time, location, and participants. Then Hubbard began to talk.

"You're a friend of Dr. John Bryne, correct?"

"Yes, of course, we're very old friends. Why do you ask?"

"You may have heard that the Bureau's forensics labs have come under heavy fire lately."

"I sure have," she answered. "*Hot Line* did a big story on it."

"Well, because of the... umm... alleged incompetence, we're in the process of recruiting independent scientific talent—expert witnesses, advisors, people like Dr. Bryne, a blue-ribbon panel of consultants, if you will. At the moment, we're looking into the backgrounds of a number of scientists, ones who have the knowledge and experience to help us put together information regarding biological warfare and terrorism."

"Really?" Vicky asked as her interest piqued.

"Yes, ma'am," Hubbard replied. "We're in the middle of attempting to interdict certain BW agents we know to have been introduced into the United States. What we've done in the past with threats like this, is, frankly, taken a relatively passive role. With all the lab flap and the fact that lately there have been a few incidents..."

"When?"

"That's classified."

"Has there been loss of life?"

"Classified, Ms. Wade. If your line of questioning continues, our little chat will have to end."

"Okay, go on, Mr. ... Hubbard, is it?" She couldn't help herself; the guy seemed a bit of a pompous ass—and, she suspected, such a lousy liar.

"Yes, it's Hubbard, Ms. Wade. What I can tell you is this: We believe that certain institutions and particularly cultural or political events with large numbers of people present will be chosen—may already have been chosen—for the application of this material."

"Why are you telling me this?"

"Certainly not as a press release, Ms. Wade."

"So?"

"As I told you, we are looking into the background of people who might help us. People like Bryne, people like yourself, in fact." He smiled that humorless smile once more. "People who have access to information, who would be willing..."

"To spy for the FBI?"

"To help us stop what could well be a catastrophic tragedy."

"Go on," Wade instructed him, glad she was taping the conversation.

"We're not asking you to do anything except answer a few quick questions about Dr. John Bryne. We are specifically interested in Dr. Bryne's assistance in this matter, and before we approach anyone, it's our routine procedure to request information about an individual's known associates. This is simply a background check."

Vicky didn't believe that for a minute, but asked simply, "What do you want to know?"

"Well, we know Bryne has been married twice. The first time when he was with the World Health Organization in Geneva. I believe his wife was also his lab assistant. I understand she died in a car crash."

"No, from what I heard, it was a hit-and-run accident. They never identified the perpetrator. I had no contact with Jack during those years, but people told me he was terribly broken up."

"Did it affect his work?"

"Of course. My God, he's human!"

Hubbard then grilled her about all of Bryne's travel, his foreign language abilities, and then about his childhood. Finally Vicky snapped at him, "Look, he never talked about growing up. Maybe once he said he was orphaned in the war, that's all. End of interview." She looked at her watch. "You know more about him than I do..."

As Hubbard made a few final notes on a pad, he realized he had to trade information. Something good. Something shocking. The dynamite material he'd discovered in Bryne's file. "Indeed we do, Ms. Wade." He smiled, and after he'd told her Jack's whole grim saga and watched her turn ashen, he announced, "Well, thanks for your time. Now it's back to basics, Ms. Wade, basics..." He tapped her tape recorder with a rolled newspaper as if to make a point.

It had been precisely ten minutes, at which point Hubbard thanked Vicky again, rose, and disappeared into the crowd.

Too stunned to move, Wade kept her seat, shaking her head in disbelief, and checking to see that her machine was still recording. Next, she reached into her bag, took out her cellular phone, and flipped it open. She speed-dialed a New York number, then turned up the recording volume on the tape machine. As the phone rang in her office, she heard the answering machine click on and went through her messages until her producer came on the line.

"Ms. Wade's office, Cara Williams speaking."

"Cara, it's me." Wade had been working with the brilliant, aristocratic Hispanic woman for four years; they knew each other well, and both played by the rules. "I've just had one of the strangest meetings, and I want to get this on record with you. I'm playing back the tape here, will you tape our conversation as well, please?"

Vicky heard the tape recording device attached to her phone being activated. "Okay," Cara told her. "Shoot."

"This happened at the Indianapolis airport, of all places. An FBI agent, Scott Hubbard, questioned me for background on an acquaintance of mine named Jack Bryne, who's a virologist with the New York State Department of Health. I recorded the interview. Hubbard was almost grilling me about Bryne's activities, about his days at the World Health Organization.... Anyway, I've known Jack off and on for years."

"Off and on?" Cara asked. Vicky could picture Cara arching her eyebrows at this moment.

"I'm taping this, Cara, and yes, we've known each other... socially... but he's also been a reliable source in terms of fascinating medical information. The guy's a genius. I ran into him on the Churchill Downs story."

"So go on," Cara said, with heightened curiosity.

"I'm convinced that the FBI's on to something at the racetrack, and now they want to know what Jack's doing here, especially after he was just in San Diego. Hubbard wanted to know where we met, Jack's religious beliefs, how many years he's been in New York, had I ever visited him in Europe, if Jack had recently spent any time in the Pacific."

"What's worrying you?" Cara asked. "That you gave up confidential information?"

"Jack and I go way back, Cara. I don't know one bad thing about him. Anyway, Hubbard wound up telling me more about Jack than I told him. All I told him was what you could get out of *Who's Who* or any good medical database, except for his first wife. Oh, and I told him we were old friends."

"Well," Cara snorted, "that'll certainly keep them coming back for more... But Vicky, aren't you intrigued by why the feds chose you, and why it's tied to the Derby story? It really makes me wonder who this Bryne guy is."

"I guess in a way I've always wondered who he was, too." Her mind drifted to the kiss they'd shared, however brief it was, then she remembered that this phone call was being taped. "Anyway, I wanted to tell you right away. I'll let you know my schedule when I'm done here. For now, we'll simply leave it that I'll be in New York as planned the day after tomorrow. Also, I want a complete search on John Drake Bryne. I want Nexis, Lexis, Sexis, and Plexis on him. Get the cybrarian in Research to pull every article, every bio, every speech. Call WHO. Call New York State. And see if you can locate any World War II POW survivors' groups. Be thorough; something's going on here. Thanks."

"Right, 'bye."

Wade rewound the tape of her encounter with Hubbard and pressed the PLAY button. The tape was blank. As Wade walked out of the airport and got to her car, she wanted to laugh at herself for thinking she could trust the FBI. That bastard Hubbard must have used a magnet. Probably in the newspaper. She paid the parking fee, then noticed the blue van Jack had pointed out, with both its sun visors down. It pulled away when she did, and though it was only behind her for a short while, Victoria Wade was no longer amused. She was angry and frightened.

On her way back to Churchill Downs, she could not get the nightmarish things Hubbard had told her about Jack out of her mind.

In all the years Vicky and Jack had known

each other, she had never had a clue that his childhood had been that ghastly. For John Bryne's World War II childhood had been spent in a Japanese prisoner of war camp, where the authorities used the inmates as human guinea pigs, experimenting on them with hideous infectious diseases.

Seated behind the wheel of the blue van, Scott Hubbard followed Vicky Wade's car for just a few minutes. The revelation about Bryne's background had shocked her, maybe even forced her to consider, if not share, his own growing interest in Bryne. In any case, he'd erased the interview, and she would be furious. An angry reporter could be very valuable. Hubbard knew he had aroused her curiosity. That left the door open for future contacts. She would start her own investigation, he was certain. He turned off when the radio car took over, but he made sure she saw him; he wanted to make his point. The FBI wasn't finished with her or Bryne.

Hubbard considered himself the type who played by the rules. When his superiors had initially decided not to run elements of the investigation by the book, he was unnerved—particularly about having to work solo. The unconventionality actually made things easier. And the case was turning out to have some interesting perks, not the least of which was Victoria Wade.

He'd seen her on television, of course, the whole world had, but she was even more

155

beautiful in person. Her green eyes had hypnotized him, her golden hair glowed, and she carried herself with athletic grace. He was looking forward to interviewing her again, not merely to enjoy her charms, but because he was sure she knew more about Bryne than she was telling, and because she wasn't asking him anything about the horses.

The FBI had been working the interstate fraud ramifications of the horse deaths since the first insurance claim had been filed. It was a routine fraud operation—the kind of investigation too junior for an agent with Hubbard's level of experience. No, he was reserved for such tough cases as the one that had started unfolding with the recovery of the water pistol. Anthrax, biological terrorism. Priority One. And then the Bryne link to both investigations popped out of the computer.

At first, Hubbard had been as baffled by the case as anyone else, because of the lack of connection among relevant individuals, victims, or witnesses. Doggedly, the FBI continued to run daily cross-matching checks on anyone linked, even remotely, to the San Diego incident and to any other FBI investigations. Eventually, Bryne's name came up cross-referenced by his flight into Indianapolis. He had been seen in the company of Victoria Wade, whose name was already on the list of individuals in the Kentucky case.

When the Priority One match was discovered, Hubbard had flown out of San Diego on an FBI flight only a few hours before Bryne

156

and was immediately updated by the Louisville agents. The FBI had known for weeks that ATV was nosing around the breeders. It always seemed to Hubbard that news people saw as much fraud and corruption as the FBI, and often knew about it first. Bryne's involvement seemed more than coincidence.

From the car phone, Special Agent Scott Hubbard called the New York office and arranged for someone to meet Bryne's plane and keep an eye on him until he arrived himself.

7

Saturday, June 20
New York City

Teddy Kameron felt and sounded energetic, refreshed, a new man—far from the silent, withdrawn neurotic he'd been in the last few months before The Vision and The Voice. If his fellow scientists were surprised by this reborn, almost garrulous Teddy, they didn't show it. One of his gossipy old friends from D.C. mentioned that the FBI had discreetly been inquiring about Jack Bryne. The friend didn't know why, but Teddy was sure it was because of San Diego.

In fact, when Kameron collected the messages from his machine, he himself heard the voice of Special Agent Hubbard. This was a marvelous development. Now all he had to do was call the agent back, cast just the right shadow of doubt on Bryne's stability, if Bryne's

157

name even came up, and persevere with his Mission.

He rattled around the two-bedroom apartment he had kept after Monica, his wife, had left him, left him at the height of his shame. The stillness of the space was profound—a furnished place in an Upper East Side doorman building, where, for all practical purposes, the anonymous city gave no one any real neighbors.

On many levels, Teddy was glad that Monica had gone—it made the Missions and the time spent in his uptown lab, his real home, much easier. Truth to tell, he simply didn't care about her departure.

They'd met in college, where he'd been the object of admiring glances from many girls; his blond good looks and gentlemanly manner had made sure of that. Yet he'd dated few and bedded even fewer; his scarred palms and strange ways always drove them away. When they dropped him, as they did, inevitably, he always cried, which made him want to strangle them; but eventually the memories went away, giving him mournful distant urges whenever their paths crossed on campus.

Monica, though, Monica was different. She was far from unattractive, an Irish redhead, an orphan who'd been raised by a very Catholic aunt and uncle in Queens. As a result, she was devout, which bothered Teddy more than a little because it reminded him of his mother. She had an air of refinement and a great desire to be a successful scientist's wife.

She was also very passionate, or at least pretended to be, assuring Teddy he was a warm and wonderful lover. Here again, his inability to come didn't seem to matter to her, since she was sure she could make him climax; she had to if they were to produce the large family she was looking forward to. Kameron supposed that in her own, social-climbing way, she loved him. He, on the other hand, felt nothing much for her—certainly not sexually—but he gave an award-winning performance, even in the sack, of being her loving husband.

The trouble began when they moved to Atlanta. Monica, a New York girl born and raised, hated the South. She hated her high school teaching job. She hated the fact that his workaholism kept them apart too many nights. She hated the heat. Most of all, she hated the fact that he still couldn't come, which meant they couldn't get pregnant.

She became more and more religious, urging him to come to church with her, filling their apartment with religious icons. Sex had virtually ceased, and he couldn't have been happier—except for the fact that she was reminding him more and more of Mom, nagging and pushing and praying.

Things improved briefly before he left the CDC and they came back to New York. Through a Church official he'd met at one of Monica's activities, he made a connection to his religious backers. As his ace in the hole, what would be known as the Kameron Test, came closer to reality, her ambition sprang to life again. Then came the debacle. The lab explosion at CDC. His fault. His career.

Suddenly, instead of the fortune she'd be expecting, there was no reputation, no work, no grants; the whole religious network cut him dead. Monica never knew about Teddy's elaborate trust fund, so for her purposes they had run through their savings and were practically penniless.

One night she told him she was leaving. There would be no chance of divorce, of course, because the Church didn't allow it, but she would petition Rome for an annulment. Teddy couldn't have cared less whether she got one or not. He had no intention of marrying again. She let him keep the apartment, certain he was never going to be able to afford the rent. He gave her half of everything she thought they had. What she never would know was that she got out just in time. Had she stayed, he would have had to kill her.

Saturday, June 20
Guilderland, New York

Bryne had been away for days, and he had arrived at the small farmhouse in the woods exhausted, yet anxious about how far behind he was at work. To his disappointment, Mia wasn't there. He had hoped to make his unexpected absence up to her immediately, and now he was not going to have the chance. He climbed the stairs to their bedroom.

Sometimes he wished for a simpler life.

160

Sometimes he wished they had more than a weekend marriage, if that. He was bitter now when the exhausting days turned into lonely nights like this one. Missing Mia was always hardest after he'd flown home to an empty bed in what they referred to as their "cottage"—which was only a half-mile from the lab and reminded Jack of the small pied-à-terre he'd had in Geneva.

Walking into the bedroom, he noticed an envelope of her pale blue stationery on his pillow. He dreaded its message, but was relieved when he finally opened it. She told him she had emergency city business that had to be resolved before Monday, didn't know how long it would take to wrap up, and was sick at the thought of not being there when he arrived. She promised to try to get back to Guilderland as soon as she could and to show him how much she loved him.

Relieved that she wasn't angry, Jack stretched out on his side, patted the space where her hips would be, and sighed as his muscles relaxed. He decided to close his eyes for a moment, then call her in New York. Only a moment...

He heard a soft ringing—far away, faintly, he could sense the bell cutting into his attention.

The phone. No. Much slower.

He tried to sleep.

He struggled to wake.

He heard the bell again, abruptly now, more like a school bell someone was swinging back and forth. He looked around and saw that the windows were open. But they were not the bedroom windows. They were the windows in the barracks.

The barracks at the Pingfan internment camp, Unit 731.

The bell rang on and on, as it always did at dawn, as it had since Jack and his mother had been sent to the camp eight months earlier.

All the prisoners were made to dress, walk to the latrine, report to the medical desk, and step up on the scales. Each was inspected and weighed, and notes were made in careful Japanese script. Then the inmates were marched into a courtyard and through a gate through which they could see out to an open field. Dozens of stakes, bearing iron manacles where hands could be secured, had been erected in the field. Each day, in the afternoon, twenty or so prisoners would be selected for the stakes. Most were Chinese, although occasionally an American or British soldier would be chosen for the experiment.

In the morning, Bryne, aged eight, was made to run around the perimeter of the camp with hundreds of other prisoners, urged on by the guards. It lasted for a torturous hour. Finally they were led back into the barracks area and given some water, rice cakes, and a thin broth of rendered fish. There was nothing to do but sit in terror and wait as the afternoon approached.

Every afternoon, a corporal, sometimes accompanied by a medical officer, would come to the barracks and line up the prisoners. Every afternoon, a group of prisoners—always including three or four of the healthiest and strongest—was chosen, examined by the doctor, then led out.

Bryne had been noticed by the medical officer many times, but he had never been selected. They all knew why. They were waiting for him to gain weight. He was tall for a boy his age, nearly as tall as many of his jailers, but still thin, not as strong as they wanted him. They were patient. They gave him tofu, fish cakes, more rice than a foot soldier. The protein saved him, the balanced diet helped him grow. At full strength, he would be perfect to test the weapons they were making at the camp.

When the officials and the chosen prisoners had left, Bryne would always climb up his bunk to the rafters and onto the highest point in the barracks, where he sat inside a little wooden cupola slatted for ventilation. From there, he could see over the roofs of the other barracks and into the field of stakes with all their handcuff rings.

He looked on as they led the prisoners out, men from one barracks and women from another. He was watching for his mother. Luckily, so far she had never appeared among them. When the people were manacled to the stakes, the doctors were driven to the field in their long black Daimler, accompanied by their assistants, who checked off procedures in large black ledgers. Next, young Jack Bryne could see the soldiers unloading boxes from the supply trucks.

Each soldier placed a box in front and upwind of a prisoner, then quickly backed off as the doctors and their assistants gathered up their documents and were driven away.

Nothing seemed to happen for a long time.

The prisoners stood at the stakes.

Some were able to sit down.

Some turned their faces away from the boxes.

Some prayed.

Suddenly a spring-loaded mechanism in each box snapped back its lid. Jack could see a puff of smoke—or was it dust?—rising from the boxes and, blown by the wind, to the prisoners. They awkwardly brushed at their faces with manacled hands, and tried to hold their sleeves over their heads.

Each afternoon was different.

Sometimes nothing happened, and the prisoners were unaffected. An hour might pass, even a night and day, and still they stood at the stakes.

Sometimes a tank truck from the lab drove out and hosed the prisoners off with a spray.

Sometimes after only an hour, the prisoners were led away.

Sometimes a squad of soldiers drove up, got out of their truck, and methodically shot each of the prisoners at point-blank range.

What never changed was that the prisoners selected for the afternoon experiment never returned to the barracks.

He saw what happened to the others.

Sometimes the little box puffed a yellowish-green cloud, and the prisoners would die an agonizing but rapid death.

Sometimes they screamed for hours. Young Bryne saw them, their mouths black, their eyes white, but he rarely heard them. The Manchurian winds blew their voices away from the camp, as certainly as the wind blew the poison smoke into the faces of hundreds and hundreds of manacled prisoners while Jack Bryne watched. It was the same Siberian jet stream that blew the Pingfan-manufactured balloons with their tanks of toxins, bacteria, and viruses from the home islands of Japan as far east as Ann Arbor.

Jack knew his turn would come, and even in his dreams he knew he wanted the bullet.

Suddenly, in his dream, the prisoners in their death throes became the dying horses at Churchill Downs, became Joey St. John and Jody Davis in their last ghastly moments, became a multitude of maddened bees, became the overwhelming horror of Turner's *Fifth Plague*. The images revolved around and around in his brain, like a carousel of horrors, until he was on the verge of—the bell, the bell, the bell! Thank God, it was the telephone. Jack awoke, shaking, sweating, and picked it up.

It was Mia, who noticed something in his voice immediately and asked if he was all right. Of course, he said yes, he was, but he'd been asleep when she called. This time, she had good news. She'd troubleshot the city problem in no time, was at the Albany railroad station, and would be with him in twenty minutes.

"Don't even unlock the door," she told him. "I'll be coming right up to bed. Don't you move a muscle. Yet."

"I'll take that as instructions from a physician," Bryne smiled. He hung up and, despite his dread of more camp nightmares, managed to drift off to an untroubled sleep.

The next thing he knew, Mia was beside him, kissing him, kissing him harder and harder. Almost immediately, he had maneuvered her lovely, pliant body under his, while her soft hands gripped the muscles of his lower back. Now it was his turn to kiss her, kiss her despite the old pain from his injured left biceps. As he slowed his kisses, she gripped him even tighter and slid her hands down toward his elbow.

Suddenly a bolt of pain tore upward across the joint and stabbed into his shoulder. Inadvertently, Mia had pinched the radial nerve where it was most exposed, and the jolt forced Bryne to pull back his arm and roll away from her and sit up.

"Oh, Jack, I'm sorry... I didn't mean—"

"Of course not, darling." He caressed her face with the hand of his good arm.

"Now I've gone and ruined everything!"

"You most certainly have not, my love, but be a good doctor and massage my wound."

As she did, tracing the scars and stitches with her fingertips, she asked him—as she had many times before—wherever had he gotten the repair work done after the hang-gliding accident.

"I know, it's the damnedest thing that I can't remember, I really can't. Elements of amnesia..."

Regarding him in the light from the nightstand, she could sense his uneasiness.

"Are you lying to me, Jack Bryne?" She knelt behind him on the bed. As the weight of the question sank upon him, she wrapped her arms around his shoulders before he could answer. "Because," she said playfully, "if I find out you were stabbed by some jealous husband or attacked by one of those poor women you've seduced and abandoned all over the globe, and that hang-gliding story I've taken on faith is—"

"Stop it, darling," he said strongly. "Believe me, rumors of my amours are greatly exaggerated." As he said it, he thought again how he could never bear to tell her the truth—about the injury, about the Russian field hospital he called a "Swiss clinic," about the American soldier who'd given him penicillin to rub on the wound after the camp had been repatriated and probably saved him from dying of gangrene.

"Okay," Mia was saying, "I'll stop with the amours, but look how upset you get. I didn't only touch a nerve literally. Something's not right with you, and if I can help—"

"I don't need any help!"

"Oh, Jack, come here." She held out her arms, and he let her hug him.

"Sorry, Mia, it's been one hell of a week."

"I know, Jack, I know," she said quietly.

"No, no, you don't. I'm not even sure I do," he began. And suddenly he understood the end of the dream, those revolving images of horror, a sort of confirmation of what he had been pondering without fully admitting it to himself. Now he knew, now he saw clearly.

"Mia," he began, "you're going to think this is crazy..."

"What's crazy, Jack?"

"The anthrax thing in San Diego and the horses in Kentucky. I think they're connected."

Mia looked interested. "Really, how?"

Jack knew this wasn't going to be easy; after all, his wife was a doctor and a scientist, and what he had to tell her sounded a lot like science fiction.

"Well." He took his time and chose his words. "Hear me out before you say anything. I saw a painting in Indianapolis, a painting by Turner called *The Fifth Plague*, you know, the plagues of Moses. The fifth plague is called the Murrain, where all the animals die. And there it was in the picture, after I'd just come from Louisville where the horses were actually dying. Everyone involved suspects some kind of sabotage."

"And..."

"And then I remembered that another plague is boils—which could be interpreted as anthrax. We know that San Diego event was

168

definitely sabotage. Someone planted a toy gun filled with anthrax where one particular kid would find it, even wrote the medical code numbers for anthrax on the handle. And lately we've been getting reports on ProMED about a swarm of bees—swarm is another of the plagues—it was in San Antonio a couple of months ago. The thing is, they weren't killer bees. They were ordinary honey bees, but something had turned them violent."

"I'm not quite sure I see where you're headed, Jack."

"This is what I'm saying. This is what I think. Some brilliant maniac—or bunch of maniacs—is using modern bioterrorist methods to recreate the ten plagues of the Old Testament."

Mia said nothing, but simply listened.

"And dear love, there are more plagues to come. And I've got to stop them, stop them myself, because nobody, nobody else will even believe this, much less act on it."

He sketched out a plan to search for the other plagues, and explained his need to share this only with her and with Drew, because he was sure that there were others he could not trust; people—or one person—planning more horrors. People he didn't want to tip off. He wanted her to understand, to help him keep faith in himself, but all he saw in her face was alarm.

She asked a little too gently, "Jack, are you feeling all right? Your nerves must be shot." He realized she hadn't believed a word, and that was the same as if she thought he was losing his mind.

Now that it was too late to take back what he had told her, Bryne assured her as well as himself, "I'm just exhausted, just completely beat."

"Jack," she persisted, "there's no danger from your exposure at the hospital, is there?"

"Mia, my love, I'm taking prophylactic antibiotics. Not to worry. I'm fine, just tired." He rubbed his eyes.

"Jack—"

"Please, Mia, no more talking now. Tomorrow. I've got to get a decent night's sleep. I love you, and being home with you is the best medicine a man could ask for."

Kissing him lightly, Mia murmured, "I love you, too, Jack," then rolled to her side of the bed.

Bryne ultimately slept, but before he did, he remembered a snippet about Moses from a sermon his father had once given. "And she bore him a son, and he called his name Gershon: for he said, I have been a stranger in a strange land."

8

Monday, June 22
New York State Zoonosis Laboratory
Guilderland, New York
7:30 A.M.

Drew Lawrence had worked all weekend to make sure the entire file of incoming "urgent" bulletins was printed out and ready for Bryne's review by seven Monday morning. He had been in Jack's office before daylight and put on the tea water, but there was no sign yet of the virologist.

Drew had also assembled a detailed summary of ProMED's activities during the past few years, to be reviewed by the federation scientists as supporting data for a new grant proposal. Time was running out. He thumbed through the spreadsheets.

Keeping the system on line with the Boston server, SatelLife, cost one hundred and fifty thousand dollars a year. Most of the other funds were for part-timers, office equipment, rent, and an elaborate telecommunications system. A bottom-line figure of nearly half a million for three years. Not a huge amount, but money The Federation of American Scientists did not have. Bryne, Drew, and the other scientists had offered free time over the years, but ProMED had basic dollar needs that weren't being met.

When Jack Bryne had arrived on the scene a few years before, there had been some minor intellectual sparring between him and Lawrence that ended in a draw. Drew knew Bryne needed him; over the years Lawrence had come to know everyone, and he helped Jack through the politics and infighting that were the drawbacks of working in a large, decentralized governmental laboratory system.

The "oubliette" at Guilderland, as Jack Bryne referred to the dungeon-like group of buildings, had suited them both quite nicely, as did the manner in which their working relationship evolved. Bryne signed off on the routine stuff, while Lawrence did the serious lab work. Both men regarded the time spent on ProMED more as a fabulous hobby than as real work.

While Jack referred to the "urgent" bulletins as the "Holy Shit list," Lawrence never did. Not him. Far too irreverent. Drew looked at the clock and adjusted his stance to ease the pain of his hip as he reached over to put the printouts and the grant proposal on Bryne's desk.

Five neat tables and two graphs summarized the work of ProMED. A dozen backup tables, charts, and spreadsheets were also available if requested, for either Bryne or the people in Washington. It was amazing to see how the system had grown in the last few years: the new presentation offered a succinct summary, while other tables and charts reported on basic administrative work, publications, notes, and a breakdown of ProMED subscribers by continent, then country.

Drew was arranging the material on Jack's desk so he couldn't miss it, when the phone rang.

"Lawrence here."

"Bryne here as well, Drew. Things going okay?"

"Ready to roll."

"Drew, would you do me a favor?"

"Sure thing, *capitán*."

"Got that summary sheet handy on slow viruses? Also the index of recent animal citations? Poisoning, bites, attacks, rabies, things like that? I have an idea that has been keeping me awake, Drew."

"Stand by," Drew told him. "I have a list right here, including animals and insects. Want me to read them to you? There's only a few."

"Yes, yes I do."

"Okay. Six rabies attacks, no big deal, the usual suspects except for a wolf in Iran. Bit seventeen people two months ago. There are kangaroos going blind in Australia, a myxovirus has been incriminated, a bird dieoff in Mexico from H_4N_3 influenza strain, seals with phocid distemper, and some miscellaneous stuff on mad cow, a new mouse disease, and tree frogs. Why do you ask?"

"Because I keep having this dream." There was something in his voice that troubled Lawrence, troubled him even more when Bryne asked, "You read the Bible, Drew, right?"

"Sure." Lawrence was a devout Baptist. "Looking for some spiritual salvation at last?"

"No, seriously, Drew. In Exodus, the fifth plague visited on the Egyptians was the Murrain, wasn't it? I saw a painting of it in Indianapolis a couple of days ago. I was wondering—"

Lawrence cut in. "The animals died, but the Egyptians were spared. Exodus nine, three. Loses a lot in translation. It could have been anything. It must have been some form of zoonosis. Came after... the swarm, I think. Yeah, the fourth plague was the swarm."

"I'm at a loss, Drew. What did they mean by the swarm? Hey, it's getting late. I should let you get to work," Bryne said absently, "but before you do, read me the spreadsheet on insects, arthropods—it's similar to the animal list we generated? I need a complete list."

"Got 'em, but it's too long to summarize over the phone. You are coming in this morning, aren't you? Or should I fax them over to your house?"

"No, don't bother, I'll be over soon," Bryne told him.

"Hey, wait a minute." Drew stopped him before he could hang up. "What happened in California? What's going on out there? An FBI agent named Hubbard has been calling you. Anything to do with the little boy?"

"I'll tell you when I get in. Oh, yes, one more thing. I need you to look up that chapter in the Swedish textbook on infectious diseases on *charbon*."

"You mean anthr-"

"That's right, Drew!"

"Does this have something to do with that communication we got from that Pakistani physician?"

"Not now, Drew. Later."

"Right. Like you said, *charbon*."

After they'd hung up, the urgency in Bryne's voice stayed with Lawrence. Anthrax? He wondered why he hadn't wanted to use the "A" word and if it had anything to do with the FBI guy. Was Jack worried that the phones were tapped?

174

And why the sudden interest in arthropods, a ten-dollar word to describe a distinct phylum of living things separate from most animals? The creatures had no vertebral column and depended on an exoskeleton to support their outer bodies. The insects and other creepy-crawlies. Small but potent, a Centroides scorpion could kill with one sting. Children in South America, India, and Australia died within hours after playing with the little creatures that looked like miniature lobsters. Arthropods also included spiders, fire ants, blister beetles, reduviid bugs, centipedes, millipedes, ticks, and thousands of others.

Arthropods, anthrax, swarms. "And exactly what has Jack gone and done now?" Drew demanded of the empty room.

Lawrence decided immediately to get out his Bible and reread Exodus, to prepare for Bryne's questions. Then he remembered the article on killer bees that the kid from Brooklyn had sent him, along with a newspaper clipping about the bee attack in Texas three months ago. Couldn't hurt to take a look at it.

The killer bee phenomenon had started more than forty years before, when a Brazilian millionaire imported into his country a new subrace of honey bee, or mellifera, called *Apis mellifera adansonii,* which had fine-tuned its ability to find flowers in the plateaus of South Africa for thousands of years. The idea had been to bring this subrace into Brazil in order to compete with other honey-producing countries, especially the United States, which got its stock of honey from effete temperate species—unlike adansonii, which was a prodigious producer of a rich honey of the double-stringed carbohydrate variety. The promised yield for Brazilian apiculture was immeasurably rich, as were the profits to be made from these African bees. But, oh, the price for that wealth.

It was only one year later, Drew read, when twenty-six entire swarms of the African bees accidentally escaped from a suburb of Bahia and headed north, mating with local bees as a new, formidable species was created, *Apis mellifera scutetella,* or, as the press would soon call them, "killer bees." By 1980, all of Brazil, as well as Venezuela and Colombia, had been conquered, and still they headed north to Central America.

The first U.S. death from the killer bees was reported in 1985. Soon confirmations of animal and human bodies covered with bees were common in the South and Central American media. Killer bees now became the stuff of Grade B Hollywood movies as well as the subject of intense research.

It had been known since 1967 that a bee's sting gland contained at least two "alarm odors"—isopentyl and isoamyl acetate. When a bee stung an aggressor, these volatile chemicals were released, alerting other bees of danger and triggering their instinctive recruiting response. Normally the response was measurable and predictable, but the cross-breeding of the Brazilian Europeanized bees with those of African origin had accelerated the power of the attractant tenfold.

The killer bee had become an accidentally bioengineered weapon, easily capable of killing the largest mammals or hundreds of people once triggered by isopentyl and isoamyl acetate, two chemicals easily manufactured either by the bees themselves or by an equally industrious chemist. Drew read to his horror that twenty killer bee stings can kill a mouse, fifty an average-sized dog, one hundred a toddler, five hundred an adult. The average hive contained 25,000 bees, yet the release of a single bee's alarm odor could recruit the whole hive, with the exception of the queen and a few drones.

By 1996, four swarm-related deaths had been reported in Southern California. It was only a matter of time, said the article, until the killer bees invaded the entire United States. The piece had been written before the Texas incident. But hadn't the boy mentioned that the Texas bees were normal honey bees *behaving* like killers?

Lawrence looked up to see Jack Bryne standing before him, tension pulling at his features, not even bothering to say hello. Pointing to a chart on the desk, he asked Drew, "Can you tell me which of these creatures swarm? Look, I know we have urgent work to do. I have to make a ton of calls, and we've got to look at these slides in my carry-on. But first, anything showing on insects? Any more insect/human animal attacks?"

"Look at the Hymenoptera, Jack, on the big sheet on top. Then sashay down the list."

Bryne looked over both sheets. Four Hymenoptera. No fire ants. That left wasps, hornets, and bees.

"What do you have on the four reports?"

"All Apis, my friend. Bees. No Vespera at all."

Bryne looked at the report:

ProMED. Italy:
Apis mellifera swarm causes evacuation of monastery.

Jack looked at Drew with an intrigued expression, then went on to the next report.

ProMED. Mexico:
Bees attack local village, donkeys scattered. No deaths reported.
ProMED. LA:
Centrolenella-induced death. Fatal alkaloid poisoning, report of single case.

He wrinkled his brow at the fatality, but it was the next report that brought the nightmare home to him.

ProMED. San Antonio, TX
Honey bees attack downtown San Antonio and suburbs.

Bryne read the horrifying description of

178

the swarm. Tens of thousands of usually harmless bees had killed seven adults and three children. He was frightened.

Could somebody actually have planned this? The bee venom would be too complicated to make in a lab. But the alarm odors? Bryne knew they could be made in any good high school chemistry lab. Gallons of it, if anyone really wanted to synthesize a substance that triggered bees to stampede, any bees, all bees: African bees or even American honey bees could instantly be turned into mindless killing machines.

And that would make three, so far: a swarm, a murrain, the boils and blains...

Am I playing a private cosmic poker game, Bryne wondered, *or is someone—some weird cult—in the process of reenacting the Ten Plagues of Exodus? Or am I playing solitaire without a full deck?*

Tuesday, June 23
Manhattan
11:00 A.M.

Surrounded by his containers of toxins, Theodore Kameron sat in his lab, logging onto ProMED. It pleased him that the swarm was still posted. *I think I'll revisit that little exploit from my work in progress*, he decided. So he logged off, typed the password LMPG to bring up the chronicle he was writing for posterity, and began to read:

April 15

Kameron had been patient. The Visions and The Voice had changed him, soothed him, energized

179

him. He had filled the fish tanks, and he sat in his secret lab taking pleasure in the rosy glow that filled the room when the lights were turned on over the water. He was in awe of how strong the blooms had grown and how they suffused the tanks with colors. He didn't need fish; the tanks held a much more formidable predator.

He knew exactly what he needed to coax the swarm to come nearer, fragrances that would call to them for miles around. And he knew too that he must be ready, ready and waiting, long before The Voice would tell him where they would fly.

It took only a few late nights to make the attractant. Kameron started with white vinegar in an enamel pot, added basic chemicals, stirred, heated, and added another reagent, then waited. When he was sure the mixture had been refined, he stored it in a small refrigerator. Earlier in the month, as instructed by The Voice, Teddy traveled under an assumed name to Texas for a trial run, trying the compound on the ledge outside his motel room window.

He waited until the breeze was right, until the warm sun heated the hives and opened the flowers. As the wind picked up, he opened the window sash and applied a few drops of the potion to the sill.

For twenty minutes nothing happened, but the breeze was picking up and he saw the crocuses and daffodils blooming outside the room and knew that the honey bees were abundant. He was patient, as The Voice told him to be, and at last he spotted a big worker bee spiraling along above the grass toward the window. Coming to rest, it began to

*dance agitatedly, circling the tiny dab of attractant.
Suddenly the bee flew up, stinger protruding, hit the
window glass with an angry buzz, and bounced to
the sill, dazed.*

*Carefully checking for others, he slid open the
window and crushed the fallen bee with a green
nylon fly swatter. It was not unpleasant. Again
locking the window, he left the room, got in his
rental car, and drove to a hardware store, where he
purchased two cans of wasp and hornet spray with
nozzles. The errand had taken no more than fifteen
minutes, but when he returned, he could no longer
see the window to his room.*

*The entire window was covered with a thick,
undulating mass of bees. Their glistening golden-
orange bodies and translucent vibrating wings gave
the massed insects an almost hairy appearance.*

*He had to keep himself from laughing as he
watched the motel clerk run up, warning people
away. Taking the first canister out of a bag, he
waved at the clerk, then began to turn the nozzle on
the swarm, which was growing alarmingly in only
the time it had taken to wrench the top off the canister. Even more bees were coming now, and before
he fired, he prepared the second canister as well.*

*With a canister in each hand, Kameron hosed
down the swarming bees. In three minutes thousands lay dead in the grass. "Better get in touch
with the manager," he told the clerk like the solid
citizen he was pretending to be. "Those bees can
really be nasty. Children could have been stung."*

*Now, at last, Teddy's patience had been reward-
ed, and The Voice had spoken. He was to go to San
Antonio with his small but precious burdens. Yes,*

San Antonio would be chastised by the swarm. He decided he would quietly squeeze a large measure of attractant at the very first church he passed. Then on to the Easter Sunday promenade along the River Walk.

Tuesday, June 23
New York City

Ah, that had been a fine piece of work, but still Teddy felt he had written particularly well about the frogs. Even now, reading it for the umpteenth time, he was impressed.

After the real success Kameron enjoyed with his power from The Voice, now this! His shipment of tree frogs arrived—all dead. His heart broke. It had been extremely difficult getting the perfect frogs, what with all the difficulties of a Panamanian export license coupled with the hazardous conditions for shipping.

But The Voice was not to be denied. Teddy persuaded his most reliable dealer to try to ship another container of arrow frogs, dart frogs, reticulated glass frogs directly from Panama, Colombia, and Costa Rica. His dealer offered no guarantees and never kept records. It was perfect.

The plan seemed so simple. Get the beautiful tree frogs. The little critters have amines, peptides, steroids, and alkaloids in their skin: batrachotoxin, gephyrotoxin, pumiliotoxin, epibatidine, and samandarine. Feed the tree frogs mealy bugs, crickets, and cockroaches. Coat the insects with powdered mycotoxins. Add a few other "organic" alkaloids. If the frogs don't die—and they rarely do—

182

they will concentrate their poisons in their granular skin glands, known to laymen as warts. He had to marvel at the tree frogs' ability to salvage toxins from tropical ants, millipedes, and beetles. In captivity, they would slowly lose their toxins, but he could provide them from his own little storehouse of protective juices—including a new one for them, his old favorite, yohimbé.

The dealer came through, but the weather in the country of origin was cooler than expected, and this second shipment also arrived dead. Now he was upset. The Voice had spoken and must be obeyed. He ordered again, praying that the third time was indeed the charm. The frogs had to come before the lice. They had to be number two.

One week later, he got lucky. Three dozen delicate black and yellow tree frogs, *Centrolenella valerior*—reticulated glass frogs—arrived at JFK, and they were alive. All had survived and were actually thriving. He could see their brilliant markings through the plexiglas cage. Yellow and black with a faint hint of orange. And he knew precisely the member of the Christian Council for whom they were meant.

Teddy, it must be known, enjoyed a penchant for disguise. When he made the trip to Louisiana, he disguised himself as a courier, wearing a wig, false nose, and sunglasses, to make sure Bishop LaPierre would never recognize him. When he arrived at the residence, he told the housekeeper he had been ordered to deliver the package personally.

Of course, LaPierre had no idea who the delivery man was. In a jovial mood, he asked Kameron to sit down while he opened the elegantly wrapped

gift. The bishop was thrilled with the wooden box.
He told Teddy that he could tell it had been carved
in Costa Rica. Inside the box—which had breathing
holes—was a small fine mesh. The bishop removed
the top of the box and dozens of the energetic black
and yellow tree frogs jumped out. His Eminence,
laughing delightedly, collected the little rascals. The
frogs were jumping all over the rectory.

It was then that Dr. Kameron regretfully took his
leave. Even as he drove away in a rented car
parked discreetly far away, he could envision what
was happening.

Bishop LaPierre must have thought they were a
present from a former parishioner who had relocat-
ed to New York and was perhaps on vacation in
Costa Rica, someone who knew of his love of frogs.
The return address read "L.M.P.G.," and he was
probably racking his brain to remember the person
when his heart began to pound and he began to
salivate. The frogs would appear to glow, although
he knew that was not possible. Now everything
would begin to shimmer. Suddenly something
would be stirring beneath his robe. It could not be.
His holiness would try to ignore the rousing warmth
and swelling in his groin, something he thought he
had lost many years ago.

Now he would be having difficulty containing
himself. He would also be having trouble breath-
ing... very serious trouble.

Teddy's spirits soared once more, and he looked
forward to his next Mission with an ecstasy he
never dreamed of feeling.

"Jack, I take it all back." Lawrence walked into Bryne's office with a sheet of paper in his hand. "I found this on Nexis."

"Now what, Drew? What are you taking back?" Bryne was poring over the ProMED budget and didn't really want a distraction, but knew Lawrence wouldn't interrupt him unless it mattered.

"Got a response on your frogs, and you're not going to believe it. Take a look at the size of this printout; there's this one guy at NIH who's written over one hundred papers on frogs and their toxins. Fascinating."

"Tell me more." Bryne put down the spreadsheet he'd been studying.

"The little guys pack a toxic wallop in their skins. They can kill a dog easily if the dog chews on one. But, and here's the interesting thing, these frogs don't manufacture venom the way reptiles do. The frogs seem to harvest the toxins..."

"What did you say, Drew? The frogs do what?" Bryne looked up, reaching for the printouts.

"That's what it seems. The poisons in their skins come from the environment, things they eat."

"Okay, and... ?"

"These frogs live on a diet of venomous insects, spiders, millipedes, wasps. And they don't digest the venom, they actually absorb

185

it, process it though their systems, and exude it on their skins."

"Good lord, you mean each frog is producing a different toxic cocktail based on what it eats?"

"Looks that way. Amazing. It seems that some, but not all, of their toxins come from stinging insects, mostly bugs, beetles, and the like. But the original sources for most of the alkaloids they carry have yet to be found, because the forests are being clear-cut, and all these chemicals will disappear. They could be used to make medicine. They are very, very powerful."

"How many frog species are we talking about?"

"Dozens, it seems, counting subspecies. I called the guy at NIH. He was quite helpful. And here's the amazing part: I told him about the bishop in Louisiana, and he already knew about him. He actually has the frogs in his lab right now. The state lab sent them to him. They're an endangered species."

"And he confirmed that the old man died from handling them, for certain?" Bryne asked, still incredulous.

"Yes," Lawrence continued, "the frogs had enough toxin in them to kill twenty people. And one other thing..."

"Oh?"

"This guy says that these tree frogs not only had all the expected natural toxins, but a new one as well. He seemed to think it was really important."

"Well, what is it?"

"The newcomer," Drew looked at his sheets, "is actually from the bark of a tree, the Corynanthe yohimbi tree. The bark contains an exotic alkaloid, yohimbé. It causes changes in the heart and blood vessels. Too much can cause blood pressure to skyrocket, tremors, even seizures. It is even supposed to cause erections, even in people who are not sexually aroused."

"That's how the guy died, with an erection?"

"That's what they told me. It could have been this yohimbé. That and all the other toxins. But the obvious thing is that frogs don't eat the bark, do they?"

Bryne nodded. "Maybe the frogs fed on insects that ate the bark. What are you getting at, Drew?"

"It wasn't exactly yohimbé. It was pure stuff called yohimbine. Crystalline pure. It created a single spike on the chromatograph. The chemical had to have been synthesized. It was commercial yohimbine preparation, this guy thinks."

"It could be, or it might be a rich natural source. Why? Does he think it's not part of the frog's normal diet?"

"Because, Jack, this tree, Corynanthe, is not found in the Costa Rican rain forest. The guy from the NIH told me that. It's only found in West Africa."

"Which means those frogs were doctored," Bryne mused. "Which means I'm not losing my mind."

9

Thursday, June 25
Zoonosis Laboratory, Guilderland

The FedEx package arrived from Kentucky at a few minutes after ten. Lawrence noted it was "smoking"; good news, it meant that dry ice was still keeping the specimens cold. He unwrapped the bulky box, carefully easing the cube of dry ice into the sink, then removed four plastic vials, which he placed by the set of slides Bryne had given him. Easy, another simple rabies series, a slam dunk—although he and Jack had agreed that processing all the rest of the material Bryne had collected from Churchill Downs was going to take weeks.

Lawrence hated the big samples, like horses. The procedure required to get to the brain was heavy-duty work—messy, noisy, and involving saws. The one moose head he'd done three years before had taken all day, and the lab stank for a week. Cows were also bad news. They seemed to look at you if you didn't close their eyes before sawing began. But this time, the brain had already been removed, fixed, and sliced and was ready to go.

It was hard to ignore Jack's theory about the reenactment of the Exodus plagues—what with the swarm, the tree frogs, even the anthrax, which could easily be a modern version of the Biblical murrain. And if the horse die-offs turned out somehow to be man-made, well... What was as hard for Lawrence as it had been for Bryne was even trying to imagine what kind of maniac—or maniacs—would launch such a grisly operation.

Drew wondered whether the FBI was also thinking along these lines. That Agent Hubbard had called Jack several times without being clear about what he wanted, but sounding, well, menacing. Vicky Wade had also checked in almost daily, sounding worried, both about the horses, which weren't testing positive for anything, and about Jack. Drew wasn't sure what was going on there either, but hoped it was all business. Bryne had been adamant that only Lawrence and Mia knew about the plague theory and wanted it kept that way.

It was then that Drew remembered the kid from Brooklyn; he had noticed the swarm pretty darn fast. What was his name? Berger, yeah, Berger. It would be good to see what the kid was up to now, better send him an e-mail.

Sunday, June 28
Brooklyn, New York
1:30 P.M.

Shmuel Berger sat by the television set, along with four other teenagers from his high school. He knew well enough that it was forbidden for an Orthodox Jew to watch such a movie as this, but it was a delicious new experience—a horror movie, and in color!

Only recently, his parents had bought an eleven-inch black-and-white set but restricted

189

its use to news and special cultural events. A VCR was out of the question.

All his new school friends' parents let the boys watch the movies that the local channels showed on Saturdays and Sundays. Of course, for Shmuel, Saturdays were out of the question. This weekend, they were running a special on old thrillers. There was no way Shmuel was going to miss at least one of the features. Late Sunday morning, he'd muttered something to his mother about visiting a friend from the yeshiva. He then made a beeline for the bus.

The movie he was watching had been made in 1971 and was called *The Abominable Dr. Phibes*. The color was terrible. Along with the other kids, he howled with laughter as a madman, played by Vincent Price, took revenge on a surgeon, who had accidentally killed the madman's son. Price went on to murder a parade of victims, the doctor's staff, one by one, using the plagues of "the Old Testament." It was corny, inaccurate, funny, scary, and... forbidden!

There was a rabbi in the movie who had been portrayed in a ludicrously inaccurate fashion. It wasn't anything like that. There was no mention of bats in the Chumash. The Hebrew characters had been all messed up as well. It was dreck, but it reminded Shmuel of the strange story about the swarm he'd sent to ProMED. It had been a while since he'd checked for a follow-up.

Leaving his friends' home, he went by bus to the Brooklyn Public Library at Grand

Army Plaza. There he turned on a public access computer. It was time to surf the wonderful, free world of the Internet. There, and only there, Shmuel could enter whatever world he chose—basic science, medical research, games, even sex; he would search cyberspace for its compelling, often forbidden thoughts, images, and ideas.

Today, though, he went first to ProMED and proudly saw the posting of the San Antonio swarm, then some other new additions that were very, very interesting—especially after that ridiculous movie he'd just seen.

Logging off, he began to surf in earnest, searching for something the experts might have missed and that ProMED would be very interested in seeing. And then he found *plaguescape.com.*

*   *   *

Sunday, June 28
Manhattan
11:00 P.M.

Theodore Kameron sat in his lab, glorying in the magnificence of his collections and waiting for The Voice to give him explicit instructions for his next Mission. Things were going well. ProMED now listed more of his "incidents" than before. There could be absolutely no connection to him—if anyone had even figured out they were not acts of God in the traditional sense, but the work of one man guided by the hand of an avenging Deity. Even better, it seemed clear that Jack Bryne himself was becoming a prime suspect for San Diego and the horses. Hubbard should be linking these events more closely any day now.

Teddy had returned the FBI agent's call, and at first played dumb when the subject of Bryne came up.

"Well, Agent Hubbard," Teddy began, "of course I know of Dr. Bryne, and we've met at various lectures and events over the years, but I really don't think I know him well enough to be of any help to you. Do you mind my inquiring about the nature of your interest?"

"Not in the least, Dr. Kameron. We're considering him for a special panel the Bureau's forming on bioterrorism. His fellow scientists' opinions of his qualifications are important to us. We've already spoken with many of your colleagues."

Teddy knew the man was lying through his teeth, but was impressed with how smoothly he was doing it. "So, Agent Hubbard, how *can* I be of help to you?"

"Would you describe Dr. Bryne as, let's say, resistant to authority? He will be working with the Bureau, after all."

"You mean, does he follow the rules? No, sir, Jack Bryne is very much his own man. Bridles under tight control, I'm told. Likes to do things his own way. But let me remind you, he does work for the New York State government, and they seem satisfied with him."

"That's true," Hubbard replied. "What about his temperament? Easygoing? Live and let live?"

"Well," Kameron took his time answering, "uhhh, no, I wouldn't characterize him that way at all. Dr. Bryne's known to be very... passionate... about things."

"Really? Bad temper?"

"Agent Hubbard, I really don't know him that well. Actually, some of my colleagues have found him quick to anger, but I personally can't say."

"You used the word 'passionate,' Dr. Kameron. Could you expand on that a little further?"

"Agent Hubbard, this is making me very uncomfortable. I've told you, I don't know the man that well."

"I understand. Just a few more questions. Now, about 'passionate.'"

Teddy sighed. "Here again, this is from colleagues, but, oh, I don't want to cost this man a federal appointment..."

"You won't, I'm sure, Dr. Kameron. Please go on."

"Actually, Agent Hubbard, there are those few in the scientific community who feel that Dr. Bryne's preoccupation with disease and poisons is morbid, almost monomaniacal—but that could stem from envy."

"What if it isn't just envy?"

"Well, actually... I don't know if I should be telling you this, but you are with the government. I spent some time with Dr. Bryne in Haiti back in the sixties, when we were both visiting fellows at the Albert Schweitzer Hospital outside of Port-au-Prince. And I'm

193

embarrassed to admit this, but we got terribly drunk one night, and he told me the story of his childhood. It was absolutely horrific."

Hubbard said nothing.

"Actually," Teddy said, "I had been nursing my drinks, while Bryne couldn't toss them back fast enough; I'm doubtful he even remembered the evening, much less what he'd revealed."

"Horrific. Really?"

"Yes, you see, his parents were missionaries in China. When World War II broke out, the whole family was sent to an internment camp where biochemical weapons were tested on the prisoners. He managed to survive, but both his parents were killed—his mother before the youngster's very eyes. I guess you could say that's where his resistance to authority as well as his interest in toxins was born. If it is morbid, you really can't blame him."

"That's very interesting, Dr. Kameron, very interesting indeed."

And I bet you already knew it, Kameron said to himself, then to Hubbard, "I do want to remind you, sir, that Dr. Bryne is a brilliant, brilliant scientist, highly regarded."

"Reminder noted," Hubbard told him. "I think that's about it, Dr. Kameron. You've been a tremendous help."

"I only hope I haven't spoken out of turn. Oh, dear. I do hope this will all be kept confidential, Agent Hubbard."

"It will, I assure you. Good speaking with you, Doctor. If anything else about Dr. Bryne

194

comes to mind, be sure to give me a call. You have the number."

"Yes, Agent Hubbard," Kameron signed off, "I'll be sure to."

Teddy was delighted with the way the conversation had gone—even better than anticipated. It was really too bad that he probably wouldn't be speaking with the FBI again—unless he could come up with something to tighten the noose that was already encircling Jack Bryne's neck.

Monday, July 6
Department of Health, New York City
10:00 A.M.

Dr. Mia Hart had already begun her epidemiology presentation, a lecture attended by dozens of doctors, student nurses, and summer interns from Columbia's Graduate School of Public Health, when Jack, glad to surprise her, snaked into a back seat of the auditorium. He could tell the audience was already galvanized, both by the subject and the speaker. Jack was always a little awed by Mia's immense personal magnetism, especially in a public forum. She might be heart-stoppingly beautiful, but above all she was the expert's expert—a scientist to be reckoned with.

Mia had projected a slide with ominous images on the big screen behind her: lovely colors, dark bluish at the bottom merging into a light aqua at the top—but a grim subject. The heading was in red, dates and names in yellow. A second, smaller screen on the right at the foot of the stage flashed to life, and the image of a knight on horseback appeared projected upon it. A knight menaced by the figure of Death. Jack recognized it as a woodcut by Dürer. His gaze shifted to the big screen, and he read:

HISTORY OF EMERGING PATHOGENS

Century	Major Pathogen	Century	Major Pathogen
11th	Ergotism	16th	Dysentery
12th	Smallpox	17th	Tuberculosis
13th	Leprosy	18th	Typhus
14th	Plague	19th	Cholera
15th	Syphilis	20th	HIV/AIDS

"So let's consider," Mia was saying, "that each century had its own bug. We can argue about being Eurocentric, but I suggest these infections in Europe early on also affected large stretches of Asia and Africa—and later the so-called 'New World.'"

Plague, she went on to explain, devastated Europe in the fourteenth century, but its origins were Asian. Many believed syphilis originated in Africa, and that ergotism came out of the Middle East into Europe and Africa—the toxin, a fungus called *Claviceps,* having been carried on moldy rye seeds.

Just then, another latecomer entered the auditorium, taking a seat at the other end of the row where Bryne was sitting. Even from a distance, the tall, gray-haired man seemed vaguely familiar, but Jack, for the life of him, couldn't place him. Maybe afterwards, he thought, he'd try to speak to him. Now his focus returned to the lecture.

"When consumed in bread made from moldy rye," Mia was telling the audience, "ergot—which produced repeated, well-documented epidemics throughout Europe—causes auto-amputations, convulsions, and dancing manias. The toxin is an analogue of what we now know as LSD... Unfortunately, the trouble here is that to cover each of these diseases thoroughly could take hours and we don't have the time. I'll be brief, but these pathogens were all calamities in their day.

"In the twelfth century, smallpox took off, particularly in Europe, where walled cities fostered its spread. In the thirteenth century, leprosy appeared, real leprosy—not the Biblical *lepra*, which refers to any disfiguring skin disease from psoriasis to measles. Now the disease that swept through Europe in the late Middle Ages was even more virulent than our present-day strain. There was justification for the proscriptions placed on the victims, although bells worn around the necks of lepers to warn healthy folks of the approach of the 'unclean, unclean,' as they were forced to cry, seem a bit excessive..."

At that moment, a beeper went off in the audience, causing a general round of laughter. Mia quieted them with a wink toward the offending student. "Although it probably means the same thing today...

"For some reason," Mia went on when the second round of laughter had subsided, "after cresting in Sweden, leprosy began to ebb during the latter part of the century. Some have hypothesized that a new affliction—aided by walled castles, along with the emergence of city-states and large urban centers—actually immunized people against the disease, which receded to its present location, the tropics."

She pointed toward the list on the large screen. "And the new disease that drove leprosy from Europe was TB. But TB with a potent twist. Being airborne and highly infectious, TB may well have crowded out leprosy by producing cross-reacting antibodies. However, this does not mean I'm advocating TB as a cure for leprosy!" The audience chuckled again.

"Now I don't think we'll get an argument about what disease dominated the fourteenth century: bubonic plague, followed by pneumonic plague, the so-called Black Death. Plague undoubtedly came from the east via the Silk Route, reaching Italy about 1325 and spreading throughout Europe, where, in a few decades, it killed twenty-five million people, a quarter of the continent. Plague was an equal opportunity killer. It probably devastated Asia and Africa as well, but unfortunately, we don't have much in the way of written records to substantiate this. But we know plague is still with us today."

Not just plague, PLAGUES! Jack thought in frustration. *If she's so knowledgeable and open to new ideas, why won't she listen to me? She's got to. I've got to make her hear me about the Plagues.*

"Now a poem published in 1530," Mia continued, "about a shepherd named Syphilis, gave the next disease its name. We know syphilis exploded in Europe only a few years after Columbus's first voyage. Could be coincidence. Could be he brought back more than gold. Although the disease came late in the fifteenth century, syphilis dominated its time as much as plague had. A killer of women, men, and babies, it was referred to as 'the large pox' to distinguish it from a lesser affliction, smallpox. As its virulence declined, it became endemic throughout the world."

Bryne saw a hand go up in the audience. A young female graduate student asked why Mia hadn't mentioned the New World. "Don't you include North and South America in your considerations?"

"Good point," Mia concurred. "The Old World epidemics were very important in the New World. When Cortez, Pizarro, and others began to exploit the Americas, they brought with them smallpox and measles. Smallpox killed forty-nine million Indians in Mexico, and measles decimated indigenous people in the Caribbean and Central and South America, not to mention native Greenlanders and later the peoples of Alaska, Central Africa, and the South Sea Islands."

She paused to sip water from a cup on the lectern, then went on, "Yes, the Old World diseases did quite well in the New World. Particularly when they had human beings helping. But let's get back to Europe." A new slide of an outhouse appeared. "Would anyone like to suggest why I chose dysentery for the sixteenth century?"

"Bad sewage systems!" someone shouted out.

"Yes! Or no sewage systems at all. You see, the whole European continent was at war; large armies, constantly on the move, with no sanitary systems and no knowledge of germ theory, soiled everything with their feces. A fine patina of fecal matter covered all the environmental surfaces of Europe—swords, sabers, shrines. Please excuse the 's' word, but dysentery was not only about a lack of shithouses, it was shit with a message for today. A few weeks ago, you had your weekly on *E. coli* O157:H7. Well, the plasmid that O157:H7. *E. coli* has acquired came from the bug that causes bacillary dysentery.

"Imagine tens of thousands of sixteenth-century English, French, Flemish, Italian, and German soldiers with a disease that eats the lining of the bowels, causes severe abdominal cramps, bloody diarrhea, high fevers, and ultimately, sepsis and death. The whole of Europe was a festering outhouse—until the constant wars subsided, indoor plumbing was introduced, and the rudiments of public health began to make an impact.

"Tuberculosis dominated the eighteenth century as both Europeans and Americans began to build great cities. The crowding, poverty, and lack of proper nutrition fostered the spread of TB.

"Over the next hundred years," Mia continued, "typhus, probably imported from

Russia, dominated the Euro-Asian world. Like dysentery, it rode on and in the bodies of soldiers who didn't or couldn't bathe. When Napoleon marched into Russia in 1812 with three hundred thousand French soldiers, most of them died of the disease. If you ask me, neither the Russian army nor the weather defeated Napoleon, but typhus did, and I bet Napoleon would agree with me on that.

"The nineteenth century," Mia went on, "unequivocally belonged to cholera, with pandemics sweeping the entire world. The highest mortality rate for a single year in New York City history was in 1832, the second highest in 1866. And that's when the first Board of Health was established in the City to prevent the spread of cholera.

"Now, last, or nearly last," Mia commented, as a slide appeared showing a graph of world-wide AIDS-related deaths starting with 1980 and projecting through the year 2000: the line shot upward in an eighty-degree angle, then plateaued into the next century. "Now, until our next seminar, when we'll address this modern plague, I thank you all."

At this point, the auditorium lights came on, the projector's lamps were turned off, and an appreciated hum of fans began to cool the sweltering room as the audience stretched in their seats.

Checking the clock, Mia asked, "Questions, comments, queries, complaints?" A few of the younger students laughed. Hands shot up. She answered questions about the 1993 plague in India. Why wasn't Ebola included on her list? What about influenza?

An arm whose gloved hand clutched a black pen was raised from a back seat and a deep voice identified itself: "Dr. Theodore Kameron."

Ted Kameron! Bryne thought. *That's who the latecomer was! How odd that only a few days ago, I was thinking he'd disappeared off the face of the earth.*

"And your question, Dr. Kameron?" Mia asked.

"Dr. Hart," the tall, handsome, soft-spoken figure continued almost diffidently, "isn't it true that the so-called emerging pathogens, these new infections are simply impossible to predict and control? Can't we say the catastrophies of the past are often simply replays of what has already been written?"

"Doctor," Mia prepared to answer, "I think I know what you're asking. Yes, I think we're constantly experiencing new waves of infections. Every civilization has its encounter, almost all have tried and failed to predict it, to outwit disease, going as far back as the Romans."

"Or the Egyptians and the Greeks," Kameron added.

"Yes, them too." Hart asked for a last question and looked for another hand.

Bryne, rubbing his forehead, stood up, introduced himself, and was recognized. Ted Kameron turned on his tape recorder before Bryne spoke: "Independent of some mysteriously driven force, and I do not mean the

Almighty... if indeed we have experienced a disease per century, don't you think things have sped up recently?"

"It's an important point," Mia agreed. "Things do seem to have taken off over the last quarter-century. Keep in mind the explosive population growth the 'green revolution' enables. Aside from AIDS, we've had Ebola, legionnaires', Lyme, Lassa, and ehrlichiosis, to name a few. I suppose it does appear that things are accelerating. My primary concern is about the emergence of an antibiotic-resistant organism— a totally impervious bacterium that might well accelerate what I call the 'Post-Antibiotic Era.'"

Bryne shook his head. "No, not really. You say 'might' happen. We *know* that's going to happen. Influenza mutates every year, it comes down to parts per billion, there are so many mutations possible. The problem is, once it starts, how can we contain it? But what I want to know is, what do you predict will be the twenty-first century's really big one? The disease our grandchildren will remember and record, as our ancestors did, as we do for HIV/AIDS. What will be the next name added to your slide for the twenty-first century? And can any prediction stop it? Will God cause it, or man?"

There was a stirring in the audience. Was this other guy a nut or a genius? "That man's right!" Bryne said, pointing to Kameron. "Every culture in history predicts its demise. What's our Armageddon?" Bryne sat down, and Kameron smiled over at him.

Along with the audience, Mia was stunned by Jack's outburst. She was worried, terribly worried. She stared straight at him, saying nothing. Ted Kameron, on the other hand, was pleased to see what seemed to be a palpable strain between them. Another woman? Or was she, too, questioning Bryne's sanity, or his innocence? Whatever, he almost pitied Bryne. A wife like that, so tough, so rigid. Teddy couldn't shake the realization that Mia Hart reminded him of his own ex-wife and his mother.

Signaling that the lecture was over, Mia thanked the audience for their attention. Students, doctors, and nurses began to file out of the auditorium, and Jack tried to fight his way through the crowd to reach Kameron, but could not get to him. With the tape of Bryne's remarks securely in his pocket recorder, Teddy was rushing to the lab to make a copy. Once he doctored it, he knew it would all be manna from heaven when it reached the FBI.

10

Tuesday, July 28
Zoonosis Laboratory, Guilderland
10:30 A.M.

Bryne sat stewing at his desk, with plenty of reasons to be out of sorts. First of all, dinner with Mia had been a disaster—Jack had ordered an extra-rare T-bone steak. Mia, who had ordered the venison casserole, was all over him instantly, reminding him of the

204

very real dangers of *E. coli* O157:H7, the bacterial mutation she'd alluded to in her lecture—which now created a new, elaborate, and quite potent toxin that caused cramps, bloody stools, fever, and in many children acute renal failure. *E. coli* O157:H7 had first come into being among ruminant herds in Washington State and was spreading to feedlot herds throughout the Midwest. After routine butchering, the contaminants were spread widely during the rendering process.

Hamburger meat was the worst because a single hamburger patty blended in giant grinders and then repackaged might contain the meat and bacteria from one hundred different cows. Undercooked burger, taco meats, and steak tartare had become lethal, but an extra-rare T-bone was close enough. The epidemic in August 1997 had caused hundreds of deaths across the United States.

Jack almost winced as he responded to Mia's attack on his choice of entree but said, "Darling, this is a very, very good restaurant. And besides, how often do I do this? I haven't had a real meal for days."

Shrugging, Mia snapped back, "Well, it's your life. I guess you've got a right to pick your poison." Then an uncomfortable silence fell as they sipped their '91 Torre Giorgi—which Jack had lavishly ordered when he imagined this was going to be a celebratory reunion.

By the time the entree was served, food was the last thing on their minds. There was no denying the distance between them. And that was before he told her about Louisiana and the strange death of the bishop. Aware that she was still disturbed and annoyed by his outburst at the lecture, he had hoped against hope he could reach her. No luck.

"Jack, all the events you've been describing lately are natural phenomena," she countered. "For some reason I don't understand, you're searching for anything, anything to support your very strange theory. Look, I bet I could find an item on the Internet about a hailstorm happening somewhere right now. Does that mean there's a conspiracy? Or locusts? Last year they swarmed in Utah. Does that have a deeper meaning? Jack, please!"

"It was the year before last. I called..." Bryne seemed distracted. Mia stared and changed the subject. They tried to enjoy the wine, returned to the apartment by ten, and went directly to sleep after a perfunctory good night kiss. Mia was still sleeping when he got up to make the first morning train to Albany.

It was nearly ten-thirty when Bryne arrived at the lab, later than he liked to get in. After calling hello to Drew and receiving no answer, he remembered Lawrence had told him he had a doctor's appointment, which would keep him out of the office all morning. Jack decided to go through the e-mail first, culling the more important notes, then putting them into some sort of order. The reports piled up, filling his In box faster and faster, and he had no magical command to stop them.

He was already swamped. He'd promised Tucker and Vicky his conclusions on the cause of the horse die-offs in a week or two and still hadn't been able to deliver. Not that he and Drew hadn't been running tests constantly. They had, but every single time, the results came up negative, for rabies, for alimentary toxic aleukia, for pathology suggestive of prions, and for the known arboviral diseases. He and Lawrence were mystified, which wasn't any help to Tucker or the horses.

Jack realized he was becoming obsessed by the plague theory that almost everybody else but Drew thought was crazy. He was sure he had identified the second plague of frogs, the fourth plague of the swarm, and the sixth plague of boils, or, in this case, anthrax.

What about the first plague of water turning to blood, the third plague of lice, the fifth plague, a murrain, the seventh plague of hail, the eighth plague of locusts, the ninth plague of darkness, and the tenth plague, the death of the eldest? Nothing at all so far. Maybe he was getting paranoid. Well, mad or not, he still had to work. He concentrated on scrolling down through ProMED messages.

Suddenly he saw something interesting. It was an e-mail message sent from someone in Florida, from a name he didn't recognize, and it read:

```
For ProMED:
Certain startling events took place
four months ago—in St. Cloud,
```

Minnesota, March 3; Bangor, Maine,
March 4; New Canaan, Connecticut,
March 5. Could these occurrences be
related? Explicit accounts to follow.
First read up on ergotism.

What in hell was this all about? Bryne mused,
struck at the dry irony of ergotism showing up
first in Mia's lecture, then in a completely unrelated way on ProMED. And who was this
mysterious new contributor? Well, maybe
this was synchronicity. Jack waited until there
appeared on the screen an article, *Ergotism,
a Brief History*, from an English newspaper, and
he began to scan it for material Mia hadn't covered.

Ergotism first dates from the Assyrians, he
read, who realized that rye, which was new to
them, was contaminated by black "pustules"
growing on the grain and inscribed its dangers
on sandstone tablets as early as 600 B.C.E.

The contaminant, a microscopic fungus, spread
by wind or insects, inoculates the rye's germinative
center. These fungal spores do not affect most
other grains, since they are largely species-
specific. The fungus, *Claviceps purpurea*, elaborates
a variety of potent toxins that may cause severe
symptoms in humans. The Classical Greeks
realized that grains infested with ergot caused
illness and death. Rye was avoided in Roman
and Egyptian cultures. Rye's introduction into
Egypt corresponds to the decline of the Late
Dynasty, a collapse that ended the civilization
around the first century B.C.E.

Bryne learned that with the rise of Christianity and the Church's relocation to Constantinople, rye began to be grown throughout Europe and used in bread and other grain-derived products. Simultaneously, the hallucinations induced by ergot also spread.

He looked away from the screen, wondering what had become of this blight, which he thought of only as a remnant of the Middle Ages. Maybe history was recycling ergotism—or maybe *someone* was...

New York City
11:30 P.M.

Kameron pulled the nylon strap around his midriff and pressed the Velcro closures tight. He wanted to be sure the electrodes made good contact. He pressed the RECORD button on his audio monitor, and the voice relay, actuated by any sound in the room, switched on. Even in his sleep, he needed to record himself: his vital signs, his moods, his diet, his excrement. He had to know what was happening to him. Science. His primary faith. He swore on his own fate to be as objective with his self-diagnosis as possible. Humanly possible.

He needed to monitor himself, for he was never able to know in advance when The Voice would call him next. He needed desperately to know what it was he was hearing. He needed to know why this was happening to him. He needed to prove before science that the gods of man were the gods of the brain. It must be his brain that spoke to him with the voice of Jehovah. It was not his own. He recorded the sounds in the room when The Voice had spoken to him before. Spoke about the blood. Spoke about the lice, spoke of the murrain. He had heard so much. Not simply his own voice, but his and The Voice of another were merged for him on the tapes. He played them repeatedly, just as he reread his notes from those horrible moments. Moments when he shrieked out the name of God, moments when he heard The Voice, The Voice of a God both powerful and vengeful.

As a scientist, he had reminded himself after the water had been turned to blood, and after the frogs, the lice, the swarm, the murrain, the boils, the hail, and the locusts, that he was responsible for documenting objectively, for the first time, the existence of God himself.

When Dr. Kameron felt that there was to be word from The Voice, he prepared himself, arranged the objective meters of medicine to survey the phenomena, what he hoped would be a record of a man's empowerment by divinity. He knew when The Voice spoke, when The Voice had chosen him, that The Voice had known that only he among all men could have the necessary knowledge to see that His Will Be Done. Would The Voice have given him the ability to speak his name if it was not proof of Teddy's own divinity? His mother had told him he was accursed. He had doubted her then, and now he knew she had been utterly wrong; he was the holiest of the Holy.

He adjusted the EEG straps and tried to relax. The Voice seemed to come every few weeks, more often now, and for three nights he had stayed home and monitored his heart, his blood, and his voice. He would always transcribe his recordings. He had been able to document all six of the "possessions," either from recall or from his tapes. With the power of The Voice guiding his memory of the wrath of God, he would dictate elaborately detailed descriptions of himself as he created, carried out, and witnessed the plagues of Exodus unfolding before his eyes, and by his hand...

After monitoring himself, Teddy Kameron delighted in making Jack Bryne wait for the explicit ergotism accounts, just on principle. The man was so arrogant, he deserved to suffer the impatience Teddy always felt when waiting for The Voice to command him. Kameron had made certain the material couldn't be printed out.

Teddy had picked up the Florida return address and name to add to his collection. The user was an eleven-year-old boy who couldn't possibly have any knowledge of ergotism or the Events. If Jack started asking ergot questions on ProMED, he would appear certifiably crazy—or, perhaps to Special Agent Hubbard, a guilty madman with the sociopath's irresistible and hubristic desire to be found out.

As he waited for Jack to read the material he was feeding him, Teddy reviewed his account of how he put this knowledge into action for the third plague:

Wednesday, April 1. April Fool's Day

It took less than an hour at the library for Kameron to locate seven mail-order suppliers of untreated rye seed, buy ten-pound sample packages from each, and promise more purchases after he'd used the sample in his latest recipe. Bakery supply houses provided lists of cereal grain suppliers, and there was always a new crop of hybrids to test.

Teddy made himself wait until evening to open the packages, then spent a fascinated hour looking over the delivery, inspecting the rye for any dark seeds. The powerful ones. Different suppliers provided varying quality as well as a range of prices; he could spot the good samples right away and promptly discarded them. The samples with even a few dark seeds were given special treatment. They already contained what he was after. Kameron scattered each new batch of top candidates in a low plastic tray.

He sprayed each with a light mist of fresh water, and covered the tray with a dark cloth. Each sample was carefully marked—supplier, date of separation, date of moisturization, number of days in dark-ness—presaging the Greater Days of Darkness that were to come.

Bryne broadened his reading, discovering that major epidemics of ergotism were reliably described in the Middle Ages—with symptoms including gangrene of the feet, hands, even the arms and legs. Some people had limbs drop off due to the intense vasoconstriction from the ergot toxins. Noses turned blue, then black, and sloughed off their faces, leaving

212

gaping holes. Women aborted, while many people developed seizures and psychoses. Whole towns were affected.

Half-crazed survivors with sublethal doses of the mycotoxins danced in the streets, some in agony from the ergot, some in superstitious frenzies trying to ward off the Devil's evil spiders, which were blamed for the affliction—hence, the "tarantella," Italian for spider. People called the disease "St. Anthony's fire," and a pilgrimage to the saint's shrine was thought to be the only cure for the pain and intense, intractable itching that herald the onset of ergotism.

Bryne stopped to make a note; the mention of itching was important.

Also relevant was the fact that pilgrimages often did effect a cure in a sense, since travelers were leaving behind their home-grown toxic breads and buying non-poisoned food along the way. Magpies were popular remedies; "four and twenty" of the blackbirds baked in a pie. By the time the pilgrims arrived at St. Anthony's grave, the ergot's effect had disappeared.

Just as Bryne read on compulsively, so had Teddy Kameron kept on working, refining the autobiography, checking his notes, recording progress, and adding to the writings in the files labeled "LMPG":

Theodore Graham Kameron took each damp, covered tray of seeds and set it in a specially built rack. Remote heat units kept the trays at a constant temperature while he waited.

Daily he added more moisture, recorded his data, and watched as the darkness spread among the rye seeds. After only a few weeks, he was positive which seeds he wanted to cultivate.

It was not simple rye seed alone Teddy was cultivating. Now he was growing the toxic ergot-producing fungi. And in quantity.

After only two days, he took the first tray from the heated rack for inspection. Teddy estimated that over 4,000 tiny seeds had been on the tray when he started. Now he divided the uncontaminated from the many new, beautiful swollen dark gray ones—festering, hundreds of them, all infested with fungi.

Each gray seed was vacuumed up with a small device Kameron had created. It was a tiny glass cylinder with two plastic tubes that came out of a stopper, and a HEPA filter that screened the toxins from his lungs. One end of the vacuum was long enough to sweep over the piles of rye like a miniature upright Hoover. The other tube he put in his mouth and sucked on. He was on the safe side. He used a water pressure vacuum attached to the sink faucet, with the out spout forced in past the U-trap of the sink. The toxins could not become airborne and drift into his breathing zone.

Each time Teddy sucked, a tiny infected rye seed flew up the plastic tube and fell into the bottom of the collection jar. He worked precisely, taking only gray ones.

When he first sampled the tray, only a few grains had been infected. On the second day, twice as many; on the third, four times. After only a week, the tray had produced more than two hundred dark gray rye seeds. All in all, they weighed less

*than a gram. They were beautiful to Kameron
because they were enough to kill two dozen healthy
adults, kill them in agony, kill them slowly, kill
them without leaving a trace.*

*It was working perfectly. In only a few weeks,
he'd created far more infected seed than he'd
expected. Yet after a quick calculation, Teddy discovered to his horror that it wasn't nearly
enough…*

Bryne had immediately decided to determine just how effectively the U.S. grain inventories were being checked for ergot. Could it really be happening again, as the phantom e-mailer claimed? Turning back to the article, he learned that Medieval Germany and France had been the most severely affected, but the Germans experienced hallucination and convulsions, while the French experienced gangrene. These ergot-infected ryes can easily produce secondary metabolites, including LSD—Mia had mentioned that in her lecture.

Affected by the moldy breads, tens of thousands of half-crazed Europeans once danced in the streets, many experiencing scotomas, flashing lights that appeared on their retinas; others saw visions of the Virgin Mary; still others marched as flagellants.

The mania spread from early outbreaks in the Low Countries across the Rhine. Catholic Europe was in crisis. Since the Church, of course, was powerless to affect the epidemic, a rampant anticlericalism developed. Monasteries were burned, bishops unseated, and protests and riots continued.

And, Bryne thought, in another hundred years, Protestantism was born in Germany.

During the Renaissance, the sale of contaminated rye had continued, spread to England, Sweden, and Russia, and did not trail off until the eighteenth century—even though a French physician had finally traced the cause of the disease to moldy rye in 1630. The article even suggested that the Salem witch trials might have been caused by ergotism. The last U.S. epidemic, it stated, occurred in New York State in 1825.

Bryne was surprised. *In my state? Where? Never heard of it.* He made another note and continued to the article's conclusion.

There were various theories put forward as to why ergotism began to trail off in Europe by the nineteenth century. The chief one was the introduction of the potato (which supplanted dependency on grains, particularly rye). The last recorded episode occurred in Pont St. Esprit in Southern France in 1951.

Ironic, Bryne thought. *Right back where it had started.*

And Teddy read on:

Driven to commence his Mission as rapidly as possible, Kameron began ordering the rye in bulk by phone under another assumed name, and waited impatiently for the deliveries to arrive.

He had plastic garbage cans ready when the sacks came in by truck. By the second week after their arrival, he had almost two hundred gallons of seed under cultivation. Eight of the heavy-duty thir-ty-gallon plastic garbage cans he'd gotten from Sears fit perfectly under the stainless steel work counter in his kitchen.

Ritualistically, Teddy would open each sack and lovingly shovel the rye into the carefully labeled cans. He misted the kernels, but before sealing these cans, he'd gently shake a few spoonfuls of the care-fully selected dark gray seeds, hairy now with the black fungus, directly on top of the damp freshly arrived seeds.

Each day he would come into the kitchen of his lab, check the heaters, take the tops off the cans, and scoop out the top layer of seed. A quick trip to the sorting table, and within ten days he had accu-mulated almost forty pounds of the grayish kernels, each infested with pure ergot-producing fungi.

Now came the creative, the artistic stage. The infected seeds went through one final transforma-tion in a food processor, which turned them into a fine dark powder resembling pepper. Teddy's stove could accommodate four large bowls filled with supermarket-purchased brownie mix. He divided the powder equally into each of the bowls, stirring and blending the contents, and then carefully poured the mixture onto wax paper.

Once cooled, the sweet-smelling dough was ready for baking—at a temperature too low to destroy the beautiful essence produced by the fungi. Then there was the cutting, packaging, and mailing. Prompt delivery was of prime importance. Ash Wednesday had passed, but the Easter holidays, after all, were fast approaching...

Teddy stopped reading his written record to look at his watch, deciding he would now send Bryne the rest of the material. Exiting his special journal file, he went on line and sent the material to Bryne's e-mail address. He was aroused by his little "dramas." He wrote them based on newspaper accounts and calls to local residents who loved to gossip—the gorier the better—but he embellished them for Bryne for dramatic effect, made them into passion plays, each with its own divine message. As the first of the files winged its way to Bryne, Kameron felt himself grow hard.

Bryne told himself to download the incoming files even before beginning to read them, but wasn't able to. Nor could he print or save them. Must have been a sophisticated hacker, this sick sender. Hmmm. He would have to read the stuff off the screen. When he did, he was utterly shocked and baffled.

Tuesday, March 3
St. Cloud, Minnesota
It had begun to snow, early for the lake country. The pastor, Thomas Matthew Ogilvie, D.D., bundled up in a down coat, gloves, and scarf, wasn't looking forward to the drive, but he had to see his doctor. The terrible itching had been going on for days.
His fingers first, then both his arms. He could not keep himself from scratching. It was worse than hemorrhoids, with the skin along his arms and legs becoming red and hot, and almost ablaze with itching. His toes began to glow, and his ears hurt. His

wife, Marlene, saying it was probably only an aller-
gy, wasn't all that sympathetic.

She hadn't been all that sympathetic in general
lately, maybe because he had put his foot down
with their spoiled daughter, her husband, and
their four children staying with them. She couldn't
wait until they could move into their new house.
Yes, Marlene was mad at him, had even refused
one of the brownies that had been sent to him
from New York City, without a name or address,
only a little "LMPG" etched on the bottom of the
tin. Whoever they were from, perhaps a former
parishioner, they were delicious, homemade. He
was glad, in fact, Marlene hadn't wanted to
try one.

Luckily, he made it through the snow to the doc-
tor's relatively easily. The heat of the car seemed to
reduce the itching, especially across his arms and
forearms.

His toes were numb—he was alarmed by that—
and his hands were colder than he had ever experi-
enced. After a while, he could hardly hold the steer-
ing wheel and began using his wrists. It was snow-
ing so hard, he could barely navigate. Almost there,
thank God.

He looked into the rearview mirror after he
made the turn into the office park. The tip of his
nose, the very tip, was as white as the snow, but it
didn't hurt. The pain would come later, he knew,
when he warmed up.

As he came into the waiting room, Ogilvie saw
one of his parishioners, Wilmot Jones, nice guy,
insurance, but very talkative. As he nodded hello,
Ogilvie felt something loose in his glove. An icicle?

*he wondered. Then he felt another icicle in his other
glove. He had to get those gloves off.*

*Tugging on the fingertips of each glove with his
teeth until they were loose, he then bit into the
wristband and peeled off the left glove. It fell to the
floor and made a cracking noise on the tile.
Without thinking, he repeated the same process for
his right glove, and heard another clatter. Both
gloves seemed to be filled with things… icicles…*

*Suddenly Ogilvie realized that Wilmot Jones was
yelling, "Jesus God, Reverend. Hey, Doc, Doc Santos!
Get out here fast!"*

*"What's the trouble, Wilmot?" Ogilvie asked, see-
ing Jones looking open-mouthed at the gloves on the
floor, then up at the minister's hands.*

*Looking down at his hands, Ogilvie could not
believe what he saw. No fingers, he had no fingers.
Only stumps, white stumps. He watched as his left
finger rolled out of his glove and hit the linoleum.
Then, impossibly, another finger shook free from
his right glove. He could see his wedding ring on
one of the cold white nubbins.*

The screen suddenly went blank. Bryne,
unable to believe what he had just read, did-
n't know what to do. He wished someone
else had seen the message. He wished Drew
were there. For the first time since he'd
worked in the lab, he actually felt afraid.
Still, there was nothing to do but check out
what would appear on the screen next. He heard
the chime of his e-mail alerting him that
another message was arriving. Bryne read

the next strange vignette as astonished as he been by the first.

Wednesday, March 5
Bangor, Maine

Dr. Kevin O'Reilly, a doctor too old to be making house calls, had been summoned by the sisters at 11:00 P.M. He had initially intended to tell Sister Angelica to take her colleague to the Emergency Room until she had mentioned the Mother Superior's name.

It sounded like food poisoning at first... He was told that all Mother Superior had for dinner was a snack of milk and some special brownies that had been delivered in the mail that day. Not long after the snack, she had complained of a terrible itching, especially in her fingers. Then spasms began in her stomach, rhythmic bouts of pain that forced her into bed. The pains began to settle in her abdomen. Appendicitis? O'Reilly wondered. Unlikely. There was only one condition that brought him out at midnight—but never to a nunnery. Yet out he went.

When he knocked on the convent's massive wooden door and Sister Angelica answered it, he saw behind her hundreds of candles. The candles were in stationary holders, in glass devotionals, on lead plates only used for special masses. Most of the white waxed candles were being held by the nuns in the order. He had never seen all the nuns at one time, or so many candles.

As special gynecologist to the Order and senior gynecologist at St. Patrick's Hospital, he knew most of them. He knew, for instance, that Mother

Superior had a fibroid, but she was well over seventy and didn't want to have an operation. This was something of much greater significance than a fibroid flareup. Some of the nuns were praying, others whispering or saying their Rosary. Many were crying, invoking the name of Jesus.

When O'Reilly asked to see the elderly nun, he was escorted upstairs to a room with ten senior nuns maintaining a vigil around the bed, where lay an extremely thin elderly woman with a swollen abdomen. The Mother Superior was in obvious pain, clutching the sheets as a wave of agony swept through her body. A nun immediately to her right wiped her brow, and another massaged her abdomen.

"Every three minutes now," a sister said. "They were five minutes apart a few moments ago."

It couldn't be happening, O'Reilly thought to himself. This eighty-year-old woman was in labor and about to deliver. It was as if she had been given an injection women in difficult labor sometimes receive, ergotamine.

"Everyone out, please," O'Reilly roared, motioning only Angelica to stay.

A quick exam with one gloved hand found a roundish dome being extruded from the birth canal. O'Reilly positioned forceps to facilitate the passage.

The Mother Superior pushed and screamed as the delivery finally took place. Sister Angelica fainted at the sight. O'Reilly felt a twinge in his chest as he saw it—the one-and-a-half-pound pedunculated fibroid she hadn't wanted to part with. It had been expelled from the woman's uterus by a violent force squeezing down on the mass long sequestered *inside. He cut the stalk and placed the tumor in the small cradle by the bedside, where one of the most faithful of the novitiates had prepared a creche and swaddling clothes, just in case.*

Bryne read on as fast as he could, but again the screen went blank when he tried to print out the report.

Can all this be real? Bryne wondered. Of course, he could check the local papers to verify if these stories had ever been released— or contact the two doctors involved. Why was he being shown this material to begin with? Maybe another entry would give him the answer. He watched the screen, and a new message began:

Wednesday, March 5
New Canaan, Connecticut
The meeting with the minister had gone extreme-ly well, and Neil Edison was elated. He and Tammy would have a church wedding in six weeks. The cer-emony would be a short one, simple, without all the bells and whistles. Reverend Phillips had been most understanding of the earnest young couple's finan-cial problems.

The minister had offered them milk and a new tin of brownies during the planning session, and Neil pigged out. He could feel it now. His stomach was full and, strangely, deep inside, it itched. When he had mentioned it to Tammy, she said it was the beginning of the "seven-year itch," and he'd laughed.

He'd used the lunch break from his computer

223

programming job to meet her at the rectory and was racing back along the Merritt Parkway. As he took a last drag on a Marlboro and flicked it out the window, the pain hit like a cannonball, then exploded in his belly.

On a scale of one to ten, this is a twenty, Neil realized right before the car lurched off the exit ramp and he passed out. Neil was lucky in a way; another driver saw the car veer off the road, found the young man unconscious, and got him to a hospital. In the ER, the surgeon and radiologist agreed that Neil's was an acute surgical condition requiring an immediate laparotomy. An otherwise healthy young man, now unconscious, with a boardlike belly probably meant a ruptured appendix. They would explore as soon as the OR was ready.

Tubes were placed in the veins of both his arms, and another tube—a Foley catheter—was inserted in his bladder and the little balloon inflated to prevent slippage. Another metallic tube was thrust into his throat. They were ready to go. The surgeon's scalpel opened his belly with ease.

The abdominal muscles were gently pried apart until the intestines could be seen through a semitransparent membrane. Something was terribly wrong—the intestines appeared to be black. They opened the belly, and a foul odor swept through the operating room.

"Takayasu's?" asked the assistant surgeon, searching the cavity, then yelled, "Look at the artery! It's empty." He was pointing to a stalk of flesh resembling a pink noodle that was blanched at the opening. The vessel had been pinched open completely, but no blood came out. "This guy's had

an intestinal infarction, like a massive coronary!"

Neil's blood had been cut off to the spiral of arteries serving the duodenum, jejunum, and ileum—the entire small intestine. The same mechanism, occlusion, was also responsible for heart attack, stroke, and gangrene in a limb. This time the small bowel had died.

"Oh, my sweet living..." the anesthesiologist broke in, and all eyes turned to him. He was sitting at the patient's head, but looking at the floor, by the scrub nurse's feet. She jumped back as if a serpent was about to strike her foot.

On the floor was the standard square plastic bag to collect urine, connected to a tube that coiled around the floor in loops and should have disappeared under the sheets and drapes to where it was attached to the man's body. Instead, the tube had fallen to the floor. The balloon was still intact. But the Foley catheter was not broken, had not been dislodged.

Neil's penis, denied a blood supply, was turning a ripe purple and was still attached to the catheter on the floor.

As Bryne read the sentence the screen went black and stayed black, and he turned off his computer.

Bryne went out for some much-needed fresh air and sunshine after he'd finished reading and had only just returned to the office when Drew Lawrence walked in.

"Drew, you've got to see this!" He turned on the computer to show Lawrence the messages and found nothing. All the material—

all record of it—had vanished without a trace.

Bryne described the three messages to Lawrence, who could only shake his head in disbelief. "It's got to be him, Drew," Jack thought aloud. "This has got to be the guy behind the plagues. He knows we're on to him, whoever he is. But why this? To prove I'll never get him—or to challenge me to try?"

Tuesday, July 14
Zoonosis Laboratory, Guilderland

July had been unusually hot, and as the first two weeks slipped by, Jack and Drew's failure to identify the source of the horse die-offs was deeply frustrating to both of them, not to mention Enoch Tucker—and Vicky Wade.

Wade had been calling every couple of days, and every couple of days Bryne gave her the same news: nothing. She'd even made two or three trips up to the lab to make sure, as she flat-out told them, that they weren't keeping anything from her. That was certainly a good part of the reason, Drew figured, but there was more to it, and it continued to worry him.

Wade always showed up in the late morning, coifed and clad as if she were about to go on camera, nosed about the lab for a while, sniffing for some element of a story, but always ended up having lunch with Jack. She had the smarts to invite Drew along, but he always claimed he had too much work to finish. Frankly, he knew he wasn't wanted, and he didn't care to be involved if there *was* something going on between them. One thing he was sure of: Bryne hadn't mentioned the plague theory to her—or she would have been all over both of them about it.

These lunches—at some posh place, bankrolled by Wade's expense account—lasted for hours. Even if Jack and Wade talked only about the mystery of the horses, they did it over wine. Jack always napped in the afternoon after lunch with Wade.

This had been a Wade day, and Jack's absence, plus the backlog of materials to be processed, mandated their working late. Two new specimens had come in from Jamestown, New York—a cat and a raccoon, both possibly rabid. The two worked silently together, fixing the material, until Bryne abruptly asked, "Drew, what do we have on lice?"

Placing a slide under the microscope, Drew smiled. "I'm way ahead of you, Jack. The third plague was lice. There's nothing worthwhile in the ProMED archives. Routine head lice is all. Have any ideas?"

Bryne didn't—or didn't have any swimming around in his unconscious that were ready to link up and reveal themselves as coherent theory. The weird ergotism episodes still haunted him. When he'd tried to contact the Florida e-mail address, he'd reached an eleven-year-old boy who didn't have the slightest idea what he was talking about. He'd mentioned the disappearing e-mail to Drew at the time, of course, not making light of it, but had decided against even bringing up the incident with Mia. It would at worst give greater credence to her fears for his sanity, and at best it would earn her disdain.

And yet there was something, something. Whoever authored those vignettes had much more information than could be gleaned from any newspaper—and much more precise knowledge of the effects of the toxin under discussion. Plus the "LMPG," which Jack remembered had been written on the handle of the San Diego water pistol. That almost certainly made whoever was sending this stuff the same person. But would he be acting alone, raining Biblical vengeance down on the modern world? After all, Jack thought, ergotism had nothing to do with Exodus. Or did it?

The clattering ring of the telephone startled him, but then, since the ergot information arrived, anything seemed to startle him. Whoever had hacked into his computer had convinced Bryne that evil—pure, malevolent evil—did indeed exist and that no one was safe from it.

"Jack Bryne," he answered the ringing phone.

"Dr. Bryne." The unfamiliar voice was hesitant and boyish, but trying to sound grown up. "I am sorry to call you so late, but I couldn't do it any sooner. I had to finish my research. And besides, the rates are lower now." He was almost whispering. "My name is Berger, Shmuel Berger. I'm a student. I've had correspondence with Mr. Drew Lawrence."

"With Drew? You said your name was Berger?"

Drew looked up from the microscope in which he was examining a slide, gave a thumbs-up sign, and scribbled Jack a hasty note, "The swarm report!"

"Yes, Mr. Berger," Bryne told the boy, "Mr. Lawrence remembers you very well. Go ahead. Tell me about your research." He heard the boy gulp.

"I believe you're asking questions about the plagues." The boy spoke with a heavy Brooklyn accent.

Bryne was surprised. His queries on ProMED had been interspersed with many other requests, but this student had seen through it. "Yes, I am, Berger. How'd you guess?"

Flustered, Shmuel blurted out, "Well, you see, there's the so-called 'swarm,' which could be wild animals, flies of some sort, or bees—like the bees I contacted Dr. Lawrence about."

Now Bryne remembered Drew telling him about Berger when he had arrived in San Diego. The kid was sharp, definitely doing his homework. "And the waters turning to blood?" Silence. "What about lice?"

"Well, Doctor, sir, that's what I recently found. The Hebraic term for lice is *chinnim*, often translated as generic 'vermin,' but the Greek *sciniphes* means mosquito or gnat. I personally believe that it was anything that causes intense itching. It doesn't *have* to be lice as we know them..."

Eureka! Bryne knew that Aristotle was the first to classify animals, including insects, one thousand years *after* Exodus. That meant that any insect or *anything* that caused itching might be responsible. It was the itching! And for all he knew, for the LMPG monsters, "vermin" might be ergotism—the last cause any contemporary scientist would even bother to look for!

After the horror of the vanishing messages, Berger's sweet, clear decency was like a breath of fresh air. "Berger," Jack asked him, "how can we get in touch with you?"

Shmuel obliged by giving Bryne his home phone number and address, of all of which Bryne gratefully made careful note. At last, another person who didn't think he was nuts—and a hell of a scholar, to boot.

"Thanks, Berger," Jack signed off. "You've been a great help. And please contact us whenever you even *think* you're on to something. Okay?"

"For sure, Doctor," Shmuel replied. "Well, I don't want to keep you." And he hung up.

"Smart kid," Jack told Drew. "Now, can you expand your net to include anything that itches, bugs or not?"

"Does this have to do with 'vermin'?"

"Might well."

"I can try Nexis. Any news article or magazine reference with the word 'itch' will come up, but please give me some time. There's going to be a lot of itching out there—allergies, scabies, shingles, dandruff, psoriasis, poison oak, sumac, and ivy. How far back do you want to go?"

Reviewing the notes he'd jotted down from the mysterious ergot material, Bryne suggested, "Try from the beginning of the year. Maybe March. Look for incidents in Minnesota, Maine, and Connecticut. Okay?"

"Done."

"Too bad we can't have it by tomorrow when our guest arrives."

"Yeah, we're finally going to confront Special Agent Hubbard. Maybe we'll actually find out what he wants."

"He claims he wants to discuss my WHO work on bioterrorism."

"Maybe it's my flaming radical past, Jack, but I never believe those guys. They never want what they say they want."

"All we can do, my friend..." Jack said breezily, still thrilled over Berger's call, "...is wait—and see!"

11

Tuesday, July 14
New York State Thruway
11:30 A.M.

Special Agent Scott Hubbard, an avid war buff almost all his life, had a special interest in World War II. His father had been wounded on Iwo Jima, and they'd often talked about it; the war in the Pacific seemed almost as real to the younger Hubbard as if he himself had fought in it. Not only did he have the complete videotaped set of *Victory at Sea* and *The World at War*, but he had studied every major battle of the conflict.

Yes, he was a storehouse of World War II information, but even he had never heard of Unit 731, the Pingfan internment camp. Not until a brief mention of it had turned up in Dr. John Bryne's file.

Hubbard was disturbed to find that there were pieces missing from Bryne's file. He asked his colleagues at the Bureau why the material hadn't been included and never got a straight answer. He had started digging and eventually realized that whatever had been deleted, parts of it went way back, before the old G–2 guys, the OSS, the old Army CWS—the Chemical Warfare Service contingent—the early precursors of Fort Detrick. What with his own growing suspicions about Bryne, plus the virologist's missing past, Hubbard needed some answers.

Hubbard drove north on the New York State Thruway in a rickety government car through high wind and heavy rain, not a pleasant journey, but his thoughts were preoccupied with a rare book he'd gotten, not from a secret source but from the New York Public Library: *Unit 731: Japan's Secret Biological Warfare in World War II*.

The obscure book, published in 1989 by two Englishmen named Williams and Wallace, had been a revelation—and not only about Bryne. Hubbard learned that under the direction of General Shiro Ishii, the Japanese had conducted industrial-scale germ warfare against the Chinese— some of the most inhuman biological experiments ever conceived. The real mystery was why the scandal wasn't more widely known. Even before Pearl Harbor, the brutal plans were operational.

In November 1941, a single unidentified plane was seen making low passes over the streets of a Chinese city called Changteh. Two eyewitnesses at the local Presbyterian hospital had watched rice grains, pieces of paper, cotton wadding, and tiny dolls floating down to earth. A week later, the city's children began to develop symptoms of plague. Plague was new to Changteh, and local reports were read with great interest by British, Russian, and American intelligence agents, who were able to trace the plane to an airfield in Japanese-held Manchuria. The plague ran its course, and the records were "lost." Nothing more had been done officially about the incident. But the records had been recovered, and Hubbard found what he was looking for.

Further into the book, Hubbard was astonished to find a reproduction of an old OSS mimeographed summary of John "Jack" Bryne's early records. This was paydirt! James and Anne Bryne and their son John had been incarcerated in three separate camps—first Mukden, then in Unit 731 at Pingfan, and finally at 731's lesser-known zoonotic station, Unit 100—the Hippo-epizootic Unit, specializing in botanical and animal pathology. The OSS summary Hubbard found in the FBI archives described the Japanese experiments conducted before and during the Bryne family's captivity. How terrifyingly close the Japanese had been to perfecting the tools for biological warfare. They had built a factory for plagues.

Hubbard read about the viruses, smallpox, cholera, typhus, glanders, salmonella.

Well before the war began in Europe, the officers under General Ishii were preparing to create an epidemic of hemorrhagic fever, and they needed the yellow fever strain for their experiments. The Japanese had tried to order a lethal strain of yellow fever directly from the Rockefeller labs in New York City in the late thirties. When that plan failed, they tried Brazil, with the same result.

A separate enterprise, Unit 100, performed many chemical and biological experiments, but its specialty was thermal exposure in winter to study frostbite and precisely how frozen limbs could be lopped off with one blow of a club. The human subjects of all these experiments were called *moruta,* "log," or the Japanese word for monkey. Most inmates were Chinese, but there were more than one thousand Occidentals— in case the Chinese might either be immune to a particular microbe or more susceptible to it. And because the Westerners, both Americans and Russians, were the troops the Japanese feared most, they desperately needed Occidentals to experiment upon.

The 731 Unit was huge, complete with its own airfield. It had been designed and built for mass production: flea-breeding incubating machines, rodent colonies, vats, dehydration chambers, and conveyor belts capable of turning out kilogram shipments of deadly freeze-dried bacteria. By 1945, over eighty pounds of anthrax bacilli alone had been produced and meticulously stored—more than enough to kill every person on earth. The survivors of the toxic experimental trials, the unlucky ones, would often become immune to dozens of diseases, so they were ultimately sent on to Unit 100, where they were used as subjects for the thermal and chemical experiments, which nobody survived.

There was no record of how Bryne's father had died. His mother's death had been recorded by a Russian major, who, once he had taken charge of Pingfan, cleared the trenches, identified the victims by the tags around their necks, then covered them with the fresher corpses of Japanese soldiers.

John "Jack" Bryne had been repatriated on August 14, 1945, after a Russian force of one and one half million troops, almost six thousand tanks, and over five thousand aircraft had relentlessly destroyed the Kwantung Army in Manchuria. For years, that was where the trail ended. Bryne's FBI file was blank from the 1945 repatriation to 1957, when his school records picked up, showing nothing out of the ordinary through 1967 when he turned up at the World Health Organization. Maybe there wasn't anything bizarre enough to merit recording. That was definitely a possibility—but not a certainty, not by a long shot. Not to an agent with Scott Hubbard's investigative skills...

Tuesday, July 14
Zoonotic Laboratory, Guilderland
12:30 P.M.

When he heard voices in the hall outside his office, Bryne was almost relieved. He'd been reviewing with Lawrence the details of the bizarre ergotism episodes, along with the additional pieces of the puzzle from Shmuel Berger's phone call. They were sitting across from each other, and Lawrence was making notes in a logbook.

Bryne was impressed by Drew's commitment, especially in light of the pain he knew his associate was suffering, for his left leg was splayed awkwardly beside his chair to help avoid cramping. Nevertheless, it was Drew who sprang up to answer the knock on the door. A moment after he went into the hall, he announced, "In here, sir."

The inquisitor who'd presided over Bryne's San Diego grilling was early. Hubbard had called again, yesterday, asking to meet with Dr. Bryne to further discuss the San Diego incident and other matters. Suspecting that the "meeting" was going to be another version of the first interrogation, Jack suggested they meet at his lab, if for no other reason than his own convenience. The agent had readily agreed, despite the drive.

Shaking hands, the two men sized each other up once again. Each the same height, both with a strong grip and steady gaze of hard-won self-confidence. Hubbard began by explaining that although he was technically assigned to Washington, he was presently based in Region II—the greater New York area—on special assignment. At that moment, Lawrence caught Bryne's eye and nodded toward the window. Bryne, distracted, looked over his shoulder and saw someone locking a car door. Someone indeed! There was no mistaking Vicky Wade. Twice in as many days?

"When it rains," he muttered, interrupting something Hubbard was saying. *What a damned morning,* Jack fumed. *First the FBI invites itself up, and now...*

Meanwhile, Hubbard calmly continued "... and so while this is basically a routine matter, I can assure you that we consider any help you may be able to give us as most welcome... Er." Hubbard finally noticed Bryne and Lawrence were concentrating on something other than what he was saying. "Am I interrupting? I realize I'm early, but I had hoped we could spend a few minutes..."

At that precise moment, Victoria Wade burst through the door. Her eyes shone as she spotted Bryne, but her gaze turned cold when she saw Hubbard. Running over to Bryne, she looked around and apologized. "Oh, Jack, I'm sorry for the surprise visit. I'm on my way up to the track at Saratoga. There's a rumor going around that some of the horses are getting sick, and..." The rain swept over the roof, making an ominous pinging on the tiles. Acknowledging both Hubbard and Drew Lawrence, she added, "Forgive me, folks, I'm on a tight schedule. Jack, could I talk to you privately? Maybe out in the hall. It's confidential."

"Hold on a moment. Everyone's running late." Jack took control of the situation. "First let me introduce you to Special Agent Hubbard of the FBI."

"Victoria Wade," Hubbard replied blandly, as if they'd never met, "I've seen you on television. *Hot Line.* I feel like I know you."

Wade, clearly deciding to keep the airport meeting between them, shook his hand, looked him in the eye, and said simply, "Nice to know you." She had been wrong about Hubbard, she realized, he could lie, and quite well. She wondered if she should tell Bryne about their meeting.

Bryne paused and looked at Wade. Something was off; she seemed preoccupied.

"Let's all sit down." Jack indicated a good-sized table in one corner of the crowded room. "We may have something in common." He turned to Hubbard. "In my opinion, both Ms. Wade and Mr. Lawrence are vetted. Whatever you have to ask me, you can ask in front of them," he said, knowing that it wouldn't hurt to have witnesses.

Hubbard was far from sure he had anything in common with Bryne. Bryne had a past that could turn you into either Mother Teresa or Jack the Ripper. The agent had had suspicions about the guy even before he knew about Pingfan, even before he realized Bryne made a habit of showing up at trouble spots.

And Bryne wasn't the only one in the room on whom the Bureau had a thick dossier. Drew Lawrence, it turned out, had been an early member of CORE, had toyed with the Black Muslims in the sixties and SNCC in the early seventies, but had allegedly left the organizations when he married, and he was now supposedly

238

an active member of an Albany Baptist church. Still, Hubbard had an early picture of Lawrence sporting a huge Afro, and although the man now looked conventional enough, who knew what his real politics were? No, Hubbard didn't consider Drew Lawrence vetted. And Wade? Hubbard was counting on the fact that anything they discussed stood an excellent chance of ending up on *Hot Line*.

Vicky could see that her presence was making them uncomfortable. She hadn't been expected, clearly wasn't wanted. The thoughts about Jack that Hubbard had put in her mind at the airport still worried her. She was torn between wanting to hear what would be said and wanting to flee the meeting. Finally she chose the latter.

"Look," she told them, "I've got to get up to the racetrack at Saratoga to interview some trainers. It's not a good time. Sorry for the intrusion." She had felt the tension in the office, sensed there was a bigger story brewing, and hoped like all hell that Jack wasn't at the center of it. What she did know was that the FBI had been following Jack or her, or both of them.

"Mr. Hubbard, nice seeing you," she told him as she got up, feeling as if she was betraying Jack by never having mentioned the meeting with Hubbard at the airport. "Drew, good to see you," she smiled, getting out her car keys, winking at Bryne, and remembering she still needed to tell him about the new development. She pulled Jack aside and whispered quickly, "Jack, Dr. Tucker has flipped out. The doctors think it was the stress of the whole thing. But he's had auditory hallucinations. They think it might be a brain tumor. I hope to heaven it wasn't something to do with the horses. I was with him! Talk to you soon," and out she marched into the rain.

The three men watched the door close, then Bryne and Hubbard took seats around the large table on which a badger's skull served as a centerpiece. Lawrence brought them all coffee, then subtly twisted the skull of the badger—*Meles*, the first rabid example of its species in the state—so that its bared teeth faced Hubbard.

"What can you tell me, Dr. Bryne," Hubbard began, "about biological warfare from your days with WHO?"

"Well, Mr. Hubbard, you've only asked half a question." Jack sat back in his chair, wondering just what Hubbard meant.

"You see, Mr. Hubbard," Jack continued, "the important distinction is that there are two *bios*, not one: biological warfare, or BW, and biological terrorism, BT. The perpetrators of either may use biological agents, but the difference in purpose and intended targets varies greatly. Which one are you interested in?"

"Both, I guess," Hubbard said, flinching as he took a sip of the hot coffee.

"Sorry," Drew apologized. "Forgot to tell you that the machine makes the hottest coffee in New York State, but when it cools, it's stronger than what you usually get from these machines."

"It's fine," Hubbard nodded. "Go on, Dr. Bryne."

"Simply put, the tactic of biological warfare is to first win a battle by incapacitating—which is superior to killing—and then to win a war strategically, over time. Incapacitating victims with *Staph* enterotoxin, for example, would cause a week or so of vomiting and diarrhea. Survivors—both soldiers and civilians—can have subtle wide-range effects. Agent Orange, for example."

"Now, Dr. Bryne, what about biological terrorism?" asked Hubbard, taking notes.

"Well," Bryne, who was idly doodling on a pad he'd brought to the table, looked up and continued. "Biological terrorism, on the other hand, wants to make a statement, a political statement, a religious statement. It makes the point by killing people, often killing as many people as possible. BT has a more localized effect, like the sarin attacks in the Tokyo subway on March 20, 1995."

"So," Hubbard asked, "one is for victory, the other just to make a statement?" He eyed Lawrence, who also seemed to know the subject well.

"But biologicals are so strong," contributed Drew, "that a terrorist could take out more than just a 'tactical' target. They can take out a city the size of New York."

"Right," Jack went on. "With BT, use of an agent is selective; it should act immediately and offer no possibility of treatment by vaccines or antibiotics. The BT target is carefully selected, well ahead of time. The act invariably has some sort of symbolic meaning, sometimes obscure, and it has to be unleashed in a symbolic place for greatest effect. Traditionally, a symbolic gathering of people in a symbolically important place."

"For the symbolic destruction of what?" Hubbard asked, wondering if Bryne was basing his remarks on personal experience or, perhaps, future plans.

"Isn't it all only a delusional symbolism of insanity?" Drew asked, watching as Hubbard turned his gaze from Bryne to him.

"Of course. Insanity. The 'true-believer' mentality. To me—to us—a planeload of people is not a symbol. It is simply a planeload of people.

"Yet," added Hubbard rather menacingly, "it's often the most insane who are impossible to stop... and to recognize."

A strained silence fell over the room until Bryne, after sipping his coffee, continued. "Now, from an individual act to state-sponsored terrorism, to BW, that's a big leap taking us in an entirely different direction. Symbolism is not nearly as important to BW as the direction of the wind."

"Meaning?" Hubbard asked.

"Meaning BW uses chemical weapons of mass destruction, and they do exactly what their name implies. Their effectiveness depends on the size of the opposition, the location—urban, rural, tropical, desert, Alpine, et cetera—and the strength of the enemy. Strength meaning the number of troops, their offensive capabilities, and their ability to defend themselves against the germs you plan to use against them."

"I see," Hubbard murmured, thinking of Bryne and all he'd read about Pingfan.

Pouring himself more coffee, Jack went on. "During Desert Storm, for instance, allied troops had all been vaccinated against anthrax. They had tens of thousands of ampoules of atropine on hand in case sarin or some other organophosphate was used. We now know that the Iraqis had anthrax and botulism toxins loaded into artillery shells, and it was a good thing they were never used, since Saddam had Type F, 'bot-tox.' The only antitoxins our troops had been immunized against were Types A, B, and E—utterly worthless against F."

"Really?" Hubbard asked, almost flinching. The first classified reports on the cases of botulism from different parts of the United States had recently arrived in New York. He hadn't even had time to read more than the summary pieces. How could Bryne know about them?

"Now," Bryne continued, "BT, as opposed to BW, is almost like a chess game, assessing the enemy's ability to respond to a specific agent and then using another, totally unanticipated one, like bot F. When each new entity—the more exotic the better—is introduced, the enemy is expected to panic." He stopped to emphasize the psychological impact.

"You see, on the subject of panic," Jack went on, "no one is going to panic much if they hear

243

that a new strain of flu virus has been discovered—after all, they get exposed to influenza every winter. But let the government try and tell the population that something exotically evil, like Ebola, is spreading, and it's a whole new ball game. Given the disease's unfamiliarity, what it can do, and the knowledge that it cannot be controlled or treated, people react as if they were living in the Middle Ages. It's more like a scene from *Mad Max* or *Escape from L.A.*"

"I hear you," Hubbard nodded.

"One thing that is consistent with the history of biological warfare and terrorism," Jack announced, "is that subsequent written records of its use remain largely hidden. The winner takes over not only the enemy but also the historical record. History is what the winner chooses to tell people."

"Could you explain that a little further?"

"Sure," Jack told him. "The losers are dead. What killed them is not necessarily what the historians will write about. And the winners will often purposefully obfuscate their use of the weaponry. Stories are denied. Disinformation is used. For one thing, using BW or BT agents could easily be seen as genocide. For another, they would want to credit their victory to brave soldiers and star generals rather than to a germ. Lastly, they may want to hold onto their secret in the event that it might have to be used again. Historians remain largely oblivious to the real reason a critical battle, even a war, was won."

Hubbard shifted uneasily. "It's not *all* covered up. I went to college at Amherst, and I know for a fact that Lord General Jeffrey Amherst left a smoking gun, not a glorious memoir, a written record that he'd destroyed Chief Pontiac and his tribes in Pennsylvania and Ohio by purposely giving them blankets infected with smallpox."

"Yes," Bryne agreed, "but for every smoking gun, there must be dozens of other instances nobody will ever know about."

"Like Pingfan?" Hubbard took the plunge and watched carefully as Bryne acknowledged the word with a poker face.

At that very moment, Lawrence stood up and reached into his jacket pocket. "Here's the best record of all." He took out a worn book, his father's old World War II pocket Bible. "The first written incident of a mysterious epidemic and warfare occurs in Samuel, Book I, Chapter Four, Verse One. The Israelites were about to do battle with the heavily armed and murderous Philistines in a place known as Ebenezer around 1400 B.C.E."

"Would you call that the first Israeli-Arab War?" Hubbard inquired.

"No," Drew explained. "The Philistines weren't exactly Arabs, but, yes, the Israelites were under attack by peoples who live in what is now known as Palestine."

"Hmmm... interesting," Hubbard mused, still watching Bryne.

"At Ebenezer," Drew went on, "the Israelites lost four thousand men, but not the war. They withdrew and called in reserves from a place called Shiloh. The fresh troops brought with them a secret weapon, the Ark of the Covenant, which became the rallying point for a counterattack."

"Wait! Three thousand years 'til the next Battle of Shiloh," Hubbard interrupted. "And Grant loses thirteen thousand men, the Confederates ten thousand. No biowarfare, just muskets and bayonets. A bloody affair, Shiloh."

Sipping at his coffee, Hubbard listened as Drew recounted how the Philistines, puzzled by the cheering of an army they had just driven off, attacked again, killing an additional forty thousand Israelites and seizing the Ark of the Covenant as a trophy. "That's when the fun began. When they got back to the city of Ashdod, the Philistines were visited by a vengeful God in what might be construed as the first record of biological warfare."

Hubbard sat up. Lawrence's knowledge of the Bible seemed a bit too extensive.

"The Philistines placed the sacred Ark next to an idol of their god, Dagon. The next morning Dagon was found beheaded, with his hands severed. Then people, thousands of them, started dying of what is now translated from the Hebrew characters as *emerods* in their private parts."

"Could they have been buboes of bubonic plague?" Bryne suggested, hearing Lawrence's rendition of the battle for the first time.

"Whatever it was," Drew explained further, "the disease then spread from Ashdod to Gath, then to Ekron and throughout the land of the Philistines for seven months. The Bible recounts that over fifty thousand Philistines were killed before their ruler finally returned the Ark to the Israelites, who, led by Samuel, defeated the weakened enemy near Ebenezer, where it all had begun. If you read Numbers Thirty-one, Verses Nineteen through Twenty-four, it's clear that the Israelites knew about contagion."

"More coffee, Mr. Hubbard?" Bryne asked. Hubbard nodded no, staring at Drew, riveted.

"Hey," Drew spoke up, "I'm almost through, but this whole thing gets even more fascinating. You see, the Philistines tried to appease the Hebrews' God with a gift of ten gold statues—five fashioned to look like mice, the other five gold spheres. When historians tried to piece together what exactly the spheres might have represented, they tended to agree on enlarged inguinal lymph nodes, a hallmark of bubonic plague." He ended his talk. "Like Casey Stengel said, 'Youse can look it up!'" Drew smiled and added, "It wasn't known until the nineteenth century that plague was carried by fleas on rodents, but the gold mice suggest that the Philistines associated the plague with mice in some way."

"Poussin put a rat into his painting *The Plague of Ashdod*," Bryne added. "How could he have known? You'd have to argue that whatever the disease was, either the Hebrews knew of and avoided it—or even knowingly brought it on their enemies. Was the Ark some kind of Trojan Horse? Attributing it to God is a nice way to avoid criticism—as I've said, a typical biowarfare tactic. Disinformation, shifting of blame, pleading innocent, all may have had their origins in the Book of Samuel. Hats off to you, Drew. I never heard that one before!"

Hubbard sat back. "Gentlemen, please go on."

Now Bryne began discussing more recent events: the tortured agony of BW through the ages—Carthaginians hurling baskets of cobras from their ships against the Romans; Tartars catapulting plague victims into Italian garrisons; Germany, England, and the United States covering up atrocities in and after both world wars. He decided not to delve into the Japanese. Hubbard's mention of Pingfan had come as a grossly unpleasant surprise. Was he telling Bryne he knew all about him? Bryne wondered.

Hubbard decided to throw in his two cents' worth, some declassified information. "Speaking of cover-ups, did you know that in the Korean War eagle feathers dipped in pathogenic bacteria were dropped from U.S. planes? And when there was an upsurge of hemorrhagic dengue fever in Cuba in the eighties—Castro claimed it was U.S.-sponsored BW, but nothing came of his charges."

"And now we have hemorrhagic dengue throughout Central and South America," Bryne replied with an ironic smile, "and it's moving relentlessly into the southern U.S. Happenstance, coincidence, or purposeful BW?" he asked Hubbard, who was making notes in a small spiral-bound book but simply shrugged.

Bryne went on, "One theory even suggests that the 1994 bubonic plague outbreak in India may actually have been caused by Pakistani terrorists. My wife could tell you about that. But no one ever got a culture of the bug to test its genealogy, which would have been interesting, if not incriminating. They could have traced it, you know."

"What about the anthrax in California, Dr. Bryne?" Hubbard decided it was time to cut to the chase.

"Needless to say, I've been thinking about it constantly," Jack responded calmly. "It appears to be a BT act. But it doesn't fit the pattern completely—no bragging notes, no threats that I'm aware of. Why Joey St. John was the victim, I've no idea. What is the Bureau thinking, if I may ask?"

Hubbard was silent briefly, then replied, "We think pretty much the same. There are other events about which I can't tell you..."

"Other anthrax cases?"

"Other... incidents... classified." Hubbard was curious to see what kind of reaction he'd get from Bryne, who seemed genuinely concerned. "In any case, Dr. Bryne, I was wondering if we might use you as a resource. I realize this may be a bit out of your field. After all, you're a virologist."

"But Jack used to do this kind of stuff at WHO," Drew broke in.

"I... we know. And by the way, Dr. Bryne, I hear you've developed an interest in ergotism. Why would that be?"

"Where did you hear that, Mr. Hubbard?"

"Oh, just around." Hubbard, for the first time that day, smiled his cryptic smile, for the informant who led him to ProMED had been anonymous.

Having absolutely no idea how much Hubbard knew or from whom he might have heard it, Bryne decided to keep his own counsel. "As a matter of fact, my wife gave a talk recently on the subject and asked me to do a little research for her. I'd be happy to send you what I've got," Bryne offered.

"I see, thanks, I'll be in touch." Again that smile. "This has been very productive, Dr. Bryne, Mr. Lawrence. Now I must go. Got to get back to the city, then to Washington." And he was gone.

Bryne was disturbed for days by the entire encounter. The FBI man was one tough customer, not the kind of guy you'd like to be on the wrong side of. It worried Jack that he already was. Plus the fact that Hubbard had gotten where he had because he was very good at his job, a specialist at knowing things he had no business knowing. First, out of nowhere, Pingfan, then ergot. It was clear Hubbard hadn't come all this way simply to talk about BT. He had been in San Diego, sent there from his office in Washington. Perhaps they really were pursuing the same track, and Hubbard's mission actually had been to assess

Bryne as a resource. Still, Jack knew that Hubbard viewed him as a suspect. Suddenly a sinking feeling hit him. He went to his laptop, got into ProMED, and, halfway down the list, found that all the horrific ergot material was back again—but this time it was attributed to him, the moderator of ProMED. He called to Drew, who came at once and began reading the material, which this time printed out. Bryne told him to delete it after the printouts were complete.

What the hell was going on? It seemed clear—a sophisticated hacker was feeding information about him to the Bureau, as well as infiltrating his whole computer system. It was at that moment that Jack realized he needed help, and not the kind the FBI wanted to give him.

He needed colleagues, thousands of professionals, people to answer the dozens of questions that he could not. The FBI had vast resources. So did ProMED. If he didn't get his act together fast, the FBI would go on wasting its time—and he'd be indicted for heinous acts he hadn't committed while the real sociopath would be free to wreak his twisted biblical havoc on the world...

Hubbard drove away from Bryne's lab elated, letting the images from the meeting sink in: the biblical references combined with the fact that Bryne's parents had been missionaries, along with the Pingfan experiences. It all fit together. Dr. John Bryne could very well be a dangerous nut who saw his mission as Old Testament vengeance. He reached for his cell phone and punched in the number of an organization very few people even in government knew about, the Special Agency for International Radical Terrorism, led by the distinguished biochemist and seasoned investigator Rear Admiral Frank E. Olde. A staff officer answered, but without letting him finish, the FBI man started talking.

"It's Hubbard, get me through to Admiral Olde." He had to wait only a few seconds. "I've just left his lab, Admiral. You were certainly right, a very worthwhile trip." He waited while Admiral Olde spoke.

"Yes, sir, I think there's a biblical tie-in," Hubbard responded, nodding. "I met Drew Lawrence. He was reading me germ warfare from the Book of Samuel. And what a surprise, Vicky Wade just happened to drop in. You were right again, Admiral."

12

Tuesday, July 14
O'Hare Airport, Chicago
1:00 P.M.

Theodore Kameron was enjoying himself thoroughly, frustrating Jack Bryne and helping guide Scott Hubbard with both anonymous tips on the Internet and direct innuendoes on the telephone. Hubbard had actually checked back with him twice, but Teddy had told him he had nothing to add to his original statement. So far,

252

the only person who seemed to be doing anything to stop him was Bryne; and that raised a bit of concern, since he was clearly starting to make accurate inquiries. Accurate, but far too late.

By now, Hubbard was probably writing up his next incriminating report on Bryne, waiting for a "smoking gun." Oh, yes, the ergotism ploy had definitely been on the right track. Well, soon there might be a little something more for Bryne to worry about. The very thought made Teddy hungry—hungry and horny.

Since his Mission was not receiving the media attention he fervently desired, he began a plan to generate some. ProMED was one tiny thing, but the networks and the newspapers were something else. His frustration was intense, and he hated to wait.

Walking to the airport newsstand, he bought five daily papers from cities scattered across the country, and *USA Today*. He found a seat in the waiting room, sat back, and began turning the pages. In front of him, a small quarter-fed TV droned on, morning weather reports alternating with the upcoming farm report. He ignored the weather, but fed money into the machine and began to read the papers.

He was not disappointed by *USA Today*. There was the long-awaited feature on the growing anthrax scare in Southern California. A feeling of divinity swept over him, and for the moment he was at peace, God's will be done. A sidebar to the article described anthrax symptoms in humans and animals. An undisclosed number of cases in zoo animals were reported, but more than three dozen adults and children had been hospitalized "as a precaution," with more to come—because the disease had a highly variable incubation period due to the spores. More cases could occur. The San Diego Zoo had been closed, and remained so.

The piece featured an exclusive profile of noted physician Dr. "Mac" MacDonald, who had been involved with the incident, warning readers to be aware of anthrax's earliest symptoms—the skin lesions, which he described as black boils that enlarge, burrow deeper into the flesh, and drain foul-smelling pus. The initial lesions would then erupt like volcanoes, spewing a highly contagious liquid.

The more unusual pulmonary form, mediastinitis, which had killed an unnamed six-year-old boy, was briefly recounted. The parents and the pediatrician refused all interviews. "Exactly what the doctor ordered," Teddy thought, "and right on time, God's will be done!"

He scanned the other papers, disappointed that news about the Kentucky horse deaths seemed scarce. He opened his laptop and did his routine quick sweep of the medical sites: WONDER, Physician-on-Line, MedScape, Outbreak, BioSpace Home Page, AgNet.

Once again the only continuing references to the deaths of the horses were in the FDA Veterinarian Alerts and on ProMED. He was pleased that at least someone—even if it was still only Jack Bryne—was following the story.

Kameron looked at his watch. Time for

the daily corn prices press release from Iowa State. And there it was on AgNet, the Speculator's Newsletter, an Internet advisory used by grain investors. He read it with delight.

July—Corn Prices Rise Sharply as Crop Failures Spread
Year's Iowa Corn Crop
HIGH IN MYCOTOXINS
Iowa State University Corn Quality Survey
Corn Surveys Show Kernel Quality Worse Than Expected
Contacts: Extension Veterinary Medicine (515) 555-8790

Ames, Iowa—Hot, dry conditions this year during the growing season raised questions about the quality and feeding value of harvested corn. The quality of this year's corn across wide regions of Kansas, Iowa, Nebraska, and Oklahoma is worse than expected.

Teddy scanned the release hurriedly, glad he could go back and read it in detail later. The point was that two separate surveys of corn taken from the field—one analyzed for lysine content, the other for ear rot and the associated fungal contaminants—had both reported higher than recommended mycotoxic levels, and that vomitoxin had also been found in the samples. Both studies also indicated that the North Central District had extensive contamination with aflatoxin B_1... Kameron stopped reading for a moment, saved the report to the hard drive, and continued.

It was no surprise to Teddy that aflatoxin

255

was the most frequently detected mycotoxin and that vomitoxin was also present. He knew this, counted on it. What Teddy wanted was information on Aspergillus. Scrolling down to the Iowa State alert, he found it.

ISU officials cautioned that the stress of drought and unseasonably high environmental temperatures this summer made much of the Midwest susceptible to Aspergillus mold invasion. Optimum environment, they stated, for aflatoxin production is 77–90 degrees Fahrenheit and relative humidity above 80 percent. Overall grain moisture between 15 percent and 25 percent is required for mold growth. Stored corn can produce aflatoxins if not dried properly or maintained at 14 percent or less moisture. Even if only small areas of corn contain 15% or more moisture, pockets of aflatoxin accumulate.

Water is a metabolite product of mold growth and the infected kernels can supply moisture to adjacent kernels, causing the process to snowball. Commercial mold inhibitors can prevent further mold growth and aflatoxin, but they cannot destroy aflatoxin already present in the corn.

When contamination is suspected, the feed and especially the corn should be promptly examined. If the corn or feed tests positive for Aspergillus mold growth on black-light testing, further tests for aflatoxin should be completed. Approximately 50 percent of the samples tested at the University of Illinois College of Veterinary Medicine Toxicology Laboratory contained 20 parts per billion (ppb) of aflatoxin. If 20 ppb or above is detected in corn, it cannot enter interstate commerce.

Teddy downloaded addresses and telephone numbers. Praise be to the Master, they told him everything he needed to know. And there was more:

One aflatoxin-containing kernel or fragment in 3200 kernels (2.2 lbs) can result in an aflatoxin level greater than 20 ppb. Feed containing 20 ppb aflatoxin can reduce feed efficiency and should not be fed to nursery-age pigs.

Running aflatoxin-contaminated corn over a sieve or screen can remove up to 50 percent of the aflatoxin. **The screening should not be fed to any livestock, as they will be very high in aflatoxin.** As a last resort, corn can be ammoniated to destroy the aflatoxin. This is a dangerous procedure, and detailed instructions should be obtained from your agricultural extension advisor before being attempted. Small batches can be ammoniated; the ammoniated corn turns brown and can then be used as animal feed.

Suddenly whatever frustration he'd been feeling vanished, for everything was perfect. The Voice had spoken, and all was clear. Jack Bryne and his infantile, heretical investigation would never come close to him. Teddy's Mission had never seemed more joyous, more certain than now, and to celebrate, he made his way to the nearest airport cocktail lounge, where he indulged himself by ordering Rocky Mountain oysters and an order of french fries plus a stinger, which seemed wonderfully appropriate to his Divine Endeavors.

*　　*　　*

```
Guilderland, NY
Moderator is repeating a request for
assistance from African and Middle
Eastern colleagues for recent sight-
ings or reports of locust swarms and
how they may have affected local pop-
ulations.
Please send any information to the
Moderator at ProMED.
        Jack Bryne, Moderator, ProMED
```

Bryne felt uncomfortable writing the brief message, knowing his responsibility was to be ProMED's moderator, not to use it as a forum for his own concerns. On second thought, ProMED had elicited fifteen responses of anthrax when he'd put Joey's case on line. All had been too late, but all had been correct. This was worth it.

He was adding "anthrax boils" to his plagues list when the phone rang. It was Drew at the Albany Public Library.

"Hey, Drew, find anything?"

"I've just scratched the surface, you should pardon the expression! That creepy report on ergotism really paid off. I did a Boolean search and crossed 'itch' with 'death.' That really limited the results. Only those reports that mentioned both words were retrieved."

258

"Fantastic, what did you find?"

"I found a considerably more 'respectable' version of that New Canaan case when the ergotism stuff appeared. It's a newspaper squib, short. Want me to read it?

"Sure, go ahead!"

March 5
New Canaan, CT. Special to the Stamford Advance.
A twenty-seven-year-old man died at Stamford Hospital of what doctors are calling ergot poisoning. The man's name has not been released by hospital authorities. According to a hospital spokesman, the man suffered a fatal intestinal infarction when the blood supply to his intestine was cut off by the drug ergotamine.

Ergotamine is used in certain migraine prescription medicines and to treat complications of pregnancy. Traces of the drug were found in the man's blood after doctors suspected foul play. Local authorities are interviewing family and friends in an attempt to ascertain the source of the drug. One official speculated that he may have been given the medicine by a well-meaning person who used it for migraine attack, and may have taken too many pills accidentally. The official also mentioned that the man was a smoker, which would have greatly potentiated the drug's effect. The man's distraught fiancée told reporters he had been in excellent health but complained of generalized itching shortly before he succumbed.

Bryne digested what Drew had read him. Was that it? Was ergotism the "lice" in the third plague? It jibed with what the boy Shmuel had said. Lawrence had not found reports of either the Maine or Minnesota cases, but how many doctors would even bother to test for a disease that had purportedly died out centuries ago? Whoever had sent ProMED the material that vanished knew his business, and a ghastly business it was.

"Thanks, Drew," Jack told him, then asked, "Just on a flier, could you do another search for 'ergot' and 'death'? You may not get anything, but it's worth a try."

"Sure thing," Drew replied. "See you after lunch."

Bryne went back to his monitor. He reviewed the ProMED archives backward, to April and May, and there it was: The bee swarm in San Antonio had first appeared on ProMED in June, but at the time it was an isolated incident. Like the frogs. Like Joey's anthrax.

Jack knew he was alone. He had to think up a way of asking for help without letting his professional audience, one of whom was very possibly the perpetrator, know that he was looking for a killer—or killers. Time was racing toward what he was sure would be the next cataclysm. He was glad he'd sent that request about the locusts. ProMED was the only chance he had. He knew he had to call Hubbard and knew he should not wait.

*   *   *

Tuesday, July 14
O'Hare Airport, Chicago
2:00 P.M.

Kameron read Bryne's request about the locusts as he sat in the padded fiberglass chairs of O'Hare waiting for the flight to Washington. He sat up abruptly as he realized Bryne was not only onto his game, he now anticipated him. Well, if this were to be a game of cat-and-mouse, Jack Bryne was becoming an admittedly worthy antagonist. And their strange connection, a sort of rivalry of the damned, Teddy remembered once more, had been established decades ago, in the sixties, on a sweltering night in a hovel of a bar in Haiti.

The young Englishman Bryne and the young American Kameron had been downing too many warm Prestige beers, chewing raw sugar cane, and ordering rum chasers—or rather, Jack Bryne had. Teddy had held back, wanting to be clear about what he might learn, but Bryne was so far gone, Teddy doubted he could remember their conversation the next day, much less thirty years later.

At the time, the two young men were working as researchers in infectious diseases, where, as Bryne put it, "In the one week I've been here, I've seen enough suffering and misery to last me a lifetime."

That afternoon, the two had gone with a professor to scrape up the toxin-ridden roadkill that polluted the Haitian countryside. Although

261

Teddy made a point of keeping to himself, he'd consented when Bryne suggested that a drink or three was most certainly in order after so gruesome a task. A farewell drink, for Teddy's tour was over, and he was leaving the next day.

Kameron made sure not to show how sorry he was that he was leaving. He loved the work. Disease and toxins truly excited him, and Haiti was the epicenter of both. He felt a frustrating melancholy, like a vacationer who has to return home before he wants to. A tremendous melancholy indeed.

Teddy knew he had whetted the Englishman's curiosity. Not so much because of his brilliance at toxicology, his incredible ability to memorize, or his tall blond handsomeness—anomalous in one so shy—but because of his hands. He had seen Bryne stare at the way his fingers always circled in on themselves, palms hidden, and at his strange handshake, which rapidly touched only fingertips, not palms.

"I see you've noticed my hands," Teddy began when Bryne was well into his cups. "Would you like to know how it happened?" Bryne nodded. "I can see you would. Okay, here goes. I was burned. I was only a child." He displayed a line of scars that went completely around the perimeter of his palm, reaching up to the underside of each finger. It was as if his palm prints had been outlined in red ink, but he opened them proudly to show how well the skin grafts had taken.

"But how—?" Bryne had blurted out.

"Oh, nothing so unusual," Teddy replied.

"My mother had been baking, and the oven door was open. I happened to run into the kitchen and tripped."

As he continued, he slowly opened and closed, opened and closed his palms. "See, the oven was scalding hot, I tried to catch myself. I put my hands out..." He paused, his hands slapped the table, the candle flickered. "Unfortunately, as you can see, the skin stuck to the metal. The palms seared onto the door, and my mother had to take a spatula to pry my hands free."

For the first time, Teddy completely unfolded his long, tapering fingers as he told the Englishman, "I've completely forgiven her, of course... I mean, she only meant to help, and anyway, she passed away a few years ago, so what's not to forgive? And after all, the doctors did a fabulous grafting job. Almost no loss of mobility. Of course, the skin they used for the grafts came from my legs so it had hair follicles, but there's not too much hair, and I can shave it."

Bryne said nothing, shocked into silence—until Teddy suggested, "And now, my friend, return the favor and tell me how you got that awful scar on your arm."

"I never tell it, try not to think of it," Bryne had said, then, "Maybe I'll tell it to you tonight, and never tell it again." And he'd gone on at length about his childhood in the prison camp, then fell silent before downing another drink.

Ah, my comrade, Kameron had thought at

the time, *we have so much in common; we are both maimed—within and without. Perhaps fate brought us together in this fabulous hellhole. Perhaps fate will bring us together another day.*

Kameron almost laughed at the synchronicity, for it had all come to pass. If it was infernal chess they were playing, the next move was Teddy's—and it was going to be good.

Now, as he boarded the plane that would take him from Chicago to the site of his next mission, he reflected on his own wondrous work. Kameron recalled Billy Pusser's rally in Virginia in June, right after he'd resurfaced. He'd attended Pusser's lectures in the old days. After he'd met the man, they'd done fundraising business together. Teddy, like many top-grade scientists, was forced to lose months each year hunting for grant money. It was an art form, and in some ways he loved it. Now he had another mission. Once the plane was at cruising altitude, he turned on his laptop, punched in his password, "LMPG," and read his own history:

1987

Since being asked to resign from the CDC before he was vested, Theodore Kameron was always in need of grant support, like any other independent researcher. Yet he was lucky, for he was good at it and knew where to look. The Bible Belt schools and church councils, that's where he truly shone. To what could this strange affinity be attributed? Perhaps his fervor, which convinced most of them to agree to his requests and promises.

*And there was an energy, a power, and a spirit
in his eyes when he addressed them. They could see
it clearly, mistaking it for faith.*

*Kameron had increased his research funds
steadily for years simply by polishing his ability to
persuade trust advisors, boards of governors, grant
committees, and cadres of lawyers how important
it was to fund his cancer research. Now that he was
so close to developing "the magic bullet," Pusser, a
lawyer with top-level religious connections, had
actually set up a meeting for Teddy with the
Christian Council—a very well-endowed nationwide
organization, comprised of everyone important to
the fundamentalist cause, among them the powerful
televangelist Cato Phipps; the most conservative
Catholic bishop in Louisiana, one Monsignor
LaPierre, who was said to be far right of the Pope;
and a California real estate developer with national political clout, Joseph St. John.*

The interview took place in a lovely mansion
in Virginia, home to an industrialist who
donated millions to right-wing Christian
causes. Pusser, the lawyer, was there somewhat
as mediator when Teddy began explaining
clearly, easily, what he was sure would be a
cure for certain cancers.

"Killing cancer cells selectively, protecting
the surrounding normal cells, that's the trick,"
he began his presentation. "I have always believed
fungal toxins hold the ultimate answer; after all,
antibiotics are all derived from fungi. Cyclosporin,
the same." When he showed how his systematic
inventory of fungal mycotoxins could be screened,

distilled, and tested on cancer cell lines, they had been impressed. When he told the twenty-five or so prominent Christians in the room that the will of God had led him to his discoveries, his audience was doubly impressed.

"And, gentlemen," he concluded, "I am only a few steps away from my goal of saving countless lives." Kameron's cure, he thought to himself, the key to untold riches.

"Now let me understand you, Dr. Kameron." The speaker was the California developer, Joseph St. John, "It kills cells—bad cells, only the evil cells, is that it?"

Kameron had nodded.

"And the good cells are saved?" Again a nod.

"But what about fetal cells?" the Louisiana bishop, LaPierre, demanded. "Will your drug kill the unborn, the growing cells, as if they might be cancer?"

"Well, Bishop." Teddy was suddenly uneasy and tried to hedge. "Like many drugs we use today, unfortunately it could not be used during pregnancy—"

"Because it would kill or damage the fetus," the Bishop broke in.

"Well," Teddy acknowledged, "it would."

"Could it then," Pusser queried him, "be used as an abortion pill, a morning-after pill, like the experimental drug in France known as RU486?"

"It could be used for that purpose, but—" He could see the horror in their eyes even before Pusser cut him off in midsentence. "Thank you, Ted, we'll be sure to get back to you ASAP."

They'd get back to him, sure they would. Of course they would. They never did. Six months later, he not only was rejected or lost funding for grants, but he was also sued and lost a patent on another drug he had developed. In one lawsuit, he was threatened with breach of contract. If it hadn't been for the inheritance stashed in the Caymans, he would have been bankrupt. Kameron couldn't believe it. All of a sudden, the Christian organizations didn't want to know the man who previously had been their pet, their darling, their scientific genius.

His wife's departure made him even more aware that his contacts had died with his contracts. Obviously, the Christian Council, in their infinite wisdom, had made him an anathema, a man who could not be trusted. Oh, he still lectured occasionally. He had come from old money, but every bit helped. He spoke to nonreligious scientific groups like the one in Aspen, where he'd first heard The Voice ordering him to take his vengeance...

And when The Voice told Theodore Kameron to attend one of Billy Pusser's conferences in Virginia, he was bemused, but of course he obeyed. To avoid recognition, he dyed his hair and grew a Van Dyke beard and wore glasses. As he drove to the rally, he remembered how lawyers like Pusser and the rest of the fundamentalists would roll their eyes when Teddy used to explain the financial benefits of a tax-deductible gift—how it conferred a ground-floor partnership arrangement when the technology was transferred to the commercial sector.

Teddy had visited money-manager conferences like Pusser's often enough to recognize the boilerplate in all the recycled speeches that filled up these lectures. Pusser paid a speechwriter for his, and it was amusing for most, even for Teddy. At least the first time.

Pusser, a big, beefy man with graying red hair and a florid complexion, had mounted the stage right after lunch. He nodded at the assembled heads of an assortment of churches, corporate general counsels, and senior partners of many of America's most prestigious law firms. Raising his hands for silence, Pusser composed himself as light applause spread across the room, then grew: Pusser had made many of these people millionaires. At last, Pusser again held up his hand to stop the clapping.

He took out a handkerchief and wiped his broad forehead, then boomed to the audience, "Thank you... thank you!" They applauded again.

He rang the side of his wine goblet with a butter knife.

"Ladies and gentlemen," Pusser began when the audience quieted, "now wasn't that a wonderful buffet?" The applause started yet again. Pusser stopped them and said, "It gives me concern to be getting such an enthusiastic greeting from a group that has been described as a 'plague of hungry locusts.'" Silence fell over the assembled.

Was he insulting them? Kameron, sitting at the back of the room, seemed to be the only person present who knew what Pusser was leading up to.

"Now don't shoot the messenger, folks," Pusser continued. "I'm not the one who called you locusts. And it wasn't the liberal press, and it wasn't the President, Heaven help him. I'll tell you who it was. But before I do, I want to warn you all: we must change that 'locust' impression. We must bring a more Christian image to the legal profession."

Pusser leaned back, confident that the remark had bonded him to the right segment of listeners. After all, he paid his speech-writer handsomely.

"Locusts. Hungry locusts," Pusser continued. "I, for one, am deeply embarrassed by the terminology. As an attorney who takes his faith and his work quite seriously, that slur, ladies and gentlemen, even from an opponent, would cut me to the heart," and he thumped his chest with his fist for emphasis.

"But the man who made that remark was no opponent, no atheist..." He took a breath. "Not a reporter." He paused again. "He was our brother...

"It was the Chief Justice of the Supreme Court, the late Warren Burger, who called lawyers 'a hungry horde of locusts about to devour the land.'"

Pusser gave the audience a moment to let his revelation sink in before repeating, "It was Chief Justice Burger. The one man who has done more than most to keep God away from our children and out of our communities than anyone else I can think of. And if Warren Burger, a colleague of the man who wants to tell us when to pray, the man who keeps the word of the Bible from the Lambs of God, well, if that man wants to call me a *locust*... why, then, I am proud to be an insect." Pusser looked around, watching the applause start as it always did, loving it.

Kameron had clapped politely with the rest.

He had heard the Burger story before.

But this time it was different.

Now it mesmerized him.

Now he knew why The Voice had ordered him to come here.

Locusts. Locusts. He looked around the audience. He saw them, the locusts, the lawyers. He felt dizzy. He felt as if he had to get away. To flee.

Locusts. Suddenly he felt the power of the Lord.

And once again The Voice inside Teddy's head spoke.

And once again, he knew what to do.

These lawyers were the voracious grasshoppers. These were the people the eighth plague must take.

These were the true locusts, cannibals who would feed on themselves.

For months, before this day, the locust question had worried him. He was not an entomologist, but he knew about *Arthropoda*.

270

Knew their toxins: hornets, fire ants, scorpions, spiders, centipedes. Their strengths. But locusts? How? He would wait, wait for inspiration. He had repeated obsessively, "*Locusts most grievous, went over the land. In all the coasts of Egypt.*"

He had remembered and wondered, and then The Voice had taken him to the answer.

He had patted his stomach and reached out for a buttered roll. Time to feed his favorite pet, the one waiting inside him, for the last time.

Late that night, as Kameron thumbed through the conference pamphlet with Pusser's face on the inside page and a brief description of Pusser's famous talk, everything was finally revealed to him. Kameron had taken a break from reading his journals, thinking again about Bryne and feeling the old thrill of the chase return. Still, he had gone to such trouble to prepare this coming plague, he simply could not let Bryne outwit him. Besides, there was still the seventh plague, or as Teddy preferred to call it, "The July Surprise." Merely thinking about it made him feel aroused and almost divine.

Tuesday, July 21
Brooklyn, New York
7:00 A.M.

Shmuel Berger climbed the gentle hills of Borough Park through a warm, soft rain. It carried the familiar creosote and harbor water smells, the odors of ancient piers and ancient cargoes. Shmuel turned his collar up nice and snug and pulled his fedora tighter. It was new and expensive, but it had "room to grow." He kept his head down, concentrating on the cracks, concentrating on keeping the rain off his glasses.

As always, when he reached the last storefront, he glanced left, almost due north up the cross-streets, and squinted at the nearby majesty of the Manhattan skyline. Its spires shot into the gap between the decrepit shops and even in the grayness filled the entire sky with sparkling possibility. For the thirty-nine steps across the street, the world was not Brooklyn; for thirty-nine steps, there were shining towers of opportunity, and he knew that now, for the first time as he walked this way, he was part of it.

Across the far sidewalk, into the shadow of the next block of stores, and only three more blocks to Or Yehuda, his yeshiva for nearly ten years. Keeping his head down, he concentrated on what was coming.

Suddenly the rain picked up. This time Shmuel lifted his head to look up at the City. He had vowed he would get there for as long as he could remember, and he had. He had gotten out. As far out as you can get at seventeen, but out. He had been a dedicated student at Or Yehuda, and the Torah was a passion. Yet every day when he crossed these streets, he longed for the mirage of Manhattan.

Then, two years ago, a miracle: he had

been accepted at Stuyvesant High School in Manhattan, the city's premier school for gifted students. He begged to be transferred, but his parents were lukewarm; Shaul and Rivka Berger, like all the Orthodox Jews of Borough Park, believed the material world snared far too many from their fold. They could see their boy now, God forbid, attempting to balance the secular and the sacred.

Praying in the local *shul*, they had always taken great pride in their son's accomplishments; his brilliance to them was the light shining in from the *ner tamid*, the eternal lamp, the light that allowed them to let him explore— as surely as the reflections of Manhattan had drawn young Shmuel's eyes from Brooklyn, and from the Torah.

For Shmuel, his neighborhood was either an enclave of the devout or a religious ghetto. At seventeen, he was still not sure which. His father was a *sopher*, a religious scribe, and expectations had always been high that Shmuel would one day assume that honored craft. The boy felt certain that one of his four brothers could fulfill the tradition more ably. He wanted Stuyvesant. His family wanted a student of the Torah. He told them with great sincerity that his love of the Torah would never diminish, no matter where he went to school.

Somehow, in the end, they relented.

Stuyvesant was heaven. Science, computer access, an entire universe of challenge. In two years he had learned much, and the time had moved so quickly. He'd thought it impossible that his former world would impinge upon his present life, yet now... destiny. Destiny had brought him to science, to prediction, to biology.

The book. He had seen his destiny in a book, but not the Torah. It was called *Microbe Hunters,* and it had sent him on the arcane quests required of a believer in the faith of science. And it told him of that same destiny that today brought him back to his old friend and teacher, his rabbi.

Splashing across the wide, wet puddles deep in the worn sandstone steps, Shmuel felt his feet fit the familiar depressions. He tipped his head back and let the water cascade over the brim of his hat and down his black topcoat.

As he reached the yeshiva door, Shmuel kissed his first two fingertips, then with them stroked the intricately carved olivewood *mezuzah* mounted on the doorjamb.

This simple act, hand to lips, hand to the tiny box high beside the massive doors, was an act of faith in his father and of the laws of his forefathers. The Jewish law—the *halacha*—mandates that every door must have such a magnificent little box, inside which was a tiny parchment, inscribed by his father, and of which his father was very proud.

Proud of the blood of Abraham, which these small gatepost talismen symbolize. For it was the blood of the lamb that was smeared on the doors of the Hebrew people in Egypt.

Fresh blood, painted on the doors in order that the Angel of Death would spare the people of Moses, the Chosen.

Standing in the rain, suddenly reticent to enter, Shmuel felt foolish. Maybe he should leave. Yesterday this visit had seemed a fine idea, but today?

He'd called the *rebbitsin*, Rav Solomon's wife, to see if he could meet with her husband, who was *Rosh Yeshiva*, the school's headmaster. He asked if he might come the next day, maybe after *shacharis*, morning prayers. The *rebbitsin* remembered him fondly and said her husband would be delighted to see such a favorite former student, even after such a long time...

She'd let the remark hang, signaling Shmuel that he should apologize for having been away, but he couldn't, and she had also relented, only cautioning him not to be late.

Now, looking through the glass in the heavy door, he saw Rav Solomon watching him from his office beside the sanctuary. Of course, Shmuel was right on time, and even through the rain-studded glass, he could see the old man's eyes twinkling. He pushed his way inside, hung up his coat, and looked sheepishly at the Rav.

"Come in, come in, Shmuely," the Rav beckoned. "And close the door behind you. We've much to catch up on. I hope we can do some learning together. It's been a long time."

Relief swept over Shmuel. Those dancing eyes, the immense and beautiful beard, the smile from heaven. He could tell the Rav was not angry by the warmth of his greeting, and he was glad to be back. Telling himself he shouldn't worry, Shmuel waited, but not long. The Rav got right to work, as usual.

"The *rebbetsin* tells me you have questions about the Torah you need to discuss."

"Yes," Shmuel responded. "But I'm not sure where to begin."

"Not sure where to begin?" Rav Solomon laughed. "You were never at a loss for words when you were a student here."

Was there a rebuke implicit in that comment? Shmuel knew that each of the Rav's words was carefully weighed, that he rarely if ever indulged in idle conversation, and that he was scrupulous in avoiding *loshon ha'rah*, gossip, because according to the Kabbalah, foundation of Jewish mysticism, to speak ill of another puts a blemish on one's soul.

Make it short and simple, Shmuel decided. "Rav Solomon, I need to have a better understanding of the plagues."

"The plagues..." The old man's eyes focused above the boy's head, seeing nothing but images from centuries past, images of suffering, images of deliverance. "A most serious business." He tightly closed his eyes as he uttered the words, going deep within himself, remaining almost motionless. Shmuel wondered if he were breathing.

Abruptly, the Rav returned to this world again. "But what about these plagues do you want to know? You were always excellent with the *Rashi* and the *Rambam*. The meanings have been well explained in the texts."

"But Rav Solomon, I need to get a better sense of how Hashem manifests Himself in these plagues."

The Rav looked at his former pupil. And waited. And wondered. "Blood is blood, Shmuely. Frogs are frogs. Locusts are locusts. What sort of deeper meaning are you looking for? What is troubling you?"

Shmuel took a deep breath. "Rabbi, please be patient with me. I have a puzzle I'm working on. A clear understanding of the plagues is important to me."

"A puzzle? After two years you come back to the yeshiva because of a puzzle?"

"Oh, no, Rav Solomon. Please, this is not a child's puzzle, but a scientist's puzzle. A puzzle that is putting many, many lives at stake."

Rav Solomon's expression softened when he saw how upset the boy had been by his disapproval. "To be a child, Shmuely, sometimes is not that bad. Maybe you should start at the beginning and tell me what this puzzle is all about."

Shmuel then began methodically describing the ProMED posting, and almost magically the story seemed to unfold against the quiet assurances of his teacher and the warm, dark study with the rain pitter-pattering against the windows.

Yes, it was destiny, Shmuel felt as he talked, somehow bringing the *shtetl* to cyberspace as he watched the smile of understanding etch itself slowly across the old man's face.

13

Friday, August 7
New York City
9:00 A.M.

Teddy scrolled to the appropriate file, the one where all the Plagues would be recounted in complete and vivid detail for all posterity. Now to record the Eighth Plague:

Billy Pusser's "locust" speech had inspired Theodore Kameron, for he now knew how useful his "intimate companion" would be. The locusts would feed, and, in turn, feed upon their brethren.

They would eat far too much. Far too many.

He was careful with the diet, careful to prepare. To help his companion, to sustain it deep within himself.

Good food was important for a strong body. Kameron ate lavishly but carefully, and he saw that all his minions did also. This one was so much more than a mere minion. Although the creature was technically hermaphroditic, Teddy treated it from the first moment as "She" and "She" alone. She was his pride and joy. Although he had never seen her, he knew she was healthy and in the prime of life.

He had picked his companion up in a market a few kilometers outside Port-au-Prince five months before, during a visit to the Caribbean. There were many to choose from, all deserving affection, but with this one—it had been love at first sight. And for only a few American dollars, the creature was a steal! He immediately threw away the pork loin that had been her home, carefully removing his new glistening *amour*, later washing her down with a bottle of warm Prestige—decades after his night with Bryne, it was still the only beer available in the Haitian marketplace.

When he reentered the U.S. on one of his many false passports, the Customs people could never suspect what he had hidden in his gut. Over a short time, she had grown into a magnificent creature, possibly eighteen feet long. The tapeworm, like Dr. Kameron, was an omnivore, enjoying fats, carbohydrates, and protein meals, and her host was giving her the best.

Now it was time to measure the outcome of his investment. He scratched out a rough equation:

150 days x 500 eggs = 75,000 total

Even allowing for ten percent wastage of progeny, she had produced nearly seventy thousand viable offspring. If, in the ideal situation, the seventy thousand were to be evenly distributed among two thousand people, each person would ingest thirty-five infective units. Often only one larva would be needed. Ten would be more than ample. Twenty would be overkill. Thirty-five would be beyond the wildest nightmare of any parasitologist. Kameron wanted more.

The new tapeworm segments appeared every

day, writhing below him in the toilet bowl. He used a stainless steel strainer and rinsed the segments—they looked like animated pieces of warm macaroni—free of fecal contaminants, then put them in the empty baby food jars with screw-top lids. Eventually, the segment's proglottoid wrapping simply dissolved in the saline solution, releasing some five hundred invisible eggs—each egg ten times as large as a white blood cell—to drift to the bottom of the jar.

The eggs were patient, awaiting liberation. For these eggs the call to generation is ingestion. The tough, resilient coating on their surface must soften in order that they shed their intricate shells, and to soften they need a bath in hydrochloric stomach acid.

The Promised Land for these eggs would be not a pig's gut, as nature intended, but a human stomach, alien yet warm and comforting. Rapidly, the larvae would encyst as they never would inside a pig. Then they would move, penetrate the mucosa of the small bowel, and drift into the blood stream. Feeding on local nutrients, drawing in nourishment through a dynamic, osmotic cell membrane, they would grow in a week to the size of a grain of sand.

Once they could swim in the extracellular fluids, looking for fertile soft tissue, they would expand, move outward—to places like the anterior chamber of a person's eye, protected by the globe of the eyeball from destructive white blood cells. Often, too, they swam into the dark, moist spinal fluid of the ventricles deep within the brain—or further on, settling gently into the soft convolutions of the cerebral cortex itself.

They were creatures of chance, and, being opportunistic, would settle for less favorable climes like the skin, the right chambers of the heart, the dense and spongy lung tissue, and frequently the unlit, sequestered places in the abdominal cavity.

Of course, the body would try to defend itself, sending forays of lymphocytes to attack the enemy, but soon the growing cyst would trick the body into perceiving it harmless, and thus be ignored by the various components of the immune system.

Unchecked, each cyst would grow steadily, relentlessly. Small at first, then ever larger, from the size of a pea to a grape to a plum to a peach then to an over-ripe orange—ultimately to the size, configuration, and appearance of a hydroponic albino tomato, which they often resembled when a pathologist would excise one from a cadaver.

Teddy's beloved creature was now a fully mature adult, judging by her daily egg production. He had cared for his *amour* splendidly, but she was still dangerous. She could turn, as women or men often do when they reach adulthood.

He picked up a glass of the fine Merlot he had opened. Was it time to say goodbye? He eyed the medication. Should he take the pill now? The miraculous drug would almost instantly start to dissolve his worm's sturdy head—the scolex, killing the mother, killing the lover, a female and male living as one, but not killing him.

Teddy turned the pill over in his hand. Only a bit of nausea, probably some diarrhea. He was dining on quail that evening. No, he would take the pill tomorrow after he collected another three hundred eggs she would exude.

And so the pork tapeworm, *Taenia solium,* would die, as unaware of her death as she had been of her life, sacrificed to the greatest cause of all...

The timing was perfect. Teddy was prepared to take the next step. The last week in August, the lawyers always gathered together at the stately Land's End resort—hidden in what remains of an immense hardwood forest — now sliced up into golf courses, riding trails, Interstate Highways, and strip mines — that once spread for hundreds of miles across West Virginia, Tennessee, and Kentucky, and began in the Blue Ridge Mountains of Virginia.

Teddy found it almost pleasant to drive up from Lynchburg, the home of *Chap Stick* and Jerry Falwell. The views were magnificent. Years ago, people made this trip by railroad and horse-drawn carriage. There were only two reasons people gravitated to Land's End. They came for their health and the golf.

With its manicured grounds and peerless food, Land's End had always been a favorite site for professional gatherings of the well-heeled, golfers, dentists, surgeons, and lawyers.

At present, specialized attorneys were meeting to discuss their successes in transferring funds to tax-exempt institutions. For them, their work culminated on the last business day before August 15. On that day, the automatic extension the IRS allows every taxpayer officially expires. Since charitable donations were governed by the limit set by law on the size of the deduction being granted, trusts, wealthy individuals, and investors inevitably waited until the last minute to write the largest possible check to their favorite charity.

Not surprisingly, pledges to the more fundamentalist churches could be significant, and often the lawyers involved in these transfers were rewarded by a percentage of the entire deduction. As summer arrived, there was much celebration among the trust lawyers who represented the many fund-raising organizations that virtually rule the economies of certain southern states. Along with foundation and investment attorneys, these trust lawyers always chose Land's End. For the golf. And the food. They loved to eat more than anything.

This group, primarily men, helped transfer an estimated 6.8 billion dollars a year into the coffers of a thousand little churches and synagogues. Little churches and synagogues with beautiful little real estate holdings and investment portfolios. In his old days with Pusser, Kameron had known a lot about this group, including the fact that since they would give and attend speeches, the entire weekend would be a deduction, a research deduction. They were lawyers, after all.

Laden with his precious cargo and in proper uniform, Teddy easily managed to mix with the florists and the food staff. He watched the lawyers promenade from their lunch tables beside the curved windows of the sunny Colonnade Room and enter the buffet line again and again.

While they were away from their tables, Teddy—eagerly accepted as an extra hand—cleared their dishes and arranged fresh silverware. The food was extraordinary. He was one of the staff who handled trays of smoked trout, wild pheasant, fresh asparagus, mountains of roasted quail; and at each diner's place the most beautiful flowers.

Exactly as flowers at lunch were given a last, freshening spray before the guests came in, so were the dinner flowers misted. Teddy was dutiful in spraying the lilies and primroses, baby's tears and staghorn ferns. Some of the water, of course, misted across the place settings and flower arrangements and onto the silverware, the bread plates, the butter knives, across the lips of the water glasses, over the endive and watercress salads, onto the napkins and dinner menus waiting beside each place setting.

The guests arrived, the napkins were tucked, the bread was broken, the butter spread, the water sipped, and the salad picked at.

A fine feast was had by all, and much merriment abounded. By the time the first of the evening's speakers rose to address the audience, everyone in the room was flushed with satiation and financial success.

That first speaker was Kameron's old friend William, formerly "Screamin' Billy," Pusser, and Kameron noted with dismay that Pusser had entered the dining room near the end of dinner and *eaten nothing*. That fucking lucky son of a bitch, he had no right to salvation. Well, Kameron assured himself that there could always be a next time. From a doorway in the kitchen, Teddy watched Pusser begin to rise and address his brethren.

"Gentleman, I have been asked to speak tonight on the issue of how American lawyers are viewed by the mass media. I decline... However, I will tell you how your profession is viewed by one far more qualified than I..."

Since his Mission was complete and he knew what was coming from the podium, Kameron quietly took his leave, excited by the prospect of how different business would be this year for so many, many locusts.

And now Teddy started a new file for the morality tales of the Eighth Plague. Teddy loved composing these entries best of all— his re-enactments of the death scenes. He knew Bryne would be fascinated. He based them all on actual occurrences, researched by calls to local people. Claiming he was from some newspaper like *The Star*; the locals always talked and talked.

Saturday, August 22
Sherman, Connecticut
3:45 P.M.

On nice weekends, the speedboats cutting the placid surfaces of Candlewood Lake can be heard well before 8:00 A.M. Among the out-of-towners whose cottages rim the lake, the chief sport is to trailer impossible two-seat muscle-boats down to the water and tear around like mad.

One of the fastest of these boats, built for ocean racing, belonged to a lawyer named Ed Rivers. His firm, Smithson and Rivers, had seventeen junior partners and, together with old Mr. Smithson, who was on retainer to the Archdiocese of New York for five different churches, the firm billed in excess of $44 million a year. When Rivers married Smithson's daughter, four Bishops had offered to officiate.

Ed Rivers was an almost completely predictable individual and his clients considered that an asset. He brought in the churches' annual donations, and the referrals made him wealthy and influential enough to attend the annual Land's End gathering. The fees enabled him to indulge in his boating.

Ed and his family had been coming to Candlewood Lake since he'd been a student at Cornell. His big, powerful racer seemed to fulfill a poor boy's fantasy of having the fastest boat on the lake.

The noise bothered some people, but they

didn't say much about it because Ed was a popular guy. He was always good for a couple of free fireworks shows. Several times each summer he would bring a party up from the City and let the landlubbers putter around on his party-float—a custom-built, forty-eight-foot houseboat with all the amenities of an Intercontinental Hotel suite plus a wide rear deck and an awning from which guests could watch him tear up the lake in his Donzi, christened "Angel's Breath."

Ed was a good boat driver, having completed racing school in Florida as well as three deep-water crossings to the Bahamas.

This particular afternoon, as Rivers made a low-speed turn past the houseboat, he could see the bartender mixing Bloody Marys on the deck. He gunned the twin Mercs, touched forty in seconds, and headed across the lake with a twelve-foot rooster tail spiking up in his wake. A few hundred yards away, he throttled back to make his turn, letting the boat drift sideways as the wake spread; behind him, the lake seemed to flatten out as if a gigantic trowel were smoothing out a waveless track for his return leg. This time, he planned to pass close beside the houseboat and give the kids a thrill.

As he turned, he felt a slight tingle in the corners of his eyes. Then each cheek seemed to be touched by an invisible electric feather, a tiny surge of pins-and-needles. Ed shook his head and rubbed the back of his neck. Suddenly, a weird headache focused and grew behind his left eye.

He rubbed his temples with his fingertips, felt better, adjusted his goggles, turned toward the party on the houseboat, and gunned the engines.

The sleek boat knifed smoothly back down the course, with the throttles half-open, the water perfect, and the boat closing in on sixty-five miles an hour.

Ed felt great.

Blue sky, fast boat, great people... What a life! Throwing his head back, he gazed heavenward. Suddenly the trigeminal nerve on the right side of his face transmitted an electrified jolt of pain as intense as a surge from a high-voltage cable.

An organic intrusion into the core of Ed Rivers's brain had been growing since shortly after the Land's End get-together. Slowly growing larger hour by hour, the cyst had inserted itself into any crevice it could find, and there were many available. Inevitably, the organism had swollen to such an extent that it pinched part of his brain against his skull, causing the crushing pain.

He head jerked to the right with agony. Involuntarily, he pulled his right hand off the wheel and clutched at his face. A new paroxysm of pain prevented him from reaching back for the throttles. With his left hand, Ed held onto the wheel for dear life. Finally, the pain lessened; he reached out for the throttles and eased them back.

As he started to slow down, guests on the houseboat noticed him holding his cheek, took their drinks, and moved to the rail. He waved, sort of... but when he reached out to slow the boat even more, the third paralyzing jolt hit him. This time, he jerked his hand straight back, and his windbreaker cuff caught on the starboard throttle. He pulled it wide open. The engines roared, and the boat leapt to life.

With only his left hand on the helm, Ed, in agony, inadvertently wrenched the wheel hard to port. The four-ton fiberglass boat heeled over sharply, going forty in seconds, and headed directly for the houseboat.

The speedboat hit going more than fifty and killed two people outright. One young attorney, inside the cabin when Ed's boat crashed through the side, saw his leg repeatedly sliced by the prop as the boat passed over him. The leg sustained so many spiral cuts that it had to be amputated at the Danbury Hospital.

The parasite that was taking Ed Rivers's life then proceeded to kill more people on shore: his speedboat passed completely through the houseboat and crossed the twenty-five yards to shore, where it left the water and broadsided an old aluminum Airstream. The boat and the trailer burst into flames. The trailer was demolished, taking the lives of an entire East Orange family. It took forty minutes for volunteers from Warren to get a fire truck to the isolated site. By that time, there wasn't much left. Ed's body had been burned extensively.

At first, it was unclear exactly what had happened. Almost overnight, the number of lawsuits filed against his estate forced the family to authorize an autopsy.

The pathologist was the first one to cut into Ed's brain and spot the gelatinous cysts, dozens of them. He saw their mouths. Moving. Still alive, pulsating inside their membranous skins like embryos which, of course, was exactly what they were...

Saturday, August 29
Bergen County, New Jersey

Barely a week after Ed Rivers's strange and tragic death, Richard and Edna Rubin were making a presentation to the Council of Elders and the Head Rabbi, official investment representatives of the more than 75,000 Jews living in Bergen County.

Richard and Edna were well aware that Bergen County's synagogues had more money to invest than many small countries and that their schools occupied the lavish, *fin-de-siè-cle* mansions of the Robber Barons. The parishioners' homes, all a comfortable walk from their temple, were uniformly beautiful, well-kept, and top-dollar.

The Rubins and their teen-aged son and daughter, not yet ready for Englewood, lived somewhat down-scale in Leonia. As they drove down the hill to their meeting, past the Stanford White Mansions, they knew someday they would move here.

Their meeting with the Rabbi and the real estate agent began right on time, and the presentation went well. Everyone seemed pleased with the information Edna had given them on repositioning the pension funds—a concept they had learned at Land's End, where she and Richard had been among the few Jewish attendees—and restructuring some real estate holdings.

Now all that was required for the money to be transferred immediately was the signing of authorization papers attached to the synagogue's trust agreements. That meant $75,000 in fees for the Rubins. By the time they left, it looked like a sure thing. They had made the twenty-minute drive back to the office via some of the most beautiful houses. Edna was already elatedly shopping for one. This deal would change everything.

Richard, on the other hand, was not elated in the least, suffering the same pulsing headaches he'd been having for a week. Edna had rubbed his temples repeatedly. She reminded him he always got the headaches when he was working too hard, and restructuring the proposal must have taken a lot out of both of them. But there was no denying the dark shadows on his cheeks, the heavy circles under his eyes. Even her daughter had noticed.

Once Richard turned off Lemoin Avenue and into the firm's parking garage, he put his head down on the wheel. Edna reached over, her cool, strong fingers loosening the knots in the back of his neck and making him feel better almost immediately. He kissed her. He felt much better. Good enough, in fact, to return to work.

From the reception desk manned by a perennially cheerful, freckle-faced redhead with a British accent, their office space afforded a sweeping view of Manhattan to the east and the Hudson River flowing south beneath its imposing Palisades. Behind a long glass wall eleven attorneys toiled in smaller offices arranged around Richard and Edna's suite.

The couple went directly into Richard's office, where he picked up the phone to call Citibank, intending to reposition the funds that afternoon. Though the headache pain had lessened, as the phone rang, the pain spiked up more intensely than ever. Thinking he was going to fall, Richard grabbed the edge of the desk. Just as he was about to cry out, the pain stopped. He took a deep breath when the Citibank operator answered and was able to request the Trust Department.

He was on hold when he realized, at some hideous level, that he was losing his mind.

He heard a screaming sound inside his head.

He was out of control.

Was it a stroke?

The ringing. The pain. The ringing.

He needed help. He tried to act. Get to the hospital. Stop the pain. But, instead, he only hung up the phone, and stood frozen.

Edna tilted her head at him in concern, but he ignored her. "No answer?" she asked, but he could no longer hear her.

He had been trying to tell her to call an ambulance, but as the words formed in his mind, they were shouldered out of the way by something in his brain.

Circuits were being disrupted.

Memories were no longer being formed.

Existing memories were no longer accessible.

Thought and speech were beyond him, and the signals that did move within his brain had no referent, no meaning, because they were no longer being processed by the part of the brain that governed reason.

Inside Richard's brain now, dozens of swollen tapeworm cysts floated into the ventricles of his cerebrum, down the cortical area controlling sensory input. Some had already begun to alter the transmission of auditory memory signals from Broca's area into the "current information" spaces.

Thoughts Richard had long forgotten were now being played back as direct instructions from a commanding voice that seemed to come simultaneously from old black and white movies and from Richard himself. He knew what he had to do. He knew the part he was destined to play.

Jumping up and taking Edna's neck in his hands he closed his fingers around her throat and squeezed with all his might. "Whore! Jezebel!" he screamed as he choked her.

She was dead in less than two minutes.

Strangely, both parts of his shattered brain seemed to be congratulating him on having murdered his wife. He thought he heard applause. Through the glass partition, he could see the terrified faces of the other attorneys as well as one of the secretaries, an attractive, prematurely silver-haired woman in her forties, on the phone, undoubtedly calling the police. She had worked for the Rubins for years, she liked them, and there was a panic in her voice.

Richard saw her dialing frantically, started out of the office, walked over to her, took her throat in his hands, and began to snap her head back and forth screaming, "Jezebel! Harlot! Whore of Babylon!" Her neck broke with a crack.

After he had dropped her lifeless body in a heap, he turned toward the others, raised his hands to his forehead, screamed, and fell over backwards.

In time, the police arrived along with the EMS workers, took away the bodies, and brought a still-unconscious Richard to the hospital. Everyone at the office agreed it had to have been a medical crisis, maybe some sort of stroke.

Richard died that night.

During the autopsy, they found the cysts studded throughout his brain. Because this was a police-related matter, autopsies were performed on the two dead women. Nothing unusual showed up in the secretary, but Edna was a different story.

The pathologist estimated that, had Richard not broken her neck, Edna would have had at best only a few weeks to live. Her right lung was almost completely filled with a glistening cyst almost the size of a baby's head, which, when it burst, would have killed her almost instantly...

Monday, August 31
Boulder, Colorado
2:00 P.M.

Twelve years earlier, Sheila Woods, of Irish descent, had married Dan Hammer, a Lutheran attorney and a man she should never have even dated. Towering arguments were the marriage's *leitmotif*, alternating with seasons of silence. Time apart was not merely welcomed, it was earned. Sheila had made sure to keep her maiden name—a prescient gesture, now that the marriage was essentially over.

When Dan would come back to Boulder from a case or a conference like the one he'd attended at Land's End, Sheila and he would meet to discuss the care of their nine-year-old son Joshua, or their upcoming separation, or who had screwed things up. They were beginning to realize that while marriage may be temporary, divorce lasts forever.

Dan considered himself a fundamentally good man, but others wondered. During the seventies, Hammer had applied an eagle eye trained at Harvard Law School to the vintage U.S. government paperwork signed when Crow, Apache, and Pawnee reservations were set up on the eastern slopes of the Rockies. He spent years digging, hitchhiking to D.C. and virtually moving into the vaults of the National Archives. When he was done, the Indians were no longer called Indians. They were called wealthy.

Drilling rights to oil deposits, copper mines, water rights, notations on forgotten documents—all were turned into fast fortunes with Hammer leading the suits against the Federal Government on behalf of the tribes.

Initially, the Establishment reviled him, but in time he, like any good Robin Hood, began to take from the rich while continuing to give to the poor. His practice came to include a wide range of corporate and church, as well as Native American, clients. Quite wealthy now, Hammer had fallen into a high lifestyle of flashy consumption. The divorce was going to be messy.

In town to pick up their son for a week in Aspen, Dan had insisted on meeting with Sheila at the new Denver airport despite the long drive down from Boulder and the problem he was having with his vision. A cataract? She had readily agreed—anything not to have Dan in her house.

To add to the annoyance, Hammer's plane was late. Sheila had sent Josh to the video counter when she saw Dan coming down the escalator, wearing lifts and carrying a big Stetson. Flamboyantly waving the hat when he saw Sheila, he noticed a couple of travelers looking at him. He ate up the attention. Sheila wished he was dead.

Suddenly, even from a distance, Sheila could see Dan's nose begin to bleed. And not a little bit either.

Although Dan didn't know it, a good-sized cyst above his right nostril, his ethmoid sinus, had ruptured. The blood flow was intense and startling enough to force him to drop the hat. He sneezed violently, producing a jet of blood that struck a woman below him on the escalator. Drops, round, red, and wet, hit the woman's coat, hit her hand, hit the railings on the escalator.

The pain behind Dan's eyes was severe, he couldn't turn away. Other cysts deep in his brain had been ruptured by the violent sneeze. He tried to stop the bleeding with his fingers, but another fan of it splattered the entire face of the woman, who had turned around. She screamed, so horrified by the bloody spray that she stepped back to get away. Her foot went into space, and she lost her balance completely. Her arms reached out as she fell, and her hand came away red— since Dan's blood was smeared all over the escalator's rubber railing.

As she fell backward, her head struck the woman directly below her. They fell forward together, and the escalator hit bottom as Dan dropped to his knees in pain. The force of their fall left the women in the direct path of oncoming passengers, and someone stepped on the first woman's hand. When she screamed again, security guards with weapons at the ready appeared almost instantly. Someone eventually turned off the escalator.

Dan himself was near screaming in agony when, abruptly, the pain stopped. When he started to stand up, a rush of light pink fluid— soupy, unlike pure blood—poured from his left nostril, causing him to gag. Then that stopped, too.

He was dizzy, his vision was blurred, and he had a headache. Still, it was better than the fires of hell Dan had just felt dancing around in his brain. He had seen inside the fiery pit; roasting there was as great a physical torture as any man might imagine. He never wanted to feel that way again for as long as he lived.

Dan was trying to stay calm as help arrived, and attempted to convey to the EMS worker that his vision was blurred and to tell her about the pain. She nodded as she checked his vital signs, clicked on her ophthalmoscope and looked in Dan's eyes.

Through the dark center of his iris her light shone normally, but, instead of passing through the lens and falling on his retina, it passed through the lens and illuminated the side of an egg case—a blury membrane of transparent tissue, shaped to fit in the space behind the lens, a tiny, barely visible sac of clear fluid floating behind the lens, obscuring his vision.

She adjusted the magnification and examined the anterior chamber and could now see through the transparent wall of the case the heads of young parasites. The ones that hadn't hatched. She saw the tiny hooklets. Tiny circular mouths. They moved...

The woman recoiled as if she'd been slapped and pulled away from Hammer abruptly. Aware that she was an EMS worker and not a physician, she reported what she'd seen to a doctor, and after that, never looked in anyone's eyes again without remembering. The things might be waiting.

Denver General Hospital's Emergency Department's chief resident concurred that she'd never seen anything like this case before and called the senior attending. They consulted with each other and immediately made an emergency call to the CDC for advice. The things, whatever they were, were alive and swimming in the chamber of the eye like tiny, white porpoises.

And, in a matter of hours, Sheila Woods got her wish: Dan Hammer was dead.

Reading his account of the horrible death the locusts suffered, Teddy was ready months ago to get to work on the Ninth Plague—the darkness which would last three days.

14

Monday, August 31
Director's Office, Zoonosis Laboratory, Guilderland
10:00 A.M.

The red hotline phone on the right of Bryne's desk began to peal.

"Arbovirus Lab," Jack barked into the receiver. He was busy, and Drew was out to lunch, leaving him alone to field triage calls with nothing to eat but a Hershey bar.

"Dr. Bryne?" a male voice tentatively asked, and when Jack said it was, told him, "This is Dr. Jerome Marlowe from Connecticut, right next door, so to speak. Hope I didn't get you at a bad time. Dr. Bryne, I'm a physician, a ProMEDer."

"Then call me Jack."

"All right, umm, Jack. I'll try to make it short. I'm with a large HMO over here in North Haven, part of a good-sized system in fourteen states: East Coast, and out West. We all get together on a telecommunication system once a week to share our cases, exchange information."

"Go on."

"Last week, our California affiliate presented an unusual case, extremely rare and, frankly, quite frightening. One in a million."

"One in a million?"

"Yes, Jack, except we've had two in the last three weeks here in Connecticut, and in this state we might see at most four cases a year."

"And what is the condition?"

"Neurocysticercosis. Pork tapeworm. I'm not an epidemiologist, but... I, or rather we, went on line and did a quick count. In the fourteen states we came up with twenty-six cases..."

"And that's about one per million Americans a year."

"Right," Marlowe replied, "but the twenty-six cases were in limited catchment areas, fourteen states, over the last two months which would be ten to twelve times the national average if it keeps up. We represent about ten per cent of the HMO market nationwide, and the time frame we're working with is about one-sixth of a year. That would make over one thousand five hundred cases a year, not one per million but about sixteen per million..."

An alarm bell went off in Bryne's mind. Neurocysticercosis was a very rare complication of an even rarer disease—an unusual event confined exclusively to someone harboring a pork tapeworm. Neither the worm nor the complications from the worm were public health problems in the western world.

The condition was now considered an anomaly even in most developing countries.

"What's your thinking?" Bryne asked, reaching for his fifteen-year-old text on parasitology.

"Either this is a bias error, an A or B error, in our clientele," Marlowe replied, "or we may be seeing a marked increase." He paused. "That's something that ProMED might be interested in—or CDC, if the damn thing gets big enough. I don't like the looks of it, but I'm not paid to do this kind of research. I'd like to turn it over to you."

Telling Marlowe he would definitely look into the matter, Bryne thanked him and hung up just as Lawrence reappeared from his lunch break.

"Drew," Jack yelled, "I need you, please—and fast!"

Drew's initial response to the call was a whistle of disbelief, followed by, "Jack, this can't happen. Unless someone is... if the numbers are correct, something very frightening is taking place."

Within an hour, they had a strategy. Faxes had been sent to all fifty states and three territorial epidemiologists requesting help:

August 31, 1998

Dear Colleague:

ProMED has become aware of what may be an absolute increased case rate of an infection that is not reportable in most states. In order to assess whether our observation may be valid, we ask your help in determining the incidence of this rare condition in your state during the last twenty-four months.

Cysticercosis, a complication of *Taenia solium* infestation, has recently been noted with an alarming and unusually high incidence in some Eastern and Western states. However, this observation may represent a bias in reporting. Alternatively, cases may actually be increasing in number, but not recognized by individual physicians, hospitals, or state health departments. As you know, the disease spectrum for cysticercosis is broad. Cases may have been seen by pediatricians, internists, infectious disease consultants, and parasitologists. In the case of neurocysticercosis, neurosurgeons may be aware of cases. Pathology laboratories, hospital discharge coding systems, and death certificate entries might be used to identify cases.

ProMED urgently requests your help in identifying any and all cases that have occurred in your state/territory during the last two years. Information without name identifiers on age, race/ethnicity, sex, travel history, profession, and outcome of cases would be greatly appreciated. We realize that some state epidemiologists may find this a difficult task. We stress that our request is urgent. We would prefer incomplete data versus a delayed reporting of complete data. Any and all information will be confidential and will only be shared with state and territorial epidemiologists. A summary of the data will be forwarded to you once received and analyzed.

Thank you for your time, attention, and friendship.

Jack Bryne, Ph.D., ProMED Moderator

Bryne had thought of going directly to the CDC, but he knew they would put up caveats and insist on lengthy peer review processes before a manicured questionnaire might be developed and then—perhaps—approved by a... bureaupath.

Sixty days, minimum, for even a rudimentary look. Sensitivities had to be respected... the pork industry, food establishments, the FDA, the media.

If the normal process were circumvented by ProMED, he thought, he could get a quick and dirty answer back in less than a week. The CDC could, if it wished, pretty up the survey if it came to anything.

Bryne knew that stats on an "unreportable condition" like this disease were not readily accessible on any database; no one kept count, and no surveillance system existed to identify a possible case upswing. Tracking it would require time-intensive work; in states like California, for instance, thousands of physicians would have to be contacted, but the Wyoming epidemiologist, Stan Dance, could call the four neurosurgeons there and have an answer within an hour. Other states had computerized hospital discharge data or mortality figures. The numbers coming in would be piecemeal: incomplete, underestimated "dirty data," research no longer accepted at the politically correct CDC. Hell, it was worth the chance!

Tuesday, September 8
Zoonosis Laboratory, Guilderland
9:30 A.M.

Ever since the neurocysticercosis request had gone out, Lawrence would barge into Jack's office with the arrival of each new fax or e-mail, like a TV news reporter announcing primary results.

"New Jersey, twenty-three cases." "Montana zip, New Mexico three." Later, "Oregon, fifteen; Illinois, seventeen!" The numbers were really beginning to grow. But what could

Bryne compare them to? Statistics on the disease had never been collected before.

After the first week they started the analysis, with Lawrence working on the raw data. On a Tuesday morning after the three-day weekend, Drew announced, "Got something for you, Jack. But before I give it to you, you better understand that the data—"

"Are raw," Bryne broke in.

"Don't interrupt. What I was going to say is that neurocysticercosis is increasing, especially in the U.S. Know why?"

"Not a clue."

"The reason," Drew announced, "is changing agribusiness practices south of the border. It's not only infecting people. It's also in the fruits and vegetables from Central and South America. The eggs of the worm hide in the crevices of the skin of the raspberries, strawberries, and melons at your local supermarket. See, Guatemalan, Salvadoran, and Honduran agribusinesses now use huge overhead aerial sprays. Great for efficiency. Bad for me and you."

"Why?"

"The more efficient irrigation sprays in Latino agribusinesses are full of fecally contaminated sewer runoff. The spray coats the fruit with viruses, bacteria, and parasitic eggs. The sun kills off the microbes, but the eggs of some of these critters survive sunshine, washing, even chlorine. So that's my read. Wanna look at the data?"

Lawrence triumphantly handed Bryne a

sheet of paper with six graphs, cautioning him that the results were incomplete, perhaps 56 percent of the actual numbers. And although only thirty-one states had responded by the end of the first week, Drew told Jack he felt they were a fairly good model of the country as a whole.

Actually, Drew was ready to predict an outcome but had waited for Bryne to ask for the crucial data, the breakout in the last graph. Did the man *see* it?

"Want a hint?" he teased Jack.

"Sure."

"Night of the living DWELs," Lawrence responded with a straight face.

"DWELs?" Bryne demanded. Some hint, he thought. Bryne watched Lawrence run his delicate fingers across his black pate and shift his weight. Hours of sitting in that chair had stiffened his joints considerably, and his hip was hurting him, but Drew continued sitting there, content to watch his colleague play with the puzzle.

As usual, Lawrence had done exquisite work; still Bryne would get the credit, despite his best attempts at proper attribution. It certainly wasn't because Lawrence was African American that he would not be quoted by the media; it was Drew's lack of a doctorate that would doom his career. Anyone who lacked the title "doctor," Jack knew, ended up on the back burner of the academic stove that warms up to degrees and fancy initials. The Commissioners, Special Projects Directors,

Bureau Directors, Chiefs of Laboratories— men, white men, with advanced degrees and impressive-sounding titles—always got the kudos. The ones who actually churned out the work—the complex spreadsheets, the sophisticated statistical analyses, the regression analyses that documented the authors' conclusions—never got the rewards. No Ph.D., need not apply. Bryne knew that sign was hung around Lawrence's neck and the necks of thousands of "almosts" like him. It took a few hundred thousand dollars and a continuing student loan debt to buy oneself out of the company store; Lawrence never could have afforded it.

"This looks good, my friend," Bryne said immediately. "Drew, you're my eyes and ears. This is very, very good. But I still don't see it. The sample may be too small."

"Not enough regional feedback, Jack, but there's almost enough... keep looking..."

The top two graphs on the paper were basic time-and-place histograms, used by epidemiologists to pin down—or, in their word, "orient"—the epidemic by asking when and where. Lawrence had assembled the numbers from the state epidemiologists and refined them into a pair of histograms. During the past two years the neurocysticercosis did not appear to increase if one looked at the United States as a whole, and the disease was not concentrated in any particular region.

The third graph, adjusted for population density, was also flat when calculated by cases per million per region. Regions were used by the CDC to monitor trends for certain diseases— heart attack, stroke, cirrhosis, influenza, and HIV. Surprising differences were sometimes observed; further questions were then designed to explain the differences and track the outbreak. None were apparent for neurocysticercosis. Dead end thus far...

Jack's eyes focused on the fourth graph. As he looked at "person" characteristics, he began to notice interesting differences: males far exceeded females.

"Not surprising, since we're looking at data about parasites," Lawrence told Bryne. "Most boys tend to have dirtier fingers, wash less, go barefooted more, tend to be more adventurous, and get into more trouble with animals... dogs, cats, raccoons, bats, and microbes, including parasitic worms." Bryne agreed.

The fourth graph also showed that significantly more adults than children were affected, which would ordinarily not be the case unless the disease was long-lasting. Some people harbored parasites like hookworm for decades, but this worm was different. Pork tapeworms usually manifested themselves in only a month or two.

When Bryne got to the last two graphs, he understood why Lawrence was focusing not only on adults, but on *who* among adults were getting the infestation, and *when* and *where* they were getting it. Lawrence had identified the epidemic by putting together fragments of information. The numbers were incredible.

"So many adults, Drew? Why? Why all of sudden in the United States?"

"Neurocysticercosis is no longer a problem in the States, Jack. Infected pigs are identified and destroyed. Meat is inspected, and pork products are well cooked because of the fear of trichinosis. Trichinosis has vanished ever since offal was outlawed as food for swine; meat is strictly inspected for tapeworm, too. So-called 'measly pork,' the term for larva-infested chops, hams, and loins dotted with whitish larval globs, is easily spotted during inspection."

"Drew," Jack asked, "when humans replace the pig as the definitive host, don't they in essence become an intermediate pig host? Wouldn't they develop larval cysts in their hearts, brains, eyes, and skin, and hundreds of parasitic 'daughter cysts'?"

"Sure. Probably happens frequently. Take a look at the next figure."

Bryne scanned the sixth graph. There had been many ways to "cut" the information Drew had put together—subsets by race, ethnicity, social class, income level, and occupation.

The last graph clinched it. God only knows how Drew did it, Bryne thought. He knew the statistics were as reliable... as Lawrence. Even so, the information shocked him.

Professional classes were preferentially infected, particularly... lawyers.

"Night of the living dead," Lawrence inter-rupted, "but not all of them are dead, that's for sure. I've made a few calls to our New York cases. Fifteen in all. Eleven available. Seven willing to talk. Sick... really sick, but not all of them bought the farm."

Bryne was amazed. "And what do they all have in common?"

"For one thing, they want to know who to sue. I call them LWELs, living white European lawyers. Not a happy bunch, but one up on the DWELs, that's for sure.

"There are a lot of DWELs out there in the United States," Lawrence added, "and no one except us, not state epidemiologists, not the CDC, not the docs and the hospitals, knows about this scourge. Jack, it's us. The confederacy of dunces that runs our balkanized health care system has no idea what's happening."

"Drew, we have to tell them. We have to do something..."

Yes, do it, Jack, then forget it, my friend, Lawrence said to himself. Then he announced aloud, "I'll make the call. I'll fax the results back to all the states. But Jack, there's an old Turkish saying... 'A man who tells the truth is chased from nine villages.' Give it up, Jack, it's not your responsibility anymore."

Relatives of the deceased lawyers were not always helpful when Bryne tried to interview them by phone. It had taken several hours, but thanks to his persistence, he had finally pinpointed Land's End.

He immediately called the manager, who,

oblivious to what had taken place, was helpful almost to the point of obsequiousness, promising to send Jack the complete three-day list of activities, plus a description of all foods that had been served.

"I must say, Doctor," the manager continued to sell the resort to Bryne, "that the attorneys had a wonderful time. Everybody does at the Land's End. You must bring your family down here sometime."

I don't think so, Jack thought, but said, "I'll consider it," then gave the manager a list of the information he needed and thanked him for help.

Most of the material arrived by fax the next day. Congressmen and senators had made keynote presentations. There were over three hundred guests. A famous comedian had entertained the lawyers one evening. The food had been particularly outstanding— venison, pheasant, free-range chicken, duck, mountain trout, spicy soft-shelled crabs flown in from Baltimore.

Scanning the bills of fare, Bryne was puzzled because there was nothing on it suggesting pig. Why? Because there had been Jews in attendance? Quite possibly. In any case, the dinner had included no pork roasts, chops, or ribs, no bacon, not even Smithfield ham, which was considered a delicacy.

Next he read through the carefully printed program, looking for something that was there, but that he wasn't seeing. And then he found it:

"Screamin' Billy" Pusser's speech.

It was meant to be a roast of sorts, gently chiding the lawyers with lawyer jokes. The title of the speech had made them all chuckle, he was sure. Taken from the line that Chief Justice Warren Burger had used in his retirement address, it warned against the new generation of attorneys being spawned. "A hungry horde of locusts," that's what he called them. A hungry horde of locusts...

Bryne shuddered. There it was: The eighth plague. The locusts had gorged and now were beginning to feed upon themselves.

Taking out his list, he double-checked. The Louisiana bishop's Centrolenella death had been the second plague, the frogs; the ergotism had been the third plague, the lice; the honey bees had been the fourth plague, the swarm; the anthrax had been the sixth plague—the boils and blains described in the Bible.

Now he added the eighth plague, the locusts. But what about the seventh plague, the hail? Or the fifth plague, the murrain—it must be the horses; it *must* be, he thought. And what of the ninth plague, three days of darkness, or the tenth, the death of the eldest? And what of the first plague, the one that had started it all? How could any human being, no matter how possessed, turn a river, turn water, into blood?

15

Wednesday, September 9
Bryne's Cottage, Guilderland
3:00 A.M.

How *could* you turn a river into blood? The question continued to preoccupy Jack until, jolted out of a sound sleep, he was sure he had an answer.

His first thought was to phone Mia in Manhattan—until he remembered it was 3:00 A.M. and she would think he was losing it, anyway. He didn't want to wake up Drew. And he wasn't about to share his plague theory with Vicky until he was ready to see it as a feature on *Hot Line*.

Drew always got to the lab early, but this morning Jack beat him by a good half-hour and had the coffee ready when Lawrence walked in, surprise evident on his face.

"Dr. Bryne," he joked, "to what do we owe this unexpected—"

"Drew," Jack broke in excitedly, "I think I've got a real lead on the first plague!"

"You're serious?"

"You bet I am. Think... think... what could turn a body of water the color of blood, of red?"

Drew mused for only a moment before responding, "Or to purple or to a phosphorescent chartreuse... Red tide, an algae!... You're thinking of some sort of toxic bloom?"

"Yep. All those beautiful deadly blossoms!

Drew, I need you to go run a Nexis search for me. Scour every available source for toxic red tides, including ciguatera poisoning, probably in the Caribbean, around the first of the year."

"Sure thing," Drew grinned, always up for a challenge. "I'll leave right now!"

And Lawrence hadn't returned empty-handed. He'd brought back a nine-month-old article from the *Miami Herald*. It was brief, too brief for Jack to be sure, but it certainly made for fascinating reading.

Miami. January. Reuters.

Dutch public health officials on the island of St. Maarten confirmed today that the food poisoning deaths of Reverend Cato Phipps, his wife, Georgianna, and their daughter, Gretchen, had been caused by ciguatera poisoning, probably from toxins found in many Caribbean game fish.

The Phipps family and dozens of his U.S. parishioners had been on a New Year's cruise. Of the hundreds of tourists, only Phipps and his family seemed to have been affected. "We deeply regret the deaths of the Phipps family," said Dr. Nick Mertens, Director of Health for the Dutch Ministry of Medicine in Amsterdam.

Dutch officials recently revealed that ciguatera toxin, believed to have come from a red snapper appetizer, had caused the deaths. The Phipps family had consumed a traditional *rijstaffel* feast of Dutch and Indonesian delicacies, given in their honor by local dignitaries, as well as a ceremonial local fish entree ordered by the reverend. The meal also included a fiery *sambal oedong,* a peppery dish that local doctors first thought had felled the family.

The collapse of Rev. Phipps and his wife and daughter, who were stricken at a banquet given in their honor, caused near hysteria among his followers, many of whom had recently joined him on his cruise, "Onward Christian Soldiers." In a near-melee following Phipps's death, numerous ministers claimed that Phipps had appointed them as their new leader before he died.

Bryne was sure U.S. officials would not have even investigated the deaths. The "Reverend" had been on a cruise ship near the Dutch half of the island of St. Maarten, which was where they would have taken the body and done the autopsy. If he wanted any more information, Jack would have to talk to Dutch health officials, either on the island or, more likely, in Holland.

Turning to his bookshelf, he flipped open a well-worn volume and opened it to the section on algae.

Ciguatera poisoning, he read, was due to a bio-intoxication from microscopic organisms known as dinoflagellates ingested by larger predator fish from the Caribbean to the South Pacific. The dinoflagellates, known as *Gambierodiscus toxicus,* are consumed by small marine animals, and the toxins are carried up the food chain to larger fish such as snapper, grouper, bonita, and barracuda.

Ciguatera could certainly kill someone, but not in a matter of minutes, unless the dose was extremely high. Bryne had friends who had once gotten mild cases during a sailing trip to Grenada, losing all sensation in their groin, some for twenty-four hours.

Bryne rapidly scanned the text. Searching, wondering. How easy would it be... ? He read on more carefully, looking for the means, the toxins. The marine dinoflagellates were only one of many phytoplankton capable of causing neurological problems—numbness, paralysis, paresthesia, respiratory depression. During the last decade, microbiologists from dozens of countries had noted variants of ciguatera on the "algal blooms" that drifted across wide expanses of the oceans and seas.

The name "Red Sea" was attributed to a bloom of *Fusarium rosaceum* centuries ago. Around the world there have been green, brown, blue, and more recently colorful purple tides in estuary waters, each with its own potent toxins. Even freshwater lakes degrade into a pale chartreuse from algae so toxic they make the ponds unsafe for waterfowl. Some marine blooms glow in the moonlight, giving tropical seas a surreal appearance.

Algae blooms produce toxic molecules simply as a by-product of their own respiration and excretion. Some algal toxins destroyed the delicate marine ecosystem. They killed fish and shellfish by the millions, denuding entire reefs, fouling beaches for weeks. Other toxins are harmless to certain fish and shellfish, although the toxins can accumulate in their muscles and gills. While the poisons would not harm the creatures, when something larger, like man, eats them, the concentrated toxins would kill rapidly.

Recent increased "blooms" of red tides had been monitored by satellites that tracked the expanding algae as they drifted over thousands of square miles of ocean. For years they were thought to be harmless. However, Bryne read, recent new and alarming data showed that the rising phosphate concentrations in seawater, caused by fertilizers and chemical runoff, often started the runaway growth, especially in warmer coastal waters; and then, accelerated by warmth from the greenhouse effect, the combination leads to the creation of huge toxic blooms.

Bryne reached over to his Rolodex, flipped to the D's, and found the number he wanted in Amsterdam. He checked his watch—too late to call Europe. Bryne reached over to his laptop. There were three on line Dutch ProMEDers, two physicians, one microbiologist. Perhaps one of them could get Bryne the government reports on the incident. It was well known, but never published, that St. Maarten had suffered clusters of ciguatera poisoning for years. Adjacent reefs were somehow conducive to the growth of the algae.

Nearby St. Bart's was free of the disease. There were no reefs to protect and concentrate the algae. Similar reefs in the South Pacific also existed: Captain Bligh had eaten raw bonita during his remarkable open-boat exodus from Tahiti and had suffered agonizing symptoms, documented in his diary, but he survived the poisoning. The Dutch (and the French in the South Pacific) had downplayed contemporary episodes of ciguatera poisonings to protect the tourist trade. The Caribbean officials clearly knew about the problem, but they were certainly not going to advertise it.

Still, he reasoned, the coincidence was too great.

Reverend Phipps and his family had died nearly a year ago, and subsequent incidents, or "coincidences," had also involved the clergy. Some of them, anyway... And the saints thing, like *Saint* Maarten's... And *San* Diego... If these random happenstances were only... happenstances. Bryne had made the leap from science to conjecture months ago, and he knew he wouldn't stop.

If the St. Maarten's incident was his candidate for the first plague—the red tide, the waters turning to blood—then it meant that the ciguatera poisonings would have had to be only the beginning. Not only was someone reenacting the biblical scenario, but he was doing it in order.

Bryne took out a piece of paper and began to reconstruct his list, sketching the associations:

I = waters to blood = red tide/ciguatera = January

He wondered whether or not to add the saints. Could the name St. John be factored in? Had their boy been a random victim? Should he look at sports teams? The New Orleans Saints, San Diego Chargers, San Francisco 49ers?

He held a legal pad in his lap sideways and began to write down the history of the last few months. He filled out a grid.

#	Exodus plague	Real Time	Who?	Where?	When?
1	Blood-water	Ciguatera	Rev. family	St. Maarten	Jan
2	Frogs	Tree frogs	Bishop	Louisiana	Feb
3	Lice	Ergotism	???	Connecticut	March
4	Swarm	Bees	Tourists	San Antonio	April
5	Murrain	???	Horses	Ill/Kentucky	May
6	Boils	Anthrax	Children	San Diego	June
7	Hail	???	???	???	July?
8	Locusts	Cysticercosis	Lawyers	U.S.	Aug
9	Darkness	???	???	???	Sept?

Bryne thought it all through again. He was proposing that some nameless madman, probably a religious fanatic, was orchestrating a series of increasingly deadly attacks aimed primarily at members of the clergy or people associated with them, like the lawyers at the Land's End meeting.

Come to think of it, Joey's father was a highly connected born-again Christian. The San Antonio swarm had gone after tourists, but only after it attacked a Baptist congregation. (And if horses were involved, that one guy, Leigh—Vicky told me that he was also a Christian fundamentalist.)

Great. But where was the hard evidence, the "smoking gun"? It was there, he was sure; he simply wasn't seeing it. But he had to, he had to see it, before the monster struck again.

319

* * *

Thursday, September 3
Zoonosis Laboratory, Guilderland

It was not yet seven-thirty on a strangely chilly morning, despite the still-summer sun radiating through a stand of oak trees across the corn stubble fields from Bryne's office windows. In Europe, though, it was just after twelve, and there were people Jack needed to reach before they left for lunch. He poured his first cup of coffee, then carefully adjusted his chair to give support to his damaged arm, which always bothered him on days like this. He began typing a request using ProMED to Jan de Reuters, one of his Dutch contacts. Could de Reuters find out what, if anything, had happened during the cruise that ended Reverend Phipps's life? Did the Ministry of Health have any conclusive evidence that Phipps and his family had died from ciguatera? How many others had been affected? Could Bryne call him? Would he rather call Bryne collect on the telephone? He pushed the SEND button, and the ProMED message was on its way.

Lawrence popped in. "You got a call from Carl Rader in Atlanta last night after you left. Something's brewing down there. It looks like there's an outbreak of botulism cropping up, some cases as early as July. The folks down there think it's another vichyssoise thing, you know, some commercial product. If so, it's going to be big."

320

"What else did Carl want?" Bryne was attentive. A call from Rader, the retired director of the Centers for Disease Control, almost always proved important. Rader had been its director back in the days when CDC stood for Center for Disease Control. The Center was the first government institution to practice politically correct lingo, changing its name and its original mission from things communicable to a broader base: anything that might be of epidemic proportions, infectious or not.

Rader had been one of the old school, the communicable disease doctors. The new Centers for Disease Control (and, later, Prevention) investigated asbestos-related illnesses, lead poisoning, environmental contaminants, and cancer clusters. Scores of microbiologists, parasitologists, veterinarians, entomologists, and bacteriologists had been either kicked upstairs or forced to take early retirement. With them went generations of knowledge.

In 1976, legionnaires' disease had been both a wakeup call that there were many, many new bugs out there just waiting to emerge, and also an early warning that attention must be redirected to the Centers' original mission. The Lassa fever outbreaks, the AIDS fiasco under Reagan, belated recognition of new afflictions like Lyme disease, and finally the Ebola epidemics in Africa and cryptosporidiosis in the Milwaukee drinking water all presented themselves to the Centers, and to Americans in general. But the old guard had retired, and the young Turks, the chronic disease experts, occupational epidemiologists, the Ph.D. spin doctors, had to be quickly retrained to deal with the new diseases. The models for these diseases were the older ones. Diseases on which Rader had cut his eyeteeth.

"Dr. Rader needs you to call him. Pronto. He's getting the demographics piecemeal. It looks frightening. He sounded concerned." Lawrence watched Bryne nod, but he made no move to pick up the phone.

"That does not sound much like Carl Rader to me. Rader's the guy who said he owed his success to one secret. That secret was indifference."

Lawrence looked at Bryne with alarm and started to back out.

Bryne was reading and rereading the old news clip. "This really is something." He held up the news article.

"Yes... Say, how long before your Dutch friend gets back to you?"

"Soon, I hope." Bryne shook his head, knowing it could be days, even weeks. He needed another source of information about the Phipps incident. Maybe call his church. Might be a shortcut. No, maybe not. Bryne was so lost in thought, he didn't notice Lawrence had left. Fifteen minutes passed, then thirty. Bryne had still not returned Rader's call when the phone rang. It was de Reuters.

"Jack, my old friend," the Dutchman began jovially, "I got your ProMED note. It's near closing time here. What's so urgent?" He stopped himself and began the obligatory, "But first, how's that beautiful wife of yours, Jack? I trust she's well. Give her my best..."

Bryne went through the preliminaries of a Dutch salutation—the wives, children, colleagues, friends, all addressed. Finally they got down to business.

"Jan, I'm curious about a couple of cases of ciguatera poisoning down near St. Maarten. Back in January. It was a cruise ship incident, I believe... Can you tell me anything about it?"

De Reuters paused, his enthusiasm about family and friends dissolving into a serious professional's approach. "Well, I could, Jack... Do you want an official response, or..."

"Unofficial, Jan, please... not for attribution..."

"Yes. Unofficial. That is why I called. I do not want this to appear in any written document, Jack. It's not coming from me, understood? The whole thing stinks. So let me begin..."

Bryne looked for his notes. This might be good... or bad.

"The first thing is," de Reuters announced, "that the family did indeed die of ciguatera. January last."

Bryne felt the hairs raise on his arms. *Stay calm*, he told himself, *these things happen*. People died of the intoxication every year. He waited.

"There was a bit of territorial nonsense. The deaths took place in international waters, but the nearest local government was us, in St. Maarten. The captain of the vessel was an Italian, with a one hundred percent Spanish crew, save for a Philippine chef. I'll tell you about the food in a minute. The ship was flying under a Panamanian flag and the captain actually tried to refuse boarding by our local officials. For about three minutes. And then Dutch soldiers and French gendarmes took over."

He paused as if he didn't want to reveal any more, but Jack prodded him, "Go on! Go on!"

"The officials talked to the chef," de Reuters grudgingly told him, "confiscated the fish, put the three bodies onto gurneys, and left them at the hospital on the island. The three Phippses were already dead... or so it seemed! There is a bit of a flap about the precise time of death... One of the unrecognized symptoms of intoxication is cataplexy. The victim appears dead, but is really not. He needs to be intubated until he can breathe for himself. Anyway, then the American embassy called, thanks to your congressmen, asking for an expeditious removal of the bodies."

"So," Bryne paused, "they died of ciguatera?"

"Yes, most unfortunately, they did, Jack. And, my friend, for obvious commercial reasons we and the French are not overly anxious to publicize this tragic event. It is bad for tourist relations. In any given year we and our French colleagues on St. Maarten, Martinique, and

Guadeloupe will often see this... plague. Our governments do not wish to promote this as a... bad press?"

Bryne understood. Coverups happened all the time. In the fifties, the Mexican government had denied that yellow fever ever passed across its southern border with Guatemala. It would have been bad for the tourist trade. Bryne remembered, almost word for word, the talk he had been asked to attend while on vacation with Mia a few summers ago in Hyannis Port. This obfuscation had been closer to home. In the seventies Martha's Vineyard and Nantucket began to report two rare diseases, both transmitted by ticks: Rocky Mountain spotted fever and babesiosis. These tourist-dominated havens finally had to admit that their island paradises posed a threat from ticks. It was the ticks' retribution, as in *Jaws*. The ticks' jaws were microscopic, but equally deadly.

He was certain there were other aspects of the poisonings that de Reuters was not mentioning...

"Jan, my dear friend, is there anything... unusual about the findings? You seem a bit hesitant. The concern about tourism is understandable, but is there something more? Something... fishy?"

"Ya, something quite fishy, Jack. In point of fact, the man and his wife did not have any fish in their stomachs. They had some rice, bread, and the minister had a good shot of Scotch shortly before his death. And they found some metabolites of cocaine in his blood, but not enough to kill him. An extraordinary and interesting American minister you once had. The wife and daughter were clean. They, too, had not eaten any fish."

"But you said they died from ciguatera?"

"They did, but not in normal physiological amounts, Jack. It was pharmacological amounts, some ten thousand times what we usually detect in fatal cases. There was no way, no natural way..."

"To get that amount into them unless..."

"... someone dosed them. And there's more. We found not only ciguatera toxin, but neosaxitoxin, gonyautoxin, and microcystin toxins. Our toxico-vigilance program is very sophisticated, Jack, but we have never seen anything like this, and I hope we never do again."

"What did you do, and what are you planning to do about it?"

"One thing we are not recommending, my friend," de Reuters replied, "is putting the event on ProMED. It may produce, what do you call it, copycatting. These algal blooms and dinoflagellates which produce the toxins can be made in fish tanks by anyone with access to the ocean, or to ponds or lakes—any body of water in which organisms grow. With proper temperature control, salinity, and light, one can harvest these blooms as easily as growing duckweed."

"Okay, I see your point."

"Jack, we told the World Health people, Interpol, and your government about this. There is no suspect whatsoever. Fortunately, there is no evidence of another incident."

Bryne thought about the implications of de Reuters's words. Of course, ProMED could be misused, could even facilitate an event. And it could be penetrated—as the ergotism episode had clearly shown. Worst of all, what if the psychopath who was doing all this was a ProMEDer himself? So many what ifs. So many questions.

Thursday, September 10
New York City
Noon

Teddy Kameron, having carefully monitored Bryne's e-mail from the week before to de Reuters, already knew what the virologist was up to. First this instinct and now this evidence told him that Bryne was narrowing in on the Phipps incident—the First Plague, the very first time the voice of God inside him had directed him to act.

The news of Bryne's relentless pursuit—this challenge to The Voice—made Kameron both uneasy yet strangely excited at the same time. The FBI, on the other hand, had bored him. They were merely apparatchiks with no imagination who followed orders like the good soldiers they were. Bryne was a different story; Bryne was a more worthy antagonist. Still, up until now Kameron had been the one in control. If Bryne was on to the first plague, he was doing so without any clues from Teddy. Not good. Not good at all.

Gazing at the beautiful, deadly algae blooming in the fish tanks, Teddy began to feel afraid—afraid of Bryne's getting too close, afraid of being stopped before all the plagues were done. No, no, he assured himself. The Voice would never let that happen. Teddy was God's agent, under divine protection. All would be well. All would be as the Divinity designed it. There was no need to think about Bryne, a mere mortal sinner like the rest.

Pouring himself a snifter of Poire William brandy to calm his nerves, Teddy forced himself to concentrate on his momentous visit to the Caribbean, now almost a year ago. Had he made mistakes, he wondered.

He had heard about the cruise on Phipps's television show, which The Voice had ordered him to watch, then waited for instructions, and they soon were given. The plan was so magnificently simple. Teddy booked a ticket on the liner as an ordinary tourist, not as a member of the Phipps group. But he'd kept his eyes open, and on that fatal final night had managed to slip into the first-class dining room before the main meal. He had seen it all firsthand, and it aroused him greatly, for although the minister "died" quickly, his last few moments were far from pleasant.

Pouring himself another Poire, he opened his laptop, entered his password "LMPG," pulled up the files on the first Voice, and reread his account of the end of Phipps and his family; they were almost ready for Bryne to see.

Friday, January 30
First Class Dining Room, S.S. Rio Roja, St. Maarten
Harbor

Reverend Cato Phipps sat with his family on the
dais of the cruise ship's first-class dining room, congratulating himself on what a good idea this little
junket had been. He had invited contributors to his
electronic church on a week's tour of the islands—
the "Sainted Islands," as he called them when he
pitched the event on television: St. John's, St. Croix,
then down to St. Maarten.

In order to join the tour, one needed to make a
substantial donation to Phipps's religious enterprise; the top one hundred pledges won places on
the tour. All in all, he'd garnered more than two
million dollars. The cruise line had paid his way
and kicked back a few thousand, and the net was
nearly $1.8 mil. Not bad for a country boy! He
smiled.

Phipps planned to make this the Last Supper in
more ways than one. That night, he planned to
ditch the wife and daughter, take the launch into
St. Maarten for a "business evening," then fly back
to Key Biscayne in the morning—having joyfully
seen the last of his family for at least a couple of
days.

The farewell meal of the cruise, he knew, had to
be especially memorable. The feast was going to be
the talk of Des Moines, El Paso, Charlottesville. He
wanted the word to spread so that next year's
cruise would make what he'd netted on this one
look like pocket change. He was thinking of

329

Europe—St. Tropez, St. Étienne, St. Raphaël... all these wonderful places named after saints. He'd have to think of some new angle to get over to Bangkok. Too bad the Jesuits hadn't gone farther into Asia.

"The fish are ready, Reverend Phipps," the steward announced.

"No Jew fish, I hope!" the reverend quipped, then asked more sharply, "And the breads?"

"They have arrived from the bakery on the French side of the island, sir," the steward told him. "Hundreds of baguettes."

"Now remember, the baguettes are only for our people, not the tourists on the second deck. Be sure that the non-church group is asked to leave before we have the meal."

"Yes, sir," the steward shot back.

As always, the reverend was watching his pennies. Since he considered himself a fair man, Phipps had made the cocktail hour open to all the passengers, but not the dinner. Over and above the rijstaffel, there was to be a special catch of bonito, wrasse, and red snapper. All the best markets on the island had been raided. The exclusive seaside resort, La Samana, would be offering beef, not fish, this evening.

Phipps planned to have two whole red snappers placed on each table, after which he would pass among the diners with a large basket of warm, fresh bread. Other baskets would be kept behind a screen, making his supply appear unlimited. Loaves and fishes. A feast of plenty. A miracle.

As he fantasized about the glory that lay ahead, Cato Phipps snacked idly on the rijstaffel, barely noticing when his daughter Gretchen stuck her finger into the thick spicy food; but his wife, Georgianna, did and slapped the girl's hand, hissing that she must use her fork. Georgianna started eating, and then offered a forkful to her little girl.

Something about the fork caught the reverend's attention, and looking at his own, he sneered. It was very hard to find quality service these days. Neither fork appeared to be properly cleaned, and his had given a distinctly metallic flavor to the food. Suddenly he felt his lips and tongue glowing hot from all the spices, then his fingers tingled—although not unpleasantly. Delicious, he thought at first.

"Daddy," Gretchen began to wail, "it's so hot! My lips hurt!"

"Take a sip of your Pepsi," he told her, and the pigtailed child obediently sipped from a large glass swimming with ice cubes, but it didn't seem to help.

"Daddy, Daddy, this tastes hot! It's burning my lips!"

"Nonsense," he barked, taking a sip of the drink. She was right.

Abruptly Georgianna slumped in her seat. Not again, he thought, that drunk this early? But then she fell to the floor and began twitching—first her fingers, then her legs and arms. As Phipps watched, his right-hand man jumped up from his chair and ran to the dais to help. Phipps tried to reach for his wife, but all at once he realized he couldn't move. He tried to lift his arms, turn his head, call for help. Nothing. Powerless, he watched his wife go into convulsions, writhing on the floor.

The dry ice sensation he'd felt on his lips now

spread to his entire face. Electric shocks followed the thick root nerves in the branchial plexus of nerves under his armpits, down through three major nerves into the tiniest fibers in his fingers. Then his privates became numb. He knew he'd uri-nated in his pants, yet couldn't feel the stream emerge. On his skin, however, the urine announced itself as boiling water across his thighs, as rivulets of molten steel streaking down his white socks and into his shoes.

Gretchen was now writhing on the floor with her mom. People were calling for doctors. Complete chaos had broken out. Tourists came into the room. Yet Phipps, who easily commanded a vast TV audi-ence, could do less than nothing now, for, like his family, he had lost the ability to remain upright. The assembly disappeared before his eyes as his trunk melted and his head plunged toward the table top, landing in the red sauce, the sambal oedong.

After what must have felt like minutes, someone lifted Phipps's head out of the peppery paste and called, "Oh, dear Lord, Reverend Phipps... Reverend Phipps?... Can you hear me?" Gently, the person leaned over him and felt for a pulse, which was far too slow and weak to be detected by an untrained hand. "Oh, no... I think Reverend Phipps is dead, too."

Somebody else shouted, "Hey, come here! Gretchen's still breathing." So they left him and turned away. "Oh, Lord. She's dying too!" someone whispered.

Phipps could hear clearly but since he could nei-ther move nor speak, he couldn't tell them he was

332

not dead. That they were dreadfully mistaken.
Already the parishioners were arguing about the
money. About who could open the safe. About the
PAC funds. The congressmen. About who would take
over.

One of the women went to Phipps and wiped his
face with a napkin. It was excruciating. Stroke by
burning stoke, the peppery paste was removed. She
leaned over and closed his eyelids, but gobs of
sauce and bits of rice remained under his eyelids.
Exquisite pain, fiery and hellish, a shooting agony
began to sear his corneas.

Dear God, it was the Indonesian peppers in the
sauce, "hottest in the world," the chef had said,
"hotter than Scotch bonnets or habañeros... They
can raise a blister on your fingers... and never,
never let them get into your eyes, Reverend."

He lay motionless now, eyes scorching, longing
for death, but his cataplexy would last almost two
more hours. He heard everything: the conniving of
his staff. Smelled everything: the fresh, acrid odor of
the body bag even as they zipped him into it. The
bag was dark and warm, and he could still feel
everything: the full, dreadful understanding of what
was finally happening to him.

Later, he could hear the zipper opening, could
feel the slab beneath him and the cool air of the
autopsy room. Blinded now, he saw nothing, but he
knew what was ahead, and if he had been able, he
would have screamed. Now the sound of steel on
stone.

Slowly and most mercifully, the muscles of his
diaphragm weakened, and he realized that he was
suffocating.

He died right after St. Maarten's foremost under-taker finished sharpening his trocar, and only moments before the suctioning began.

Early September
Zoonosis Laboratory, Guilderland

Jack's conversation with de Reuters had produced a stunning revelation: not only had he found the first plague, a toxic algal bloom, but it had happened last January, eight months ago, seven plagues ago. This madman was on a schedule! Next he dialed Rader in Atlanta, who luckily picked up immediately.

"I may have something for your collection of weird occurrences, Jack," Rader began without pleasantries. "Been following your ProMED stuff. Now I have something that does not make any sense at all, even to me."

No lack of humility there, Bryne noted. "And what would that be, Carl?"

"Botulism, Jack."

"Botulism! It happens. What's up?"

"Not your specialty, I know, but in your ball-park. Our illustrious new class of Epidemic Intelligence Service fellows and the FBI are still trying to figure it out. The point is, we've had dozens of bot cases all around the U.S., especially in and around last July, but some as recent as a month ago."

"FBI?"

"Yes, Jack," Rader continued. "It looks like a purposeful act. We told the FBI a week ago. For obvious reasons, they asked us to keep it quiet."

"Are they doing their own investigation?" Jack knew he'd be getting another visit from Hubbard.

"Yep. Anyway, some cases are fatal, but not all. None of the people canned their own vegetables. The incidences are isolated by time, place, and person. No evidence of wound botulism or, for that matter, common food. The state health departments went through the entire drill—foods recently eaten, common restaurants, canned and commercial foods. The FDA boys did a sweep in a few cases. Got you guessing, Jack?"

Bryne was sure Rader had an answer or a partial one and was teasing him. "Do I get only one guess?"

"Go ahead. If you get the answer right, you can open door number two."

"Ministers."

"Bravo! I should have known... Jack, keep your guessing quiet or the FBI will be stopping by."

"They already have, Carl, but not about botulism; what's up?"

"There's something serious coming down, Jack. Ministers or their families, including kids, are the only risk factor that stands out. How did you know?"

"I'm just guessing, but did any of them ever take a cruise to the Caribbean?"

"Now what kind of nonsequitorial question is that?"

"It's relevant, Carl, believe me."

"Okay, if you say so. I'll see what I can

find out. Next question, Jack. How did they get it?"

This really wasn't Bryne's field, Rader had been right, but he did know that except for a rare puncture wound like tetanus, which introduced spores from the soil, botulism requires special conditions to form toxins. He remembered an outbreak of infant botulism which had been caused by formula containing honey made from flower nectar that contained spores bees brought back to the hive, spores so potent they survived in the honey even after routine heating.

"I have no idea," Jack admitted, "other than the fact that most botulism in adults is food-borne."

"It wasn't from food." Rader clearly liked this guessing game. "And after the CDC identified the toxins, we knew it wasn't from a pharmaceutical source."

"A what? Somebody actually sells the toxin?"

"Company in California. It's used to treat cross-eyed people and control eye muscle spasms. The thing is, the company shows no record of any unusual sales, and the toxin they make is only Type A. The stuff we got here is one hundred times more powerful, a mix of A and B."

"But don't you have to eat it or inject it?"

"Usually yes, but they found something else. Dimethyl sulfoxide—DMSO. The DMSO allowed the toxin to be absorbed directly through the skin. Someone—or some fanatic group that has yet to claim credit—mailed the toxin in small globe paperweights to dozens of unrelated, unconnected people."

"But mostly ministers."

"Correct. The globes were souvenirs from a ski resort called Padre Mountain, sent anonymously as presents."

"*Padre* Mountain. Whoever's doing this has a warped sense of humor?"

"You might say that," Rader replied. "Anyway, when the victims shook up the globes, the bot toxin leaked out, and the DMSO allowed it to penetrate intact skin. The incubation period was often a matter of minutes. Bang, instant botulism, like instant coffee."

"How many cases?"

"Still counting. It's dozens so far, Jack. And there may be many more than those being picked up on the reporting system. If some old duffer comes in DOA, the local ME or coroner is going to attribute death to heart attack or a stroke. Jack, we're dealing with a man-made epidemic here. And whoever he is, he's mixing a nasty cocktail."

"Any idea why?" Bryne remembered reading that Phipps had been trying to steer the Republican Party agenda.

"None. But here's a funny thing. The bot cases have appeared in Florida, Indiana, Kentucky, Mississippi, Missouri, Nevada, Ohio, Tennessee, and New York. Now the FDA, not wanting to alarm people, made a public statement that a batch of Padre Mountain glass globes contained a salmonella—not a bot—contaminant. In response, they were sent over forty globes from other states—all, it turns out, from ministers."

"Were these ministers okay?"

"Yep. When we tested the globes, they were completely clean. Oh, I should add that when you turned over the booby-trapped globes to make the snow fall—"

"Snow! These were snow globes?" Bryne made a note to himself: "snow = hail?"

"They were. But the point I was making was that on the bottoms of all the toxic globes was a four-letter code."

"Let me guess," Jack mused. "How about 'LMPG'?"

"How the hell did you—"

"What about ICD codes?"

Rader's sudden silence conveyed his amazement. How could Bryne know all this? He was either psychic or... He would have to call the FBI after they hung up. He was concerned more than ever, almost frightened now. The sociopath killing people with botulism couldn't be Bryne. Yet he knew too much.

Bryne was equally frightened, but for a far different reason. The number of victims per plague was growing steadily. A sophisticated toxin had been sent to scores, perhaps hundreds, of ministers, but only half appeared to have been targeted, and they were scattered by time, place, and person. The rules of epidemiologic investigation were simply not working. But this was a madman, he told himself, not a plague. He rubbed his eyes. There was an awkward silence. Then Bryne spoke.

"When can you fax me the list of states—both those targeted and those that were spared? I'd like to take a look at it." Rader had been hoping Bryne would request the lists. He needed help. The computers at the CDC and FBI had come up with nothing.

"I'm worried... but I'm happy you'll try to run the numbers for me. Do you have a new program up there, Jack?"

Bryne looked at Lawrence. He had been listening. "Yes, I do, Carl, a very sophisticated one. One of the best."

"What is it, Jack?"

"It's a big dark secret, Carl." Bryne hung up, never guessing that his "big dark secret" would soon provoke Rader to make more than one call to the FBI.

Lawrence waited by the fax machine as it beeped. Suddenly he noticed that Jack was smiling. Smiling broadly, a rarity these days.

"Jack," Drew asked him, "why so happy?"

"Because, my friend," Bryne answered, "We just found our seventh plague!"

A few moments later, a single sheet slid out of the fax machine:

States Where Botulism Recovered	States with No Botulism
FL, IN, KY, MI, MO	AL, AR, CA, CT, ID,
MS, NE, NY, OH, TN	MA, MD, NH, NJ, PA
OR, SC, TX, VA, VT, WA, WV	

16

Friday, September 4
Zoonosis Laboratory, Guilderland

Nearly all the UPS and FedEx drivers knew and liked Drew Lawrence. The Guilderland lab received stacks of packages daily, and they always insisted on giving him a hand with the bulkier deliveries. Lawrence was finishing a cup of tea when he saw the FedEx truck coming up the drive. Checking his watch, Drew noticed it was considerably after 10:30, the usual morning delivery time. He could see the embarrassed look on the new man's face as he pulled up to the delivery door behind the BL–3 lab, the rabies lab.

The rain that had started at dawn, then stopped, was falling again. Undeterred by the weather, Lawrence immediately went outside to help unload. The driver climbed into the back of the truck, checking each box with his hand-held scanner and handing out the packages to Lawrence, who stacked them on the loading dock. They were almost done when the driver suddenly froze.

At first Lawrence saw nothing out of the ordinary, only a routine white package, probably Tyvek wrapping paper, about the size of a case of wine. It was tied with string and, like most of the packages sent to Lawrence these days, had been wrapped in bright orange biohazard tape with its distinctive red clawlike circles.

The driver turned to Lawrence, obviously concerned.

"This one's sprung a leak, man." He gestured with his thumb at the white package. As he moved out of the light from the truck's interior, Lawrence could see thin streams of vapor seeping out of the edges of the package. Smelling nothing, he reached out and put his hand in the cloud, which bounced harmlessly off his fingers.

"Don't worry, happens now and then. Nothing wrong with this package," Drew joked, "except it's a little heavy for some people." He hoisted up the package easily and swung it awkwardly back into the lab, leaving the driver to bring in the rest.

Lawrence signed for the deliveries, put the packages on a small handcart, and made his way down to the refrigerator in the examining room. He filled out a short series of notations in the "samples received" column of the logbook, and transcribed the serial numbers on the various vials, containers, Baggies, test tubes, and slides, sorting them into categories based on degrees of urgency.

A critical request from Long Island for a rabies analysis headed the list. A little brown bat had bitten a preschool girl on the ear during an evening hayride in Sag Harbor. After killing it, the girl's father had been smart enough to preserve the bat and contact the Suffolk County Health Department. Hasan, Bryne's old friend in Riverhead, had forwarded the tiny, mangled creature, still frozen in a Baggie, along with an urgent note.

Lawrence understood that virtually every case was an emergency to someone. Not much difference, he well knew, between waiting for the results of a rabies test or a biopsy—when it came to fear.

He put on his mask and gloves, prepared the tiny autopsy table, thawed the bat in warm water, opened the bat's skull, teased out the brain, and dipped it in a small beaker of antibody-tagged fluorescent dye. Minutes later, he delicately sliced through the brain and took it across the lab to the microscope with the ultraviolet wavelength exciter.

He switched off the other lights, bent over the sample, and looked for the radiant explosion of green and yellow fluorescence that would indicate a mating between the rabies-specific dye and the rabies virus in the brain—if the virus was there. Holding the lamp closer, he adjusted his eyes to the eerie purple glow suffusing the lab from the black light, and looked into the bat's brain.

Nothing glowed. Negative.

He switched off the black light.

Drew would check more thoroughly later, but he felt sure he would get a true negative. Knowing what it would mean to the little girl and her parents made him feel wonderful. He decided to call Dr. Hasan immediately and complete the paperwork afterwards.

As he punched in the number, he checked his watch. 11:15 A.M. Drew apologized for being tardy and was told by a grateful Hasan that on the contrary, his speed was amazing. Lawrence hung up feeling that he had not only helped the girl, but also Jack Bryne and ProMED. Dropping the bat's body into a metal container and its pea-sized brain in another, he gave them to his lab assistant and told her to do the extended test, then refrigerate and inventory the samples.

Next Lawrence turned to Tucker's latest batch of specimens next, knowing Bryne would want the results as soon as possible. He wheeled the cart containing the samples into a larger lab and carefully placed all six packages from Kentucky on a long stainless steel counter. He put the steaming white package into a deep sink, then snapped on a set of large overhead lamps.

Drew's eyes had always given him trouble, and he was grateful for the bright lighting. He rubbed his forehead between the heels of his hands. His eyes hurt, his head hurt, his hip hurt. He went to a first aid cabinet, and took four aspirin. Lawrence regarded aspirin as a lifesaver.

Removing his old tortoiseshells, he held them under the water at the sink, meticulously washing the lenses in soapy water before cleaning his hands. Then he took out a fresh pair of latex gloves and pulled them on.

Drew reached down for the white package and began cutting the wrapper. Thin wisps of carbon dioxide were still seeping out. As he sliced through the Tyvek, more of the curling gray plumes escaped. He ignored them.

343

The box contained an ordinary red-and-white two-gallon picnic cooler whose edges had been carefully sealed in orange biohazard tape, with two small perforations at either end to allow the gas to escape. Lawrence cut away the tape and tipped back the lid.

Inside the cooler were six small, compact blocks of gently rounded dry ice, each roughly half the size of a cigarette pack. As Lawrence watched, the blocks continued to shed frigid carbon dioxide with such urgency that the heat of the conversion warmed the rock-hard ice from a solid to a vapor, instantly, never slowing down enough to become liquid.

Drew, well aware that the frigidly hot surface could burn like an electric wire, picked up a set of tongs to put the first pieces of ice in another sink, a sink that happened to have a defective washer. As he set down the dry ice, a fat drop of warm water hit the top of one of the pieces. Instantly, the warm water accelerated the sublimation into a mini-explosion, and the ice shot across the stainless steel basin as if it were actually alive. Turning away, Drew raised a forearm over his eyes.

The sink had now become the cauldron of a witch's brew, with silvery plumes of liberated gas coiling over the edge and drifting to the floor. Another plume of water vapor wafted toward the ceiling as Lawrence, unconcerned, returned to the samples.

He opened the specimen box inside the cooler and quickly inventoried the ten small circular glass jars inside. Each was roughly three inches high, sealed with a black plastic screw top, and bore a small paper label with a series of notations—the name of the horse, of the owners, a file name for the specimen, and the animal's death date—which Lawrence duly recorded. Some jars contained a small brain section removed from the hippocampus, others from the cerebellum, and still others from the pons.

These samples had the potential to reveal something as important as an entirely new rabies variant, or only the ordinary raccoon strain he was used to seeing. There were three paraffin blocks to be made into microscopic sections to check for Negri bodies. Bryne would also want to be able to examine the samples for spongiform changes indicating prion-induced damage. Maybe this time they'd actually come up with something.

During the last ten years, Drew Lawrence had put together more data for rabies comparisons—raccoon, skunk, bat—than almost anybody else in the U.S.; he was the resident expert. Since Bryne would have wanted Lawrence to be certain to run these tests himself, he set to work.

Drew would never admit it—he took too much pride in his scientific objectivity—but secretly, desperately, he wanted these horse brains to be full of rabies so that Jack could put this growing obsession behind him. There had to be some logical reason for the die-offs. *Now Lawrence, let the instruments speak for themselves,* he reminded himself, *let the will of the Lord be done in the lab as it is everywhere.* Soon he was dutifully working through the samples one by one.

Lawrence had first put on his protective head gear, mask, gloves, and gown, then taken each sample to the paraffin bath. He infused the samples with hot wax to firm the spongy brain tissue, which resembled cooked cauliflower, so that later, when it cooled, it would be ready for the microtome.

The first eight jars were opened, sampled, processed, and closed normally. The work went well. Each time, Lawrence was particularly careful to avoid exposure to the tissue, opening the glass jars under the BL–3 hood, putting the contents into the wax, and proceeding directly to the next sample bottle. Although he had been immunized against rabies, he knew that there were other bugs out there waiting.

He had imprinted the eight preparations, placed drops of a fluorescent dye on each, and set them on a stand to dry. He was puzzled. The samples seemed strange almost from the start. Each time he put the brain tissue in the wax bath, he noted visible differences in the samples. At least superficially, they were unlike any rabies samples he'd ever seen. Judging by the cerebellum sections, he was not even sure all the samples were horse brains.

After he closed the eighth jar, he placed it back in the shipping cooler. Two more samples, and he would retag the lot and put them on a shelf in the lab's immense walk-in refrigerator, where they would wait beside hundreds more, possibly for years, until the lab received a final disposal order for the specimen containers.

Lawrence had lifted the ninth sample jar out of its styrofoam compartment and was about to open it when the speakerphone squawked to life. It was Bryne, asking Lawrence for an update on the Suffolk bat; the Commissioner of Health had received an angry call from the father of the girl.

"Negative on the bat," Drew told him. "No fluorescence, nothing to worry about. I already talked to Hasan. And Jack, on the new shipment from Churchill Downs, we'll have most of the early results around ten tomorrow."

"Thanks, Drew, I doubt we'll see any new rabies, but I'd like to play around with some new tagged morbilliform antibodies. But that can wait." He paused, then asked, "Say, did Vicky call? I was hoping she'd have some encouraging news about Enoch Tucker's condition."

Lawrence chose not to answer directly. "I'm going to phone Churchill Downs about those specimens soon enough. Would you like me to tell you the results first? So you can pass them on to Vicky Wade?" Lawrence constantly ribbed Jack, but this time there was condemnation behind it.

"I'm finishing up a journal article. I'll be at the work station," Bryne said brusquely, annoyed by Lawrence's moralistic tone—it wasn't as if he were cheating on Mia with Vicky, after all. A few lunches hardly constituted adultery. Besides, pushy as she was professionally, Wade would never force herself on a married man. "It'll take the rest of the day. But yes, let me know if anything pops up."

He signed off, and Drew went back to work. He checked the clock. Still too early to be sure. He reexamined the first sample, playing the black light across the specimen.

Nothing.

He turned away from the first samples and went back to the hood, where the ninth jar waited.

As a precaution, he put on a fresh set of gloves, but while he was pulling them on, he felt his nail nick one of the fingers and slightly tear the latex.

He looked at the glove. Such a tiny tear.

There was almost no chance rabies had killed these horses, and he was already running late. What was the harm?

Slow down, he lectured himself, and peeled off the damaged glove, threw it away, and slipped on a fresh one.

Returning to the hood, he picked up the jar with the untreated fresh brain material, taking hold of the glass jar in his right hand and the plastic lid in his left. While he was twisting off the lid, the speakerphone squawked again.

"Drew, you still there?" For a moment, Lawrence felt a flood of irritation at this second interruption from his boss.

"Right, I'm here," he answered, backing away from the hood.

"Drew, sorry to bother you, but would you

have a moment to come in here and look at something?"

Even over the speakerphone, Drew heard a change in Jack's voice. Before it had been businesslike; now it sounded incredibly... bleak.

"Be right there, Jack," Lawrence shouted, limping away from the sample, picking up one piece of dry ice with the tongs and carrying it over to the sink.

With his gloved hand, he moved the sample jar next to the ice to keep the temperature stable, then placed sample jar nine, still unopened, onto the ice block.

As he turned away, another drop of water hit the dry ice, and the spurt of smoke rose again. He pulled off the gloves and headed for Bryne's office.

The office was dark. Bryne sat in front of his computer screen, vivid with an image of the Japanese atrocities in Manchuria. Lawrence was shaken. Jack was supposed to be working. Why this? Why now?

"Did you know, Drew? This site accuses most of the senior doctors in modern Japan of having worked and trained at this place called Unit 731 during World War II." He gestured at the screen with his thumb.

"I have visited that web site..." Lawrence felt as if he were confessing a reprehensible act.

"I was at that camp when I was a child. Did you know that, Drew?"

"I knew. Somebody at a departmental

meeting mentioned the web address a few weeks ago. I was curious so I bookmarked the site. I hope it doesn't cause a problem."

"Of course not. We don't have any secrets. I'm merely surprised it's common knowledge. I tried to keep it to myself."

"Jack, it's like surviving the camps in Europe. It's a badge of honor... I'll erase the bookmark. I'm very sorry. I meant no offense."

"None was taken. I was simply surprised when I saw it. Brings back many memories..."

"Jack, I've got those samples to finish."

"Of course. Sorry, Drew..." Bryne waved him away.

Lawrence started back toward the lab, then, needing to put closure on the incident, again opened the door to Bryne's office. Drew could see the barb-wired barracks of Unit 731, could see the highlighted text, could see Jack reading as he scrolled downward.

The light from the computer screen gave Jack's face a pale, sickly sheen. Even in the dimness, Drew could see tears coursing down his cheeks as he shook his head slowly from side to side, reading the words and scanning the horrible images.

Lawrence wanted to walk over to Bryne and put his hand on his arm and pull him away from the screen, but he was sure Bryne would have none of it. Tears that had to be shed were being shed now. Jack must be alone with his grief. He closed the door, quietly.

Back in the lab, Drew pulled on his gloves and replaced his mask. He had been right: not a single sign of rabies was showing in any of the first four samples. A faint vapor was still enveloping sample nine, and he leaned down to look at it. Same as the others. He was sure this time.

It wasn't rabies, so he decided not to take this specimen over to the hood. Drew leaned over the sink and took the jar in both hands. He gave it a twist, and the lid turned—much too easily.

Drew felt something tear inside the jar, and the lid seemed to be moving. Minute condensation was forming inside the container. *Spoiled! I should have left it near more dry ice.* He opened the cap another quarter-turn.

More minute bubbles, faster, more pressure. The lid was now spinning by itself, vapor jetting out from around the cap soaked his gloves and they slipped. The lid hissed off the jar like a diamondback rattler. A fine mist blew out around the edges of the cap with enough force to send the contents shooting up out of the sink, almost as high as the overhead lamp.

"Whoo-ee," Lawrence gasped. "Man, this one's ripe!" But he had seen worse, especially in the summer when boxes arrived without refrigerants.

As a precaution, he washed his hands and changed his gloves. Rabies most unlikely. What about this prion thing? No, he also doubted that. Drew wondered whether or not to tell Bryne about the accident, then opted against it, reminding himself that his colleague was spending the day secluded in his own private hell.

The muscle aches, fever, and chills started while Drew was driving home. The pain began in his shoulders, then moved to his lower back, quads, and calf muscles. The sweeping chills alternating with feverishness announced another bout of flu, his third within the last decade. Lawrence had developed a dry cough that would become wet and ropy within a few days.

He called Jack that night, at home, exhausted and apologetic. "Jack, it's Drew. I've got to take a sick day, probably Monday. The flu hit me a few hours ago."

"Drew," Bryne told him firmly, "by all means, you stay right where you are." Lawrence would never call in the evening if it wasn't serious. "Be sure to take a lot of liquids."

Bryne's apparent concern struck Mia, who looked up. He mouthed the word "Flu," and she frowned in sympathy.

"Say, did you get a flu shot this year?" He realized this was adding insult to injury, since Drew stayed away from the New York State Health Department clinic as if it were quarantine.

"Is this an official inquiry, Dr. Bryne?" Drew wheezed, then broke into a fit of coughing.

"I was pretty sure you skipped it again."

"I'm okay. I'll be better in a few days."

"Seriously, Drew, that cough sounds nasty.

If I were you, I'd call Dr. MacKenzie. He'll see you in a minute."

"Naw, I'll be all right. Have a good weekend," Drew managed to say before coughing again.

"Righto, Drew, thanks... You get well now, and listen, there's absolutely no reason to be stoic. Call MacKenzie."

After they hung up, Bryne sat on the edge of the couch thinking of Lawrence—of his safety, of the risks he took working in a marginally adequate BL–3 lab.

Stop being paranoid, Jack lectured himself. *After all, Lawrence hasn't handled anything hot for weeks.*

Sunday, September 6
The Cottage, Guilderland

At eleven forty-five on Sunday night, Bryne got a call from the chief of the New York State Wadsworth Laboratory, C. DeHavenon Lyman.

"Jack, I didn't get you up, did I?" He had, but didn't wait for an answer to the question. "There's a problem, Jack, down at JFK. The quarantine folks have a sick racehorse that came in on a flight from Saudi Arabia. Temp one hundred and four, respiratory rate sixty per minute, flared nostrils, sweating, and beginning to foam."

"Any preliminary diagnosis?"

"The quarantine vet's thinking *perdesiekte*, African horse sickness. But it's too soon to say. Anyway, the owner's some oil sheik, and he's

353

ringing every bell in Washington. The commissioner called me to let me know the guy's flying in his own experts. And the Plum Island medical director—he's a vet—is driving in from Suffolk."

"Plum Island!" Jack thought. "That's unusual!"

Plum Island is the United States's premier research station for exotic, foreign, and potentially dangerous animal diseases—the only facility on the East Coast with the technicians, laboratory, and—most important—the ability needed to screen the country from importing the countless emerging pathogens.

The Department of Agriculture had taken over the small, isolated island off the northeast tip of Long Island, rumored to have been a biological warfare facility, from the Defense Department back in 1954. There were those who still believed it was a cover for CIA experiments, but no one really knew for certain.

"Why's Plum Island getting involved?"

"I'd like to know myself, Jack. But it is the only federal quarantine facility for animals in the States, and it's an hour or so from JFK. That makes some sense."

"And that's it?"

"Between you and me," Lyman confided, "CDC selects its investigations, as does the Agriculture Department, or for that matter the CIA. Please do not quote me, but there may be some problem with biological agents."

"Are we talking BT?" Jack pressed him.

"Well, Jack, if somebody from Washington

thinks this horse is carrying some kind of exotic infectious agent, then all this hoopla makes a lot of sense. I need you to go down there and sort things out, protect New York State's interests."

Terrorists with a contaminated horse could do a lot of damage, but Bryne considered it more likely to be something out of the mountains of East Africa. African horse disease was real, and a real threat. No need to conjure up international conspiracies.

"Agreed. I'll go."

"Thanks, Jack. I appreciate how bloody inconvenient all this must be." *You don't know the half of it,* Jack thought, glancing over at Mia, who had also been awakened by the phone call.

"Thank God it's almost fall," Jack mused. "So many mosquitoes at JFK now." But he was praying, *Please, not another plague.* He thought about the African horse disease, about how easily it was carried by mosquitoes, of the miles of marshland surrounding the airport.

"When do you want me there, Chuck? It's midnight..." He watched Mia get up, slip into her robe, and walk out of the room. "You're trying to say immediately, aren't you?"

"I told them you're coming. Kiss Mia goodbye and try to get the first train to the city so you can make it to JFK Quarantine in the morning."

After he hung up with Lyman, Bryne walked downstairs to the living room and found his wife apparently asleep on the couch. He touched her shoulder, and she looked up, shielding her eyes. He started to tell her what was going on, but she interrupted him.

"Do it, Jack. Whatever it is, do it. I'm too tired to hear any more of your excuses." And she turned away from him.

Bryne sighed and headed back up the stairs. Unplugging the phone and the answering machine, he lay back on the bed and rested, grateful there would be no more interruptions that night. At dawn he woke, dressed, packed an overnight bag, and prepared to race to the station for the New York train. On his way out, he pulled the cover over Mia and locked the door behind him.

In his haste, he had forgotten to reconnect the phone and the answering machine. He never got the call from Drew's frantic wife, Elise.

Monday, September 7
Kennedy Airport
11:45 A.M.
Bryne arrived at the large animal quarantine area at Kennedy Airport just before noon. It was a separate building, well away from the main terminals, filled with crates of shrieking parrots, bleating lambs, whining dogs, and other terrified, unidentifiable animal cargo.

Almost immediately, an airport guard tapped Bryne on the shoulder. "Dr. Bryne," he said firmly, "I've been asked to summon you in connection with an urgent matter. Please come with me."

356

"Now, what the hell?" Jack asked archly.

"Please, sir, come with me," the guard answered firmly.

"Now hold on a minute, officer. You're with airport security, right? This is an animal-holding facility, right? Well, then I'm the man in charge here. I run the New York State rabies lab.... Who do you think has authority over this investigation, anyway?" Bryne had gotten angry and hadn't even noticed the powerfully built man in the greens of a U.S. Army colonel walking up behind him. The man reached out and tapped Bryne on the shoulder.

"Dr. Bryne, I believe I'd like to answer that one if you don't mind. Stand by a moment.."

The Colonel flipped open a cell phone and punched in ten numbers from memory. Bryne watched, incredulous, as the officer asked the person who answered to put him through to Dr. Lyman. The Colonel passed the phone to Bryne and folded his arms.

"Chuck, what the hell's going on here?" Bryne asked. "I'm standing here with some damned lieutenant...."

"That's *Colonel* Dan Edwards to you, Sir. Special Pathogens, Ft. Detrick..."

Edwards let the impact of the title sink in.

"Jack, listen to me." Lyman hissed into the phone. "I can't talk, right now. I've got Washington on the other line. Do what Edwards says. He's been to Plum Island, now he's in charge of the federal investigation. Don't ask any questions. Call me later. Sorry..."

Lyman hung up, and Bryne handed the phone back to the Colonel.

Edwards took Bryne aside. "Dr. Bryne, we believe Dr. Tucker may have found the cause for the deaths of the horses. He said it was *Stachybotris atra*—a mycotoxin in the bedding straw. We're checking it. But Tucker's hospitalized. He's mad as a hatter."

"Mycotoxins?" Bryne gasped. "Moldy straw! Of course! But what about...?"

"That's all I can tell you now. Please, Doctor, go with the guard..."

The security officer motioned him to follow.

Jack tried to speak but Edwards had already turned away.

"Maybe I'll see you later, Bryne," Edwards yelled over his shoulder as he walked toward a group of men and women examining a stallion.

As he followed the guard out of the building, Jack's thoughts were centered less on his predicament than on Drew's. Vicky, who was in Louisville, had reached him minutes earlier on his cellular phone to tell him Enoch Tucker's condition had worsened. When Bryne mentioned that the last set of samples Drew had processed might be late since he had the flu, she sounded puzzled.

"Jack," she told him, "I've been working really closely with the vets down here, and I'm positive they haven't shipped you any samples in the last few days!"

358

Months before, Kameron's journey to Kentucky had been perfectly timed, as had his divinely ordained research for the perfect microcosmic vehicle for the ninth plague. His recent trip to Washington had proven the efficacy of the virus on a grand scale. If he wanted to strike at Bryne, which of course he did, what better way than through his treasured colleague, his eyes and ears, Drew Lawrence? By now the FedEx package from Louisville had surely reached Guilderland, contents properly prepared. And besides, the steamboat trip down the Mississippi to Memphis for his next adventure had reminded him of the Nile.

"'*Ex Africa sempera liquid novi*,' quoth Pliny; there is always something new out of Africa." He had felt strong, felt potent, as the package slid down the conveyor belt to begin its journey to Drew Lawrence. "Good-bye, my friend," he had called silently to its lethal contents, "ancient as your African birthplace. Find a new home now. Land bridges, mammalian reservoirs, insect vectors won't be needed anymore."

This particular virus had descended from a progenitor thousands of years older than itself. Now Kameron's new "friend" had become a new genus in its own right, a stable mutation characterized by a distinctive conserved polymerase domain, slightly different from the other Arenaviruses—Machupo, Junin, Guanarito, Sabiá, as well as the Phleboviruses that were its descendants. It was a full member of the Bunyaviridae, a close cousin of hanta, yet very much its own species.

Kameron had learned the secret that the Rift Valley had kept for millennia, until 1918, when reports of a new sheep and goat disease first surfaced. Then, in Kenya, the disease that would come to be called Rift Valley fever had spread, carried by a variety of mosquitoes and all manner of other insects, to humans, tens of thousands of humans.

Outbreaks swept through Egypt in 1978 and Mauritania in 1985. Besides mosquitoes and insect carriers, scientists found other modes of infection: direct contact, aerosols, even the wind—the khamsins from the Sahara. The disease caused epizootics throughout sub-Saharan Africa every fifteen to twenty-five years.

Ah, but the African mosquitoes! *Dambos*, shallow depressions in the earth, afforded Edenic breeding places for the Aëdes mosquito. The virus was passed between the mosquitoes sexually like a venereal disease, and could be transmitted transovarially by the female to thousands of her eggs like a congenital disease. The Aëdes eggs could easily avoid desiccation, even in a hot, dry climate, as they waited for the rare rainstorm to free them from the crusted dirt.

The disease was devastating in mammals, striking cattle, goats, sheep, camels, water buffalo, monkeys, and man. The effects included abortions and stillbirths, and a particularly fetid diarrhea that ended in death.

When humans first contracted Rift Valley fever, most first experienced flulike symptoms. Then the complications began—jaundice, hepatitis, and bloody diarrhea, as well as hemorrhages beneath the skin and into deeper organs.

What made this particular disease appropriate to the Ninth Plague, the darkness, was that it also caused small arteriolar leaks in the retina, and there the ruptured retinal vessels would jet microscopic spurts of blood into the eyes' clear vitreous humor. Images would turn pink, then red; then blackness descended.

Victims were blinded for days, some even permanently, especially if they thought they had contracted the flu and started taking a goodly amount of blood thinners, like aspirin…

Drew Lawrence was the perfect subject for Rift Valley. Kameron had learned enough about the workings of the lab to know that Lawrence handled all the samples, no matter to whom they were addressed. With that Kentucky postmark, there was no way Lawrence wouldn't process the package immediately.

The Voice, of course, had spoken to Teddy of Rift Valley fever in the larger context of Washington, which had already been set in motion. And yet it seemed divinely inspired to smite those closest to Teddy's enemy, his pursuer, Jack Bryne. That Drew Lawrence was a firstborn son only served to give Kameron's personal mission enhanced validity.

Teddy knew that the end game of the infernal chess match he and Bryne were playing would be the breaking of a spirit, the loss of hope. Blunt a man's spirit, and he leaves the field, bloody and bowed. Yes, Drew Lawrence was an excellent move, even inspired. He almost had to pity Dr. John Bryne for Lawrence's demise, and for who would be next.

17

Monday, September 7
New York City
9:30 A.M.

In order to be certain his prototype had worked, Teddy had called the lab at Guilderland and asked for Drew Lawrence, claiming he was an old school friend from the city who happened to be in Albany. When Lawrence's lab assistant came on the line, she told him Mr. Lawrence was out sick.

"That doesn't sound like Drew," Teddy had joked. "He hardly missed a day of school in his whole life."

"Well," the young woman replied without the least trace of humor, "everybody gets the flu sometimes." She asked if he wanted to leave his name, and he said no, he'd try Drew at home to see how he was.

Kameron, of course, did not call Lawrence at home—if he *was* at home and not in intensive care—or the morgue. Now that he knew all he needed to, he sat down at his laptop, entered his LMPG password, and began to record for posterity the recent events in Washington.

On the final Wednesday before the Congressional recess, the New Christian Response Caucus from the House and the Senate's even more powerful Visionary Christian Conference were holding a much-anticipated, much-publicized joint session.

For the first time in American politics, a group of bipartisan reactionary Christian legislators had agreed to meet and approve—or "bless," as they had come to call it—all manner of funding proposals both Democratic or Republican, without first going to committee and without a floor vote. Power was shifting, and with it was a transfer of money away from the coffers of government. A multibillion-dollar mandate was in the works, and at some point, the separation of church and state was being blurred.

These people had power. They had conviction. They had, Teddy Kameron told himself with a chuckle, both blind faith and blind ambition.

The meeting was called for 10:00 A.M. As members of the delegation began filing out of the Senate and House chambers, where they had passed their own resolutions to adjourn early, press galleries were buzzing with news of the Counsel for Christ, as the members were calling themselves.

Moving in groups of three and four, they made their way to the basement of the Capitol and boarded the small underground railway that connects Congress with the office buildings across Constitution Avenue.

The Caucus was to meet, ironically, in the same room where the McCarthy hearings had been broadcast across America in the early days of black and white. This gathering would be closed to much of

363

*the mainstream press. The Counsel had its own digi-
tal cameras, reporters, and focus.*

*The goal of this session was to extract loyalty
oaths from the heads of all grant-monitoring agencies. "Balanced" approaches toward Darwinism
would increase funding parameters of a particular
agency. Positive approaches to biomedical research
with fetal tissue would gut a program's budget
faster than a fire could blaze through an abortion
clinic. Certain things needed to be made crystal-
clear to some administrators. Teddy felt that the
darkness he was going to supply, the Ninth Plague,
would be more on target.*

*The oak-paneled hearing room was alive with
faith and fear as the moderators from the Caucus
began taking their seats while senior representatives
from the major research centers shifted nervously.
These executives had been strongly urged to support
Counsel positions. They would be testifying with
their own brand of blind faith. On the other hand,
the "humanists," those disciples of godless science,
would be facing the lions.*

*The hearings opened with a benediction, followed
by initial prayers. Large groups of reporters with
their camera, sound, and light personnel had turned
the hearing room into a mass of taped-down wires,
braces of microphones, video recording equipment,
and the associated debris. The reporters, film crews,
and local interested citizens, Teddy Kameron among
them—how simple it was to forge a press pass and
dress in jeans, Nikes, a T-shirt, baseball cap, and
tinted glasses—all staked out their camera angles,
claiming their turn.*

Since it was going to be a long session, the

reporters were grateful for the coffee, donuts, apples, pastries, and soft drinks that seemed to appear magically on the trays of Congressional staffers while their masters raised the circus curtain.

A row of heavy chairs had been pushed back against the far wall to make room for lamp racks. The area was a mess, littered with crumpled food bags, styrofoam coffee cups, cellophane sandwich wrappers, used napkins, and designer water bottles. Nobody paid the least attention to a brown paper bag resting on the floor against a radiator. Nobody, that is, except Teddy Kameron, who had placed it there.

This particular bag contained a warm, half-empty sixteen-ounce bottle of ginger ale, some candy wrappers, and a handful of soiled Kleenex, all of which seemed to have been recently used. Nobody would have opened the soda bottle, even if they had looked in the bag. The fluid inside got warmer and warmer as the hearing proceeded.

Inside the plastic bottle, Teddy had placed a small pellet of dry ice, which had begun melting rapidly as the temperature climbed. By now, the walls of the plastic container were stretched as tight as the skin of a snare drum. Teddy made sure to move away quietly, out of the coming line of fire, as even more of the dry ice turned into carbon dioxide.

The first witness, His Holiness, Bishop, and Very Reverend Michael Deven of the First Church of Woonsocket, to be introduced by the Republican senator from Missouri, was delayed for a moment;

flashbulbs popped as the senator rose. There was a bit of a hubbub as a protester tried to shout something and was instantly removed from the room. Then all eyes turned toward His Holiness, making his stately, self-important way to the central table.

There was, for a brief moment, what passes as a hush in Washington. Even more lights came on. Jackets started coming off in the heat. The bishop prepared to read from his Bible.

At the precise moment the Very Reverend Deven raised his head to speak, the plastic bottle exploded, the screw-on top shooting out of the bag and rising ten feet in the air.

People around the perimeter of the room crouched down as if they were under fire. Three of the Congressmen dove behind the heavy desks built specifically to protect them from any attack. In seconds, three Capitol guards burst into the room, joining their colleagues already in the chamber. All of them were reaching for their guns.

A cameraman standing on one of the chairs near the radiator tried to restore order by shouting, "It's okay... It's okay... It's only a pop bottle. It's so hot in here, it must have blown its top. No problem!" He sprang off the chair and made his way over to the remains of the bag.

There was a sizable rent in the side of the plastic bottle. The cameraman could see the torn metal ring where the cap had blown completely off the bottle. Thin white vapor was seeping into the air, and the watery fluid at the bottom of the bottle was still fizzing actively. There was no odor.

As the security people started toward him, he jumped back on the chair and waved the shredded

366

bottle over his head. "Take it easy," he yelled, "it's only a soda!"

By then, heads began to reemerge from behind the Congressional dais. A woman on the right side of the hearing room began to clap. Slowly the general applause began to swell, the cameraman holding the bottle aloft as if it were the head of Medusa. Motioning the cameraman forward, the Bishop blessed him as cameras flashed.

The cameraman was called over to the senators' table, and his hand was shaken by every one of them, followed by every representative.

Presently someone proposed a short prayer, and thanks were given to God for the relief of everyone's fears. In truth, the hearings went so smoothly that soon the entire delegation adjourned, many making their way back to their home states to worship in their churches and arrange the agenda for their year-end fund-raisers.

By midnight four days later, a total of fifty-seven people who had been in the hearing room had come down with the flulike symptoms. The more prominent congressmen who had remained behind in the Capitol had been taken directly to Bethesda Naval Center, but at the Center, routine tests for influenza Types A, B, and C were negative. Also negative were tests for paraflu viruses, mycoplasma, chlamydia, legionnaires', psittacosis, and even hantavirus. The experts were baffled by what was now referred to as "Cong-flu." All they were certain of was that the disease was now air-borne.

By Sunday, the cameraman would be dead, and by the end of September the bishop would be blinded by a retinal hemorrhage, right before he experi-

enced a grand mal seizure. Within hours he would be comatose, and soon after he would die.

Kameron tracked his results, and one week after the bottle exploded, a good seventy or eighty attendees of the session were ill with the mysterious sickness. Most would have scattered from Washington to their homes across the country. Each case would be thought of as an isolated event. Much later, they might come to know there was a link, but by then it would be too late.

Monday, September 7
JFK Airport Security Station
Queens, New York
Noon

The security guard held open the door to reveal a spare, dim room, adorned only with flickering overhead fluorescents, grimy windows, a small blackboard, a couple of chairs, and a desk where Scott Hubbard sat.

"This is a surprise," Bryne said as the guard departed, closing the door behind him.

"How was Quarantine? Everything under control?" Hubbard didn't get out of his chair as he motioned toward another for Jack.

"Under control? I have no idea. Your guy grabbed me the second I walked into the building. Is there really a sick horse, or was this a setup to get me here?"

Hubbard said nothing, further frustrating Jack.

"Look," Bryne demanded angrily, "why the hell is the FBI even here? I've been called in as part of my job, which has no relationship

368

to yours. Or do you suspect BT? You honestly believe I'm a terrorist, for God's sake?"

"We know you're not some crazed fanatic, Bryne. Forget about that," a statement which made Jack feel all the more certain that Hubbard's words belied his theories. "Look, meeting you here beats driving to Albany, and to make sure I didn't miss you, I had security pull you in once you arrived."

He rose, walked over to Bryne, and offered him his hand, which Jack gingerly shook. "Good to see you again." Hubbard smiled that strange, cryptic, cold smile. In return, Bryne harrumphed.

Undeterred, Hubbard continued, "We can talk here, or we'll drive back to Manhattan together and talk in my office on Worth Street. I just need to ask you a few questions. Okay? Downtown?"

Bryne realized—as Hubbard wanted him to—that the Bureau had also run a security check on Mia, whose office was also on Worth. But why had he come all the way out to Kennedy to meet him?

"Is this official?"

"Quite official." Everything about Hubbard, including—or especially—his doggedness, was annoying Jack. Well, whatever this was about, he might as well get it over with.

"Okay, let's go."

"Good man," Hubbard had the nerve to pat him on the back. "I'll fill you in while we drive. You're quite a popular guy with my friends, and I've got some friends in very high places!"

What in hell was going to happen next? Jack wondered uneasily as he let the agent lead him away.

Monday, September 7
Manhattan
9:00 A.M.

Teddy usually stayed where he needed to be, in his secluded uptown makeshift lab, writing and planning and waiting for The Voice. Today, however, he had work to do.

Despite the breeze, he opened the bathroom window above the tub, adjusted the mask of the PAPR—positive air pressure respirator—and, as a test, crushed an ampoule of smelling salts beneath his nose. He couldn't smell the ammonia. Good. The mask had a tight seal, which meant he was completely protected. Next he put on rubber gloves, pulling them up to his elbows, and was careful to flush the ampoule down the toilet.

The curtains ballooned out, fluttering in the air, and the breeze caught the edges of an old map pinned to a wall as it sucked warm room air past him. He bent over the tub and mixed the corn mash slowly and carefully, like a thick porridge. Sliding the paddle through the fifty gallons of toxic slop took muscle power, and every sinew in Teddy's arms strained with the effort of his Mission.

He was especially careful with these preparations. Less than six days ago, he'd mixed two pounds of purified lysine in the bathtub, and now it was time to test the batch. The lysine accelerated the metabolic process. Would the mixture be strong enough now?

Taking a long, thin pipette from a cabinet, he drew off less than a drop of fluid, then transferred the droplet to a three-gallon container of deionized water and began to create the decoction.

Through a Lucite transfer chamber in the top of the new container, he added a minute drop. He agitated the bottle in his arms, then withdrew a drop of what appeared to be clear water from the bottle and mixed it with another three gallons of deionized water. He had created a dilution equivalent to adding a grain of sand to a beach—a ratio of dilution that exceeded all homeopathic requirements, that even approached Avogadro's number.

Now Kameron was ready to test the mix, to see if he had diluted it too many times. If it worked, the concentrated, unadulterated mash would be ready at last. Taking a fresh syringe out of its wrapper, he locked a fine number 27 needle onto the hub. Slowly, carefully, he drew out less than one milliliter of fluid from the neck of the bottle, then turned toward a cage sitting on the toilet seat.

From the cage, Teddy took a plump, silk-furred white rat, picking him up expertly by the loose folds of skin on the back of his neck. The rat began squirming.

Teddy always took care of his animals before he killed them. To him, they were much more than experimental subjects. Some were truly pets with names. Even the ones that had to be sacrificed would be remembered. This one was named Elvis.

He held the syringe behind his back so as not to frighten Elvis if he saw the needle. Placing the rat on a small digital scale next to the cage, he recorded his weight on a laptop computer next to the scale. Elvis sat up and blinked at him. Teddy stared back. Weight, 275 grams—nice fat one, like the King.

He picked up the rat again and kept it suspended while with his free hand he slid open the plexiglas cover on a large empty fish tank, then placed Elvis in the center of the tank. The rodent stood on its hind legs and looked around, twitching its pink nose. Teddy partially tightened the airtight lid over the top, as Elvis peered up at the enclosure. Teddy set his timer.

Lovingly, Teddy expelled a gossamer stream of the dilute fluid from the syringe into the tank but away from Elvis and closed the lid completely.

Nothing was visible.

Kameron snapped off the bathroom light, and then reached over to pick up an ultraviolet lamp.

He switched it on and held it over the tank.

A pale green filament seemed to float downward toward Elvis.

The rat reared up on his hind legs.

Curious.

Teddy held the black light closer.

The aerosolized fluid, still giving off a pale

green glow, was inches from the rat. Twenty-six seconds had passed. Suddenly Elvis froze. Stiffened. Screamed. Teddy looked at the clock. Twenty-eight seconds.

Writhing in convulsions, traumatized, Elvis suddenly corkscrewed himself into a white knot of pain. Biting his own tail, red pulses of blood trickled from his nose. Then he died.

Thirty-five seconds from start to finish, Kameron noted.

Strong enough for Elvis, perhaps, but not nearly strong enough for those to be sacrificed in the tenth plague. Not nearly strong enough material to kill the eldest.

Teddy watched the green vapor lingering above the dead rat for a moment or so, then turned away. The bathtub contents were fluorescing. He turned off the lamp and flipped on the bathroom light, double-checked the clock, and recorded the time.

Reaching into a cabinet, he drew out the ammonia bottle, removed the syringe from the top of Elvis's cage, and placed it in a dish. He covered the needle with ammonia, then drew more of the ammonia into the syringe and sprayed it into the cage with the dead rat.

He turned off the overhead light and relit the black light once more, watching the faint green glow from the toxin fade as the ammonia neutralized it. It faded promptly and went out.

Verily, the Tenth Plague would be perfect. Glory to God in the highest.

Twenty-six Federal Plaza once boasted a giant Brancusi-like sculpture in its open plaza, and a fountain that had been a popular meeting place for outdoor lunches. After the World Trade Center bombing and before Oklahoma City, the structures had been decommissioned. A semipermanent open space remained until someone in Washington determined what kind of barrier might best be placed in the spot to protect the building from incendiary crazies. Security was tight, and entering the building had been a hassle, even with Hubbard leading the way.

Hubbard's surprisingly small office had a pleasant view. On the horizon, one could see the magnificent spider web patterns of the East River bridges connecting Manhattan to Brooklyn.

The special agent had been polite enough on the drive in, distant, not aloof, but all business, including running a tape recorder, when he began questioning Jack.

"Dr. Bryne," he began, spinning in his swivel chair. "Your name has come up in the oddest places." He held up a thick file. "Your dossier's most remarkable, your C.V. impressive. Especially remarkable: your childhood experiences at Pingfan—or as much as the old OSS and CIA has allowed to appear in the file. Do you remember any of that?" He thumbed through the file.

"I wish I could forget every bit of it." Bryne

was becoming infuriated. "But *that* couldn't be why I'm here; the subject of my childhood never came up in San Diego or when you visited the lab."

"Right. Two children died of anthrax in San Diego, that's why I was there. The entire incident became my assignment. I need your help is all. That's why we're here now." Hubbard paused, he was prepared to share classified material with Bryne to gain his trust. "What if I told you there might be other events, other unusual situations, involving biological agents?"

"I'd agree with you," Bryne said, assuming he had nothing to lose and a lot to gain if the FBI was pursuing the same path he was.

"You would?"

"I would. It's just a theory. No hard evidence; but I also think I may have most of the what, when, and where—perhaps even the who."

"Continue." Hubbard was glad the tape was running as Bryne explained his theory.

"First, I believe the anthrax incidents are linked to the Kentucky horse die-offs. No humans were affected; no evidence of foul play. Everyone I've talked to about it so far thinks it was merely bad luck."

"And you don't think it was just bad luck?" Hubbard mused.

"Then there are all those botulism cases."

Hubbard abruptly sat bolt upright.

"And by botulism," Hubbard was opening a manila folder as if to check his facts, "you are referring to the cases Carl Rader told you about?" Bryne had the distinct sense of being scrutinized.

"Yes, I've known Carl Rader for years. He's comfortable trusting me with confidential information."

"But you knew about it even before Rader told you, didn't you?" It was only now hitting Jack that an old friend had informed on him to the feds.

"The Bureau worked with both the FDA and CDC on those botulism poisonings." Hubbard was increasing the pressure. "It was never made public. So how did you know?"

"I did not *know*," Bryne insisted. "It was only a calculated guess. I guessed the victims were ministers, that's all."

"That's quite a guess. Rader thought so, too, that's why he felt compelled to call us," Hubbard told him.

"Look, it's not the first time the clergy—or the clergy and their more enthusiastic parishioners—have been targeted." Bryne's anger was vying with his frustration. "The anthrax is also tied into it. Joey St. John's father is a powerful member of the fundamentalist Christian Council."

"Okay. Go on."

"Want another unbelievable 'guess?'" Bryne persevered. "Remember the squirt gun in San Diego? It had the anthrax ICD numerical code on it and the letters 'LMPG.' Rader told me those snow globes had the botulism symbol carved into them—as well as 'LMPG.' Can you tell me that much?"

"Classified. But continue, I want to hear this theory of yours… "

"Sure, sure I will." Bryne paused. "But it's after twelve and I have to call my wife; I have to call Drew Lawrence."

Hubbard stared at Bryne intensely; was this going to be a genuine shock—or a feigned surprise? At the very least, it would be a test.

"Dr. Bryne." Hubbard's expression had abruptly turned somber, which was more frightening somehow than the humorous smile. "Dr. Bryne, there's some very sad news I regret having to tell you. Drew Lawrence passed away this morning."

Bryne stared at Hubbard. Hubbard stared back, impassive, then told him, "Mr. Lawrence died at Albany Medical Center. The cause of death was a complication of influenza."

Jack shook his head in disbelief. Lawrence dead? From the flu? Something inside him insisted he should have been told sooner. Then it struck him that Hubbard had known about it for hours, even at Kennedy. He wanted to rip the man's lungs out.

"You son of a bitch," Jack roared, "you knew about Drew! Why didn't you tell me? Did you really believe I did it, did any of this?"

Trying to calm him, Hubbard said quietly, "I wanted a controlled environment, Jack, I…"

"Well, control this." Jack shot up from his chair and towered over Hubbard. The Special Agent was shocked, almost frozen. It would have been easy to grasp his throat and twist it, like the chickens he'd seen killed at Ping-fan. Grasp, twist, pull off the head, drink the blood. Hubbard reached for his pistol, but what Bryne finally grabbed was the phone. Hubbard did not interfere.

Drew Lawrence's son, Ali, answered Jack's call to the townhouse in downtown Albany. Shocked, not knowing what to say or how to say it, Bryne stumbled through apologies, condolences, offers of assistance. Then Ali's mother got on the line with the medical details.

Drew Lawrence's muscle aches, shaking chills, and high fever, she told him, preceded his delirium, and finally Drew screamed "red out," meaning he was going blind. "The ICU doctors told me he had all sorts of complications. He went completely blind at the end," Elise Lawrence told Jack sadly, but with her customary dignity and reserve. "They said all the aspirin he'd taken made it worse."

Lawrence had been transferred to the ICU, she continued, but he had begged to talk to Elise, to whisper a good-bye in her ear. Suddenly he had looked up at the ceiling as if he could actually see something nobody else could. "At least I was there," she ended.

"Have you thought about the funeral, Elise?" Bryne asked gently. "Is there anything I can do?"

"Yes, Jack," she replied, and for the first time he could hear the tears in her voice. "Come to the service at noon on Wednesday. Ali and I have decided to hold it in Manhattan, where

Drew's family and friends are. Can you make it? We need to talk, but now I have to lie down."

Bryne was squeezing the phone so tightly that his knuckles had turned the color of parchment. He hung up. He knew what had killed Drew as certainly as if he'd seen the lab reports himself. Rift Valley fever. It had blinded men since before the ancient Egyptians; it was what Drew himself had suggested as one of many possible diseases that would bring on the three days of darkness, bring on the ninth plague.

It was happening. It was really happening.

Bryne sat down finally after hanging up the phone. He put his head in his hands, took several deep breaths to compose himself.

"I'd like to call my wife now, if you don't mind. She's supposed to drive down this morning from Albany. "

"No, no, of course, go ahead. But then... " Then Hubbard said challengingly, "I'd really love to hear you explain all this."

Bryne simply stared at Hubbard, his eyes narrowing before telling him, "I could spend hours giving you my theories, but I'd prefer to present them to a considerably larger and more informed audience. After I speak to my wife, I intend to arrange a meeting with you, among others, but also with other health experts who are Mia's colleagues. You can bring your less-than-helpful friends, if you'd like. This, I think, is not a small problem. It's a problem that may affect the entire New York area."

Jack finally reached Mia on her cell phone as she was heading back to New York and he was taken aback by Mia's brusqueness, That was, until he told her the dreadful news about Drew, then he heard her begin sobbing into the phone. He knew without asking that for the first time she was now going to consider his "mad" theory plausible, even probable. She cleared her throat and asked, "What can we do?"

"I need a big favor, Mia, whether or not you're upset with me personally." He explained the rudiments of the meeting he wanted held. "It's urgent, Mia. I need your help. I need you. I think that a terrorist has targeted the city. Can you get the NYPD and the Mayor's Office of Emergency Preparedness, maybe some of your colleagues from New Jersey and Connecticut? I'm here now with the FBI."

"What are you talking about, Jack?"

"Drew's dead, Mia. What killed him was either meant for me or as a warning to me. What is next, I think, is meant for the entire metropolitan area."

"Oh, Jack, this kind of talk worries me. Are you sure you're—"

"Mia, for God's sake, do you need to see a city like New York attacked before you'll listen to me? Maybe you'll listen to the FBI or the CDC—they're pursuing the same track I am." Hubbard watched as Bryne misled his wife.

Mia, chastened for the moment, told Bryne such a meeting would be difficult to arrange, but not impossible. She would talk with the

Health Commissioner. It would take time, though, to get the principals together, maybe two days. Tuesday was too soon. The meeting could conceivably be held at the New York Academy of Medicine on Wednesday afternoon, following Drew's funeral. She suggested the location because if the session were to be sponsored by the City Health Department, she explained, it would have to be held on territory neutral to all state and government agencies. He agreed.

"Mia," Jack finally told her, "thanks so much for going along with me. I know you think my theories are nuts."

"Not as nuts as before Drew," she replied with new concern. "And honey, if there is a madman out there, he could be after you too. Please promise you'll be careful."

"Believe me," he responded, "and that goes for you too, my love."

"Sure," she said, then added, "and Jack, I feel so sad for you about Drew."

"I know. Thanks for caring. See you soon."

Next, Bryne called his boss, C. DeHavenon Lyman, and told him he'd be back that evening, but would be taking personal leave again on Wednesday for Drew's funeral and the meeting Mia was arranging. He assured Lyman his lab would be functioning, somehow, by noon the next day.

"Jack," Lyman responded, "I can't tell you how bad I, no, how bad we all feel about Drew. The trouble is, we've got a new public health crisis exploding up here."

"Let me guess, Chuck. A virulent new strain of influenza."

"How the hell did you know?"

"It's probably what killed Drew."

"Good God! Do you think so? The CDC has alerted all state labs to be on the lookout for it. May be a shift from H_3N_2."

Lyman went on to tell him that a dozen prominent members of Congress had come down with an acute viral illness on Sunday, some even earlier. Several had been hospitalized. Some had gone blind. Lyman had to get the state's Axelrod Lab in Albany cranked up for a mass influenza screening—although he was short on staff and anticipated thousands of submissions. He might have to pull some of Bryne's technicians to help out.

"Jack," he concluded before hanging up, "be sure to call me when you're back in your lab. You and your staff may be needed."

Bryne hung up and turned back to the FBI man. "Hubbard," he told him, "I need your help. Now. And maybe some help from your friends here in the federal building."

"And you get my help when I've heard your story, Bryne. Not before."

Jack tried to organize his thoughts. Drew's death. The congressmen. The package Drew had received. Jack decided to tell Hubbard about the package, the one Vicky insisted they had never sent. "The story explains why I need your help. You'll see." Bryne walked to the blackboard in the corner, an old slate model big enough for the ten Roman numerals Bryne chalked in on the left side. Then he filled in the biblical plagues and what he considered the corresponding contemporary afflictions:

I	Blood/water	red tide/toxic algae
II	Frogs	tree frogs
III	Lice	ergotism
IV	Swarm	honey bees
V	Murrain	
VI	Boils	anthrax
VII	Hail	botulism
VIII	Locusts	???
IX	Darkness	???
X	Death of Eldest	????

After he'd finished, Bryne went back to IX, erased the question marks, and wrote in "Rift Valley fever."

"If I'm right about Rift Valley fever, we're in trouble. It's another Old World disease," Bryne explained. "Like African horse sickness, it's only found in Africa and it's contagious like flu, but it's deadly. Aside from being spread by mosquitoes, it's also spread by droplets, sprays, and coughing. And, unlike AHS, it affects humans. I'm almost positive that's what killed Drew."

"And why is that?"

"The blindness. Rift Valley fever's most significant complication is retinal hemorrhage, which causes temporary, sometimes permanent blindness. It's the three days of darkness. It's the Ninth Plague. Drew's wife told me he went blind before he died..." Bryne felt the salty sting of his own tears.

383

Tapping his pencil on a notepad and watching Bryne unfold a handkerchief and wipe his eyes, Hubbard suggested, "And now you think somebody's given this fever to members of the U.S. Congress?"

"I don't know. It's only a theory. If you want to find out, call in all the federal hospitals, the CDC, Walter Reed, Bethesda. Why not call Fort Detrick? They can do virological testing for it in their BL–4 labs and might be able to find out whether Drew and the congressmen had the same thing. But they have to think Rift Valley fever in order to test for it."

"And what if it is?" Hubbard wanted to know. "Just how contagious is it? Is it going to spread?"

"It spreads like flu, and if my theory is correct, this is worse than plain old RVF. Even with the feds' help, we may be in way over our heads. It's treatable—if you're looking for it and you're fast enough. But there's no approved vaccine."

Hubbard listened, wondering if he was dealing with a Savior or a Satan, but knowing he had to be very careful. "Dr. Bryne, I can promise you that I will be at the Academy of Medicine for your meeting. I'll be able to round up some people who can give us a hand with this. I'll also tell them about your Rift Valley theory."

"I can go now?"

"Stay in touch. Call me tomorrow."

Bryne turned away, paused, then faced Hubbard one last time. "Hubbard," Bryne said, "thanks for believing me. Now that Drew's dead, I'm afraid you're the only one who does."

After Bryne left, Hubbard called Washington and started looking for the common factor linking the Congressmen and found it—the Christian Caucus meeting. He ordered every piece of garbage taken from the Rayburn Building in the last week sifted by hand. The exploding soda bottle had been found twenty feet down in a cold, wet landfill near Anacostia. Overnight, seventy-five federal marshals had picked through sixty cubic yards of Washington, D.C. garbage to unearth it. Carved into the plastic bottom with a sharp tool were the letters "LMPG," and below them was the ICD number 066.3, which designates Rift Valley fever—exactly as Dr. Bryne had predicted.

Hubbard now had one remaining problem: how to convince his superiors about Bryne's innocence. The virologist couldn't have been in Washington and Albany at the same time. Unless there were others. Had Lawrence been one of them and then changed his mind, wanted out? How was Victoria Wade involved, if at all?

And what about that kid from Brooklyn, the one the Bureau had monitored after they'd wiretapped Bryne's lab? And what about Mia Hart, his wife? She was a physician whose specialty made her a perfect candidate. Food for thought. Food for thought.

A series of calls to Washington brought Hubbard an update. FBI agents, National

Security Agency reps, and Secret Service agents all had the same information, all were aware of the anthrax and botulism incidents. The CDC and FDA had been persuaded to announce that a recall of crystal globes "contaminated with salmonella" had produced both harmless globes and others containing lethal amounts of botulinum toxin in the fluid.

Next, Hubbard put in a call to the admiral; Olde was on the line in seconds.

"So, Scott, how did it go?" the admiral asked with his usual gruffness.

"Well, Bryne seemed to know a lot more about several of the situations than he should. The botulism cases, for instance. He claims he didn't know anything for certain before Rader told him, then made calculated guesses based on previous episodes—the clerical connection, for instance."

"Do you believe him?"

"I'm not one hundred percent convinced, Admiral. He seems like a normally straightforward guy, but if he's a sociopath, it could all be an act. And get this, he's claiming something called Rift Valley fever is the cause of both this Congressional illness and his lab assistant's recent death. Bryne's sure he was murdered."

"But why would Bryne be a suspect in the murder of his closest friend and associate?"

"Logic tells me he wouldn't, Admiral. And logic also tells me he would have had to be in many different places at many different times to commit these acts—and his whereabouts are thoroughly accounted for."

"And where does that get us?" the admiral demanded.

"It gets us to a guy who's innocent, or a terrorist, or who's part of a group. Maybe Drew Lawrence was part of the group and wanted out, so Bryne had no choice but to kill him."

"Scott, are we targeting an innocent man?"

"Bryne still fits the profile, Admiral. That traumatic background, expertise in BT, an anti-authoritarian attitude, and some pretty unflattering reviews—anonymous and not—from his colleagues. I'm simply not prepared to write him off yet. And at this point, his knowledge actually is a help."

"Then stay close to him."

"Of course, Admiral. Like a shadow."

18

Monday, September 7
Mia Hart's Apartment, Manhattan
10:30 P.M.

Unlocking the door to her apartment, Mia Hart threw down her bags, ran to the living room sofa, and sobbed. There was so much to cry over. She found it hard to come to terms with the irreplaceable loss of Drew—not only Jack's dearest friend and colleague, but a man of extraordinary character and her staunch ally. God, his poor wife. At least the children were grown. She wouldn't have to raise them on her own.

If the theory that Jack, the FBI, and the CDC were all pursuing proved correct, Drew had been murdered by a madman who might very well go after her husband. That she'd doubted Jack so vehemently for so long had strained their relationship almost to the breaking point, and now she desperately regretted her behavior.

Here was a man she loved and admired with all her heart, and she had made him feel less valued, less than trustworthy. Would Vicky Wade, she wondered, have reacted the same way? Probably not. Wade would probably yell "Full steam ahead" and follow Jack to Hell and back without a qualm. But Jack had made certain to share his theory only with her and Drew; she knew he didn't want a *Hot Line* feature on the plagues. So Mia would never know precisely the reaction of this other woman, a woman she couldn't help but consider a rival.

She sobbed for Drew, she sobbed for her folly in not believing Jack, she sobbed for letting the bonds of her marriage weaken, thereby allowing room for a Vicky Wade in Jack's life.

Then she forced herself to stop the tears and get down to the work of planning the meeting Jack had begged for. Her first call was to Elijah Kent Wyatt, III, M.D., president of the New York Academy of Medicine, to outline the problem and request a meeting room for Wednesday. Appreciating the urgency of the situation, Wyatt agreed to arrange it.

Hart's calls to Trenton and Hartford produced mixed results. Out-of-state travel had been severely curtailed by the pinched budgets of New Jersey and Connecticut health agencies. Even though the potential problem might indeed threaten the greater metropolitan area and the risks would be shared by all, these state agencies wouldn't commit to the meeting. Jack had suggested that if she encountered resistance, she should call Special Agent Hubbard.

While Hart was talking to Dr. Wyatt, Hubbard was calling Juan Verde, the senior Public Health Advisor for Emergency Preparedness three floors below him in the federal building. Verde was eager to attend the Wednesday meeting and promised to enlist his FEMA colleague. He thanked Hubbard and promised at least two representatives from his area of responsibility, the U.S. Public Health Service. Region II, his jurisdiction, encompassed all five contiguous northeastern states.

As disappointed as she was that Jack would be taking the late train to Albany that night, Mia decided she wasn't going to show it. Instead, she suggested dinner at a brasserie in the West Village they had loved in better times. To her delight, he jumped at the idea.

They were both pleased to find that nothing had changed at La Vieille Auberge—the same dimly lit farmhouse walls, the same warmth from the patrons and waitstaff, the same scrumptious food and superb, affordable wines.

Almost instantly, she and Jack were as relaxed in each other's company as they'd been at the beginning of their marriage. Despite the tragedy of Drew's death and the horror unfolding around them, they'd found a place out of time where they could hold hands, kiss across the table, and even start to make plans about babies.

Jack felt as if he had awakened from a strange dream in which he and Mia had grown apart. How in the world could any man in his right mind, even a workaholic, resist Mia's intensely sensual appeal? All the times, all the places they'd made love coursed through his mind, adding intoxication to the wine. Suddenly he wanted her more than ever. Suddenly he thought of spending the night in town, but he knew he couldn't. There was too much to see to at the lab.

As they regretfully agreed it was time to get him to Penn Station, he grasped her hand and told her, "Darling, I won't be gone long, and when I come back, we'll start acting like everyday normal people who are madly in love and can't keep their hands off each other."

"I can't wait," she smiled as he paid the check. On the sidewalk before hailing a cab, they kissed lavishly, caressed in the cab, and, when Bryne had to get out, kissed again, both feeling stirred and full of promise.

At about nine-thirty, Dr. Hart got a callback from Hubbard, who seemed more interested in talking to Jack before he left for Albany than in talking to her. She did mention that although he'd missed Jack, he'd be pleased to know the arrangements for the Wednesday meeting were set.

After she hung up, Mia sorted her mail and eyed the package the doorman had presented her with when she returned from dinner. She'd been mildly surprised that FedEx would make a delivery so late, then forgot about that because the package itself was damned curious, and it was not addressed to her.

Addressed to Jack, it weighed under a pound and was meticulously labeled in nonsmear black ink, complete even to the nine-digit zip code. There was no mistaking that the handwriting was a woman's—neat, precise, professional.

She lifted the box and shook it slightly. No movement or sound from inside.

Not too small for a bomb, she reasoned, but Jack wasn't likely to draw the Unabomber types. *Calm yourself, it looks harmless,* she told herself. *It's just that Jack's obsession with all the outbreaks is contagious. You hate his caution,* she chided herself, *and now you've developed your own case.* It was only a FedEx package, maybe even a present; and it had a midtown Manhattan return address.

She placed the package on the hall table, intending to call Jack about it the next day, then went to her desk.

An hour passed. All she could think about was the female handwriting. *Vicky Wade!* Every instinct in her body assured her of that. And just when she and Jack were reigniting their marriage.

The package was clearly addressed to Jack. Did being his wife give her the right to open his mail? How would she feel if he opened hers?

Eventually she found herself back at the hall table, staring at the package.

She knew she had made up her mind an hour ago. She slid a small box out of the shipping envelope, and took it with her to the sofa and placed it in front of her on the coffee table.

The symmetrically folded gift paper unwrapped easily to reveal an even smaller box—a gift shop white, unembossed, and tied with a ribbon, to which a tiny envelope was attached by a thin white string. She opened the envelope first and gasped.

"For Jack," it read, "you'll think I'm being 'corny,' but since we've gotten to know each other again over the last few months, I'm positive you'll love this divine scent."

It was unsigned, but Mia was sure exactly who'd sent it. That goddamned Vicky Wade. The bitch bent on destroying her marriage, on making Jack her own. She'd even had the nerve to send it here, where Mia was sure to see it. Goddamned talking head! She was definitely going to have a word with Jack about this!

"Let's see what tacky taste the bimbo has," Mia said aloud, shaking the package. It sounded like a box of rice. She tipped it as she lifted the lid, and the contents almost cascaded onto the floor, but she reacted in time and opened it more slowly.

What sounded like rice were decorative kernels of ornamental Indian corn—red, yellow, pearl-colored, orange, purple, and black—which had been used instead of styrofoam pellets as packing material. How cutesy! Pawing the kernels aside, she unearthed a small olive-green bottle cast in the shape of an ear of corn, with each individual kernel sculpted into the glass.

A silver atomizer was attached to the top, and a delicate label affixed to the bottle read A-MAIZING GRACE. Worse than cutesy. Saccharine. Hart sprayed a wisp of the cologne on her left wrist and sniffed the aroma. It wouldn't have been her personal choice. She hated to admit it, but the scent was nice, very nice. It smelled like new-mown hay, like corn, like field grasses. And it was from someone who probably would have preferred her dead.

Jack's train would arrive in Albany past midnight. She could stay up and call him. Maybe he'd call her. Maybe she'd tell him about Vicky's outrageous behavior, maybe she'd wait.

By one in the morning, he hadn't phoned. Mia, still irritated about Vicky, decided to call it a day. She rewrapped the gift box, put it back on the hall table, and got into bed. She was already half-asleep when she decided not to confront Jack with Wade's gift. At least not right away. Getting up groggily, she removed the package from the hall table, stashed it at the very back of her lingerie drawer—the last place he'd ever look—and went back to bed muttering, "Revenge is best served on a cold platter."

As she drifted off, she was vaguely aware that the inner portion of her wrist where the cologne had lingered began to feel warm, then warmer, then almost like a sunburn. Already half-asleep, she hardly noticed it. By the next morning, the redness had almost disappeared.

Wednesday, September 9
Manhattan
11:45 A.M.

The first two tropical depressions had come early to New York—a pair of quick storms back-to-back in less than ten days, strewing trash and draping broken tree limbs over most of Manhattan. The streets were awash from overflowing sewers ripe with garbage, and the fetid waters became barriers between parked cars, meters, trash barrels, and the shifting mounds of recycled papers, plastics, and construction debris that formed moats between the buildings, the sidewalks, and the streets.

Everywhere, life in the city had become more difficult; flooding had narrowed the streets, making crossing many an impossibility.

Exiting Penn Station, Bryne winced as a blast of hot air, twisting and wet, spiraled through Manhattan's open West Side streets.

From a cool, dark sedan, Scott Hubbard watched as Bryne finally managed to hail a cab. He started the car.

As Hubbard pulled into traffic heading up Eighth Avenue at 34th Street, he concentrated on keeping Bryne's cab in sight while it headed north.

The taxi driver cut expertly through the traffic backed up around Columbus Circle, although Bryne was scarcely aware of it, and worked his way into Central Park. Turning northeast, above the empty skating rink, carefully passing tourists in horse-drawn carriages, the cab swung past fading sycamores and long furrows of trapped water.

Lost in grief, Jack watched the sculpted walkways outside the cab turn slowly into a vision of the vast, even fields outside the lab, the view from Lawrence's window, where they had seen many wonderful autumns, where they had shared so much.

For Lawrence to die this way was almost unbearable. And, oh, God, Jack remembered, what about Elise? And the kids? How alone they would all feel, and how alone he felt himself.

Mia was too tied up with the meeting to be there. Vicky had called with sincere condolences, but was stuck in Louisville. And the support he really could have used, Drew, well...

He took a deep breath and checked his watch. Late. Clenching his jaws, he came back to earth and saw the cab was still in the lower Sixties. They might make it. Part of it, at least. He had to find Elise...

Bryne dragged himself painfully up the church steps; because of his carry-on bag, his damaged shoulder, and the dampness, his body had the same sort of right-side imbalance that Drew suffered with all his life.

Jack felt a wave of pure grief burn into his eyes and stopped climbing. Setting his bag down on the concrete steps, hearing the slow, sad processional music from within, he leaned on the railing for support. Alone, fearful, the tears were a relief.

Soon, he made himself stop weeping. Drew was dead. That part was over. Bryne's duty now was to pay his respects, to find Elise and the family. They would be expecting him. Above him, the door swung open, and a black man's hand beckoned him up the stairs.

Bryne heard the choir raising their voices for his friend and realized the service was almost over.

Suddenly, at the huge oak doors, Jack was afraid, overwhelmingly afraid, of who else might be inside waiting for him. He hurried inside.

He could hear one tragic, beautiful basso profundo singing with the voice of an angel, singing with the torment of Moses, singing,

"Tell o'… pharaoh… to… Let… My… People… Go… !"

The revelation almost took him off his feet. Let My People Go. *LMPG!*

Panicked, he wanted to flee the church vestibule and turned toward the doors at the rear, only to see someone slipping out early to avoid the crowd. Someone familiar. Someone like—Teddy Kameron. Teddy Kameron? *I must be hallucinating,* he told himself. *Why would Kameron be here? He's not here. It's somebody else. Why am I imagining this? Why am I even thinking of him now?*

He turned back to the front of the church and watched the family pass behind the casket, saw Elise, her head high and proud. Searching.

Their eyes met.

The procession passed.

Bryne waited.

Ali Lawrence, a tall thin man dressed in a somber suit, came to Jack's side. "My mother needs to talk to you, Dr. Bryne," he said softly. "Please, she asked me to bring you out to the car."

Bryne followed the young man out of the church and down the steps while the casket was being loaded into the hearse. They walked together to the limousine, and Bryne looked in to see Elise's tear-stained face. When he reached for her hand, she stopped him.

"Drew wanted me to tell you something, Jack. He knew he was dying, and he whispered to me..." She shook her head, sobbing.

Bending over Elise Lawrence, Bryne asked, "Elise, what was it? What did Drew say?"

"Drew said, 'Elise, tell Jack, tell Jack I got it. Tell him the answer to the last puzzle, the globes. It's Memphis and Goshen. Memphis and Goshen. Goshen was passed over by the

Angel of Death. Remember to tell him.' And then, Jack, he died in my arms."

19

Wednesday, September 9
New York Academy of Medicine, Manhattan
1:00 P.M.

The third-largest medical library in the world is housed in a venerable stone building on upper Fifth Avenue facing Central Park. Although unknown to most New Yorkers, the New York Academy of Medicine serves as host to medical societies, specialty groups, and Nobel Prize–winning health leaders from around the world. Today it was hosting a small but diverse group of medical, law enforcement, and military experts.

Located at 103rd Street, the Academy lies near Manhattan's geographic center. The participants in Dr. Hart's meeting were converging on the building from all directions.

East of the Park, Mia Hart, accompanied by CDC Epidemiologic Intelligence Service Fellow Mike Cuccia and Lt. Winokur, a veteran New York cop, had only a few blocks to walk from the Lexington Avenue subway; the locals knew subways were the fastest way to get around the city. Lt. Winokur had been asked to attend the session because he was part of Operation Archangel, the city's emergency response team, activated whenever a terrorist threatened Manhattan or any of the other boroughs.

They walked past the grim and characterless housing projects surrounding the elevated tracks of Metro North, trudging through streets infested with garbage from storm-clogged sewers. This neighborhood could be rough, and Winokur's presence made Mia feel a bit more secure. She thanked him generously when he offered his arm as they crossed a large puddle. It was a charmingly old-fashioned gesture; besides, she was feeling a little woozy, and she used his arm to help steady herself.

A mile south, the New Jersey Health Department physicians drove through Central Park, finally exiting the ring road at 102nd Street. It had been a long trip up from Trenton on a dreary day—all for a meeting Dr. Hart had been quite vague about, revealing only that it involved an urgent health threat to the tristate area.

From the north, walking briskly down from Harlem to the Academy, Bryne was energized by fear and the two new revelations: LMPG and Drew's deathbed statement. He hoped Shmuel Berger would be there with the transparencies.

A few blocks away from the Academy, four large men who were crammed into a black sedan drove up Madison Avenue, and turned west on 103rd Street. "Why do we have to meet way up here?" asked a red-headed man in a trench-coat. "Afterwards, it'll be hell to get a cab, and I do not relish waiting for the Fifth Avenue bus."

"You can always ride back down with us, Ray," the driver suggested.

"No way, Jose. This is sheer torture!"

They parked in a lot near the Academy, piled out with evident relief, and began walking toward the building.

"*Almost* too wet for muggers," said one of the men, wearing a blue raincoat with two silver stars on each shoulder. Rear Admiral Frank E. Olde drew his collar tighter as the group fought another gust of wet wind barreling across from the park. "Yeah, the perps probably won't be out tonight. These days, you're more likely to get run down by a maniac rollerblader than get shot in a robbery."

The admiral was accompanied by Army colonel Dan Edwards sent in from Fort Detrick; Dr. Juan Verde, the Public Health Service's Region II Chief; and Ray Flynn—the red-headed man who'd complained about the ride—from the Federal Emergency Management Agency. Although Flynn had heard the buzzwords "BT," "imminent threat," and "bomb" coming out of Washington, he was still surprised that the colonel and the admiral had chosen to appear. He was even more surprised when Special Agent Scott Hubbard, looking grim, rendezvoused with them outside the building.

The emergency session was to be held on the second floor of the massive structure, in a meeting room overlooking Central Park. Outside, it had begun to rain again. The lights along the building's west side flickered across the dark expanse of the Park's foliage, giving the scene an autumnal cast.

Mia Hart was able to take Bryne aside before the meeting was called to order. "Jack, I'm sorry I couldn't be with you." She seemed shaky, her eyes sunken, not quite herself, but Jack attributed it to the shock of Lawrence's death. "I wanted to go to the funeral. He was such a..." Her voice trailed off for a moment, then she seemed to gather strength and went on. "He believed you. Now I believe you, too. Terrible things have happened, will continue to happen unless we... Jack, I love you so!"

Bryne loved her, too. Now that she finally believed him, was with him again, it was like the old days. It was a blessing. When he introduced her to Shmuel, she responded with genuine warmth. "Shmuel has a show for us, and it makes everything tie in," Bryne said. "We'll go set up." He and Berger went to the meeting room, and while Bryne chalked up his list of plagues and their causes, Berger put an overhead projector on the table and turned it on.

"Dr. Bryne, please, I need to focus. . ." the boy said.

Bryne finished and moved aside, and the projector lit the blackboard.

Each Plague that Bryne had written in chalk matched perfectly with the Hebrew characters for the words that Shmuel Berger had translated. The Hebrew letters had been painstakingly inked onto acetates, and for many Plagues the boy had also found the Egyptian hieroglyphics and the text of the Admonitions of Ipuwer. The Plagues had a written record that went back, without interruption, to the time of the Pharaohs.

Elijah H. Wyatt III, President of the Academy, was a tall, elegant man, perfectly dressed in Brooks Brothers pinstripes, a white shirt, and the Academy's official blue-and-green-striped tie. His brief introductory remarks assured the attendees that the Academy was open to all government agencies and ready to assist in any way that might protect and defend the city's health.

"Dr. Hart," he concluded his statement, "would you outline the agenda? The City's Health Department called this meeting."

Bryne noticed with growing concern that Mia seemed even more fragile than when they'd first spoken a few moments before. She gave only a weak smile as she opened her briefcase, took out some papers, and walked rather slowly to the microphone. Leaning against the podium, almost as if for support, she began to recite a list of infections that began with the San Diego anthrax incident.

At one point she faltered and looked at Bryne. "Now I'd like to ask my colleague, Dr. John Bryne, to continue, since this is his concept, and he is more intimately involved with the theory, his theory."

She sat down and Bryne, giving her a reassuring look, stood. He crossed the room to the large, freestanding blackboard.

"Thank you, Dr. Hart and Dr. Wyatt," Bryne began. "I first want to thank Dr. Hart and the City Health Department for arranging this meeting on such short notice, and the Academy for hosting it.

"Agent Hubbard, also my thanks to you for arranging for your federal colleagues to join me.

Lastly, I'd like to introduce a researcher who has provided critical data to this project, Shmuel Berger. Shmuel, would you stand, please?" The boy rose diffidently, aware that the audience of notables was puzzled by his presence.

Bryne then turned the blackboard around so that the group could all see what he had sketched on it before they had arrived.

#	Bible	Event/Poison	Date
I	Water to Blood	Phytotoxin Poisoning	January
II	Frogs	Centrolenella death	February
III	Lice	Ergot toxins	March
IV	Swarm	Bee venom	April
V	Murrain	Mycotoxins	May
VI	Boils/blains	Anthrax	June
VII	Hail	Botulism	July
VIII	Locusts	Neurocysticercosis	August
IX	Darkness	Rift Valley fever	September
X	Death of Eldest	Unknown	October?

"As you can see, we have a series of events during the last nine months which, although ostensibly unrelated, may, in fact, be related."

"Now," Bryne said, "we'll lower the lights a bit and I'll show you how it all ties together." Berger put the acetate in, and each of the Plagues was linked to the Bible, to the Torah, to a bit of papyrus thousands of years old, and to the humiliation of a pharaoh.... When the lights came on, Bryne addressed them. "The focus of these events is the same as the mission of Moses. Someone wants to lead his people out of bondage. He leaves a code:

LMPG. What does it mean? I'll tell you: It means 'Let My People Go. . . ' And this guy is right on schedule."

"Hold it," shouted Flynn, the man from FEMA, clearly skeptical. "Do you mean to say that those... those things like anthrax are linked to..."

"Let him go on," Hubbard interrupted the interrupter.

"Thanks, Scott." Bryne said, then, taking a sip of water, he glanced at Mia, who seemed to be growing paler by the minute. She really looked ill. Still, he had to continue.

"I am not a religious scholar and I'm not a detective, either," he admitted to the assemblage, "but, with Mr. Berger's help, I do know my Old Testament—at least in terms of similarities between recent medical events and what is generally referred to as the Ten Plagues of Egypt in the Book of Exodus."

The audience stirred, hummed, and buzzed, perplexed by the statement. Was the guy nuts? Had they come all this way in all this weather to listen to a crackpot?

"Don't jump to any conclusions until I explain," Jack urged, understanding their skepticism. "As early as last summer, when only a few of these events had been played out, I began to suspect that somebody out there was reproducing plague after plague in their biblical order. For God knows what ends."

Nelson Rigg, Associate Curator of Egyptology at the Boston Museum of Art, world-renowned expert on ancient Egyptian necrology and mummification, stood up to be heard. His present job, visiting researcher at New York's famed Metropolitan Museum, was a real plum. It came with a great deal of authority, and, frankly, Rigg enjoyed throwing his weight around. For him, this meeting was a genuine pain in the butt, wasting his time when he preferred to be back at the Met where he belonged.

"Look," he began gruffly, "I was ordered to come here by my boss because you needed an expert on Egyptian history. Now if this meeting is headed where I think it is, you don't need me. You need Cecil B. DeMille. The whole Exodus story is nothing more than legends and conjecture."

"But at one time," Jack asked him, "there *were* Jews enslaved in Egypt, weren't there?"

"Of course," Rigg admitted, "but we can't document the existence of Moses, much less any factual events that correspond to these plagues. The parting of the Red Sea, the exodus—all myth. Might as well be fairy tales."

"But the events of the last nine months are quite real, Dr. Rigg," Bryne parried.

"Perhaps, but I can't see how I could contribute." Picking up his overcoat on the chair beside him, Rigg made it clear that he had no time for such unacademic foolishness. "You might benefit from a young rabbinical student, but not from a curator of Egyptology. We differ in our views." And he strode out, a study in pomposity.

Colonel Dan Edwards from Fort Detrick asked to be recognized. "And so, in theory, this Rift Valley fever is number nine?" Bryne was relieved: Rigg's remark was being ignored.

"Right, because it caused the days of darkness, the blindness," Jack explained.

"Well, then," Edwards demanded, "where in hell did he get the virus? It's BL–4 level. Very few people have access to it, even in the U.S.—only us and CDC."

At last, Jack realized, he was talking to an expert in BW and BT. Finally, he was being taken seriously. He didn't want to appear to be guessing when he answered.

"To be honest, Colonel Edwards," Jack began, "I don't know. If you made me guess, I'd say from an Iranian, an Iraqi, a Russian. But I'd rather not speculate."

"What about those frogs?" asked Lieutenant Winokur, pointing. "Can they really kill anybody??

"They certainly can. They certainly did. I've got corroboration on that one."

Winokur nodded, and Bryne continued, "Lieutenant, the reason I asked all of you here is that I have every reason to believe Number Ten is going to be big. Let's look at the sequence. The earlier episodes involved a rather low body count, two or three or four individuals. Recent attempts have affected more and more people—probably even more than have been reported."

"Dr. Bryne," Scott Hubbard spoke up, "could you fill everyone in on the religious connection?"

"Good point, Mr. Hubbard. Most of these

phenomena have involved religious groups or individuals related to such groups. It doesn't seem to matter to whoever's doing this what particular religion, as long as the victim is politically conservative. What does seem to matter is that the causes of these incidents are almost exactly the same as the biblical causes. And in the same order."

"And you think the next one, the tenth plague, will be in the form of bioterrorism?" asked Cuccia, the CDC Fellow.

"It stands to reason. Look at the list. Most of the methodology involved toxins—ciguatera toxins from marine algae, poisonous tree frogs, bee venom, mycotoxins from moldy hay, anthrax endo- and exotoxins, botulinum toxins, and anaphylactic by-products of a tapeworm parasite. Granted, we didn't uncover them in the nice orderly way you see them on the board... "

"May I interrupt for a moment, Dr. Bryne?" Admiral Olde's voice carried the power his rank required, and all eyes in the room turned to him.

"Certainly, Admiral," Bryne replied, glad to have his input.

"Let it be known," the admiral continued, "that if what I'm about to say gets out, whoever leaked it can look forward to IRS audits from now to the Second Coming. Bryne, we might have another answer for the horses, which would let us fill in number five."

"Some kind of mycotoxin?" Bryne guessed.

"No," the admiral went on. "I'll try to keep

this simple. Koch's postulates were recently fulfilled by a very brave friend of yours, Enoch H. Tucker. He was either accidentally or purposefully infected by an agent that also contributed to killing the horses—it's an RNA virus, not a toxin—and Tucker confirmed that by diagnosing his own illness. God bless him."

"For God's sake, what got to him?" Bryne asked.

Hubbard watched Bryne carefully.

"I'll turn that over to Colonel Edwards," Olde said.

Edwards was considerably younger than the admiral, but he had the same air of authority. "Briefly, it's called Bornavirus, a virus named after a small village in Saxony where an infection restricted to horses and sheep was first recorded two hundred and thirty years ago. Again, no big deal until it was shown to jump not only species, but orders—from mammals to birds, for instance, which is worrisome. Its mode of transmission is unknown. Could be by mosquitoes into birds, transexually for ruminants, and no one knows how it's gotten into humans or how fast it spreads."

Oh, shit, Bryne thought.

"In Germany scientists are now worried about routine transfusions," Edwards went on, "since Borna antibodies are showing up regularly in a small percentage of their blood banks..."

"That seems impossible. We haven't heard about it at CDC," Cuccia tried to interrupt, but Edwards rode right over him.

408

"... In blood banks, the same way AIDS did in 1983. It may be the big one we've been worrying about."

"What are the symptoms, Colonel Edwards?" Bryne asked.

"Borna causes encephalitis in sheep, a slow-wasting neurological disease—so-called 'staggers'—in horses. Until recently, it was exclusive to European and African horses and sheep, but recent surveys show that over 2 percent of Japanese horses are also now infected, and it's spreading. Like rabies, it's a viral infection and, like mad cow disease, no one has ever identified the agent under a microscope. Now it's showing up in house cats! We do know by antibody tests that it's an RNA virus like rabies."

"There's proof positive that's what Tucker has?" Bryne asked softly.

"Now there is, thanks to Tucker himself. According to the Plum Island vets, all Churchill Downs sera were positive, as was the serum from the horse at Kennedy... as is Enoch Tucker's blood," Edwards continued.

"That means the horse deaths honestly were simply 'acts of God,' not the fifth plague?" Bryne asked, disturbed.

"Not at all, Dr. Bryne. The Kennedy horse, yes, probably. But we've learned the Kentucky horses were purposefully dosed with both mycotoxins *and* Borna."

"Tell them the thinking of the Plum Island staff," the admiral broke in.

"Those racehorses were given contaminated hay laced with *both* agents. The horse titres suggest massive doses of Borna, probably through the noses, perhaps in feed bags."

"So we've got ourselves a new pathogen, eh?" Dr. Wyatt said. "Never heard of this one."

"Right, Dr. Wyatt," Edwards turned to him annoyed, "and in 1975, no one had heard of Ebola, hanta, or HIV. Can you imagine a 1975 novelist dreaming up an African virus transmitted by sex and drugs that destroys the immune system and kills millions as it spreads around the globe? No one would have believed it."

"You're right again, Colonel," Wyatt admitted.

"And guess what? Bornavirus may have the same implications as HIV, except that it causes mental illness. Horses, sheep, and domestic cats don't have demonstrable personalities. When they get to the final stages of the disease, they stumble, and their behavior changes. But what are they *thinking*?"

"Oh, come on," Cuccia implored. "This is not real."

"Okay," Edwards fought back. "Fact one: Bornavirus has been considered a real disease since 1776. Fact two: Case control and peer review studies in Germany, Japan, and recently the U.S. support the contention that Bornavirus antibodies are found in twelve to fourteen percent of manic-depressives and schizophrenics. Look... I could go on... but it is clear that the Kentucky horses died of either mycotoxins or this Borna disease or both and that they were purposely infected."

"With all due respect," the admiral interjected, "can we concede plague five? Perhaps our terrorist used two agents, fearing that one of them would fail. We're still missing number ten, the death of the eldest. Bryne's point is that the tenth plague could easily make what happened in Congress look like nothing."

"But why call us?" the disaster engineer from FEMA asked.

Bryne glared at the man. "Because I think the big one—number ten—is going to happen soon, and it's going to happen here."

"Why here?" the admiral demanded.

"New York and Washington are prime targets, symbolic targets, and that's what bioterrorists like. He—or they—have already done D.C., so that leaves the Big Apple." He paused. "Also, I've come to believe that whoever is doing this may have ID'd me." Jack tried to smile as Hart looked up, pale and worried.

"Wait a minute, Bryne," Edwards said. "You're claiming you've been targeted? How?"

"Well, I think our maniac has been following ProMED messages—that's my Internet medical forum. We track diseases, emerging pathogens."

The colonel and the admiral exchanged glances. They knew about ProMED.

"And recently I've sent out many open questions asking discreetly for information on these events. Any one of more than ten thousand subscribers could be our man. Also, ProMED is mirrored by at least three online Web sites, so there would be no way of knowing when someone might have picked up one of my messages. But I know I was targeted," he added, thinking of Drew.

"Interesting," was all that Edwards said.

"Look," Jack said, wanting them desperately to hear him, "my dear friend and colleague Drew Lawrence may have been murdered by this spree killer, this new Moses, with his toxic packages. He sent one to me at the lab! Drew opened it." There was a hitch in his voice. "Drew may have given us another piece of the puzzle," Jack told the audience, collecting himself.

Trying to hold her head up, trying very hard, Mia digested the information that Drew had been killed by a package sent to Jack. A package sent to Jack. Then she remembered the heat on her wrist and the redness and now... *Oh my God,* she prayed, *let it not be true...*

Bryne was still speaking, "Elise, Drew's wife, said his last words were meant for me."

"How so?" asked the colonel.

"The problem with the seventh plague, the 'hail,' was that in eleven states, snow globes filled with botulism toxin and spiked with DMSO caused dozens of deaths, while in twenty-five other states, people, mainly clergymen, received globes that were clean, without any bot toxin in them."

"And?" pressed the admiral.

"The critical difference between the two groups was that only the botulism victims' globes had the letters 'LMPG' printed on the bottom. Subsequently, people in some states began receiving both types, only *some* the ones without any botulism toxin inside. I'm told the FBI hasn't come up with an explanation, but it's clear he's sending us some kind of message."

"We've not released the names of the towns or the states for fear of frightening the public," Hubbard added. "The recall seems to have worked."

"And now Drew has given us the explanation. It's all so clear. Three little words…" Bryne paused.

"For God's sake, man, what are they?" Hubbard practically shouted.

"Memphis and Goshen." Jack fell silent, then repeated the words for emphasis. "Memphis and Goshen. Pharaoh and the ruling Egyptians lived in Memphis, and the Hebrews lived in Goshen. The Hebrew lands were spared by the hail, while the Egyptians were killed by it. That's what was in the globes. The hail."

"That must be it!" Cuccia had taken a list from his pocket. "All the bot victims lived in towns or villages named Memphis, like the first guy in Memphis, Tennessee. If we look at the actual town—not the hospital or tertiary ICU where they were treated—we'll find that they all come from places named Memphis!

"And the ones that received harmless globes all lived in places named Goshen and they were spared." A hush fell over the room, all were momentarily lost in thought.

"May I ask a few questions?" Admiral Olde's

authoritarian voice echoed once again through the room.

"Yes, sir," Bryne said with sincere respect.

Olde was both a physician and a biochemist and, along with Edwards from Fort Detrick, would be in a position of unique importance if BT or BW broke out in America. No two physicians had investigated more incidents of bioterrorism—most of which the public never knew about—than Olde and Colonel Edwards. Their specialty even had an acronym, IRT—International Radical Terrorism.

Since the World Trade Center bombing on February 26, 1993, the Admiral had worked closely with the FBI, CIA, NSA, and Army BioWarfare in attempting to predict and prevent acts of terrorism involving everyone from Egyptians, Iraqis, Israelis, and Palestinians to U.S. citizens. The sarin attacks in Japan had prompted the OEP and FEMA to go on the alert in New York City during the fiftieth anniversary of the United Nations, and Olde had seen to it that every EMS vehicle in the city had been given enough atropine to treat two thousand people. He still expected a copycat incident.

Bryne knew of the admiral's work, but before today had never met the man.

"Dr. Bryne," the admiral began, "have you given any thought to how your group or person delivers these toxins? You list nine events. The bees raise obvious questions about execution. Of course," the admiral continued, "there are alarm odors that, I assume, could

414

be synthesized. But the others—the phytotoxins, live anthrax, the Borna and fungal toxins given to the horses, the botulism and neuro-cysticercosis cases—how were these people infected?"

"We've known since June that the anthrax bacilli were loaded in a squirt gun. The good Reverend Phipps and his family ingested food that must have been doused with a concentrated solution of phytotoxins. The algae produces toxins that cause a red tide—the waters turn to blood," Bryne explained. "The cruise ship was crowded, and the cocktail party before the dinner afforded anybody the opportunity to tamper. By the way, clearly only the Phipps family was targeted, because it would have been just as easy to kill the entire group. But it was the first plague. Perhaps it was more of an experiment."

"Go ahead," urged the admiral. "You're building my case."

Bryne had no idea what Olde's case might be, but Hubbard seemed to understand. He continued, "The tree frogs normally have almost enough toxins to kill a human being, but these were also juiced up with a variety of alkaloids and poisons, some of which are never found in wild tree frogs. The botulism, as we know, was delivered in glass globes, suspended in DMSO and a saline solution. The tapeworm eggs could be sprayed or painted on plates or silverware at Land's End; you wouldn't have to poison the food itself."

"And?"

"The Rift Valley that killed Drew Lawrence

415

came in an aerosolized specimen jar; he breathed in a spray. We know that the congressmen were exposed when a plastic bottle exploded, releasing the virus throughout the room."

"May I, then?" The admiral went to the blackboard and added a fifth column to Bryne's list. He quickly interpreted the data:

Blood	Algae	food	SPRAYED
Frogs	Frogs	alkaloids	SECRETED
Lice	Botulism	toxin	SPILLED
Swarm	Bees	venom	INJECTED
Murrain	Mycotoxin/Borna	straw	DOUSED
Boils/blains	Anthrax	victims	SQUIRTED
Hail	Botulism	bottles	LEAKED
Locusts	Worms	silverware	SPRINKLED
Darkness	Rift Valley	virus	AEROSOLIZED

Hubbard nodded. Everything clicked into place. He raised his hand. "The admiral has provided us with a critical new way of looking at the profile of our man. Now to me it seems as if it must be one person, and not a group. And that this individual is a male."

"And what makes gender such a certainty?" asked Bryne.

Admiral Olde took his pointer and tapped the board.

"This part of the pattern fits exactly with what we know about serial or spree killers in general. They very often have a problem with either urination or ejaculation." Olde used his pointer to draw the audience's attention to the right side of the evidence chart and continued.

"Notice the use of fluids, sprays, squirt

guns, aerosols. Our man, and I agree it is probably one person, may have trouble peeing. Perhaps ejaculating, who knows? Hence a loner, almost certainly a man."

Hubbard pointed at the board. "Don't we need to address the religious issues as well? I think we need an advisor who can tell us more about religious fanatics."

Admiral Olde nodded agreement and asked Bryne to comment, but before he could answer, Olde held up his hand and stopped him.

The heavy oak door had creaked open.

A secretary peeked in. "Excuse me, but there is an urgent call from FEMA headquarters." She looked around expectantly.

The man from FEMA started to rise, but before anyone could say anything, a furious Admiral Olde leapt to his feet and shouted angrily.

"Close that door, young woman," he bellowed. "I distinctly said no interruptions... did I not?" he shouted. The admiral was redfaced. Terrified, nodding frantically, the woman stepped back and pulled the door closed with a bang. Everyone looked at Olde.

"People, I am absolutely adamant that nothing that we have talked about here go any further than this room. I have the authority to detain any one of you regarding this matter, and I intend to do so if that is what it takes to keep this quiet. Is that clear to everyone?"

A beeper went off. The engineer from FEMA reached for the device on his belt. He looked up at Olde.

"Go on," Admiral Olde said. "You heard me." The man excused himself from the meeting.

"Now, Dr. Bryne, about the religious tie-ins, if you don't mind," Olde prompted.

"Well, again, it's not my field, but even if there are Old Testament motives in this past madness, I feel like we're still playing catch-up." He answered, "We still have no clue about the tenth plague."

"Well, let's review what we do know. A plague that kills only the eldest and in a matter of hours. Let's imagine what really happened in Egypt. And what sort of BW agent can do that today?"

"Mr. Berger and I do have a theory," Jack admitted, "but it needs work. Could be linked to famine, to a lack of food. It would start with the algae—the red tide. First the Egyptians lost the fish, then the animals. The wheat and barley would then have been destroyed by hail or consumed by locusts. We figure there was anthrax or glanders or typhus or all of 'em. People were sick, desperate, probably close to starving. They must have eventually resorted to raiding stores of preserved foods. I think if we have a person who wants to contaminate a harvest with a toxin, we have not even begun to imagine—"

There was a knock and the FEMA representative, clearly agitated, reentered the room. "Sorry, folks," he announced. "I have to leave." Pointing to Olde and Hubbard, he added, "You two as well."

"What's going on?" Olde demanded.

"You're not going to believe the timing." The FEMA man had turned ashen. "An entire four-silo brick grain elevator in the middle of *Memphis*, Tennessee, just blew up. Explosion rocked the entire city. We've gotta get down there now, bad weather or not. Casualties are massive, and the emergency rooms are swamped. They're saying it's worse, much worse than Oklahoma City!"

The meeting dissolved in chaos. Cuccia ran to a phone; Olde, Edwards, and Flynn were engaged in an intense discussion, while Dr. Wyatt was silent with amazement.

"A grain elevator?" Bryne mused. "They blow up?"

"And how!" said Hubbard. "Think that's *it*, Jack? Think it's the tenth plague?"

Bryne didn't even hear him, for his complete attention was suddenly focused on Mia. Obviously in distress, she was turning a pale grayish color. He started around the table toward her, hand out to check her pulse, but before he could get to her, her head snapped back and forth, and she slumped to the table.

Oh, dear God, no. Please, no... Bryne prayed silently. *Not Mia, not her, too.*

As Cuccia and Shmuel Berger came around the table to help, Bryne shouted, "Don't come near her! Don't touch her! Call nine-one-one!" He knew how toxic she might be, but she was so sick. She was slumping, about to slide off the table onto the floor. "Get nine-one-one, damn it!" he yelled to Wyatt. He reached out for his wife, heard her moan.

With blazing clarity, he saw that the angel of death had passed over him again. Whatever it was, whoever it was, he would again be spared. Fearless, he took her body in his arms, squeezed her hand gently, and kissed her.

"Help me, Jack," Mia whispered.

"I will, my love," he answered, knowing with a horrible certainty that there was almost nothing he could do—except to hunt down the monster who had done this... and tear his heart out.

Wednesday, September 9
Mt. Sinai Hospital
Manhattan
4:00 P.M.

The EMS vehicle, when it finally came, bore Mia to Mt. Sinai Hospital, five blocks south of the Academy. Bryne rode with her.

E.R. doctors immediately took blood specimens, set up an intravenous drip, and ordered stat consultations with a team of specialists. Bryne had been with her the entire time.

After what seemed to Bryne to be hours, but was really far less, Mia had been moved to Intensive Care, where a senior resident now joined Jack as he stood by her bedside.

"Dr. Bryne, can I see you outside?" Jack nodded, squeezed Mia's hand, and told her he'd be back in a few minutes.

Once outside, the resident pulled no punches. "It's her liver, Dr. Bryne, that much we know. It looks like acute fulminant hepatitis. Frankly, the first set of bloods are off the wall. I'd like to ask you a few questions."

Bryne reeled. This couldn't be happening. "She's been immunized against hepatitis A and B," he responded without needing to be asked the questions: he knew tham all too well. "She's not on any medications, no recent foreign travel, no family history of liver disease, no exposure to toxic chemicals..."

The young doctor nodded, then told Jack, "I'm sorry, but, as you can tell, that doesn't give us any source, and we can't do a biopsy because the liver is too severely damaged. We'll have to wait for the next set of blood tests. Unfortunately, that'll be in six hours. You can stay with her, but don't exhaust her. We might have to consider a transplant."

Bryne returned to Mia's side and pulled the curtain around the bed. It was just the two of them.

"Jack." She reached for his hand. "I'm so sick. Have they run my bloods? I feel exhausted. What's going on? Can't you tell me?" She licked her dry lips with effort, then settled back against the pillows.

"Let's concentrate on your getting better," Jack said as he kissed the palm of her hand. "Let's think about that wonderful future we were talking about the other night at dinner. I know we've drifted apart, and it was my fault. But that's over. We're closer than we've ever been, and I can't wait until you're out of here and we can begin our wonderful new life. I love you, darling, with all my heart."

"And I love you, Jack, every bit as much." She smiled despite her weakness.

"Rest, my dear," he urged her gently. "Sleep if you can. I'll be here. I'm not going anyplace."

Suddenly Mia raised her head as if she had remembered something, something important. "Jack, I don't know what this is, but I know how I got it. Exactly like Drew."

"Like Drew? What do you mean?"

"I mean... Jack, could you get me some water? My throat's parched." He did as she asked, realizing how difficult it was for her to speak.

After he held the glass for her and she'd sipped a few drops, Mia continued. "It happened Monday night after... I dropped you off at the station. When I got home... the doorman handed me a FedEx package... addressed to you."

As she motioned for more water, Jack felt a chill go up his spine. "Addressed to me?"

"Yes... I wasn't going to open it, but... I thought it might be important... and..."

"Darling, what was it?"

"It was..." she licked her lips, "... cologne... atomizer bottle... with a sexy card, from a woman... I thought Vicky Wade... I was furious..."

"You didn't spray it on?"

She nodded. "Not much... just a bit on my wrist... but... it was enough... Had a reaction... heat, redness... Now this..."

"But if you only put on a bit, perhaps you didn't get the full—"

"Jack," she seemed momentarily to be gathering strength, "I'm a doctor. I know how sick I am."

"Mia, where did you put the damned box?"

She concentrated for a moment, then told him, "I packed it back up... and I think, I was half-asleep, I left it out on the hall table... so you couldn't miss it... Get it... on the hall table."

"I will, I will, my love..."

"Jack, I love you very much... End this evil before it destroys you... destroys..."

"Mia, darlin'," he told her, "I have to believe, have to hope, it is over. This new thing, the explosion in Memphis. That's it. That's the tenth plague."

"Maybe," she whispered. Even as ill as she was, Mia's mind was as sharp and combative as ever. Jack realized how much he'd missed that lately when they'd barely seen each other, might miss it for a long, long time to come. "But there's one thing wrong... The explosion's too early... Your schedule says it should be next month..."

"You think it's a red herring? To throw us off his trail?"

"Yes—or just a prototype... a rehearsal..." She was growing weaker again, he could see it, weaker than ever, but she managed to tell him, "... Had an idea... wrote it down for you..." and then her eyes closed, and she slept.

Hours passed, or days, or weeks, or years, as Bryne sat by her bedside, watching her in a fitful semi-coma, still beautiful as she faded rapidly away. Paralyzed by regret for the last months of their marriage, by guilt because this

423

thing that was happening to Mia was his fault, and by grief, by far too much grief. Bryne neither slept nor ate.

When she was conscious, he held her in his arms, tightly, as if the act could make her whole again. He told her that he loved her over and over, and, ill as she was, she still occasionally managed to smile in return.

Then, at some time outside time, she didn't wake, but slipped fully into the coma as her breathing became shallower. Now Bryne began whispering in her ear how much he loved her, hoping she could hear him. He did that as she visibly worsened, seeming to lose dimension—as if her spirit was preparing to escape her body. Jack was vaguely aware of doctors and nurses slipping in and out of the area around Mia's bed, checking gauges and dials, but doing little else. There was, after all, nothing they *could* do. Mia's murderer had seen to that.

He was alone with her when the end came. She had been lying motionless, barely breathing, when suddenly she gasped—as all the air left her body—and trembled. A bell began ringing somewhere, and the nurses appeared instantly. They didn't need to tell him she was gone. Bryne knew Mia's heart had stopped—and his had broken.

20

Thursday, October 1
The Cottage, Guilderland
6:00 P.M.

Mia and Drew had been gone nearly a month, and Bryne, for whom days took weeks, was living like a hermit in the small house near the lab. Their deaths had caused a great wound to open in his soul. Emotions long suppressed—the prison camp, his mother's death, and then Lisle's, and now poor Mia's—suppurated in that wound, making him physically ill. Again, he envied people like the St. Johns, who had their faith to comfort them, while he had no solace at all. In time, he hoped, the compulsion to avenge the deaths of his loved ones would bring him back on track; if faith was absent, maybe rage would rush in to replace it. But that had not yet happened.

As he roamed the cottage, finding Mia's presence everywhere, he was assaulted with guilt and bitterest regret. He had put her life, her happiness, second to his work, and the price had been much higher than he ever could have dreamed. Why, he wondered, did the angel of death strike those closest to him while leaving him unscathed? Why was he not taken?

He couldn't face the lab without Drew. Lyman had understood and given him a leave of absence. He stayed in the cottage and drank too much and ate only when it occurred to him that he was famished, then making a quick trip to McDonald's—but never when he'd been drinking; he didn't want more deaths on his conscience.

Many people had called to express condolences. He tried to sound like his normal self, but he was sure he wasn't fooling anyone, especially Vicky Wade, particularly after three or four scotches. She was seriously worried about him, he knew that, but he insisted that he couldn't be around people right now. She seemed to understand.

Then Vinnie Catrini called. Bryne and the pediatrician had been communicated on the Internet when Jack had returned from San Diego, but he hadn't heard from Vinnie personally in quite a while. Before the terror started. He'd meant to check in. Afterwards, he didn't have the strength.

"Jack, good to hear your voice." Catrini began, "I was so deeply sorry to hear about Mia. She was someone I admired tremendously." His voice seemed older.

"Thanks, Vinnie," Jack replied, "Coming from you, that means a lot."

"So how are you doing?"

"Truthfully? Not great. What about you? Why didn't you answer my e-mail?"

"Here's a little surprise," Catrini answered. "I was somewhat under the weather—with anthrax. I'm actually still in the hospital, but the prognosis is excellent. They're springing me next week."

"Vinnie, no!"

"Yep, it hasn't been fun and games. But Jack, there's an upside. If you can catch the bugger early enough, it's treatable. I'm going to be fine. I hope you're being watched for this thing... Now listen, Jack, when you're feeling up to it, get your ass on a plane and come on out to see us!"

"Maybe I'll do that. When I'm feeling up to it. Vinnie, I'm glad you're OK... truly glad." And after Catrini had once again expressed his condolences, they promised to stay in closer touch and hung up.

Somehow, Vinnie's call was good medicine for Jack. Maybe it was merely the fact that someone good, someone decent, had beaten death—or that sociopathic agent of death. Whatever the reason, Jack began to focus more on Mia's illness, looking for an explanation.

When he'd gone to Mia's apartment, as she had begged him, there had been no box addressed to him, or anybody else on the hall table. The note she'd mentioned she'd written for him in the hospital had also not turned up. Now Jack had to wonder if both had been figments of her delirium.

Bryne and his in-laws had agreed that there would be no formal funeral, that a simple memorial service after things were settled would be a better idea. The family promised to see to Mia's apartment, her personal effects, and her clothes. Meanwhile, the police, the FBI, and the Medical Examiner were still looking into what would soon officially be considered a poisoning.

Once the Medical Examiner's office had gotten involved, chaos reigned. They initially told Jack that Mia's appearance suggested hepatitis B or C, or a chemically induced fulminant hepatitis. At that point, a doctor from the Poison Control Center was called into the case.

A few days later, an official from CDC, along with Admiral Olde, met with Bryne, and they told Jack it hadn't been B or C, but perhaps another type of viral hepatitis, perhaps G. Or even exposure to something toxic like carbon tetrachloride.

The City's Commissioner of Health intervened, and an autopsy had been ordered immediately. Pathologists had taken less than eighteen hours to make the diagnosis: toxic hepatitis, probably not viral.

Sanitarians from the City Health Department and Food and Drug Administration technicians took every food specimen from her refrigerator, garbage can, and pantry, questioning Bryne and Mia's friends and neighbors about where she ate and shopped. Nothing showed up.

Poison Control staff examined the bottles of cleaning agents, Clorox, ammonia, detergents, window cleaner, drain cleaner, and any other products found underneath the sink. Nothing showed up.

Bryne was interviewed by toxicologists, detectives, sanitarians, and an FDA senior scientist who came up from Washington. After a week of confusing and sometimes vituperative exchanges with low-level bureaucrats, the

Medical Examiner's office finally had a definite diagnosis: Dr. Hart had either consumed or been given a lethal amount of purified aflatoxin.

The poison had been sufficient to kill a thousand healthy adults. The question remained as to how she could have ingested the poison, and who had given it to her. Jack thought again of her story about the cologne, but no such package existed in the apartment, he was sure of that.

Mia had believed the Memphis incident was only a rehearsal, and she'd been right. She herself, the firstborn in her family, had been the victim of the Tenth Plague. Surely the killer had started again. It was far from over.

The telephone rang, and Jack, distracted, picked it up immediately.

"Dr. Bryne, this is Shmuel Berger," said a young voice. "I heard about your wife, and I said a prayer for her. I'm very sorry."

Bryne muttered his thanks, then changed the subject. "Have you done any more research, Berger?"

"Oh, yes, Dr. Bryne," Shmuel said excitedly. "It was your question on the Tenth Plague. Well, I... I finished it."

"Berger, what do you mean, 'you finished it'?"

"You were asking what the causes might be in a real time, today. Well, I think I have the answers."

Bryne was growing more and more focused. "Tell me."

"I went back to the New York Academy of Medicine, you know, the big medical library."

"That's a good start. And..."

"The librarians were helpful. They were able to hook me up with the Library of Congress right there on the computer. I was able to use a program called GratefulMed to do the search. For free." He paused again. "The printouts... cost a lot."

"How much?"

"Twenty-seven dollars in all."

"I'm good for it, Berger. Continue, please."

Eagerly, Shmuel went on, "Well, Dr. Bryne, there are a lot of theories about the plagues. Already, I've found nine references. The earliest was a book written in 1810. The librarians allowed me to look at it in the Rare Book Room, but it wasn't helpful. However, some of the more recent papers were."

"Which one was the clearest?"

"Well, the best ones were by Hoyte, Schoental, and Marmal."

"Okay, now, can you tell me exactly what they said about the Tenth Plague?"

"Yes. Well, they all have different theories. Hoyte thought it was due to salmonella, some kind of massive food poisoning..."

"Forget it, what about the other theories?"

"Hoyte and Schoental thought it was mycotoxins, but Marmal was a lot more specific about the toxins..."

Bryne froze. That had to be it. How could he have missed it? It was right in front of his eyes. Literally. Mycotoxins. Of course. And someone else had already figured this out. Years ago. Who was this guy Marmal?

430

Suppose whoever was doing this had read the paper? Been inspired by it? Guided by it?

"Shmuel, is the name spelled M-A-R-M-A-L?" Bryne was taking notes now.

"Yes, sir."

"Now tell me more about the mycotoxins."

"Well, sir, the theory says that the feed grains the pharaoh put into long-term storage in case of famine were probably contaminated with mycotoxins. The grain had been stored improperly, it was wet and moldy from hailstorms and infected by locust feces, and it began to rot. Then famine came, worse if you remember they had already suffered through nine plagues, a fish kill when the river turns to blood—which was really a red algae bloom—the frogs, the livestock..."

"Shmuel, get to the point."

"Yes, sorry. So the Egyptians were starving, and they broke into the grain houses. The first ones inside breathed in the mycotoxins in the air and died within hours. Others ate the moldy grain, and that's what killed them, people and livestock."

"But the eldest, Shmuel? Why the eldest humans and the animals?"

"Because the eldest—the elders—were the ones in power. They broke into the granaries first and, because they needed food, fed the larger animals, who were ready for slaughter, first."

"Yes, yes, makes sense. But then... ?"

"Since the mold was on top of the grain, the

first ones—the rebel leaders, the older ones—all got dosed the worst and died. But they let in fresh air, and the grain deeper down didn't have mold and was safe to eat."

"Berger, you've done great work! Anything else? Where did Marmal's paper appear?"

"In a medical journal called *Caduceus*, Spring '96. Marmal stressed that the mycotoxins were actually inhaled—airborne. And it's still happening."

"Where? When?"

"Staten Island, '97—they had to close a library. And in Cleveland, Ohio, 1994. Eight babies died from breathing moldy air. Marmal says the CDC found this huge black mold growing on the basement walls. Ducts and heating fans in the babies' rooms forced highly contaminated air right over their cribs."

"Shmuel, my friend, you've done me an enormous favor by solving a big problem. Thank you and please, please, Berger, stay in touch."

"Of course, Dr. Bryne," the boy said proudly. "Let me give you my address and phone number so you have it handy."

As soon as they hung up, Bryne knew that Mia had been killed by aflatoxin: the aflatoxins preferentially infect moldy corn exactly as ergot only infects rye. He also speculated that it somehow must have been aerosolized, sprayed or scattered, perhaps through the ventilating system.

Had her death been some kind of prototype experiment? A trial run for a much, much larger event?

Oh my God. He suddenly remembered the grain elevator in Memphis. Had anyone checked the grain for toxins? Would anyone even think a grain elevator loaded with mycotoxins could be used as a terrorist weapon?

Bryne tried Hubbard's number in Washington, but got only voice mail. He left an urgent message, and had no better luck with the FBI in New York. He called the CDC and got a Fellow-on-Call who was polite but mystified by Bryne's attempt to explain what he wanted. He called Carl Rader; his daughter said he was vacationing in the Caribbean. He called the Food and Drug Administration and was told to call back in the morning.

Finally, Bryne got up, put on his robe, went into the garage, and locked the overhead doors. Then he walked around the house locking all the windows and doors. Then he tried to sleep, but all night the house made noises he had never heard before. For perhaps the first time since his mother's death, Dr. John Bryne was terrified.

Friday, October 2
Albany, New York
8:15 A.M.

At quarter after eight the following morning, Bryne stood outside the Wadsworth's Axelrod Library, waiting for it to open. Twenty minutes later, he had a copy of the *Caduceus* article in his hands.

Marmal had indeed proven that airborne mycotoxins could have caused everything from

433

King Tut's curse to the illnesses that are prevalent among museum curators from years of bending over moldy old books and documents. The librarians and museum workers would simply inhale the exotic ancient fungal toxins deposited on the old papers and papyri centuries before.

The article's ingenious explanations for each of the ten plagues electrified Jack. He rushed back to the cottage to call Hubbard and found a large box addressed in Mia's younger brother's handwriting waiting for him on the porch.

He tore open the box and inside found an envelope containing a note signed "The In-Laws" that asked how he was doing and whether he needed any help. It was short and terse, and sounded like a good-bye.

The rest of the box was filled with Mia's personal possessions—legal papers, purses, wallet, Filofax, keys, framed photographs, toiletries, shoes, lingerie—*and a small package addressed to him.*

There it was, unearthed from where it had rested undisturbed for weeks. Mia, he theorized, must have put the package on the hall table and then, maybe half-asleep, changed her mind for some reason and moved it, probably to the back of her lingerie drawer where she usually hid things. By the time she remembered the package, she was so sick, she must have forgotten she'd hidden it.

He went quickly to the garage and got a pair of rubber gloves, a roll of duct tape, and two large plastic garbage bags. Holding his breath, he put on the gloves, taped the whole large box shut, then tied it inside a garbage bag, then another.

He washed his face and hands with strong soap and rinsed out his nose, throat, and mouth with tap water. Carrying the box in the plastic bags, he walked to the lab. When he arrived, he put on a gown, latex gloves, and a HEPA mask, turned on the ventilator fans for the BL–3 hood, and entered the rabies room, where most of Lawrence's equipment was still in place. It saddened him, and for a moment he forgot his fear.

Come on, come on, he urged himself. He opened the box, and extracted the meticulously wrapped package. Jack was relieved to realize that Mia's family had not been exposed; he could see they had not even opened the wrapper. Carefully he cut the tape and opened the box. Next he removed the perfume bottle, put it underneath the hood, and turned out the lights.

After his eyes became accustomed to the dark, he switched on the ultraviolet Wood's lamp. The color was a crisp purple neon that turned the neighboring lab tables an eerie indigo. Moving the perfume bottle under the hood, he pointed the Wood's lamp at the side of the glass.

It was what he had expected, only worse. Fiery, evil. With a thin, cold illumination of pure malevolence, the thing glowed as if magically electrified, giving off a grim, vibrant light almost bright enough to cause flickering shadows in the room.

The color was green, a perfect chartreuse, phosphorescent—shimmering with death and damnation. Bryne knew, without turning the bottle over, that etched on its base would be the code for aflatoxin and the letters "LMPG."

When Bryne called Hubbard again, he was told only that the Special Agent was in the field. He was denied Hubbard's beeper number and was asked blandly if there was a message. Jack wanted to smash the phone, but tried to convey as best he could how critical it was that he reach Hubbard as soon as possible. And there was no one else to call.

Killing time while waiting, hoping, praying Hubbard would call him, Bryne began the painful process of looking through Mia's things. Wearing gloves and a mask, he thumbed through her Filofax, combing the entries from the days before she died looking for the note she'd told him she'd written. How had he failed to notice how sick she was? The entries became fewer, sparser and less legible. She had not even been able to take notes at the meeting. No wonder she was confused about where she'd put the package.

There was one item of interest from the day of the meeting, probably made during it: an exclamation point beside a shaky drawing of a boxlike little church with a tiny steeple. She must have sketched it as best she could only minutes before she collapsed. Noticing the book was splotched, Bryne held the Wood's lamp on the stain; it glowed, faintly, but it glowed.

Suddenly the phone rang. Hubbard had

called him back. Jack started to tell him about the perfume, realized he heard a hum and felt the connection falter for a second. He was being taped—or, at least, others were listening in on the conversation. Bryne was past caring. Filling Hubbard in rapidly on the discovery of the toxic perfume bottle, Jack went on to tell him about his fears for the Memphis, Tennessee, grain explosion.

"Jack, hold up a second... Stand by a moment," Hubbard stopped him. Bryne thought he heard Hubbard talking to people before he came back on the line.

"Look, Jack," Hubbard sounded grim, "before you go any further, I've been authorized to tell you Memphis is being considered a BT incident. No one else is to know, understood?"

"Of course, Scott."

"Okay. Local authorities suspect the routine ammoniation process was tampered with. Either the grain wasn't mixed enough, or the ammonia used to decontaminate the fungal contaminants normally found in the product was inadvertently overused. In any case, the explosion blew grain over ten square miles of the downtown area."

"And the explosion killed how many people?" Bryne asked, realizing that for days now he'd stopped reading newspapers or watching TV.

"One hundred and thirty from the blast alone, but that's not all, Jack. Whether the explosion was accidental or not, it wasn't the only thing going on."

"What do you mean?"

"The grain itself was of inferior quality, infected, moldy, grade DDD. Even ammoniated, it couldn't be sold in the U.S. How and why the product became this contaminated, we do not know."

"I assume you checked the owners, and the growers and the truckers, and..."

"Sure. The paper trail was unbelievable, and then it died. Whoever did this paid in cash under an assumed name. Pretty good job."

"Hmm... Go on."

"Sometime during the last quarter, this mysterious someone purchased this inferior lot but paid premium money for it. He had no plan to resell. The grade BBB grain was left in the silo and somehow deteriorated. There could have been a leak in the ceiling. The trouble is the fungus doing the fermenting was something called *Aspergillus*."

"Got a species on that?"

"Yep." Bryne could hear Hubbard fumbling with papers. "It's *Aspergillus flavus*, a pretty pure culture..."

"That doesn't happen in nature, Scott."

"It doesn't?"

"No. Usually it's a whole mix of fungal contaminants. Sounds to me like someone inoculated the grain with a starter, like making bread with yeast. And listen, for Christ's sake. Some medical scholar named Marmal wrote about what the plagues may have been two years ago!"

Hubbard ignored Jack's remark, and kept

438

on about the grain. "But before the detox could begin, the elevator exploded and sent the stuff downwind. Right now, as we speak, Memphis hospitals are still admitting people with what appears to be toxic hepatitis—but not as bad as your wife's case."

"So Mia got the concentrated stuff?"

"Sounds like she got pure aflatoxin, a distillate... It's like comparing near-beer to Napoleon brandy. Compared to your wife's exposure the explosion showered a relatively dilute solution over those twenty thousand people. Only a few dozen got sick."

"My God."

"And Jack, we do not think it's over. Near the elevator, we found a canister of gas that had been labeled 'ammonia,' but it was really chlorine. If someone switched the containers, that could easily have caused the thing to blow. Possibly an honest but horrible mistake."

"Ammonia confused with chlorine?" Bryne exclaimed. "Don't they color-code the tanks?"

"There's no universal coding for the tanks. OSHA is not happy with that. Every company uses its own colors, which is why this occurred. Fortunately, rain dissipated the hypochlorous acid, we think, but the reaction between a strong acid and a strong base would be enough to initiate the explosion. Once the grain became airborne, the chain reaction was set in motion, and the thing went up like a thermonuclear device. They were two blocks from a twenty-three-acre retirement village."

"Oh my God. The Death of the Eldest!"

Bryne paused. *Had it all come true?* He tried to concentrate, to be practical. "Any suspects?" he asked.

"Nope, I told you the paper trail went dead. We've got crime scene units and explosives specialists all over Memphis. They think it was your guy. Looks like Mia was the prototype, and Memphis the Tenth Plague—the toxic grain, the elderly victims, the target with religious symbolism. Now all we've got to do is catch him."

Bryne was listening, but it was hard to concentrate. *Maybe it's not the Tenth, maybe the rain messed up his plans. He has to see if these things will work before he goes after the real targets.* Hubbard was telling him things he already knew. He thought he heard footsteps in the hallway outside the lab. He pulled the phone away from his ear. Nothing.

"Jack, you there?" Bryne put the phone back to his ear. "Jack, there's something else. You don't have to do it, but... "

"'You'd be most grateful for any cooperation I might... '"

"No, Jack!" Hubbard's tone brought him up sharply. "This is not about 'you help us'; this is about 'we help you.'"

"Just find Mia's killer, Drew's killer. Stop this maniac!"

"Jack, listen to me," Hubbard drove on. "That's my point. I'm not going to scare you needlessly, but this is grave. What makes you think he's done? We don't know near enough about this guy to say you're safe. He apparently tried to get you at home and at work. Do you really think he's finished trying?"

"What do you want me to do? Should I come down to the city?"

"No, for God's sake, don't come here. And don't go home. Don't open the mail or any more packages. Leave the lab. Drive down to the Ramada Inn and get a room. Call me when you're checked in. Don't go out, and don't order room service. I'll send someone over. No more than a couple of hours."

"This sounds like a bit much—"

"I'm not debating this, Jack. I'm trying real hard to protect you."

"All right," Bryne relented. "I'll do whatever you say."

"Good, do it now," and he hung up.

As Jack had suspected, there had been an audience. Hubbard had been using a speakerphone, and the people Bryne heard him talking to were eight in number, all standing around the Special Agent's desk.

"Well done, Hubbard." The senior man in the room reached out and shook Hubbard's shoulder. "Sounds like he's coming in. Is the room ready?"

"It was ready last night, Admiral Olde," said Hubbard, smiling that stony smile.

Friday, October 2
New York City

Teddy Kameron longed to include the deaths of Drew Lawrence and Mia Hart in LMPG as part of Divine inspiration, but he knew he shouldn't; only those acts ordained by The Voice were to be set down for posterity. His personal vendetta with Bryne was quite another matter. But, oh, what pleasure those two deaths had given him. And the sequential nature of them! First the best friend, then the wife. Kick an enemy when he's down, and the game turns in your favor. Ah, yes, these sad events would slow Bryne down considerably—a great boon when the best of Teddy's Missions were about to come.

Sitting in his lab reliving the deaths of Drew Lawrence and Mia Hart, Kameron felt an enormous hunger overwhelm him. Fetching caviar and champagne, he ate and drank until he felt himself grow hard, then ejaculated in a stream of triumph.

*　　*　　*

Bryne left his lab with his gloves still on, slipped them off as he drove, and threw them in the back seat. He reached the Ramada, checked in, feeling rather foolish, went up to his room, washed his face and hands, and dialed Hubbard's number.

"Scott, I'm in the room. How long do I have to stay here?"

"Jack, do me another favor..."

"Another—"

"Humor me."

"Okay."

"Stay calm and remain seated."

"What?"

Bryne didn't have time to react as the door

to the hall and the two adjoining rooms flew open and armed men in biohazard moon suits burst it, pointing their weapons at him.

"Raise your hands!" one of them shouted.

Another held an automatic to Jack's chest while a third took the phone from his hand. Putting the phone to the side of his helmet, the man yelled, "Got him. No resistance. Yes, I understand."

A fourth man opened a duffel bag and tossed Bryne a moon suit. "Put it on."

"What the hell?" Jack started to get up, but a hand pushed him back.

"Put it on right now, mister."

As Bryne put on the suit, the men never lowered their guns and never spoke.

When he was dressed, they motioned him to the service elevator, followed him inside it, and rode with him to the basement. Waiting there was a black van with black windows and a U.S. Government license plate with tiny black numbers. They all got in, and the van barreled out of the garage.

In under fifteen minutes they arrived at the New York State Air National Guard Wing. The van drove directly out onto the runway. Two of the men got out with Bryne, and the three of them boarded a U.S. Ranger Blackhawk helicopter; they were airborne in seconds.

During the entire trip, nobody said a word. Jack reverted to staring blankly at the Hudson River Valley spread out below him. In less than an hour, the chopper landed at the East River Heliport and was met by another black

443

van with three more armed guards inside, all in moon suits, all silent.

With sirens blaring, the van drove south and into the basement of the federal building. Byrne, still in the moon suit, was taken inside and left alone in a virtually empty room, stunned that all this had happened only hours after he first saw the toxin in Mia's perfume.

A speaker on the wall squawked to life, and Hubbard's voice announced, "Jack, forgive me..."

"Let me guess," Bryne addressed the voice. "You were only following orders..."

"Help me out here, Jack. There are people here who have to talk to you. Urgently. We plan to run a few tests on you, maybe keep you overnight, so you can get the hell out of that suit."

"What tests?" Jack was pacing up and down, furious and confused. "What the bloody hell is going on? Am I under arrest? I demand to—"

"Calm down, buddy," Hubbard's voice continued. "See that door over on the far wall? It opens into a bathroom. Go in, use the soap we put there. We want you to fill up the test tubes with blood samples. You can draw your own blood, can't you?"

"Of course I can, but why—"

"Time for questions later, Jack. We also want urine and stool samples. There's a Fleet's enema if you need it. We want you to take the antibiotics we've left for you. Now, as I said, we're going to run some tests, and we need your cooperation. You'll find clothes in there.

When you're done providing the samples, take a shower, dress, and return to this room. Then wait."

"No!" Jack practically screamed. "*You* wait. I want some answers, damn it!"

"Do we have your cooperation? The tests won't take long. *We're* prepared to wait..."

"Wait until what?"

"Until we get the specimens..." Bryne looked around—the room was bare.

Bryne, finally, opened the door and did as he was told. Hours passed. He sat stunned, deeply uncertain, deeply threatened, reliving a nightmare... *Hiyiku!... Hiyiku!...* He could hear it again and again as his mind drifted back to the secrets of childhood, the ones he had shared with no one, not even Mia.

Jack is at Pingfan, still a child, still terrified that his mother will be chosen, day after day of that terror. And then one day, she is. From his rooftop vantage point, he can see her with the other women, hands tied behind her, being marched to the pit by soldiers carrying rifles and bayonets. Not the stakes... the pit!

Scrambling down from atop the barracks, he runs toward his mother, but barbed wire separates them. There are shots. He wiggles underneath the wire. The women are falling into the pit.

His mother screams, he's past the first wire, he runs toward her. But the guard sees him and knocks him down with a rifle butt, and he falls with his face at the edge of the pit. He sees what is in the pit, bodies of both humans and animals, flies everywhere—his lungs are seared with the ammonia from decaying hooves, methane from decaying flesh. He sees his mother climbing on top of the swollen belly of a rotting horse, trying to struggle out of the mire, climb clear of the dead and dying human guinea pigs.

Some victims are covered with bright red spots, umbilicated red and orange pustules, weeping sores. Smallpox.

The color on other corpses is the chalky white of profound dehydration. These bodies swim in a fecaloid broth of watery excrement. Cholera.

On top are the ones without red spots or white skins, healthy—except for the foul black fluids leaking from open sores in their armpits and groins. Plague.

He sees his mother, still alive, and starts to crawl toward her. But again a guard kicks him in the ribs, pulls him to his feet, grabs his hair, and drags him away screaming. Behind him, Jack hears more rifle shots and the sound of the bulldozer pushing dirt into the pit.

And then he realizes for the first of what will be many times that the angel of death has passed over him, that he will not end up in the pit. That for him there will only be heartbreak, not death. For he hears the screaming of propellers: fighter planes, MiGs, olive green with red stars, three rockets hung on each wing. Russians. Right above his head, so close he sees their nose guns flame.

The Soviets are strafing the field, liberating the camp. The guards start to run as parachutes appear above. And Jack runs back toward the pit, but again the same guard hurls him down, aiming the silver blade of his bayonet. Jack manages to roll away, but not far enough.

The point of the bayonet enters his arm in the crook of the elbow. The guard bears down, cutting the flesh. The point hits bone. Razor-fast, the blade slides down Jack's arm, under the muscle, ripping the biceps, the point emerging just above the shoulder. The guard wrenches the blade toward his neck. Jack sees it coming, turning toward his face, missing. Passing beside his jugular, the tip sinking into the ground right behind his ear.

More strafing. The guard spits and runs, leaving Jack pinned to the earth by the bayonet, struggling against the blade, struggling for the pit. Helpless, flailing, screaming until he faints.

Pinned like a specimen ready for dissection. Where the Russian soldier finds him less than half an hour later... Jack never even felt the blade slide out.

"*Svobodo! Svobodo!*" the soldier tells him. "You are free, free—and alive."

Finally, the speaker came on again. Bryne was told to leave the containment room and proceed across the hall. He opened the door to the other room, where, sitting around a table, were Scott Hubbard, Admiral Olde, a bunch of people Bryne had never seen—and Vicky Wade.

What was Vicky doing here? She seemed as confused and upset as he. Had they yanked her in here, too? Had they tested *her*?

Hubbard rose. "Jack, I have to apologize for our treatment of you and Ms. Wade today. There are things you don't know, things that will help—"

Admiral Olde held up his hand, and Hubbard stopped speaking immediately, giving the admiral the floor.

"Dr. Bryne," Olde began, "this is not a legal proceeding, but I want to go over some facts with you. Now, can you confirm or deny the following? One, you served as chairman of a WHO committee dealing with response to BT acts, correct?"

Bryne nodded yes.

"You dropped by Indianapolis and bluegrass country on your way back to California?"

He nodded again.

"You have been hypothesizing about a recent cluster of botulism cases with Carl Rader, formerly of the CDC?"

"That's correct. You know all this! What the hell... " Bryne sputtered.

"You have recently been asking for terrorist information and toxins on an Internet medical forum called ProMED, which you moderate?"

"Now wait one damned minute!" Olde ignored his protests.

"Are you the moderator of ProMED?"

"Yes, yes, I am, but that doesn't..."

"Did you not send faxes to fifty state

448

epidemiologists asking about other cases of cysticercosis?"

"Yes, and I gave the results back to them. The CDC should have them by now. It looked like a national outbreak."

"We know. We traced it to a common meal served to the victims. Were you ever in Bath County, Virginia?"

"No, now what the—"

"Where you recently at JFK Quarantine?"

"I was, but what... ?"

"A few more questions, Doctor. Your assistant, Drew Lawrence, a man recently killed by Rift Valley fever, was he not also once a Black Muslim?"

"That does it," Jack said rising to his feet. "Who the hell do you think—"

The admiral held up his hand, and this time Bryne quieted down with difficulty.

"And is it not true that your wife recently died from what now seems to be a toxin?"

Bryne nodded again.

"So, knowing all that, can you see any reason why we would not want to get you in here?"

Jack had had enough. "Okay, I get it. I'm being charged with a crime. No, with nine, no more than nine, heinous crimes. I'm going to be brought up on death penalty charges again and again. You brought *me* here to be your scapegoat because *you* can't find the real maniac!"

"On the contrary," Admiral Olde smiled, "we brought you here to tell you, Dr. Bryne, that you're a free man!"

"What?" Bryne was almost speechless.

"Dr. Bryne," the admiral explained, "the samples you just gave us ruled you out. That's what we were waiting for. You see, whoever is doing this has been living with a tapeworm in his gut, yet your serology is as negative as is your stool specimen. You're clean."

"Of course I'm clean. What's going on here?"

"We have a report from the Armed Forces Institute of Pathology you'll be interested in. They've analyzed seventeen specimens recovered from victims of the neurocysticercosis outbreak, the one you and Lawrence uncovered. You would expect differences between the worms that caused all these cases. After all, if someone even gets this worm infection, it would normally be considered a rare, unusual situation. Random."

"And in this instance?"

"AFIP docs were able to perform DNA landscape homologous sequencing and they believe that all the cases were from the eggs of one worm. A megaworm."

"Go on."

"The cysts all matched each other exactly, a ninety-seven percent homology. We had to find out if it was from you."

"What now?" Jack asked after he'd stopped shaking.

"Now we give you all the help we can, and you help us find the guy. Any theories?"

And suddenly everything came together in Jack's mind—all the little links that had floated unconnected now coalesced into a theory, complete with a man's name, but he wasn't ready to propose it without hard, cold proof.

"Okay, listen. When you were looking at me, you were really looking at the wrong type of scientist. I'm a virologist, but I think you'll agree the guilty party is some kind of obsessive perfectionist who's also skilled in *toxicology*—a psychopath at worst and a sociopath at best, somebody who can readily acquire or create these toxins has to have a great deal of education and expertise."

"So what's our next step?"

"Can you run a check on toxicologists, the way you did on virologists, if I may be so bold? Maybe even pathologists, parisitology specialists; vets. Maybe look for people who got canned from some corporation, maybe a med school faculty member who cracked up and got fired, any people with long-lasting grudges against the world—especially if they think of themselves as geniuses. You might find someone who may subsequently have had a negative connection to at least a portion of the victims, even in passing—a business proposal that fell through, tenure denied, fired from some kind of school or organization with religious connections."

"Sure, we'll try that," Hubbard agreed.

"Next, I'd try to find out if any of the victims served together on any review panels or in any such association. If they did, they may link up to our man. I'd also look for someone who'd been out of touch pretty much since January. He had to have the freedom to move around from crime scene to crime scene."

"You got it! Anything else?"

"Well, yes. I was thinking of the ergotism toxin. The person had to grow a lot of moldy rye, many, many bushels at least. And I bet if we track down large shipments delivered to a single address over the past few months— I'm guessing an unconventional address, not a bakery, perhaps a residence—I bet we might find out where the maniac lives."

"Well, it's worth a shot, sure."

"Right, 'cause if we can get into the place, *and* we can find his computer, maybe we'll learn what's going to be next.

"Let's hope so, Bryne," said the admiral. "But we're convinced there's more to come."

"Like what?"

"Nothing certain yet," Hubbard replied. "Well, maybe something. There's a big religious Unity Conference being held in New York the day after tomorrow. It's going to attract most of the big shots of most all the major religious groups—Catholics, Protestants, Jews, Moslems, everyone. It would be a natural for our guy. It's a two-day affair, and as I said, it begins the day after tomorrow."

"And, before then... " Jack contributed, "I suggest we get our collective asses in gear!"

21

Saturday, October 3
New York City
10:00 P.M.

Bryne paced his small room in the Lexington Avenue hotel where the Bureau had put him up, waiting for the experts to come back with some hard stuff on their killer, whom every instinct in his body now told him was Theodore Kameron.

That *had* been Kameron at Drew's funeral, a psycho showing off in plain sight, saluting Bryne, no less, a greeting from the man who was working overtime—probably with anonymous tips to the FBI—to frame him. Now Jack had begun remembering vague things from long ago, from the Schweitzer Hospital in Haiti, where he had heard strange tales of Theodore Kameron's obsession with exotic toxins. The hospital staff had merely thought Kameron strange, but the Haitians considered him very, very bad luck and dealt with him only because he paid such good money for "samples." Bryne and Hubbard shared information as it came in.

Theodore Kameron, an expert toxicologist, had indeed been retired by CDC, and had started in on fundraising sessions with Billy Pusser, a lawyer with big-money, right-wing, pseudo-scientific religious connections. Pusser, Joseph St. John, Bishop Gaston LaPierre, and other victims had all been members of an organization called the Christian Council, which after months of promises and delays had not only turned Kameron down flat for grant money, but ruined his ability to raise money from any other fundamentalist coffers, much less reputable secular organizations.

From last January to June or July, Kameron had ostensibly been out of the country on a sabbatical in Europe, but if he had, it wasn't under his own passport.

Under pressure from Bryne, Hubbard admitted he had talked early on to Kameron, among many other scientists, that he hadn't been particularly damning or particularly complimentary, either. In fact, Kameron's response had been mild compared to many others. Hubbard's admiration was grudging but real as he told him how many establishment types considered Jack at best a free spirit, at worst a radical and a rebel, capable of who knew what, and how many were quite vociferous about it.

Hubbard smiled when he told Bryne how many had also used the word "brilliant."

When the anonymous tips about Jack's supposed guilt first started, there were a lot of other, more hostile people Hubbard had suspected, even checked out. He'd only made routine inquiries about Kameron. The man seemed adept at leaving little to go on except good alibis.

Teddy's present whereabouts were even more of a problem. He didn't return messages on his answering machine, and the doorman of his building said Kameron hadn't been around for weeks. They had examined the East Side apartment for evidence, but it was clean.

The key to cracking the case was discovering where all that rye had been delivered, and that was taking longer than expected.

Meanwhile, Bryne spent time making discreet inquiries by phone and Internet about the Unity Conference. Hundreds of dignitaries would be in attendance at ceremonies that would mark an ecumenical reaffirmation of fundamentalist beliefs—services encompassing all denominations. Included would be a citywide celebration with flags, fireworks, and fountains, complete with full security precautions.

Next to the newspaper story he was reading was a photograph of the Andrus fountain, which was reopening because Mia had worked out all the complex sanitary engineering procedures. It saddened him deeply to think she wouldn't be there to see it.

The accompanying article described how the fountain would now be safe, a beautiful addition to the New York skyline. Jack read how generous contributions had rushed construction so that the debut of the renovated fountain would mark the culmination of the Unity Conference. Laser lights would make the two-hundred-foot geyser one of the most beautiful nighttime attractions in the city. Installed on its own little island in the East River, the fountain was not yet ready. There was a base, actually only a big metal cube, on which a tapering tower with a lattice stairwell was attached, pointed skyward. It looked exactly like a little church. Sunday would mark its opening night.

Sunday, October 4
Metropolitan Museum of Art, Manhattan
5:00 P.M.

The high-collared vestments chafed Dr. Kameron's neck each time he turned his head. Soon he was rotating his entire upper torso to avoid the friction, and it gave him an even more regal, stately air. He had loved dressing in the armor of God, and as he shifted the unfamiliar clothing around on his body, he regretted he hadn't worn it earlier, for practice.

The mitre itself, three pounds at least, gold-embroidered, crossed with fine lace and intricate gold ribbons, was more than a foot high. His robes had been stitched together from strips of the finest white velvet. The white symbolized the purity of God. The sleeves were adorned with various crosses: the Aryan fylfot, a Chi Rho, the Cross of Lorraine, a Greek cross, the Clavis cross. Smaller medallions were sewn between the crosses: the Patonce, the Maltese, and Moline crosses of the Crusaders.

A cowled shawl of heavy yellow twill, the yellow symbolizing sovereignty, was draped over his shoulders. It bore gold piping, reinforcing the theme of supreme nobility. Silk stained a deep indigo: royal purple, the color of authority, was stitched inside the hidden sleeves and the cowl. He wore a heavy silver Patonce cross and a large golden ankh on a chain around his neck. Everything fit him perfectly, the gold mesh gauntlets, the fur boots from Florence, the chambray clerical ascot, the staff.

Dr. Kameron carried a thick curved rod of solid mahogany, wrapped around the center by a band of sterling silver.

The top of the shaft was coated in a silver jacket that curved open at the top, bending back like the microscopic *Aspergillus* fungus. The name of the fungal genus had been derived from the ecclesiastical instrument, the aspergillum.

A guard at the Metropolitan Museum of Art helped Dr. Kameron climb out of the back of the limo. Tipping his cap, he escorted the bishop to the red carpet leading to the hall of dignitaries. Security was heavy, but his fake credentials were impeccable. When he told the guards he was Bishop Lansing, come early to bless the breads, he was treated with great respect.

Dr. Kameron nodded, raised his right hand, pinky outward toward the guards, his thumb toward his breast, and passed the man a silent benediction. Attendants signaled the way at each turn in the hallway. He found the Temple of Dendur and moved toward the placid waters of the fountains, as smooth as the Nile, and stood in the moonlight that came through the enormous glass building that houses the Temple.

A Temple to the false gods...

He was ready.

He heard The Voice for the tenth time, and he knew he was invincible.

He raised the staff in his right hand and stood, arms fully extended, his white robes gleaming in the pale light coming over the temple walls.

The Voice told Teddy that the eldest of all the pharaoh's people must pay. Not the elders alone. The eldest as well.

Teddy knelt down, his hands clutching the heavy shaft, then rose, took his staff, and held it across his body. He walked toward the temple of pharaoh, beyond the wreckage of Rome and the layered hypocrisy of today. He made his way up past the goddess of death—Mut—up into the Temple itself where the breads were displayed. He could see the tables set with the ceremonial loaves, and he stood, breathed deeply, and admired them all.

He held out his arms and raised his shaft and waited as the room quieted. The few servers stood still. Some bowed their heads. Reverently he passed above the breads, hundreds of them. Whole wheats, pine-nut breads, long-grained rice breads, semolina breads stacked one atop the other. He blessed them all.

When he showered the attendants with the holy essence of his silver-headed shaft, they nodded their heads toward him in thanks for his benediction, for his blessing, for his consecration of the bread. And he was almost finished now.

But there was someone he still needed to meet. The raiment of his faith and the light upon his face opened all doors.

He climbed into the modern-day temple of efficiency. Huge ducts carried regulated air for the preservation of the countless antiquities.

He passed the locked storage areas, the computer rooms, the conservation labs. Museums had become business ventures, and the Met was one of the best. The halls were plush, the carpets quiet. Teddy strode silently through the heart of the museum. He could see lights beneath the doors of only a few of the offices.

He was at peace, yet energized, driven by The Voice.

He sighed again. This was his destination, his Mission, the Department of Egyptian Art. High on a balcony, the department abutted the Temple of Dendur. He could see the breads. All was quiet inside the Temple, perfect.

Outside the Temple there was a brief flurry of activity. Soon the Patriarchs would be coming. For the biggest, most prestigious feast of the year, perhaps the decade. Certainly of their lives... Uniformed waiters and waitresses pushed their carts back and forth at the entrance to the banquet hall. Security was everywhere, but The Voice gave him free access. When he had asked directions to the office of Dr. Nelson Rigg, the famous Egyptologist and the highest-ranking museum official there that evening, he was given an ID badge and directions immediately.

There was no noise as he swung the door inward.

"Dr. Rigg?" His voice was friendly, inquiring.

"I'm Rigg, yes. But the museum is closed. Don't you see? How did you get in here? Who are you?" Rigg stood up.

Dr. Kameron stepped into the light.

"Please, be at ease, Dr. Rigg, I am with the reception committee for the Temple of Dendur event this evening. My name is Kameron, Dr. Theodore Graham Kameron. Please excuse the interruption, but I noted your name on the door plate, and I recognized it. May I... ?" He came in a bit further.

Rigg seemed off-base, unsure of how to react.

"Dr. Rigg, I have read some of your articles..."

"All right."

Dr. Kameron came forward, stopped, gently closed the door.

"You're part of the ceremony this evening?" Rigg asked, indicating a seat, but Dr. Kameron stood.

"Oh yes, I just finished blessing the breads with this." Kameron held out the silver inlaid aspergillum for Rigg's inspection. It was similar to the ones with which the Pope conducted special blessings at the Vatican, but larger, more elegant, and with a glow apparently caused by droplets of water seeping from the scores of small holes in the head. "Now all the breads are blessed, and I have nearly fulfilled my mission."

460

"Mission?"

"Oh yes, my mission. But I had hoped to talk with you about your research, if I may. Do you have a minute?"

Rigg looked at his watch. Less than an hour and a half until the Unity Conference services began at the cathedral. This conversation would be brief.

"Well, yes, then, certainly. A moment, Father... Er... You said that you had heard of me?"

"Why, yes. You assisted with that *Time* magazine article, didn't you, the one that had the cover story, 'Is the Bible Fact or Fiction'?"

"Of course. Where do you think those silly reporters got their information? From Yahweh? From my perspective, the Israelites were not even recognized as having been in Egypt until the so-called 'Israel' stele in 1200 B.C. That would put them well after Moses and that crowd. Moses, Aaron, the Exodus, the Sinai, the Ten Commandments. They are merely fictionalized accounts of a broken people. Like the Ipuwer papyrus, a woeful lament for a time that may never have existed." The Exodus is simply a fable, Your Eminence.... Would you not agree?"

"No." Kameron, furious now, loomed over Rigg. He watched as Rigg's hand moved toward the telephone.

"Oh, please, I mean no harm," Kameron said softly. He reached over and covered Rigg's hand with his own. Rigg felt the stubble on Kameron's palm and froze. "Don't be afraid," Kameron said calmly as he eyed the vacuum socket in the wall. A flexible tube and its nozzle lay by the cabinet. He walked over to the tube and inserted it into the central vacuum system. The connection purred on. Rigg turned to dial his phone.

Dr. Kameron raised the heavy aspergillum and smashed it crunchingly against Rigg's skull.

Sunday, October 4
Upper West Side, Manhattan
5:00 P.M.

The spine of living rock that bisects Manhattan Island emerges as an exposed cliff at Morningside Heights, where a huge outcropping of gneiss running due north for many blocks is crowned with one of the largest, most beautiful churches in the world, the Cathedral of St. John the Divine. The twin spires of the Cathedral rise straight up from the bedrock, soaring 400 feet in the air.

Throughout decades, the Cathedral has sheltered scores of ecumenical movements; today, in this magnificent Gothic setting, issues of hunger, of health, and of charity would take precedence over dogma for the worshippers.

Bryne was reading the extensive program listing the Unity ceremonies and festivities to Hubbard as the agency sedan crawled north from the federal building through crowded streets toward the Cathedral.

The vision of the gathering on this particular October evening was to express the symbolic devotion of all the world's churches to all the world's children by vowing to rededicate and enlarge the efforts of each church to provide the bread of life for children everywhere.

Soon they would arrive, the ministers, pastors, priests, rabbis, and monks, carrying banners emblazoned with iconic numerals, images of sacred animals, and plants. Japanese, Chinese, Greek, Arabic, Hebrew, Cyrillic, Native American, Aboriginal, and Christian symbols of life, perfection, regeneration, and faith were represented. Decorative motifs depicting lions, bulls, fish, doves, olive branches, and passion flowers were woven into splendid textiles made of silken threads and golden brocades, Maltese silk, wire purls, spangles, braids, elaborate fringes, faille, satin, and velvet.

Special coaches and limousines had been reserved, and the finest facilities had been made available. The needlework of thousands of hands adorned these sacred garments. The prelates wore elaborate orpheys, chasubles, complex stoles, ornate maniples, Dalmatic tunicles, copes and hoods. Each leader carried a mitre, burse, alms bag, or small banner with his coat of arms. The massive vault of the Cathedral, filled with the aroma of incense, candle smoke, and herbs, had been transformed by the interplay of colors, shapes, and reflections from the banners of the world's great religions. Pews reserved for the Patriarchs were fitted with elaborate sterling silver bud vases, each with enough water for the sprays of living seed grains to cling to life. Flown from nurseries around the world, arrangements of decorative plants lined the candlelit hall of the great Cathedral. A recurrent theme appeared to be grains: rye, spelt, sorghum, rice, corn, and many more: wheat, barley, and alfalfa. There were bunches of bulgur, sacred quinoa, and blooms of rye and caraway; and everywhere, sheaves of multicolored hybrid corn and exotic native maizes. From each church in every land had come the sacred loaves and arms full of blessed grains.

First the grain, then the bread, and so with the ceremony. From the world's largest Gothic cathedral, the religious leaders would then pass to one of the world's oldest places of worship, the Temple of Dendur.

The Catholic Archdiocese of New York had been the source and inspiration for the meeting, which had taken three years to organize and prepare. Its hallowed purpose was to bring together all religions for a reestablishment of fundamental beliefs. Paradoxically, religions intolerant of one another had found unity in a common belief that governments had gone too far in restricting faith. Now the major religions would begin in earnest to guide, to force, to demand that people return to core beliefs. With government running out of control, religion had to be the world's guiding force as humanity approached the Millennium.

The Catholics who had spearheaded the convocation joined with the Jews—Conservative, Orthodox, even the Hasidim had accepted. Protestant Christian sects had followed. Eventually there were Muslims, Buddhists, Sikhs, Taoists, Hindus, Shintoists, Animists from sub-Saharan Africa, and their Native American counterparts. All would try to discard their differences to be part of the Unity Conference.

And what cause made them come together? What concept would allow diverse, fractious groups with splintered agendas to unite and to correct the heartless ways of their godless governments? Simply this: food. Bring the Staff of Life to the children of the world.

Cardinal O'Neill from Dublin proclaimed his blessed vision in a flyer distributed to the media and all welcomed guests. Bryne had picked up a copy and read, "... buried in the tomb at Thebes. It was the ancient Egyptians that discovered the leavening process, using one of God's smallest creatures, a simple fungus which we now call yeast. The very name for Egypt comes from the old Greek word to describe that ancient land. *Artophagoi*, which means 'the bread eaters,' Αρτοφαγοι, was the source, the inspiration, the name given to the wellspring of the staff of life, bread. The churches of the world will now assemble to decry famine, to unite all religious groups under one banner, to celebrate and bless the food that allowed all to live, and worship, and thrive: bread."

They parked the sedan in the security section and made their way to the steps.

Jack stepped lively, shivering, and turned up his collar. He thumbed through Hubbard's background file on the Unity Conference again, and glanced at the bishop's pamphlet, this time focusing on the Cathedral's upcoming ceremony, trying to imagine how Kameron would see it. It starts with all gathered in the Cathedral for the blessing of the grains. From each great church a living stalk of food grain came symbolically to the Cathedral, then to the Temple of Dendur, where each Patriarch would receive the breads.

The Unity Service of Spiritual Commitment was to follow, drawing on tenets from all the faiths. The grains were to be blessed in unison. That initial ceremony was to be followed by the Procession of the Patriarchs, a solemn March of Commitment that would bring all together at the Metropolitan Museum for the final dedication of the breads and the banquet.

In front of the Cathedral, an NYPD van containing dogs and their handler sat idling beside the curb. Admiral Olde had asked specifically to have them brought in. Hubbard and Bryne could see a big black Labrador, focused and ready, and a pair of beagles. The Labrador was used to find smuggled foodstuffs: cheeses, meats, and citrus fruits interdicted by USDA agents working at JFK. The big dog had first been sent directly to the Metropolitan, where they had already swept the museum's galleries and halls; it had found nothing, and was brought to the Cathedral to join the bomb-sniffing beagles.

Bryne and Hubbard, entering the vestibule through a small side door, blinked in the semidarkness as their eyes adjusted. Bryne, desperate, leaned back and looked up, vertiginous, almost overwhelmed.

Looking ahead he could see the Cathedral's pews and altar decorated with the symbolic seeds of fertility and reaffirmation: the grains of the world. It only was ten minutes before the procession would begin.

"It could be anything in sight, Scott, but I'm not a booby-trap expert and I'm not a toxicologist. Just look at all the baskets of grain. Tell me it's coincidental..." Bryne suddenly felt himself talking far too loudly. Embarrassed, he stopped. He had been standing with his back to the four immense main doors, and again he looked up into the towering Cathedral, past Hubbard, far above, up into the distant comforting spaces soaring above the altar, sensing the echo. Hearing the cavernous warning, scoffing at coincidence, he started to try again...

"Listen, Scott..."

Hubbard saw it coming.

"No way, Jack! Don't even ask..." Hubbard hissed. "I can't call this ceremony off. Now *you* listen: there hasn't been any sort of threat, there's no warning. Nothing back-channel... nothing."

Bryne looked at the security forces sweeping the side aisles with metal detectors. "What about the congressmen?" He waited for an answer.

"See it my way... please. I'm not going to tell the leaders of half the churches on the planet they can't come into this Cathedral tonight because Jack Bryne thinks it's dangerous."

"I would... if I could," Bryne muttered.

"Well, instead," Hubbard gestured toward the cross, "shall we have a little faith?" He started toward the nave.

Bryne sighed, "Sure... if it works for the FBI, why not? Might as well... faith?"

Hubbard and Bryne walked up to the baptismal font, and as they turned toward the main aisle, the two beagles, the black Lab, and the dog handler trotted in through the massive front doors and stopped. The handler settled the Lab by the doorway and began working the two small dogs first, pointing them into the pews, sending one dog forward covering each row of seats; the beagles worked quickly, methodically. The Lab, always obedient, remained at the entrance lying down, waiting its turn.

Bryne and Hubbard trod silently on the thick red carpet placed for the dignitaries as Cathedral staffers beckoned them. The mighty organ began to swell with the opening bars of Handel's *Israel in Egypt*; final preparations had begun. A Cathedral official, hands outstretched and close to distraction, came over to them.

"Gentlemen, if you please. Could we move this along? I really must start seating people. If we don't hurry, I'll never get the Patriarchs into..."

"Thanks for your patience, padre," Hubbard said, trying to calm the man down. "One more sweep with the Lab and we're done here." He motioned to the dog handler who was finishing with the two beagles. "Take them out to the van," he said, "and then run the Lab. Thanks." Hubbard turned to Bryne and shrugged.

Bryne shook his head impatiently. "You've got to stop this... Something's not right... I'll take one more look around." The deacon scurried through the entryway to placate the crowd.

A breeze wafted in as the door opened and shut, making the candles dance. The sheaves of grain also waved. Bryne saw baskets, smelled the grain.

Grain. Everywhere.

Not bread.

The grain was all that was here in the Cathedral.

Not the breads!

That's it, Bryne thought, shocked, as he paced toward the nave below the vault of the church. *None of the bread is here at all!*

It all became clear to him, as crystal-clear as the fresh chill from the opened door: the menace was at the Metropolitan Museum, and as the banners of a hundred sacred sects shimmered in the flickering light of the Cathedral, Bryne was as dazzled by the simplicity of the threat as he was by the vast sea of scarlet and gold stitched into the pennants waving above him.

It's the bread the Elders are going to lay hands on, to share. To eat! It's the bread they're going to take home with them. It's the bread that's been contaminated, not the grain!

He and Hubbard had to get to the museum as fast as possible. They had to leave immediately. He had to make Scott understand...

He could see Hubbard standing at the door beside the Lab. *He's like that dog,* Bryne thought; *he's not going to leave here until he does exactly what he's been told.* Bryne made his way back to Hubbard, took him by the arm, and guided him, protesting, toward the doors and out onto the steps.

"Listen, Scott, I've got it. I think I've figured this out. It's the bread. Kameron poisoned the breads. Think about it. The breads. Over at the museum. Not here. Come on, we've got to go."

"Go? Are you nuts? They're all coming in now." Hubbard pointed out toward the canopied carpet where Bryne could see the first limousines starting to arrive. "Don't you see?" Hubbard insisted. "We can't leave."

"*We* can't leave? *We*? Maybe you can't leave, Scott, but you can bloody well stay here and watch *me* leave."

"Jack, wait..."

Bryne ignored him and turned away.

Hubbard stepped in front of him. "Jack, you don't even know what you're looking for. All the priests are coming here, for God's sake. I can't leave here. Can't you just wait until we do the sweep with the Lab?"

"How can I make this clear to you, Scott? It's got to be the breads. That dog's not going to find a damn thing. I'm out of here!"

"Jack, wait..."

"I'm done talking, Scott. Don't you get

470

it?" Bryne stepped around Hubbard and started to trot down the steps.

Hubbard reached out and grabbed Bryne's left biceps, trying to stop him. His fingers dug into Bryne's arm, and scar tissue grated over the nerve.

Bryne felt the pain. Felt the rage. Felt the frustration. He almost lost control. "Let me go." Bryne said it slowly, distinctly, and threateningly. Hubbard's eyes tightened. "That hurts." Bryne looked down at Hubbard's fingers wrapped around his arm. Hubbard looked at Bryne's fist.

Both men froze, then relaxed. Hubbard dropped Bryne's arm. Bryne unballed his fist, but said nothing. He turned away and walked, shaking with anger, pain, and frustration, toward the street.

Hubbard cursed as Bryne went down to the curb; then he turned away from the doors and started back down the steps after him. Suppose he *was* right? Hubbard could imagine the admiral's expression when he tried to explain how he'd personally screwed up.

"Jack, wait..." he cupped his hands to his mouth and yelled. He might as well have been yelling into a sandstorm, given the wind. He could see Bryne near Amsterdam, approaching a parked cab and then talking to the first driver. Hubbard yelled again, then cursed. Too late. Bryne never heard. The FBI man turned and went back up toward the Cathedral.

The dog handler, having secured the beagles,

waved and came running up the steps to work the Lab, but Hubbard stopped him. "How long is this going to take? I've got to get down to the Met."

"Ten minutes, tops. If we do a quick sweep."

"Fast as possible. Fast as possible!" They headed inside.

Bryne was furious as he peered through the cab's window at the turbaned driver. When he knocked on the glass, the driver waved his hand, flicking his fingers toward Bryne as if trying to dislodge a bit of lint, then the driver shook his head. He was going nowhere.

Bryne knocked harder and motioned for the driver to lower the window. Again the driver waved him away and turned on the "Off Duty" lamp on the roof of the cab. Bryne banged on the window with his palm. The driver rolled the window down half an inch. "Off duty," he finally said in a thick Indian accent. "Can't you read English?"

"It's an emergency... I'll pay you whatever you ask. I've got to get downtown. Please..."

"*Tomar ma kuttar shathe gumai,*" the cabbie muttered under his breath as he began to roll up the window. It was Bengali for "Your mother sleeps with the dogs," and he said it in a dialect that Bryne had spoken since Cambridge; it was as base an insult as can be offered without offending the Koran. Bryne could not stop himself. He wrenched open the door and grabbed the cabbie by the shoulder of his jacket. He catapulted the man onto the street, jumped into the taxi, and drove off.

Swearing, the cabbie regained his footing and looked around. He saw two policemen in a blue-on-blue squad car parked in front of the Cathedral. Screaming with his white *tupi* headdress unwinding over his shoulder, he ran toward them. As he pointed at his disappearing cab, Bryne turned east down West 113th Street toward the rocky cliffs that separate Morningside Heights from Harlem, and disappeared behind St. John the Divine.

Hubbard barely missed seeing Bryne's scuffle with the cabbie. He and the dog handler were inside, heading toward the Lab. They saw the dog curled up exactly where he was when he had been told to stay. The handler called the dog; it raised its head slowly and struggled to get up. It shivered violently, and its head collapsed on the marble. The handler rushed over and knelt down. The dog was breathing hard, its deep dark eyes looking up at its trainer, fearful. It tried to wag its tail, and its haunches trembled with the effort. It retched a thin yellow bile. Again it tried to stand, and failed. It retched again—blood this time. The big dog's head shivered and sank to the stone. It stopped breathing, and with a last whimper, died.

The handler sobbed. "Not Zak, he was the best dog I ever had."

Hubbard reached down and grabbed the man by the shoulder. "Listen to me. Where else has that dog been, exactly where?"

"Only the Met. He worked the Temple. Didn't find anything. There's nothing much there, 'cept the tables of breads."

"Did he sniff the breads?" Hubbard held his own breath as the man answered.

"Sure. I told you. He's the best... Hey! Hey, wait a minute..."

Hubbard had started running for the entrance, shouldering his way through the incoming crowd, pushing aside a towering Zulu priest, clothed head to foot in the skins of animals. He also elbowed his way past a priest carrying a silver crucifix and did the same to a band of monks in saffron robes, devotion shining on their faces in spite of the assault. He got through the entrance just in time to hear the taxi driver screaming and pointing to Bryne driving off in the cab. Sprinting down the steps, Hubbard passed the policemen trying to calm the driver. As Hubbard got closer, he could hear the man screaming about his taxi and pointing to the cab as it roared away.

Hubbard ran to the squad car. "Officer, I'm Agent Hubbard, FBI." He flashed his ID and pointed at the taxi. "Follow that cab." He got in, the policeman hit the lights and siren, and they cut across four lanes of traffic in pursuit.

The steering wheel of the big old Chevy was worn smooth by the grip of many hands, and the front end trembled as Bryne heaved the cab into a shuddering turn at the end of 113th, heading south for Amsterdam. He fumbled with the wiper controls on the end of the turn-indicator lever, and managed to turn left while signaling a right. He moved the lever again and activated the windshield washer. As the spray cascaded across his vision, he narrowly missed hitting an old man at Frederick Douglass Circle.

He saw people raising their arms at him. He was afraid, until he realized that he was being hailed, not cursed. He jammed on the brakes as the light went against him, and was forced into the turn lane for the southbound route down Central Park West. NO! Wrong way again! He needed to go east to Fifth and *then* south to the Met. He peered out the side window to see if the entrance to the Central Park Ring Road was open. If it was, he might be able to cut across, even go the wrong way around the circle, and then cross back to Central Park North and clear the park. He craned his neck looking for a gap in the traffic, but by the time the light had changed, there was a steady stream of traffic blocking a left turn, and angry drivers in the cars behind him honking at his indecision. He wanted to punch somebody, anybody...

Jack looked in the mirror and flinched as he saw the blue and red flashers of a police cruiser heading toward him from Cathedral Parkway. Not looking back, he floored the Chevy and ran the red light, swerving right, finally southbound at 109th Street, doing forty. Hubbard, watching Bryne drive like a madman, told the cop to shut off his flashers and siren. He had no intention of killing Bryne by chasing him.

Crossing yellow lines and passing slow-moving cars, Bryne narrowly avoided a northbound M10 bus as it pulled away from a stop at 108th. He racked his brain trying to remember the cross streets that lead to the transverses through the park, and cursed again when he found that the 106th Street ramp was one-way against him, and blocked by police barricades, which meant the ring road was closed. Swearing, he continued south.

The downtown traffic lights were staggered in his favor. He had opened distance between himself and the police car by the time he crossed 96th Street, the eastbound entrance to the Central Park transverse. He had not seen the police car since 110th; he had a chance if he could just cross the park to Fifth Avenue, but as he tried to turn left into the Transverse, he saw the eastbound cross-park traffic backing up. Cursing, he cut south again, heading toward midtown.

At 86th Street, the squad car finally caught up with Bryne and cut him off, probably saving his life. Hubbard, terrified, had pointed, "Oh, no, he doesn't see the NYNEX truck." Picturing the wreck, he could almost feel the upcoming impact and his face drained white. At the last moment the driver of the squad car turned on the sirens, and hit the accelerator. They lurched forward. Bryne saw them coming from the side, flashers and sirens ripping his attention away from the intersection. And then he saw the westbound truck. Wrenching the wheel to the right, he slammed on the brakes and slid through the intersection sideways. The front of the cab hooked the rear bumper of the truck, metal screamed, and the cab did a complete 360 before it jumped the curb and slid across the sidewalk, shattering a bus shelter in a shower of broken glass.

Hubbard ran over and pulled open the passenger door. "Are you all right?" Hubbard demanded.

"Yeah, yeah, I'm all right," Bryne said, shaken but unhurt. "I guess I lost it." He looked at Hubbard. "I guess I'm under arrest."

"Not yet, smart guy. But you're pushing it..."

"What's going on?"

"You called it once again! The Labrador died right in front of us, before he could even start to sweep the Cathedral. He had been at the Met." Hubbard paused.

"The Lab?" asked Bryne, near shock.

"Dead. You were right, don't you get it? Whatever the toxin is in, or on, it's got to be at the Metropolitan, and we've got to get there. Let's go. Can you walk? I already know you can't drive."

Bryne was not even listening. He reached over and took Hubbard by the arm to steady himself, slid out of the cab, and stood up, relieved he felt so little damage. They got into the squad car and in less than eight minutes were at the Museum.

22

Sunday, October 4
Metropolitan Museum of Art, Manhattan
6:15 P.M.

Racing up a flight of stairs from the Met's basement garage, Hubbard and Bryne almost knocked over a priest striding downward, his eyes fixed in so heavenly a gaze he didn't even notice them. As they followed the red velvet ropes through the Greek and Roman galleries and across the vast, empty lobby, the polished marble space echoed with their footsteps.

The stairways and corridors to the Museum's many galleries were darkened, but the path to the Temple of Dendur was well lit, with attendants positioned along the route, smiling and nodding as Bryne and Hubbard ran past. Soon the two men arrived at the four massive cut-stone pillars that marked the entrance to the Egyptian Wing.

They continued to sprint by the elaborate turquoise ornaments from a pharaoh's burial chamber, gleaming alabaster hawks and wrought-gold cobras, and on into the shadowy hallway leading to the Temple.

Entering the immense room, they stopped abruptly. The space itself was dark, but the Temple was bathed in the pale light of a cold, full, autumn moon, and the gallery's glass walls and ceiling created the illusion that the Temple was outdoors. Moonlight on the Temple of Dendur had been mesmerizing worshippers throughout the ages, and Bryne was no exception. Beautiful, tranquil, ideally proportioned, the hand-carved sandstone Temple seemed to float six feet above Bryne's gaze, borne aloft on an enormous platform of black polished granite.

The source of the astonishment that rooted Bryne to the entrance was the illusion that there was not one but two temples before him. It was the transparent wall that did it. Bryne realized that the room itself, six stories high, was composed of huge sheets of floor-to-ceiling plate glass. At night, the glass became invisible, pitch dark, and so, on the tilted wall of the gallery, there appeared a perfect mirror image of the Temple—a second structure, shimmering back at him, seeming to draw him somehow closer to the banks of the Nile, an illusion sustained by the reflecting pool surrounding the Temple.

The waters of this pool—a hundred feet long, twenty feet across, perhaps thigh-deep—formed a concourse for visitors, just as the Nile had once brought the faithful when the Temple was still in Egypt.

Bryne's eyes began to adjust, to measure the room. To cross to the Temple itself, to rise to the cut stone platform it floated on, he and Hubbard would have to walk two hundred feet either left or right and mount three low steps. From the pool, reflections of the moonlit Temple glided sinuously, mysteriously toward them.

Hubbard noticed Bryne swaying a bit and asked him if he was all right. Jack looked down at the steady granite floor, took a deep breath, and nodded over toward the surface of the pool. "Scott, look." He pointed at the pool, for reflected there was not only the Temple, roof, and stars above. There were also the images of bread, more bread than anyone could have imagined, and tables, dozens and dozens of long folding tables set end-to-end, over two hundred feet of them, neatly arranged above the reflecting pool, separated by the platform from the water.

All the loaves were on the tables. The entire Temple had been surrounded by a rectangle of breads, a collection of breads such as the modern world had never seen, and might never see again. The tables had been freshly prepared. The room was filled with the aroma of dozens of bread factories, a sweet, seductive smell from a magnificent display of sourdough loaves, Italian breads, Spanish chorizo breads, Grauaus from France, Hungarian black breads, German pumpernickel, sesame-topped breads from Turkey, *arépas* from Colombia, Mexican tortillas, glazed Viennese rolls, Israeli matzoh, Middle Eastern pitas, Afghan flat breads, spongy oyster breads, Meteils from Brittany, primitive bricks of Anglo-Saxon Pullman bread, Irish soda breads, Provençale fougasse, Russian bagels, Ukrainian bialys, and Polish babkas.

Breads were shaped and twisted to make windmills, lanterns, sheaves of wheat, bunches of grapes, ribbons, bows, bells, animals, and fishes. There were tricornes, casquettes, *courrones lyonnaises,* powdered *boules tresées, pattes d'ours, pains spirals, fers à chevals,*

480

l'auvernats, pithiviers, croissants, fendus, pouched tabatières. Cornucopias, infundibula, woven baskets, floral designs, gingerbread houses, crèches, harvest presentations, farmer's fields, cocky roosters, giant country loaves, breads made with apples, apricots, prunes, raisins, dried fruits, cider, carrots, herbs, olives, seaweed, steaming loaves reeking of garlic and onions, bacon breads, hazelnut, walnut and almond breads. The giant room smelled of yeast, fresh-baked bread, and a pungent odor of vaporized alcohol, the essence of kneading, shaping, proofing, and baking.

Noting the brace of caterers' assistants scurrying around the area, Bryne and Hubbard rapidly circled the room's perimeter. The narrow walkway was bordered on the left by six man-high carved rock cats—enthroned deities, with women's breasts and feline faces—and on the right by two matching figures: a gleaming black cat representing Mut, Goddess of Pestilence, and a chimeric figure with a man's body and a ram's head, Amon, God of Fertility.

"Whoa! Slow down!" Hubbard yelled as Bryne raced past the loaves barely out of reach across the pool, but Bryne ignored him. As they turned toward the steps, he began rummaging in his pocket for his black light. Suddenly the ceiling lights began to grow stronger—like the sun rising over the Temple.

"What's all this light for?" Jack asked.

"They always turn up the lights at these functions," Hubbard explained.

"Well, it's no help to me. I need to have it dark." Bryne waved the black light at the FBI man. By the time they reached the steps and crossed the reflecting pool, the gallery was growing brighter and brighter. Hundreds of loaves lay before them on the first table. Bryne turned on the lamp and passed its pale purple glow across a loaf.

Nothing. He moved on. Still nothing.

"It's much too bright for this thing to make the toxins show up. You've got to get them to lower the lights, Scott."

Hubbard gestured to one of the museum attendants, who walked over from his post by the Temple entrance. Showing the man his FBI ID and badge, he ordered him to darken the room.

"I can't." The attendant shook his head. "See, it's all on a timed schedule... I can take you to the lamp panel, but I need Dr. Rigg's authorization. See, it's for the cameras; they start setting up in about ten minutes." He gestured to a small picture window, where the first TV and video camera technicians were arriving.

"I don't think I need Dr. Rigg's authorization to turn down the damn lights," Hubbard bellowed. "Where's the switch?"

The clearly conflicted attendant finally said, "In the equipment room, downstairs." He indicated an access door. "But I'm not allowed. Nobody's allowed to change the timers. Not without—"

"Hubbard," Bryne urged him, "Just do it!"

"No, no," the attendant pleaded. "Let me get Dr. Rigg."

Hubbard reached out and grabbed the man. "First you show me that panel, then you take me to Rigg. Jack, you stay here..." Taking the man by the elbow, Hubbard headed past the pool to a hallway and disappeared.

Bryne waited. And waited. Eventually he could see his shadow soften, and the first bank of quartz-halide spots began to grow darker. Yes, the light was definitely fading. He turned the black light on a table of Metiel breads from Brittany. Still nothing. He walked around to his left, past tables of bread in the shape of bear claws, horseshoes, and turtles; row upon row of beautiful caps, crowns, and braids.

Soon the Temple was almost as dark as the night outside. Bryne bent closely over the breads, shielding the light with one hand. Then he saw them.

Glowing faintly, hard to make out, but real: tiny dots, bluish-green, unmistakable. The deadly mycotoxin molecules were everywhere.

In the black light, the breads had taken on a sickly pale blue aura of toxic luminescence. Bryne stood up and swept the beam of his lamp to the next table. Glowing.

He went to the next. Even stronger. Globs of evil aqua-colored fluorescence dotted the breads. As the gallery darkened toward black, it was quite clear to him that the mycotoxin was on every single one of the loaves.

Bryne backed away, switched off his lamp, and looked down at his hands and at the tables. Where was Hubbard?

He stood in the darkened room waiting for

an inspiration, and it came to him: the Memphis grain disaster had shown him how to neutralize the toxins. First soak the bread in the fountain, all of it.

He grabbed a napkin, dipped it in the pool, triangled the sopping rag over his face, and tied it behind his ears. He jammed the wet cotton into his nostrils, hoping the moisture would trap the dust.

Then he started.

Taking a deep breath, Bryne began working with the first table on his left, the one nearest the Temple. He looked at the seemingly benign bread, bending down as if in supplication, while he carefully gathered the corners of the tablecloth in each hand. Slowly, smoothly, he lifted his arms, stepped back, and pulled gently, steadily, gathering the cloths together, tenting them, raising them, raising them. Soon the rich, heavy, deadly loaves began to topple and slide.

He braced his feet and tugged backwards with all his strength: the entire table of breads spilled backwards, cascading over the far side of the table and splashing into the reflecting pool.

Bryne grimaced, hurled the tablecloth into the water, and moved to the other tables, repeating his performance. There were many tables. The breads were weighty, and he was trying to move faster and faster.

He had cleared only a few tables before a caterer took note, and an old burly guard did a double-take at the tall, agile, masked man moving like a lunatic from table to table, throwing hundreds of loaves of bread into the water.

The guard shouted, then started running, but Bryne was on the far side of the pool, and hundreds of feet separated them. The guard, already getting winded, reached for his radio, which somehow slipped through his fingers, bounced off the granite, cracked, and lay silent. He began to back toward the entrance, then stopped, stood still, and watched Bryne in action.

Jack, working feverishly and oblivious to shouts, fully expected to be tackled from behind at any moment, so he pushed himself to work harder and harder.

As he neared the Temple entrance, he glanced up between the upstretched arms of the cats of pestilence, the Muts, into the main doorway to the gallery; it remained empty, and he still heard no alarms. He hurried, faster, faster. Time seemed to blur. As he pressed on, the Temple grew even darker. But where was Hubbard? Security would be arriving any second.

Hubbard, true to his word, was going to meet with Dr. Rigg. He heard a motor purring inside the office and could tell the door was unlocked, but it seemed stuck, as if a weight were pressed against it. He sent the terrified attendent for a guard to help push.

At first the door began to slide slowly open, less than an inch. Hubbard could clearly hear the noise now: it was the whine of a central vacuum. Then a draft of air hit him, carrying the faint, exceedingly sour, almost fecal smell of dead meat, fermenting blood, malevolent organic gases.

Hubbard almost retched, but he pushed harder, and the door slid back enough so he could enter.

The guard watched, but went no further; he had smelled the odor too and reached for his handkerchief. Once he saw the shock on Hubbard's face, he backed away.

Hubbard was looking at the staring, bulging, swollen eyes of a corpse, but the face that had been Rigg's seemed shrunken from within, like a raisin. His mouth was drawn open in a rictus smile, his skin drawn tight as a mummified pharaoh's. Rigg had been eviscerated from behind. Hubbard knew instantly why the vacuum was on.

Rigg lay on his side, hanging by his tie from the doorknob. His body had been used to weigh the door closed. Hanging beneath him, bloody and still connected, was the silver nozzle of a powerful central vacuum cleaner. A thick gray hose snaked across the rug to the wall connector, howling metallically, straining to draw more fluids from the body.

Hubbard backed out of the room without touching anything, ordering the guard to call EMS and to turn off the central vacuum.

As he sprinted back to the gallery of the Temple of Dendur, he used his cellular phone to call for backup.

In the darkened Temple, he found Bryne, who was just immersing the last of the breads.

Jack turned away from the pool and bent over, palms on his knees, trying to catch his breath.

"Jack... " Hubbard called to him.

Bryne saw Hubbard running toward him. He fought for breath through his improvised dust mask and shouted in a muffled voice, "It's all toxic! Contaminated... Get a mask, a cloth... cover your face." He double-timed off the platform, past the loaves floating beneath him, and pulled Hubbard toward the stairs, back to the control room.

"Cleaning closet," he yelled to Hubbard. "Take me to the cleaning closet. Hurry. It's our only shot."

"What?" said Hubbard. "What are you *DOING*?"

"Ammonia, I've got to find enough ammonia to neutralize the toxins in that pool." He pointed back at the loaves, but he kept moving.

"Tell that guard to close off this gallery..."

Hubbard located the supply room, and in a service closet, they found racks of janitorial supplies, waxes, polishes, cleaners, disinfectants, soaps, cases of toilet paper, and at least four five-gallon plastic drums of ammonia. Taking a hand truck over to the shelves, Bryne and Hubbard wrestled the canisters onto the cart.

"Go get that elevator, Hubbard. Show 'em your gun if you have to."

Hubbard had the elevator waiting when Bryne arrived, and they rode upstairs to the gallery. Tearing the tops off the big spouts, they used the hand cart to roll along the pool, tipping the cans carefully to let the ammonia penetrate into the murky water, clogged now with rafts of soggy bread.

Gagging and retching from the fumes, the men struggled to keep the barrels emptying smoothly. They then stood back, almost overcome with nausea from the fumes.

The doorway to the Temple began to fill with guards on the run, NYPD blues, and a host of other professionals; the SWAT team would be close behind. Hubbard opened his wallet, flashed his ID, and trotted over toward the NYPD point man where the security force surrounded him. Bryne kicked the last of the containers into the pool and watched the remaining ammonia bubbling into the water as they sank.

He needed air, and turned for the entrance.

He retched, head pounding, and staggered, but he kept moving. He had to have air. He tried to untie the soggy knot holding his mask.

"Hey, you!" It was the old guard who had tried to stop him before, pointing at Bryne. "Stop him, *he's* the one who did it!"

Bryne, stumbling, turned toward Hubbard to explain, but Scott was arguing with a sergeant. It was all a haze. He tried to run. Air... get outside.

At the gates of the gallery, Jack stopped. His eyes were burning, his every breath a gasp. At last the mask came off. He saw black spots everywhere. He was spinning, sick. Black spots, moving, pointing at him. He could hear, but faintly. He gasped. Black spots. He tried to keep walking. Air...

The muzzles of seven semiautomatic police pistols were focused at the center of his chest. Bryne looked around. Hubbard was not in sight.

"Freeze!" shouted the cops.

Bryne grinned. *How theatrical. Me? Freeze? I'm just going out for some air.*

He stepped forward.

He heard the safeties click off.

He tried to walk...

And then, as the fingers on the triggers began to tighten, Bryne did the two smartest things he had ever done in his life.

First, he raised his hands in surrender. Then he fainted.

The next thing he was aware of was Vicky Wade kneeling beside him and Hubbard screaming at him.

"Jack! Damn it, Bryne, wake up. I need you!"

An EMS tech leaned over Bryne, put a hand behind his head, and elevated it. Jack heard the crack of the smelling salts ampoule as the medic prepared to wave it under his nose.

Bryne struggled. "No, not more ammonia... No more..."

Suddenly, Bryne was fully awake. Retching.

Hubbard had another EMS worker bring him water. Gasping, he drank it gratefully.

Ten minutes later his head had cleared. He and Hubbard sat in the security office, reviewing videotapes from the security cameras mounted all around the Met. Wade, who had been covering the event, had wanted into the meeting, but Hubbard had given her a definite no. The videotape was in color, and depicted the front of the museum; a small window displayed the time in hours, minutes, and seconds.

"Look, Jack." Hubbard sat up. "That's him, isn't it?"

"Run it again. Any shots of his face?"

As they played the tape again, one of the museum workers told them, "He's the one who came to bless the bread. The caterer's people told me."

"Jack, Jack, listen to me," Hubbard urged him. "Who is it? Who is it?"

"Who do you think, Scott? It's Kameron."

"Goddamn it," the FBI man groused, "we walked right past him!"

"Yup, this guy's been hiding in plain sight," Bryne commented.

"I'm going to call my people to see if there's anything yet on where the rye shipments were delivered," Hubbard told him. "Let's take the guy on his own turf."

Hubbard took out his cellular phone and walked a short distance away, his back turned. When he finished, he was grinning.

"Bingo!" he told the astonished Bryne. "A lot of grain merchants are never going to forgive the Bureau for ruining their weekends, but we got it, Jack, we got it! We can find the creep at 699 East 83rd Street, Apartment 15A."

The super, like the building and the neighborhood, had seen better days, but he was sober enough to open up as soon as he saw badges and a police escort. The tenant in 15A was a loner, bothered nobody, traveled a lot, but didn't go out much when he was there—except today, when he must have been going to a costume party, and in a limo, yet. But they'd just missed him. He'd been carrying a lot of packages and had left in a van.

When they finally got to the place, they confronted six heavy-duty locks. The super's key inserted in the simplest one admitted them immediately. Not a good sign: If Kameron hadn't bothered to lock the locks, he might be gone for good. Expecting some sort of trap, the police officers slipped on latex gloves, and drew their weapons—better to be safe than sorry.

The apartment was dingy, almost empty. The space that passed for a living room featured walls hung with hundreds of images of fountains: recumbent mermaids, pissing putti, standing fish, garden sprinklers, kitchen faucets, spigots, nozzles, fire hydrants, hoses, watering cans; all manner of liquid-spraying devices—plus etchings of waterfalls, calendars of streams, photographs of the Trevi Fountain—and the Indianapolis Museum of Art. There was even a postcard of the Turner painting pinned to the wall.

Bryne's peripheral vision caught something, and he called to Hubbard, "Look, it's

491

a leather feed bag, see. The straps are folded in the bag. He was there, at Churchill Downs!"

There was a single drawing table in one corner of the room, but nothing on it. The kitchen was bare, and when one of the cops opened the ancient refrigerator, he found racks of test tubes and baby food jars with mold growing in them. He started to slam the door, but Bryne stopped him. The officer had overlooked in the butter bin a medicine bottle labeled PRAZIQUANTEL with instructions for treating tapeworm. Bryne warned the others not to touch anything, then gently closed the refrigerator door.

A glass-paneled door, painted over in lime green, led to an even smaller chamber, almost a closet, where another door had been left ajar. A policeman used the tip of his shoe to open the closet. There he found shelf after shelf of neatly arranged objects. "Jesus, look at this. Are all those things rubbers?"

After scanning the display, Hubbard nodded, and eased the door shut, pointing to another door, to another tiny room with sixteen fish tanks against the wall. But none contained fish; some, full of water, and some glistened with slime crawling up their sides. In one dry tank, hundreds of mealy bugs squirmed and spasmed in sawdust. On the wall was a map from a 1939 edition of a *National Geographic* article entitled "The Ancient Holy Lands: Tracing the Flight of the Israelites from Egypt to the Promised Land." Bryne noticed a protective orange HAZMAT space suit with its plastic hood and a small positive-pressure respirator unit crumpled up and thrown into a corner.

The far door led to a bathroom. Locked. An officer yanked on the knob, but Hubbard ordered him to stop. Bryne noticed the PAPR breathing device next to the door. He turned out the overhead light and switched on his pocket-sized UV penlight, suffusing the room in the familiar purplish glow. He walked to the door and placed the light next to the keyhole. Immediately the color changed from purple to green, and a wisp of vapor curled out of the keyhole toward the policeman.

"Get back," Bryne shouted. "Let the HAZ-MAT people take care of this room. They'll earn their pay in there. What's down here?"

They now followed a long hall to the bedroom. The door was open, and Hubbard motioned the others to follow him. He turned on the light switch, and they could see a telescope on a tripod and a pair of binoculars on the sill.

Standing alone in the middle of the bedroom was an illuminated museum case, four feet tall, inside of which stood a scaled-down model of the Andrus Fountain. Bryne now knew exactly what Mia had been sketching, what she wanted him to see—the fountain in the East River, the perfect setting for the Tenth Plague.

Bryne moved to the window and looked through the telescope, which was pointed downtown toward the southern tip of Roosevelt Island—he could barely make out the Fountain, but he knew nonetheless. This time, this plague, Kameron's target was the entire city of New York—the Memphis, Sodom, and Babylon of the New World Order.

"This is it, Scott," Jack announced to Hubbard. "This is the big one. The fountain! The grain elevators were just a prototype. Don't you see? Same toxin, same plague. He's going to use the aflatoxin until he can complete every plague."

Again Bryne bent over the telescope, adjusting the focus. Now, he could see the fountain clearly.

"Scott," Bryne told the FBI man, "we're going to need a massive supply of ammonia—immediately!"

"Okay."

"But the diluted bottled variety isn't going to hack it," Jack added. "We also have to figure out some way to keep that fountain from going off. If there's enough toxin involved, Kameron is going to kill thousands the second it activates. You've seen the winds. A plume of toxin would carry for miles."

"Exactly what do we need?" Hubbard looked at Bryne, then at the policemen, who stood by helplessly, as if expecting Bryne to save them.

"There's not enough dried ammonia anywhere I know of," Bryne declared. "See if the fire department can help. The HAZMAT team, maybe... Floyd Bennett Field, that's where the city stores all its emergency response chemicals."

"Do it," Hubbard ordered one of the cops. Then, seeing a computer work station on a table, he added, "And confiscate that while you're at it!"

"Listen, Scott," Bryne continued. "It's going to take a tank of compressed ammonia or a bag of anhydrous ammonia, a big one, hoses, couplings, a goddamned plumber's tool bag at least, a real-life plumber if possible, and a damned good boat."

"Why not a chopper?" Hubbard asked.

"Think, Scott," Bryne told him. "If we're too late the chopper will just spread the toxin."

Hubbard retrieved his cellular phone from his pocket, called the admiral, got a green light, a Defcon One, and together he and Bryne headed for the East River, racing against time with a madman.

9:40 P.M.

Tied at its mooring, the sturdy, thick-hulled police launch bobbed easily in the cold waters near the East River boat ramp. A thin iron footbridge took Bryne and Hubbard over to the dock—an old, all but abandoned berth on Seventy-Ninth Street, where boats had once set off conveying the sick out to the old Metropolitan Hospital directly across the river on Roosevelt Island back when it had been known as Welfare Island. Bryne gazed over the dark, oily water at the tortured ruins of the crumbling, abandoned facility.

Together they heaved a tool bag on the deck of the launch, then jumped aboard. Hubbard spoke with the skipper, who told him that a bagged block of anhydrous ammonia was on the way upriver from the Governor's Island facility across from the Statue of Liberty. Hubbard suggested that the Coast Guard launch rendezvous with the police boat near the Brooklyn Bridge, and then carry the special cargo back up the river after he and Bryne were left on Roosevelt Island. it was agreed, and the launch cast off.

Bryne watched the island approach with an anticipation he could barely contain. Vengeance. Pure, perfect vengeance. Vengeance was his by the laws of God and man, and he meant to claim it.

23

Sunday, October 4
7:00 P.M.

When Kameron left his hidden lab, he had driven carefully down Second Avenue and out of Manhattan over the Fifty-Ninth Street Bridge into Queens. Precisely on schedule, he doubled back along the waterfront through the ruined gates of an abandoned bakery. Tracing the route he had rehearsed many times before, he pulled past the crumbling loading bays and over to the steel bulkhead beside the water's edge. He turned off his van and rolled down the window. The ground fog was thinning, and as the mists of autumn were swept from the East River, Teddy could see the Andrus Fountain outlined clearly by the lights from the U.N. complex. He watched the river

496

churning north filling the narrow channel, and saw the flotsam swept along by the currents. The East River was only half a mile wide at this point, and now it was all that separated him from the two million people on Manhattan Island. He could see his boat rising with the tide, safely moored beside the piers. He checked his watch. The tide was perfect—it would be high soon—and he could start the loading.

Knowing he would never return to his lab, Kameron had copied all the files and records from his workstation to CD-ROM, duplicating all his biographical material, his formulas, his codes, his patents, the numbers of his bank accounts, and all the charts, recordings, photographs, lab tests, and bibliographies, the sum of his life's work. He had copied certain of the files that he wanted Bryne and the FBI to find onto a new hard drive and installed it in his docking station. Then he had taken his old disk drive out to the fire escape, doused it with alcohol and set it on fire. Everything he had accomplished, and everything that had made him what he was today, was on two CD-ROMs. He slipped them into his jacket, set the security cameras and left the lab.

He had kept his laptop with him, and as he sat in the truck waiting for slack water, he turned it on, dialed his password into his cell phone, and logged onto the Internet. He accessed his network at the laboratory and activated the cameras above his monitor. Nothing out of the ordinary. He relaxed. He knew they were close now. He had almost laughed out loud at the Met when Bryne walked past him. He replayed the surveillance system records from the lab with excitement. On the screen of his laptop he could clearly see inside of his lab. While he sat in Queens, a digital camera swept the lab in Manhattan every fifteen seconds, storing the images and downloading them to Teddy. Since the Internet connection had been set up through his cell phone, there was no way for the police to locate him, even as he waited for them.

He was looking forward to observing Jack Bryne. If he had guessed correctly, Bryne might even break into the lab while he watched. Perhaps, Teddy hoped, he might even see Bryne and Hubbard read the stories of his great achievements. As Kameron waited patiently for the next step in the grandest, most inspired of all the plagues, he slipped a CD-ROM into his laptop and scanned through the files until he came to the Prologue of his autobiography, drafts of the toxic words he had tried to use to describe his life, to define it, to explain it, and to glorify it. The words were his attempt to memorialize his own existance. He looked upon them for what he knew might be the last time, with the steady hope that he might still be nominated for a Nobel Prize. He waited for the selected files to come up on his screen, savoring the smells of the river, enjoying the skyline. He could see a Moran tug, diesels straining, heading downriver towing a barge against the tide. Ah, New York, always at work, he thought, and, smiling, he started his autobiography.

PROLOGUE
   It is said that great men's genius must be attributed to their mothers. Theodore Graham Kameron is no exception to that dictum. Who knows what he might have become but for the religious hypocrite who had gone to the trouble of bearing him—only to cane, burn, and humiliate him for reasons that were baffling to him as a child, and unmanning to him as he grew. She hated him, she pronounced his blond good looks diabolical ("Lucifer was golden as the sun—like you, Theodore!"). She would force him to learn a new lesson from the Bible every day, would punish him for every mistake, would strip him and read the passage to him over and over until he could say it with her, and then say it without her. She would make him stand naked until he learned it perfectly. She always had the belt for small mistakes, and the sink for more serious misbehavior, or forgetfulness. He could recite every Psalm by the time he was three, and he would learn them or she would hold his face underwater in her bathroom basin until he did. Even when he was older and had not learned the

daily lesson, he was told to stand naked for his punishment. She would taunt him about his scarred palms and his body. When he grew older still and first dared to touch himself, she had begun to burn him to make him stop, to mock him for his huge penis. To survive, he wandered into the world of his dreams, of his ambitions, where he was safe from her prying hands, painful cane strokes, and the iron. She went too far with the iron. The bandages usually meant he would keep his hands away from himself, but eventually there were blisters, infections, and then there were the burns on top of the infections, and then the time had come when she knew she would have to take him to the doctor, and she knew she had to hide the scars on his fingers. She knew they would see, those doctors, and so finally she turned on the oven, let it come to broil, and called the boy into the kitchen. Mrs. Kameron said a prayer as she opened the oven, grasped his wrists and pulled the boy to the door. He remembered the words all his life as she pressed his hands to the searing steel and turned all his burns into one. She had told him that she was doing this for God. Screaming that God never wanted him to abuse himself, she swore she would see to it that he never did it again. Teddy could smell himself burning, but he fainted, gasping in agony, before he could even scream. He had been eleven and he never touched himself again. And he never could come to orgasm unless he tortured and killed small animals or executed even more elaborate destructions. And he never had peace anywhere but in his dreams. Those dreams were always about the two things in life he wanted to be.

The first was an actor. He knew he was good at pretending. He pretended all the time at the private school that his mother was the widow of an insurance executive. He pretended that she was a good mother, just a little strict, which was why he couldn't make friends like the other kids—he had to go right home and "be the man of the house." He also pretended to laugh when someone told a joke and to be kind when it suited him. Yes, he would have made a great actor.

But the theatre was anathema to his mother; she was one of those who still believed actors should never be buried in consecrated ground. She knew he had the devil in him, and the devil dined on pleasure. So no school plays. No movies. No television, when it came along.

The second thing Teddy Kameron wanted to be was either a scientist or a doctor, especially the kind that spe-

cializes in the creepy-crawly wood-
land things he'd been obsessed by for
as long as he could remember. His
mother believed neither in evolution
nor science, and she could barely tolerate going to a doctor. Telling her he
was interested in healing softened her
a bit. So she let him go to the library,
where he spent days, then years,
studying not healing but death—toxins and poisons—making notes she
never saw, doing experiments in a
deserted tool shed on the edge of the
property that she never visited.

By the time he graduated first in his
high school class and had gone on full
scholarship to Cornell, he was more
knowledgeable about toxicology than
many of his college instructors.

When he was in Ithaca, she was
dividing her time between California
and her farm in West Virginia where
she kept her horses, far enough away,
he figured, that she could no longer
torture him. But it wasn't true. It was
as if he carried her inside his head, a
head buzzing with the drone of
repression and damnation despite the
distance. Her letters, actually
religious tracts, seared his scar-thick-
ened palms. Her piteous phone calls
begging him to come to see her made
him physically ill for days. He returned
the letters unopened, and begged her

not to write, not to call, but she persisted; it was his punishment for leaving.

That was when it occurred to him: although she considered him the devil's spawn, a disciple of Onan, it was really she who was the damned one, she who deserved the punishment. Finally, while still an undergraduate, he made a long-delayed trip home, ostensibly to reconcile.

The prodigal son returned. He embraced her, worshipped with her in church, and even bought some rare and beautiful specimens for her fish tank, the only thing outside of her horses and the Bible that she loved. That first night, while she slept, Teddy had crept downstairs and, with a chill of delight, added merely a drop or two of the colorless ciguatera toxin he'd extracted from a two-kilogram red snapper and brought west specifically for the occasion.

Next morning, her screams awakened him. He knew what she had found. He walked calmly to the bathroom and watched himself in the mirror, naked as she always insisted. He turned on the water and filled the sink, and without touching himself, he ejaculated. "Look, Ma," he said aloud to his reflection, "no hands..." before he joined her downstairs.

Pretending to be as mystified as she at the massacre, he comforted her until it was time to leave. Overwhelmed with hunger, he stopped at a diner on the way to the airport and ordered enough bacon, eggs, pancakes, and coffee for two people, relishing every bite.

Two months went by without another word between them. Then, suddenly, the call came from California. She was dead of a myocardial infarction. Teddy had hoped the death of her fish really had broken her heart. Although her money was a godsend, it was too bad in a way that she wasn't still around, to die of shame at what her little boy was up to.

Teddy had not needed his mother to tell him he was different; he'd always known it, but he thought of himself as "special" rather than merely different. Of course, his Divine Selection for the Missions proved him right. To the world, even as an adult, he seemed rather shy, a most brilliant loner, good-looking but detached. Actually, few knew how detached. He was a man of limited but ardent passions, romantic love not being among them. He was passionate about his work, which was the best of him, passionate to make a contribution, to be remembered.

Since the commencement of the Mission of the plagues, since he had first heard The Voice, as a scientist he had become committed to keeping detailed records of his achievement. His contribution to history would be astounding, and he eventually wanted the world to know about it.

He stopped reading—convinced he had shown his mother properly. He concentrated; Kameron had spoken to the cause of his madness, his toxic mother, and he needed to address the nature of the toxins themselves, why they had obsessed him, why he had become the scientist he had, and how he had come to be infected. There is such a bond between genius and madness that only one who has experienced both could ever hope to explain either, hence his need to concentrate. Hence the work in progress, the work he had created to document, explain, predict, and control, not only madness or cancer, but Divinity as well...

Teddy looked up from his laptop. He had heard something. He closed the screen a bit to reduce the glare inside the van. He saw nothing save the rising tide, he heard nothing more except the sounds of the city. He opened the laptop and accessed the cameras in the lab, scanned the rooms, saw nothing, and shut down the connection, pleased. He switched his screen back to text entries and continued to read, scanning Chapter One, skipping ahead, and finally settling into Chapter Two.

~ II ~

Tragically, in Dr. Kameron's life as well as for others, even today, important medical discoveries are kept from the community through greed, dogma, and stupidity. Galileo knew it all too well, as did Theodore Graham Kameron. Because of the bigotry around him, the scientific world would never be aware of the Kameron Test. One of the world's foremost yet least-known toxicologists, Theodore G. "Teddy" Kameron, Ph.D., spent most of his life searching out the organic toxins of the world. Dr. Kameron committed himself to this quest because he knew that the fundamental engines of death held the secret of life.

Dr. Kameron devised a test combining the magnificent insight of Sir Alexander Fleming's observation of bacterial inhibition by a penicillin mold and Bruce Ames's discovery that simple petri dishes could serve to determine the presence of cancer-causing agents. The Kameron Test, as its discoverer liked to call it, also used a petri dish, but it could rapidly screen a vast range of common environmental agents to assess both their antimicrobial and anticarcinogenic potentials.

With this test, Kameron systematically screened scores of insect and snake venoms; he tested thousands of soil specimens, isolating bacterial and even fungal toxins that would inhibit microbial infection and even, he believed, malignant cell growth. He had been unsuccessful for seventeen years until he ventured into the Third Kingdom of microbial chimeras and griffins: the phytoplankton and algae.

It was Kameron who had hypothesized that phytoplankton would be the most efficient and powerful of all toxin-producing species. Truly toxic phytoplankton, like the red tide dinoflagellates, *Pyrodinium bahamese*, produced powerful chemicals that easily killed small fish. Strangely, the bigger predator fish that ate the smaller ones did not die. They accumulated the toxins in their muscles, exactly as tree frogs that ate poisonous insects concentrated the powerful poisons into their skin glands, storing and magnifying their potency. And both the fish and the tree frogs used the toxins for their own defense.

Still other phytoplankton killed the bacteria that prey on them selectively. Kameron believed these toxins could be made into an entirely new class of antibiotics—safe immunosuppressant agents to treat cancers, leukemias, and much more.

And, almost inevitably, after nearly two decades of trials, he had found just such a naturally occurring phyto-toxin in an obscure brackish-water algal bloom. It was not toxic to normal cell lines, but it killed bacteria across the board, and its chemical structure had never even been defined.

When he reluctantly gave the sub-culture to his sponsors at the Christ-ian Council, they had assured him that the senior members of their ruling staff would take his find to pharma-ceutical companies, even lobby for government funding. He had fully expected an uncontested patent, a directorship, stock options, a nomina-tion for a Lasker Award, perhaps the Nobel a few years down the line. He told his wife they would soon have everything—limitless money and fame. And then one day he found his lab had been locked when he arrived.

And then the whole thing had col-lapsed upon him, a house of cards blown down by bigotry and hypocrisy, and he was a ruined man. He lost everything—his wife, his status, everything—except the bulk of his sizable inheritance, which he'd pru-dently kept in an off-shore account in the Caymans.

And where emptiness had once been, there now burned a fiery hatred crying to be unleashed upon the world.

He read the words he had written many months ago, and he was astounded at how fitting the passage of time made it all seem, for it was his knowledge of toxins that offered the best hope for the world, and it was toxic religious dogma that had nearly destroyed him. Treat a toxin with a toxin, he reminded himself...

And he moved back into the files where he had stored his earliest records, the drafts of his descriptions of the first moment he became aware of his madness. It had always amazed him how he had lost his mind in a roomful of people and nobody had noticed, except him. He scrolled down through his diary until he found the January entries. January, only ten months after the accident at the CDC, and the start of the end, he thought. *That's longer then the virus took to affect Tucker, wonder if he knows,* Teddy ruminated as he found the chapter and opened the file. He read slowly, making up the rave reviews:

FRIDAY, JANUARY 2
It had been strangely warm for a January afternoon. But while the air was still cold in the central lecture hall, it was more than fifty outside. Kameron was almost shivering, but

not distracted, as he lectured to the elite group of fellow toxicologists. He'd given parts of his talk before, yet today, as he began to describe the new toxic impact of the modified double helix, the image seemed to come off the screen in front of the slide projector and undulate toward the center of the ceiling, where it circled near the fresh air vent.

To the end he continued with his lecture almost automatically, even fielded six quick questions about the presentation, talking at length to most of his colleagues about how to improve research tactics at their various labs. But during most of these conversations, he watched, quite distracted, as the two awe-inspiring images, visible only to him, interacted above the audience.

The serpentine double helix coiled, danced, and twined in the air, seeming to have substance and life, yet it had to have been unreal or the entire assemblage would have reacted. As it was, they were remarkably oblivious. With the lecture ended successfully, and with many reciprocal thank-yous, the helix writhed still. And then the coils of the helix slowly turned into the body of a huge green serpent. He could feel the panic rising within him as he watched the snake—so he commanded himself to leave the hall in search of fresh air.

As the doors opened, a shaft of crystalline high-altitude sunlight cut through the side of the dimly lit lecture hall, and he found himself forced to turn back, to see if the light had pierced the serpent. The helix had become so reptilian, so terrifying, he knew he was close to hysteria. His chest was heaving, and he needed to flee.

Yet he felt compelled to see if the sunlight would destroy this, what, hallucination? Vision? Divine sight? And instead of walking on outside, he looked back. And there it was still: the serpent swirling upward in an undulating spiral. The double helix uncoiling, he thought in horror, still staring up. *Natural mutations no longer important. The entire helix can now be recreated in the lab. My collections irrelevant. All my work meaningless. How can I ever restore it? How?*

Now the coils were becoming the body of the snake that wraps the staff of Caduceus, and the coils parted while he watched.

And as certainly as the one snake became two snakes, the two sentient parts of his mind fell apart. Reason and superstition separated. He saw with a terrible clarity that the snakes derived from the one Great Snake in the Garden—but had now chosen to become two: the Original Sin of his enemies and the Original Vengeance that is mine, sayeth the Lord.

It was at that moment that he knew he must perfect his means and strike back at his foes. He heard The Voice and it filled him with a terrible resolve and an overwhelming realization, knowing that all the pieces of the puzzle fit at last.

"Let My People Go... " he heard his own voice speaking Scripture.

It was then at last that his sense of conscience left him.

If those idiots on the Christian Council could believe in the Scripture as a literal document, then he could part from his civilized ways and raise a biblical hand to smite the two-faced sinners who had destroyed his life and his career, smite them with "the fiery serpent of the Israelites."

He had vowed to himself with a Voice he did not know was his, and it frightened him more than anything he'd ever experienced. It was the sound of pure compulsion: for Kameron at that moment, and every time he would hear that Voice for the rest of his life, would be hearing the Word of God Almighty. How strange, he thought, that God would reveal himself to a man who believed in nothing but The Void. How strange and how wondrous. By the faithful he had been betrayed, only to be granted the purest faith of all.

Someone's hand was reaching out into the space between the snakes and Kameron's eyes. "Teddy, dear boy, are you all right?"

Kameron had nodded earnestly. He knew what to do. How to do it—all that purifying horror.

The Voice had made it perfectly clear.

Teddy read the last sentence and realized that despite the cool air, he was sweating. He checked his pulse. He wished he could draw his bloods. Had it just been the reading, or was he having another moment with The Voice? Unsure, he took several deep breaths, relaxed, and put the thoughts from his toxic mind behind him. He liked to think that what he had learned above all was perseverance, and that as a scientist it was only by example that he could hope to prove his point, so it was a pleasure for him to review how he had persevered, and how he would prevail.

There was a shattering roar as a helicopter shot by above the river. Teddy watched it go over with a smile. He knew that as long as the helicopters were still flying, they hadn't figured out his plan. He looked at the river. The current was slowing, and a gentle chop flecked the surface. Teddy realized it was almost time to travel again, but he had time to read his favorite chapter.

~ XXIII ~

Theodore Kameron always loved air travel. Travel had been at the core of his life, and he welcomed every departure, each arrival, the planning and the reflecting. He routinely flew the Atlantic and the Pacific, and enjoyed working aloft. And he loved local, short-haul travel just as much. He actually preferred the feeder routes that let him make connections to local buses, ferries, and trains.

In the past, travel was imperative because he had his collections to change and samples to package; each trip to another small-town drug-store was an exercise in American society that left him alternately amused, enraged, and intrigued.

The threat of lost luggage was, of course, the fly in the ointment, so he never checked anything, choosing instead carry-on or FedEx, DHL, or Parcel Post, to help him stay on schedule. The common carriers moved his heavier samples, books, clothes, cameras and slide projectors, trunks, crates of records, stacks of journals, collections of grain samples, slides in carousels, photographic film in canisters, and unedited papers in storage cases.

This was the most efficient way of moving his esoteric equipment. After all, what was left of his speaking circuit required presentations to more than twenty professional seminars a year—to fellow toxicologists, drug companies, medical schools, and researchers at several of the National Science Foundation Research Centers.

He had been a respected figure in the scientific community, having published over 150 peer-reviewed articles, co-founded a prestigious medical journal, and discovered five new bioactive alkaloids.

He also owned one of the world's largest collection of organic toxins, and harvested samples everywhere: from snakes, lizards, tree frogs, toads, insects, spiders, tropical bird feathers, from the mouths of the duck-billed platypus, from fresh and saltwater fish, dozens of bacteria, and various brightly colored algae blooms, and toxins from dozens of species of molds, slimes, galls, mushrooms, and microscopic fungi.

His talks about alpha−1 adrenergic antagonist affects of ganglionic nicotine receptors had been filled by colleagues in the pharmaceutical industry. And his work on the use of mycotoxins in therapeutic application was always exciting. Then, suddenly, and for no apparent reason, he stopped talking about the work anymore. There had been rumors about CDC developing a secret biohazard lab dedicated to highly classified material, there had been talk about a BL–5 hazard. His fellow toxicologists always wondered, but the truth is that he had been changing, even before the Aspen revelation. While behind his back, colleagues blamed the changes on the accident and on his dismissal from CDC. A centrifuge had failed: Kameron had taken full responsibility. He had exposed an entire lab, had been working on material not assigned to his grant program, and had a very real chance of having contaminated himself. It was this risk-gene behavior that marked all of Kameron's life, and ultimately doomed his career at CDC as well as made his betrayal by the Christian Council inevitable.

Even before the Borna spill, and many months before the first revelation, his compulsive behavior, his dedication, his perseverance began to take over. Perhaps as part of an unconscious preparation, he was lecturing less, much less, and traveling more to expand his toxin collection. He gathered samples in orchards, in ditches, at fish markets, zoos, live-stock auctions, butcher shops, florists, furriers, barber shops—any-and everywhere.

In the lakes, by streams, along nature preserve paths, in animal shel-ters, at grain elevators, from apiaries and the swamps of Africa, he was always collecting samples. He gath-ered them from tsetse flies, mosqui-toes, black flies, the eggs of sand flies, salivary glands of stable flies; the inner carapace of snails, the slime left by slugs, and the scales shed by reptiles. His studies had taken him to Zaire, Vietnam, Haiti, Sri Lanka, the Himalayas. He gathered dirt from the lawn of the Phebe Hospital in Liberia, retrieved scat from São Paulo's Her-petological Institute, set his pick into the guano of New Spain's bat caves and the tundra of the Falklands. His only lasting fame occurred at the other end of the globe—a small peak beside a huge mountain in the Brooks Range actually bore his name. Why was he there? For the polar bear droppings, and the intestinal microbes they contain.

He had begun his toxin collection as a graduate student years before. Explore a single pinch of soil, see the dirt, swimming with microbes. It was his idea to collect soil and scat specimens, tag them, and systematically store them during his trips, lovingly depositing them year after year in the secret New York apartment where he kept his lab.

But there was a problem: what could he store his precious samples in when he was on the road? Early on, wooden matchboxes were plentiful, but when they were no longer given away by bars, hotels, and candy stores, he realized another uniform storage container was needed.

Then, in the men's room at a seedy motel and grill, came the answer: a metal machine bragging, SOLD FOR THE PREVENTION OF DISEASE ONLY. At that time, he believed his mission was to *prevent* disease, and the silver quarter in his pocket purchased a rubber—the first of thousands of prophylactics, which would all be filled with twenty-gram samples taken on his extensive roadside stops and endless journeys abroad.

His was one of the largest and most impressive collections of condoms ever assembled: Fourex's, Trojans, Ramses, X-cellos, Spartans, even three rare Golden Pheasants in their metal tin, displaying caravans decorated with "ships of the desert," Arabs mounted on the beasts, and a phallic cactus in the background; a Mickey Mouse with little ears from Amsterdam, a scrolled dragon from Bangkok, red ones, blue ones, one that glowed in the dark. Some had attachments— the ticklers; newer ones had ribs and reservoir tips. But his favorite remained an old tin of Ramses, a tiny Egyptian landscape painted on its cover, colorful hieroglyphics, and two seated figures of Ramses himself, enthroned and enrobed, holding a suggestive curved scepter long enough to reach over his shoulder. Each one was filled with a specimen, labeled with the date and place of acquisition.

At some point, he always told himself, he would process the specimens for evidence of a new fungal species, test the growth for its antimicrobial potential. He would find what no one had found before, grow it, refine the by-product, sell it. His very own antibiotic!

The years sped by, and the work was never done, but the condoms remained. Earlier catches sometimes required repackaging. Mickey Mouse lost an ear. Latex is perishable. The more expensive brands, many of sheep gut, while more porous, were almost indestructible. Newer brands were best.

Since Kameron was only human, he wondered, from time to time, why he did it, hoping against hope that eventually the purpose of the collection, its predetermined destiny, would be made known to him.

And then came Aspen and the Vision and The Voice, and he knew he must abandon the magic bullet derived from a mycotoxin, forget antibiotics, forget the healing fungi. He saw then, and he saw even more clearly now how to use the precious toxic specimens for another purpose. A divine calling.

He looked up from the screen as his laptop chirped. There was a motion-detector in the floorboards outside his lab, and Teddy knew he would be seeing the intruders in his lab momentarily. He touched his keyboard rapidly. The lab came into focus.

He watched as Bryne, Hubbard, the NYPD, and the HAZMAT team began to stream into his apartment. It was time to go. He turned off his laptop, putting the CD-ROM in his pocket. He stepped out of the van, walked over to the water, and hurled the laptop as far as he could into the East River.

Kameron's boat, which was tied to the dock, bobbed among the waves as he diligently loaded the tanks, untied the bow, and slowly headed into the turgid water.

Teddy was ecstatic with anticipation, but he moved carefully, aware of his priceless cargo: three large plastic drums containing seventy-two pounds of pure distilled, highly concentrated aflatoxin.

The east wind was rising perfect for his Mission. Nothing could stop him now from fulfilling the ancient twisted dictum that The Voice had inspired him to carry out: Live by the Book, die by the Book.

24

10:50 P.M.
East River, New York

After Bryne and Hubbard climbed onto the shore, a policeman on the launch had handed each a large four-battery flashlight. The beams only cut through the ground fog a few feet ahead. They could hear the boat speed downstream, making for the Coast Guard vessel that was heading north with the canisters.

They maneuvered their way through the ruins of the decaying hospital, stumbling toward the far end of the island. Crossing southward, past the highrises and Goldwater Hospital across the last paved road, they glimpsed the fountain at the far end on a small breakwater a few yards from the island's southernmost tip. Bryne noticed with alarm that the area was too rockbound for the police boat to moor by the fountain.

There was more than enough light with the moon nearly full, and more coming from the Goldwater Hospital behind them and Manhattan

521

across the water. As they clambered over the girders, cement slabs, and steel of yet another crumbling hospital, the mists began to shift, and a breeze picked up from the east. There were stars. They could see the city highlighted clearly, from the exclusive apartments of East End Avenue and Sutton Place to the sleek facade of the United Nations building. Off to the east, Queens began—elongated, flat, surprisingly dark and forbidding.

Crawling over the partially collapsed hospital was treacherous, but it was the only direct route to the fountain. Long ago, this place had been the city's first pesthouse, where victims of smallpox, typhus, and leprosy were isolated behind the moat of the East River and its treacherous currents. Eventually it had been replaced by Metropolitan Hospital, a mile north. This original pesthouse, vandalized now and almost destroyed, had become an eyesore and a dangerous place. From the FDR Drive it looked like a haunted castle.

Basements, tunnels, and underground shafts were hidden beneath the stunted trees and weeds that covered the island's south end. Rotten boards, collapsed stairwells, and a plethora of metallic shards that had once been wheelchairs, examining tables, and outdated electrical fixtures lay covered by soil. The metal protrusions alone could easily puncture shoes or hands. A wrecked copper cupola on the ground had turned from verdigris to brown as the trees and bushes enveloped what little copper the scavengers hadn't stolen.

Past the debris Bryne could see the fountain—a cubelike structure anchored in concrete to stabilize it against the tremendous shock when the full explosive force of the water jet was activated. Its placement seemed precarious—a mini-island of some four hundred square feet, built of granite blocks, which appeared to be only a few yards from the shore.

All of a sudden Bryne heard a sharp, creaking sound and immediately crouched down. He was quietly turning back to check on Hubbard when there came a sudden crash, followed by a loud, "Oh, shit!" Then more rotten timber crunching and splitting, then another scream from Hubbard, then silence. "Jack, watch out! Everything's rotten."

Making his way toward Hubbard's voice, Bryne directed the flashlight over the area and spotted what looked like a pit. When he crawled to the edge, he could see Hubbard looking up at him, his right foot twisted at a horrible angle.

"I've broken my damn ankle!" he shouted to Jack. "Go on without me!"

"No, I'll climb down and get you out."

"There's no time, Jack," Hubbard insisted. "Come back when you're done."

Bryne paused, knowing that Hubbard was right. "Okay. I'll phone for a helicopter, if I make it in time. You stay put!"

Hubbard waved Bryne away. "I'm not going anywhere!" he shouted.

Grabbing the tool bag, Bryne stood up, turned, and crept back to the copper cupola alone. Peering through the louvered holes, he viewed a scene that took him back many years ago to Manchuria: the shards of metal sticking up from the soil and the dark pilings of the abandoned pier reminded him of the stakes in the ground at Pingfan—and brought him back to reality, to urgency.

The fountain was at least two hundred more yards past the cupola. Jack heard the river slapping against the rock and nothing else, saw the water—dark and fluid on his right. Sizable pieces of flotsam creaked slowly northward, while the bigger objects—a bookshelf, a crate, dozens of rotting boards—lay motionless, stranded by the tide.

Bryne had to cross the open space to get to the fountain. It was now nearly high tide. After a few brief moments of slack, the East River would reverse itself and head out to sea. The far side of the island was surrounded by a barrier of granite riprap, but its eastern side offered an approach to the giant steel box housing the fountain's generators, motors, and filtration system. He headed south.

Bryne had looked at the plans for the fountain with Mia months before. He knew how it worked, knew what he had to do, but could he get there before the system activated, providing Manhattanites with a sight that would literally take their breath away? A cascade of lights, lasers of all colors, would be bounced off the soaring, powerful stream of water, changing colors as they illuminated the theme of religious unification. It would indeed be a pillar of fire.

Again, Jack reviewed what he knew about the fountain. It was mounted on one end of a large concrete block, bolted to a broad pyramid of concrete blocks and pylons that had been stacked on bedrock. It was a man-made island supporting a structure that looked like a church—exactly as Mia had drawn it.

Projecting outward from an opening in the middle of the cube was a tapering copper tower shaped like a giant fire hose nozzle, aimed straight up at the night sky like a piece of artillery. It was at least fourteen feet tall, with a nipple-shaped collar around its tip and a small ladder welded to its side. Bryne noticed that debris had already collected around the cube's footings. Would he, or anyone else, be crazy enough to try to leap across the water?

It was then that he saw the motorboat tethered behind a boulder on the small spit of land. Only the dash lights were on, its bow pointing south, its stern drifting upstream. A powerful engine running at idle, if Jack judged correctly, burbled a gray plume of exhaust that trailed off to leeward. Kameron!

Bryne had to get to the fountain, had to get there now. He played a brief beam from his flashlight on the sickly industrial green surface of the steel cube. Both bolts and welded seams outlined its edges. On the east side of the cube, there was a hinged access door with a stainless steel lock the size of his fist hanging from the hasp. The lock had been cut open, and the door was partially ajar. Bryne kept moving. If he could get inside, he knew he would have to find the correct valves and an easy way to control the holding tank.

Ahead were only a few slick yards of rock. The slack tide gave the river a deceptive calm. He tested his footing and decided to jump, using a stranded crate bobbing in the eddy as a stepping stone. Momentarily, it supported his weight as he hurled himself from the granite to the crate and then, surprised at his own good luck, up onto the small island and the fountain.

Picking up a piece of rusty iron rebar, he quickly dropped it, the skin of his palm cut deeply by the crooked metal. It clanked on the blocks as a gust of wind nearly knocked him down. It was nearly midnight. He put out his flashlight. In the New York gloom, the river's reflection illuminated back the towering skyline above him.

Staying low, Bryne climbed up to the door and looked in over the sill. Just a quick glance and he pulled back. No light inside. The box was easily big enough for two to stand on. The far end of the room had ended abruptly at a mesh wall. Metal. Behind it sat the motor for the giant fountain and a control panel that looked like the fire wall of a steam locomotive. There were dials, valves, pumps, and workmen's tools scattered about the base of the wall.

Bryne could easily step up and pull himself over the lip of the door and he would be inside a room the size and shape of a freight elevator. He waited, listening, the wind swirling off the water, the steady lapping tide, the hum of traffic on the FDR almost drowning out the sounds inside the pump room. Nothing happened.

Finally he turned on his light again, nudged the door, and shone the flashlight inside. Again nothing. He looked in. On the far wall he could see the gauges and handles, each labeled with stenciled red paint: NOZZLE DIAMETER (CM), TRAJECTORY (DEGREES), COLUMN HEIGHT/POWER (M/PH). He climbed inside.

Below, at the base of the pump control box, a stainless steel funnel emptied into a drain that disappeared into the base of the nozzle block. Next to it was an intake valve used to secure a male nozzle. Strapped to the inner wall were two fifty-five-gallon barrels labeled "SODIUM HYPOCHLORITE 5% CAUTION." A prybar was hanging from a hook on the wall, along with a shovel and an industrial-sized broom. He heard nothing. Saw nobody. He clicked off the flashlight, blinking in the darkness.

Bryne reached for his black light and fanned its beam around the cube's interior. In the corner, glowing an eerie ultraviolet, were a pile of rags, a yellow ball of discarded newspaper, some empty plastic grocery bags, and an oil can. He flashed his light into the corners. Nothing. The gauges looked untouched.

Then, inside the mouth of the funnel, he noticed the glowing luminescence again, now undulating like a will-o'-the-wisp in a swamp.

Oh, God! The glow was stronger here, a distinct bright greenish-yellow color emanating from a few faint smudges about the size of teardrops. Stooping to examine them more carefully, Bryne immediately recognized the granular mixture: crushed corn.

He found the main valve. The last one seemed different from the others. Looking more closely, the last threads were shiny. He realized that the large valve had been unscrewed, backed off at least five complete revolutions. It now stuck out from the pipe by more than half an inch, and it was glowing green.

The control valve had been opened well past its maximum; if the fountain was turned on now, its plume of water was going to shoot more than one thousand feet in the air, three times as much as the "MAX PERMISS PRESSURE" indicated on the gauge.

He turned off his UV lamp and snapped his flashlight beam back on. The light blinded him momentarily.

Suddenly Bryne heard the hinge creak and the door closing behind him. Blinking frantically he pulled the broom from the wall and thrust it against the doorjamb before it could fully close. The broom's handle torqued as the door was nearly slammed shut, but Bryne thrust it farther out the door until only the brush remained inside. Someone was pulling on the handle, trying to yank the broom out the door.

Bryne relaxed his grip, and the brush spun out of his hands and twisted, the head jammed.

He lunged for the prybar and smashed it against the metal walls. The broom handle dropped to the floor. Bryne jammed the bar into the door and forced it wide open.

He could hear footsteps crunching on the rocks, slipping on the concrete slabs, moving away from the fountain. He sprang through the door and after the man he knew had to be Kameron. The beam of Bryne's flashlight raked the black water as he sprinted ashore. Almost to the boat, the dark figure clad in black jeans, black shirt, and black running shoes slipped and fell to the granite as Jack tackled him. Both men went down hard, struggled to their feet, and faced each other.

"Well, well! If it isn't my old Haitian drinking buddy!" said Teddy. "How's your mom?"

Bryne was stunned by the emptiness of the man's eyes and by the hatred radiating in the man's words. And yet he made no move to resist, none at all. The move was Bryne's, and it was driven by pure rage.

In the name of vengeance, in the names of Drew and Mia, Bryne raised the metal bar he carried like a ceremonial sword and thought, *Give him what he wants, kill this piece of...* and then he stopped.

He remembered a glimmer of another time, a glistening bayonet. Screaming, *"Hiyiku, hiyiku! I'll kill you, I'll kill you."* And that was exactly what Bryne screamed as he slammed the point of the bar down, striking Kameron's right flank with all of the hatred in his heart. Blood appeared on Teddy's black garments, and he went down. Bryne raised the rebar again, *Hiyiku! Hiyiku!* and thrust it into the supine man's chest, and, straining with both arms, jammed it deep into the thin muddy sand, so hard that the bar embedded itself in the ground beneath him.

"You're too late to stop me!" Kameron growled. He struggled against the bar, and howled in pain.

"You think so, Kameron?" Bryne yelled to the pinioned figure. "Your Tenth Plague will never come off! We're going to stop you."

Kameron seemed beyond caring. He lay back on the sand, grimacing with pain. Suddenly he shuddered, gasped, and then his mutilated palms fell open, lifeless, his arms spread outward, crucified.

That was when Bryne heard an engine and recognized the red and green running lights of the police launch. Its powerful arc lamp almost blinded him as it outlined Bryne and Kameron against the side of the fountain.

"Dr. Bryne, we're here!" yelled the skipper. "Where do you want the ammonia? We have a big block here, it's all we could find."

There were only a few minutes left. Bryne tore himself away from Kameron, securely pinned to the ground, and pointed toward the metal cube, and shouted, "It'll be enough! Come in as close as you can. Get the bag ready. If you can get close enough, drop it on the big rock by the door there. I'll only need five to ten minutes, then we have to get the hell out. And keep the choppers out of here. If the fountain does blow, they're the last things we need buzzing overhead."

The tide had crested and the river was slack, almost smooth, glossy and iridescent in the moonlight. The launch approached on the leeward side, and two officers dressed in heavy gear lifted the forty-pound bag of anhydrous ammonia over the launch's gunnel and rolled it onto the granite. They headed for the ladder.

"What about him?" one of the cops yelled, pointing to Kameron.

"Let him rot in hell! He's not going anywhere," Bryne cursed. "We have to get the ammonia into the holding chamber. There's enough toxin in this fountain to kill every man, woman, and child for ten miles downwind. We have to neutralize it. Only this ammonia can do it!"

"But there's all that chlorine in the holding tank!" the HAZMAT officer cautioned. "If you add ammonia, it's gonna react..."

"That's putting it mildly," Bryne told him. "But if it blows, it won't happen until after the ammonia has done its work. It needs time to seep through the corn mash. We'll be out of here by then."

"And if you're wrong?"

"Then we'll all turn to salt in the middle of the explosion."

"God in Heaven!" the first officer said. "Well, let's get on with it!"

Bryne helped roll the heavy block to the edge of the door and push it inside the small room. He stepped in and ripped the bag open. The ammonia immediately began to react with the moist air, creating an eye-stinging vapor. He dumped the entire contents into the funnel and watched as the granular particles sank into the holding tank below. He scrambled out of the metal pump house and jumped onto the launch. The engine roared.

"Dr. Bryne, Dr. Bryne," a policeman screamed. "He's getting away!" Somehow, unbelievably, Kameron had managed to pull free from the bar and was running toward the cube, then climbing onto it and up the ladder until he stood, arms out, atop the funnel.

"To hell with him," Bryne shouted. "He'll be blown to Kingdom Come in a couple of minutes. Get this thing pointed south!"

At that moment, the first wet rumble came from the top of the metal cube and thick steam vented in plumes from the open door and around the main nozzle, where it engulfed the top of the pump. In the vapor, Bryne lost sight of Kameron.

"It's going to blow!" the captain of the launch was screaming as he wrenched the wheel and opened the throttle.

The nozzle on top of the cube gave off a short, thick, explosive, belching geyser. A heavy, veiled plume wafted downward directly toward the boat. The vessel began to drift backwards, pulled now by the shifting current. As the skipper powered toward the rocks in a tight turn, the engines whined.

"Keep clear of that cloud," someone shouted, but it was too late.

"Don't smell it!" Bryne yelled. The thick ribbon of smoke curled and snaked its way down to the river, enveloping the launch. Even though those aboard held their mouths shut, everyone began to cough uncontrollably. It was in their noses, their eyes, their lungs.

Bryne rubbed his burning eyes. Flames of pain licked the back of his throat. His lungs hurt, but this was the familiar smell of ammonia, and it told him everything would be all right. He'd done it. The ammonia must have suffused through the sop of purified aflatoxin Kameron had unloaded into the funnel in time to neutralize it. The question now was whether the ammonia would still react with the chlorine at the bottom of the holding tank. If so, the first explosion was going to be only a prelude.

"Get us out of here fast!" Bryne yelled. The launch caught the tide and sped south.

Looking back one last time, he was sure he saw Kameron standing on the fountain, arms still outstretched. Even knowing that the man was doomed didn't diminish the strange fear that crept though Bryne. Suddenly the first lasers cut the sky and converged above the fountain. He looked at his watch. Two minutes to spare.

Precisely at midnight, the first incredible geyser of water exploded upward, rising almost instantly above four hundred feet, then pluming higher and higher. Right on time, all the converging lasers changed color one by one and stabbed through the clouds of steam:

red, yellow, and blue. Faster and higher the plume shot, far past its limits and higher still.

Beacons based on the bridges in Queens and Manhattan strobed the giant geyser, abruptly cutting off and on with perfect synchronicity, and then all beams focused at once above the fountain, and they captured the tremendous explosion. A circular blast of blue-white light blew the plates off the steel pump cabin and sent the brass nozzle straight up into the night air like a rocket, followed by an incendiary cloud hundreds of feet high. The explosion's intensity and the flash of light momentarily blinded Bryne. He fell back in the launch as it roared south, away from the falling debris.

Almost immediately, another smell washed over the men in the boat—the aroma of hypochlorous acid, the pungent smell of a swimming pool that has been overdosed with chlorine. Bryne, wet, shivering, hands bloody, almost collapsed from the smell.

Fifteen minutes later, virtually the entire population of downtown Manhattan was carping about the deteriorating quality of the city's air; but everyone had agreed that the light show was spectacular.

25

Monday, April 26
Bryne had been taken directly from the police launch to Bellevue Hospital. Hubbard had been rescued by a HAZMAT team; his ankle was badly broken.

Jack was treated for exposure and for the damaged hand, which ultimately required skin grafting. Vicky Wade remained at his bedside until the doctors told her he would recover. Afterwards, she visited almost every day, often with Shmuel Berger, who always brought Jack huge portions of luscious food prepared by his mother, who guaranteed it would cure him.

Throughout the bleak winter, Jack had kept up with Hubbard as the search for Kameron's body—or body parts—continued. The confiscated work station had been accessed, using "LMPG" for the password. They read the suicide message he'd left for them. Teddy's journal had alternately sickened and fascinated everyone who had clearance to read it.

The contents of Kameron's strange little apartment revealed additional documents and letters, among them the rejection notice from the Christian Council and files of subsequent other rejections. In the end, few had known him, few had liked him, and no one would miss him.

Bryne went home and tried to carry on.

Six months had passed since the fountain exploded, longer than two normal seasons, but this relentless winter, deep and determined, refused to surrender to spring. For Bryne, it was the longest winter of discontent since China. A few days in California had helped. At last now, by April, he was beginning to sleep soundly.

Bryne had been frequently asked to the

city by Hubbard and the NYPD to discuss Kameron's MO. By March there had been no trace of Kameron, and Bryne relaxed. He'd seen Vicky a few times for lunch, but she'd been respectful of his mourning, and never suggested drinks or dinner. She also hinted she had a wonderful secret, if he could only wait a while.

And so, one Monday morning in late April he was in Manhattan for a meeting with Vicky, Shmuel Berger, and Scott Hubbard at Hubbard's tiny office in the federal building. He had been early and looked down on the plaza from a window in the waiting room.

Below, at street level, Federal Plaza swept in an arc around the face of the skyscraper. Throngs of people striding to work dodged building maintenance crews planting flowers in a large circular bed where modern sculpture had once been.

Pleasant blooms formed rings of thick colors: triple bands of alternating orange and blue flowers, the colors of New York City. In the center were hundreds of tulips in reds, whites, and blues. A rich background of grass, pale green, vulnerable, announced that life had officially returned to the sidewalks of Manhattan.

Bryne looked down at the people below, intently carrying on complicated lives: all were coping with problems that could overwhelm them, and all were struggling for peace of mind. Yet he could see the spring in their steps.

New Yorkers! He shook his head. They were oblivious to what had nearly befallen them.

Bryne was aware that they would rather not know. They were, for the most part, caring and trusting men and women. Oblivion or denial, he asked himself. Which comes first?

He had done his job. He had stopped a new plague, the mass poisoning of the city. Was it merely a preamble for the big one of the next century? How many Teddy Kamerons were out there? Bioterrorism was easy, countries and populations trusting and vulnerable. The unthinkable could become fact in an instant.

As he stood alone waiting for Hubbard, thick clouds began to cast dark shadows over the mall, and the New Yorkers picked up their pace. Spatters of rain, big spring drops, began pelting windows and cutting into the grime. Pedestrians flipped newspapers over their heads and started trotting to their destinations. People bunched at crosswalks, huddled and unprotected.

As the brief downpour lulled itself into a shower, a mounted policeman appeared on a magnificent white horse. The man and his beast moved as one, forming a moving blockade that stopped downtown traffic in front of the building, allowing the drenched people to cross the street for shelter. As suddenly as it started, the rain stopped.

The policeman finally moved out of the intersection to a parking space, dismounted, and tied the horse's reins to a meter. Bryne saw him pull off his slicker, unsnap a rain protector from his cap, and place them in a cylinder, which looked like a quiver, and tie it in place behind the saddle. Inexplicably, the sight induced in Jack an overwhelming and frightening sense of *déjà vu*.

Bryne watched the rider stroke the mane of his animal, shaking the water off his hand. A few pedestrians stopped to admire the horse. One woman in particular put out her hand and gently stroked the horse's nose. Bryne looked closer. It was Vicky Wade. Early as usual. As he observed her, a teenager in a long black coat appeared from the subway exit and went over to her. Shmuel Berger. Also early. As the two greeted each other and walked toward the building entrance, the sky darkened again. Bits of debris swirled across the streets: newspapers, coffee containers, and brown bags twisted and danced through the air. The rain was sudden and intense.

The policeman shielded his eyes, though he could see the horse beginning to shy. He put his foot in the stirrup, grasped the pommel with his left hand, and started to swing into the saddle. The horse stepped sideways. Suddenly a shaft of sun appeared in the midst of the rain, catching the gold in the officer's cap and shooting a bright beam of light directly into Bryne's eyes, stunning him.

The image of the horse and rider made him blink involuntarily. He refocused. The rider was now fully mounted. Bryne blinked again as near darkness returned, this time with a flash of lightning followed by a massive crash of thunder. Bryne's sense of *déjà vu* had nearly the force of hallucination.

The horse rose on his hind legs, ears back, nostrils flared, eyes wild, its hooves clawing at the sky. The rider's entire body was outlined as the uniformed officer fought to stay in the saddle. The rider struggled, the horse reared again, and the policeman regained control.

For now the animal was reined in firmly; the moment of panic had passed. Bryne leaned on the window, looking down and sweating. Something chilled him to the bone, and he had no idea why. He was still breathing heavily when the door opened and Hubbard walked in.

"Are you all right, Jack?" Hubbard asked. "You look terrible."

"Sure," Bryne finally answered. "I feel like someone just walked over my grave... That's all." Bryne paused. "Any news on Kameron?"

"Not a thing—still no body or even body parts." They walked to Hubbard's office.

"You know, Scott," Jack suggested, "it doesn't really matter whether or not you find a body..."

"Really, why?"

"Look, Kameron certainly did exist, but all these unspeakable events could have occurred without a maniac, without a terrorist."

"What do you mean?"

"Look at all ten plagues: toxic algae blooms, mycotoxins in crops, foreign animal disease importations, ecological intrusions—we don't need a madman to concoct these events. We're doing a pretty good job all by ourselves."

"Oh?"

"Our risks will not go down. As my old professor Josh Lederberg always said, 'It's not if they will occur, but when and where.'"

At that moment, the door opened and Vicky Wade, Shmuel Berger, and a Bureau secretary walked in. The secretary put down a tray of coffee, and left.

"Scott." Bryne presented Shmuel to the FBI man by saying, "This is the guy that actually cracked the case. Agent Hubbard, you know Shmuel Berger, official ProMEDer." Hubbard pumped the boy's hand.

"Now, we all know," Hubbard smiled, "it is you, Shmuel, and not Dr. Bryne who deserves the Bureau's thanks. I cannot tell you, my friend, what a pleasure it is to find the man who finally gave us the clues we needed."

"Glad you could make it, Berger." Bryne shook his hand also, then, smiling, looked at Wade. "Any word on Tucker? I hear he's doing better."

Wade hesitated before answering. "He definitely has Bornaviral infection. He was morbidly depressed for months, and the shrinks just attributed it to his failure to diagnose the horses' deaths. But he's the one who diagnosed it! Did you know he actually infected himself with an inoculum from one horse and kept notes?"

"My God!"

"Yes, and the notes and diaries provide key insights into a patient's brain and mind as he developed an insidious progression of thought disorders. They eventually progressed almost to schizophrenia. Finally, because the health commissioner interceded, neurologists at the university took over."

"And found?"

"An MRI showed degeneration in parts of the brain different from the scans of routine schizophrenics. It had a true organic cause. They tried some of the newer major antidepressants, and the antiviral medication amantadine. It's used for influenza A and Parkinson's. He came out of it almost overnight."

"Is he back to normal?"

"Pretty much so. He continues to publish, but his titres show he's carrying the virus. Enoch Tucker, as you first knew him, is a changed man, but he's doing okay. *Hot Line*'s planning a major piece on him *and* Borna for this fall. We think it's a major breakthrough in psychiatry. Imagine, an infectious cause of depression, maybe even schizophrenia!"

Abruptly, Wade changed the subject. "Now, Jack, we're here so you can give Shmuely your congratulations!"

Bryne was puzzled; what congratulations? He was aware that Berger and Wade had been communicating over the Internet on some project. He could tell they made a great team, but both had been intensely secretive about their work.

Wade saw Shmuel begin to blush and turned to him. "Shmuel, please tell Jack and Scott what you've done."

Shmuel turned an even deeper shade of red,

then collected himself and pulled out a letter from the editors of *Caduceus*. "They accepted our paper! It's going to be published in the fall!"

"Might I ask what paper?" Bryne asked, tweaking him a little.

"It's about the ten plagues and Exodus. The paper by Dr. Marmal gave me the idea, and I finally persuaded my rabbi to work with me on it. We decided on joint publication. He'll be senior author."

"Would you like to tell us your idea, Berger?" Hubbard asked.

"Oh, yes. The whole thing was a result of Dr. Bryne's ProMED request, not to mention his recent, er, adventures, so to speak. You see, the Jewish Passover feast celebrates the Hebrews being 'passed over' by the angel of death during the tenth plague—forty years before the Hebrew people found the Promised Land and became Israelites."

"And so..." Bryne was honestly curious to know more.

"Well," Shmuel continued, "the Hebrew people had been living in Goshen, miles from the pharaoh and the Egyptians in Memphis, and so they were spared most of the plagues, especially the last four. The Hebrews had healthy animals, good crops, and were certainly not starving. They had no need to raid the storage facilities to get supplies. That's what kept them from being exposed to moldy food."

"Your paper is on that?" Hubbard asked. "That's interesting. You're saying the Hebrews weren't starving?"

"No, they weren't. Our paper explores the symbolism behind the foods eaten at our seder, the traditional Passover meal—the meal consumed the night all the Egyptians were about to die of the tenth plague."

"And?"

"It was the passage about the firstborn that got me started," Shmuel explained. The Hebrew for firstborn is ΘΛB, which translates to 'first fruits.' When I showed Rabbi Solomon, he was fascinated with the interpretation. Maybe someone dropped the last letter, so that 'first fruits' became 'firstborn.' Who knows?"

"It's intriguing to contemplate, in any case," Vicky commented.

"Then I began to think of the seder meal. Today we eat a number of foods, all symbolic of the Passover. But what did the Jews eat back then? That's what I had to find out. It really got me thinking. Rabbi Solomon, too."

"Come on, Shmuel, stop teasing us," Bryne smiled, watching the boy blush again. "Tell us about seder."

"First," Shmuel continued, "we have the shank of a newborn lamb on the table. A lamb too young to be infected with anthrax. Second, fresh herbs, which are newly grown—no mycotoxins. Third, we taste a bitter root, usually horseradish or celery. It grows underground, and it would also be protected from hail, locusts, or even from mycotoxins."

"Isn't there more?" Bryne asked.

"Oh yes, Dr. Bryne. Many. Roasted eggs,

and a mixture of saltwater, walnuts, apples, honey, and wine, a mixture called *charoset*. Although other foods are served, the most important symbol of the seder plate is... " He paused for effect, looking around the room at his elders and savoring the moment.

"Matzoh!" Jack whispered. Of course! Matzoh. It was so simple.

"That's right," Shmuel said. "Unleavened bread. A bread which *must* be made without using yeast. Remember, now, yeasts are fungi. Supposedly the bread, the matzoh, was made in haste, to escape the wrath of the Egyptians. But my rabbi and I now believe it was made without yeast on purpose, because the yeast in Egypt had gone bad. It was full of a mold, a fungus. Toxic fungi..."

Bryne shook his head in amazement. All so obscure, all so obvious.

Shmuel went on, "Because the matzoh didn't have any yeast, there were no mycotoxin contaminants. The Hebrew people led by Moses were spared death because they knew about the yeast, the fungi, and indirectly, about its poisons, the mycotoxins. They knew how to avoid them."

Wade broke in. "And it doesn't change the tradition at all, only makes it more miraculous. Shmuely and I asked the mycologists in Indianapolis and Peoria to document the research and get citations from medical libraries." Wade smiled as the boy blushed again. "Now show them the spreadsheet."

The boy unrolled a hand-lettered sheet of

paper that indexed every scientific cause suggested for the ten plagues. Bryne looked at it, stunned. He saw how Jewish and Christian specialists had tried and failed to bring scientific meaning to the plagues.

He saw that specialty groups had individual explanations for selected plagues: entomologists discussed lice, the swarm, and locusts; veterinarians debated the significance of frogs and the cause of animal deaths; climatologists theorized on the hail and the cause of the three days of darkness; ecologists talked of bloody water; epidemiologists focused on boils and blains and explanations for the sudden deaths.

They were all experts preaching to their own choirs, publishing in their own parochial journals. ProMED, a forum for all specialists, might open discussion and exchange ideas to prepare for the big one. The sentinel system might even work to prevent another epidemic, or an ecological disaster.

Wade noticed Jack's signal. "Shmuel, please close your eyes. Jack has a little present for you."

Bryne grinned. "Go ahead, Shmuel, close your eyes."

Shmuel clenched his lids. Bryne pulled a brand-new laptop computer out of his briefcase and placed it in the boy's hands. He opened his eyes and stared down with obvious delight.

"Thanks to Dr. Enoch Tucker," Bryne began, "one wonderful older gent in Louisville. This came to me. Now, technically, it's against state policy for me to accept gifts, but you can, Shmuel."

The boy couldn't believe his eyes.

"I put a ton of software on it for you, Berger. It's fully loaded, with GIDEON—straight from Israel—and Netscape. It's got a Checkpoint firewall, VetNet, Medline, ToxNet... and of course ProMED, where I hope you'll be working in a few years."

He passed Shmuel the laptop, a battery-powered GEO/POS model with a cellular link to the Internet, a 5.4 gig hard drive, and 128 megs of memory.

"Try it, Shmuel, it's yours. It's still set for my password, so you'll have to register your own."

"You mean it's really mine?" Shmuel ran his hands over the case and snapped open the cover. He found the power switch, and light washed onto the screen.

As Bryne looked on, Berger stared, overjoyed, at his future. The boy tapped the keyboard again, and the desktop icons blinked into focus. Shmuel accessed the link to ProMED, and in seconds was on its home page typing in Bryne's password.

Suddenly the screen went blank. Just as quickly, it flashed on again, and a brilliant spray of colors flared across the screen. In seconds, an exploding star was displayed—beautiful, tragic, familiar, terrifying.

"Neat screen saver, Dr. Bryne," exclaimed the boy.

"Thanks. It's from the Hubble—supernova

in the Crab Nebula—forty million light-years away."

Shmuel turned the laptop around so the others could see.

They smiled. Suddenly the screen darkened for a second, there was a pause, then a menacing black-and-white image from centuries ago appeared where the supernova had been. An image more familiar and threatening than the first. Another screen saver? Shmuel wondered.

Jack leaned toward the computer, focused on the image with all his concentration, and felt the grip of twin dreads: first, the terror he'd felt when Vicky had told him all those months ago that the package that killed Drew hadn't come from Louisville; and second, the chill he'd just felt moments earlier, that very morning, watching the horse and rider rearing in the shattering lightning.

He had seen the computer's image before, and he knew what it meant. It was Albrecht Dürer's print of *The Four Horsemen of the Apocalypse*, now almost five centuries old. At the bottom of the screen, text began flashing: "*Albrecht Dürer... German... 1471–1528... Date of woodcut... 1498.*"

Suddenly Bryne could swear he saw the second number of the date start changing, and the "4" in "1498" began slowly melting until the year below the engraving became... 1998.

As suddenly as it had appeared, the image faded and disappeared, leaving only a blank screen. Bryne started to speak, then stopped himself and nodded at the boy to go on, but he wondered if the others had seen his fear, had seen the message sink home.

Dr. John Bryne didn't need "LMPG" on the screen to understand that the Eleventh Plague was still to come. He realized now that he was about to do battle with a dead man.